SMALLWORLD

DOMINIC GREEN

FINGERPRESS LTD
LONDON

Smallworld

ISBN (pbk): 978-0-9564925-3-1

Published by Fingerpress Ltd.
Printed and bound in the United Kingdom by Lightning Source.
First Edition.

Production Editor: Matt Stephens
Production Manager: Michelle Stephens
Copy Editor: Madeleine Horobin
Editorial Assistant: Artica Ham

www.fingerpress.co.uk

FOR ALLYSON

CONTENTS

white man steal my gravity

t was the third morning of dia 2,148 of the New Calendar when Free Enterprise came to Mount Ararat. The ship, an ugly, functional workhorse of a model whose examples tended to have serial numbers rather than names, touched down with typical Tetsushuri concern for local sensibilities in the South End cemetery, knocking forty gravestones flat with the blast. Had the crew of the good ship *PLD38227* thought of anything beyond ticking their way down the list of prescribed actions for landing on a prospect, they might have wondered why such a large graveyard existed on a colony listed in navigational records as only three kilodia old and only one hundred people in size. Indeed, the cemetery filled a sizeable percentage of the southern hemisphere of the planet, if the words 'hemisphere' and 'planet' could be said to apply. The South End of

Mount Ararat was considerably smaller than the North, containing rich veins of radioactives which poisoned the soil for any crop other than corpses and made EVA without protective clothing hazardous. In earlier ages, a crew of prospectors might have been greatly interested in striking such a lode, but the Tetsushuri Microgravity Mining Company did not concern itself with seams of any mineral of any size less than a cubic kilometre. What *PLD38227*'s crew were searching for was something far more profitable.

Thus it was that, some time after three of her house's windows had been put in by the vessel's landing jets, Shun-Company Reborn-in-Jesus saw three heavily pressure-suited figures trudging with difficulty through her vegetable garden up to her front porch, trampling precious sprouts, potatoes and Jerusalem artichokes with their magnetic space boots. The Garden Devils stared sightlessly from the undergrowth as the intruders passed.

The back door knocker was in the shape of a grinning devil. The EVA team leader did not give this a second thought as he took it in a sausage-fingered fist and rapped hard on the metal. All the doors and window frames were metal. This was unsurprising: the one tree he had seen through his thick triple-glazed hermetically-sealed helmet had been a single anaemic cherry blossom growing in imported soil in what passed for a village square.

When Shun-Company opened the door, the spacepersons stood suited on her threshold and said nothing. This was because the Tetsushuri Mining Company procedure for EVA on worldlets less than one hundred kilometres in diameter specified vacuum suits were to be worn at all times, and vacuum suits did not have external speakers. Who, by definition, would hear the sound in a vacuum? Communication, the procedure clearly stated, should be either by radio or, in an emergency, by touching helmets. Removing one's EVA suit was unthinkable.

Shun-Company, meanwhile, who communicated by yelling at her seven small children at the top of her voice, and whose house contained neither radio nor thinking machine nor electric vacuum cleaner by edict of the blessed First Arkarch, simply stared obediently at the floor, and said nothing, as was only right and proper with strange heathen male visitors

Eventually, after the entire Reborn-in-Jesus family had gathered behind Shun-Company, gazing goggle-eyed at the golden-faced newcomers, the team leader plucked up sufficient courage to remove his helmet, revealing a thoroughly anticlimactic human face beneath it.

"Good day," he said. "I represent the Tetsushuri Mining Company, without prejudice." He had no idea what the phrase meant; it was simply in the procedure to say it. He nodded to his team; uncertainly, they removed their own helmets and sniffed the alien air.

Shun-Company curtseyed, an archaism which nonplussed the EVA team, fifty per cent of whom were female and twenty five per cent homosexual, in line with demographics.

"Good day," she said. "The master of the house is currently absent. We have real tea. Would you care for some?"

Senior Planetometrist Wong sipped his Real Tea thoughtfully. He had now had every single junior member of the Reborn-in-Jesus family squirm all over his meteorite-resistant knees, and was doubtful whether the rickety Genuine Old World Wood armchair he was sitting in would continue to take the weight of himself and his suit combined. His mission on this new world was fact-finding; he had so far learned that Shun-Company had feared that her first child, Unity, would be her first and only due to the high level of ionizing radiation on Mount Ararat, hence the name. Hence, when her second child, Testament, had been born, she had felt the need to commemorate the birth by bestowing a name which referred to a divine entity which came in two parts. The same logic had led, as God had blessed the family with five more children, to the naming of Magus, Apostle, God's-Wound, Measure-of-Barley, and Day-of-Creation. Planetometrist Wong, who had been brought up to regard families having more than two children as morally perverted, was currently feeling the skin crawl on the back of his neck. How did these people imagine such a rate of population growth was sustainable on a planetoid not twenty kilometres long?

A gigantic fly, its wings whirring like engines, buzzed in through an open window and lowered itself onto the saucer of Wong's teacup. The fly was shiny and metallic in lustre, green as burning copper. Wong watched it in horror. It was unthinkable for insects to exist in space; he could only speculate as to the insanitary condition of the ship that had brought the settlers here. How many diseases might one fly carry? Did flies sting, or was that bees or locusts? He attempted bravely to ignore it.

The Master of the House, he was informed, was out searching for the family's only goat, which had last been seen perilously close to the South End Chasm. The EVA party themselves had travelled here in their rover across what Planetometrist Wong learned was called the South End Saddle, the only safe way to cross the chasm and visit the Cemetery. The Chasm surrounded the South End on three sides, was a kilometre deep, and was populated only by rock hyraxes and magpies, two of the only species to have survived First Arkarch Duke's beneficent release of genera when the colony vessel *Utanapishtim* had arrived on

4

Mount Ararat three kilodia ago. Planetometrist Wong reflected, as he sipped his tea and watched little God's-Wound Reborn-in-Jesus crawl *inside* the EVA suit of Junior Gravitographer Shankar, that this explained the bleached and magpie-picked skeletons of two Himalayan yaks and one honest-to-God elephant that the team had passed on its way here.

Planetometrist Wong expressed great interest in the geology of the Chasm. Was Mrs. Reborn-in-Jesus aware that it represented a tectonic boundary between what had once been two entirely separate planetoids loosely cemented together by their own weak gravity? Now that those worlds had been slammed rudely together by a massive and anomalous increase in planetary mass, the Chasm was the only remaining sign that they had once been distinct worldlets. Shun-Company replied that yes, she had heard that this had once been the case. The Anchorite had told her children so. And was Mrs. Reborn-in-Jesus aware, continued Planetometrist Wong, of the reason for that sudden mass increase? No, she was not aware. There was no cause for her, as a woman, to be learned in astronomical matters. However, she had heard her husband speak of a Mononeutronic Sphere Which Encompassed the Centre of Gravity And Was Probably Surrounded By A Shell of Electron Degeneracy, which lay buried at the bottom of the Chasm. The Anchorite would of course know more about the subject, having once been an educated man. However, the Anchorite would see nobody, preferring to keep to his cave on the upper slopes of the Chasm, and spoke only to those who confined the length of their conversation to 'Good day, Mr. Anchorite, sir', or who had genuine reason to speak to him. The Anchorite's definition of 'genuine reason' was, she added, set by the Anchorite himself. He would, however, speak at great length to children.

All this information was delivered by Mrs. Reborn-in-Jesus with her head respectfully lowered, gazing at the unadorned alloy floor plates. The Planetometrist noticed with minor disquiet that the home-made cup he was drinking out of was decorated with a zoetrope of grinning devils, despite the fact that the parlour was also hung with enough crosses to crucify an entire congregation of very small Christians.

The EVA Team made their excuses and rose to leave. They were growing hot inside their suits with the helmets removed: the suits' environmental controls would not work with the helmet seals unlocked. One of the team, Asahara, had removed her suit entirely. Planetometrist Wong glared at her severely as he gave the order to re-seal helmets and depart.

When the team returned here, he reflected, it would be neighbourly of it to bring back some of *PLD38227*'s own supplies, not least for his own sanity. The Real Tea had been brutal in its reality. He suspected that the family only took it out whenever visitors from space happened to alight on their worldlet, and that visitors from space had not alit for a very long time.

The rover's electric motor cut in, and the wheels ground coarse-grained regolith that admitted water like a colander. How these people managed to farm such soil, Planetometrist Wong had no idea. The team set off back to their ship, which was cramped, crowded, reeking of anti-odorants, but nevertheless, after an hour spent in the Reborn-in-Jesus household, home away from home.

Mr. Reborn-in-Jesus was a man whom a lifetime of hard struggle against gravity, radioactivity and a sun that gave off little but heat, had toughened until he resembled an unsmiling, two-metre callus. What passed for fields on Mount Ararat were, as fields always were on red star planets, strung with lines of cheap UV lighting filament, powered by solar arrays at the end of each furrow. The furrows were seeded with genetically-modified crops, usually a variant of the omnicompetent potato, which cost a farmer a good deal of his annual yield every time he purchased a new batch from his local Agribiz ship. The UV filaments were a sop to technological necessity; without them, no crops could grow here. But from the rusted iron implements, pocked by cosmic ray trails, sitting in the fields, it looked as though everything apart from the UV in Mount Ararat's sere fields was powered by the human hand.

Captain Adeti of the Tetsushuri Mining Fleet, Kranion Sector, had once prided herself on being able to run further, faster, than Phidippides. She had been born in gravity; she had been weakened by kilodia of living in free fall. She had sacrificed fine muscles and an Amazonian physique for her career. Currently, despite the fact that the man facing her had been burned out like a spent venturi by the heat of plough-pushing, seed-planting, stone-clearing, and ditch-digging, Captain Adeti was uncomfortably conscious of the fluid still puddled by overlong exposure to microgravity in her once powerful ankles. Her ankles, despite being supported by elastic stockings, were painful now that an unaccustomed six-newton gravitational field was pulling on them. A promotion from field grade would buy her a posting back in gravity, perhaps even back on New Earth, New New Earth, or Earth; but to earn a promotion, she had to make quota. The centre of mineral exploitation and exploration, now that Earth had been mined out, was now New Earth, and exploration therefore proceeded accordingly to the constellations that could be seen in that planet's sky. The constellation Kranion had so far proven to be an unmitigated prospecting disaster. The *PLD38227* held nothing in her specimen tanks but gold and diamonds, the former of which could be extracted cheaply from seawater on Earth, the latter of which could be made out of coal by the tonne using the Popol Process. Here on Planetoid 23 Kranii 3X, however, she believed she had discovered a thing which would make her quota ten times over and put her behind a desk within constant spying distance of her untrustworthy husband in Kibera on Earth, for life.

"Mr. Reborn-in-Jesus—figuratively, you have a mine of, uh, substances greater in value than weapons grade uranium beneath your feet."

Mr. Reborn-in-Jesus nodded politely without anything resembling a mad look of greed seizing his features. He tapped a paperweight, horribly radioactive uraninite ore encased in lead glass, that sat on his writing desk beside the table. "We are aware that there are radioactives on our world. We conducted a survey when we first arrived." He reached behind himself to the lightswitch and dialled the light downwards. The mineral sample in the lead glass fluoresced evilly.

"Uranium oxide," said Mr. Reborn-in-Jesus. "But we cannot mine it out. There's only a few cubic kilometres of it, and to remove it would be to unbalance our little world's centre of gravity. Mr. Battista assured us this would happen."

"Mr. Battista?"

"The Anchorite. Lives in the South End Chasm. Keeps himself to himself," said Mr. Reborn-in-Jesus. The Captain was left wondering whether there was an unspoken implication that the Tetsushuri Mining Company should do likewise.

"It's, ah, not the radioactives we're interested in," said the Captain. She set her devil-handled cup down on an occasional table—the house had furniture for every function—and pulled on her business face. "Mr. Reborn-in-Jesus, have you never wondered how a planetoid only twenty kilometres across can have an atmosphere?"

Mr. Reborn-in-Jesus frowned. "Well," he said, "old Arkarch Duke always claimed it was down to the Providence of the Lord. But on account of how I have an honours degree in Natural Science, I tend more towards the 'there is a nugget of degenerate matter two thousand million million tonnes in mass ten kilometres beneath my feet' explanation. There was once a companion star to 23 Kranii, a stellar-sized object Mr. Battista refers to as Easy Pink, and it was knocked out of orbit by a hypothetical object passing through our system, which Mr. Battista is fond of calling the Q Ball. We can infer this from the specks of hypermassive debris hereabouts which occasionally collide with agribiz ships and cut them in half."

"The oxygen fires are pretty when the ships get cut," said little Apostle Reborn-in-Jesus, with an acetylene light in his eyes.

"Who is this Arkarch Duke?" said the Captain, nervous that this unremarkable rock was proving to contain far more people than she had anticipated.

"Our leader," said Mr. Reborn-in-Jesus. "The man who brought us here to Mount Ararat, Lord rest him."

"What sort of a name is Arkarch?"

"Not a name,a title. The Arkarch used to claim it was an old Earth title meaning 'master of the ship', though I suspect he made it up. He took my family out of a seventy-cubic-metre tenement in the Selvas Favela in Manaus and gave us the stars. Now, alas, he is dead. He died four years after landing."

"A lot of people," said Captain Adeti, "seem to have died four years after landing."

Mr. Reborn-in-Jesus shrugged. "It was hard adjusting ourselves to the ways of this place."

"Are you not concerned that your crops might fail, that a solar flare might drive background radiation even higher than current levels, that there might be a meteor impact or a flash oxygen imbalance caused by a bacterial mutation? Your family could *still* all die."

The dirt monkey shook his head. "We have adjusted."

To be true, this appeared to be the case. Mr. Reborn-in-Jesus was the same colour as the regolith he farmed, like a clay model of a man baked from Ararat sand in a red solar furnace.

"Mr. uh, Reborn-in-Jesus, we believe that the centre of your world could contain a neutronium mote equal to one half-millionth the planetary mass of Old Earth. It might be as big as a beach ball, the largest commercially exploitable neutronium chunk yet discovered. The value of such a find would be incalculable. Neutronium is induplicable on a financially viable scale, and essential in nanomedicine, femtoelectronics, and weapons manufacture. A share of the profits of mote extraction, if you moved your family offworld, would easily pay for a far larger, more fertile plot of land on a developed colony planet—"

"We do not want a developed colony planet," said Mr. Reborn-in-Jesus. "God led us here."

Captain Adeti fidgeted in the unfamiliar wooden chair. "Have you considered another possibility? The collision with, uh, Q Ball might have been enough to compress certain components of Easy Pink below their Schwarzschild radius. The mote inside Mount Ararat might be a collapsar, steadily growing. You and your family might be sitting on a time bomb. Now that we are drilling in the South End Chasm, we will be able to provide an answer to that question."

"Which I never asked," said Mr. Reborn-in-Jesus. "How long have you been drilling in the South End Chasm?"

The Captain had no need to consult a watch; the time came up on her retinal HUD on command. "Around five hours now. Did you get your goat?"

"No. I suspect the Devil has taken her. It will be expensive. I'd only recently had her impregnated."

"Soon, if you take our offer, you'll have goats from your front door to the horizon. The world will be paved in goats." The Captain looked up around the room at the cavorting devils carved into the coving. "So, as well as God, your sect's teaching encompasses a belief in the Devil."

Mr. Reborn-in-Jesus stared back with a dull sullen eye. "No, it does not. But the Devil exists regardless."

"STOP! WHAT THE DEVIL ARE YOU DOING!?"

The man had appeared from the rocks above as if they'd given birth to him, his head a mass of hair like a bull baboon's, waving stick-thin arms that looked to consist solely of bone and nerve fibre, wearing only a light-reflective kaftan. He had nothing on his feet at all—the soles of his feet, Planetometrist Wong imagined, were probably tough as goats' hooves by now.

"This must be the Anchorite," whispered Social Correctness Officer Asahara. "Evidently he is no Buddhist."

"Perhaps those of his religion believe cutting a man's hair takes away his strength," giggled Junior Gravitographer Shankar from her position at the telemetry station. One kilometre below them, on the end of thirteen linked windings of superfine line, the sampler drone had located itself on a flat plane of rock visible on the station monitors. It was now on its second section of drilling down towards the C of G, which the Forward detectors clearly identified as a concentrated mass well above the density limit of electron-degenerate matter.

The Anchorite tumbled down the rocks like a corpse down a waterfall, pausing only to yell, scream and wave. Finally, he dropped to the ledge where the Sample Team had set up shop with the rover's prospecting module, winched down from a hundred metres above on the vehicle's emergency towing cable. He fell onto all fours, more like an animal than a man.

"Stop," he said. "You have no idea of the danger of what you're doing. Please desist."

"You would be Mr. Giovanni Battista, I take it?" said Planetometrist Wong. "Might we exchange public access data?"

The Anchorite shrank back into a wary crouch. "I have no census data," he said.

"But *everyone*," said Planetometrist Wong, "has census data. The chip is implanted in the corpus callosum at birth."

"Unless," smirked Correctness Officer Asahara, "the birth is *unregistered*." This carried with it an implication of deviant non-compliance with central census legislation or, even worse, of birth beyond the Accepted Frontier, where only fanatics and enemies of right and good authority originated. Perhaps unsurprisingly if he was indeed an illegal, the Anchorite did not rise to the accusation.

"We are engaged in an operation the Tetsushuri Company has great experience of," assured Planetometrist Wong. "For a man with a pick and shovel, it would indeed be dangerous. But we have tried and tested procedures."

"Gravitational attraction is increasing steadily," said Junior Gravitographer Shankar. "As expected. Don't believe what's down there to have a super-C EV." The gravitographer spoke in code to keep vital information from the mudballer; frustratingly, he seemed to understand more than a mudballer should.

"I'm well aware of that," snapped the Anchorite. "It's a ball of neutronium no larger than a space hopper. Do you think I don't know what neutronium is?"

From the telemetry station, Gravitographer Shankar's tone too grew sharp. "I'm getting some very odd readings here. Density is much lower than expected. Neutron-degenerate towards the core, of course, and electron-degenerate in a shell around that, but between the two—"

Gravitographer Shankar tapped SCO Asahara on the shoulder and directed attention from the figures at the base of the screen to the TV picture at the top of it. The picture glared white.

"Vulcanism!"

Wong shook his head. "Impossible on a world this small."

"Could such a large nugget cause vulcanism in the rocks around it?"

Wong considered the idea for a microsecond. "We have documentary evidence of over a thousand instances of neutronium-cored planetesimals. It's never been observed. What's the recorded temperature?"

Asahara glanced at the screen. "Uh...you could walk around in it. Weird coincidence...gravity's Earth normal at that depth too."

"Turn down the gain on the photosensors," said Wong.

The brightness adjusted downwards.

Wong stared into the screen.

"What the hell is THAT—?"

The picture went out; and no attempts at diagnostics and random juggling of settings by Shankar and Asahara could convince it to come back.

*

"Ma'am, the planetoid is hollow below a depth of three kilometres."

The surface of Mount Ararat hardly rotated. The ring surface of the unnamed planet above, on which Earth or New Earth might be peeled and hung out to dry numerous times like pattern wallpaper, swept towards Captain Adeti so thick and golden out of so close a horizon that it seemed impossible she could not step up and walk on it.

"You realize, Zhong Zhi, that if this planetoid were any larger, this view would be quite unfeasible."

Wong nodded. "Tidal forces would drag it apart. Only something this small, with this powerful and localized a gravitational field, can orbit within the rings intact."

Adeti bent down to the child at her right. The child had walked the thirty kilometres from Third Landing to the prospecting ship out of sheer curiosity. The crew had been feeding it Low Fat Ice Cream Simulant.

"What do you call that planet hereabouts?" she said, pointing up at a third of the visible sky.

"Naphil," said the child. "You're sitting on my uncle Forswear-Dalliance's gravestone," it added.

"Oh," said the Captain. "Sorry."

All around her, headstones lay smacked flat like dominoes. So many, in so short a time...

Wong broke in impatiently. "Ma'am, there is also breathable air down there. Shortly before the drone lost contact, it broadcast successful tests for oxygen, CO_2 and nitrogen. The readings for all three gases were even higher than the ones up here on the surface. Uh, ma'am? You're not wearing your EVA suit, ma'am."

High above, a set of stars skated overhead in a perfect V-constellation—the components of the prospecting vessel that

14

weren't required on a planetary surface, the FTL drive, interstellar fuel stages, and deep space navigation fit, temporarily discarded as extra payload.

The Captain looked down from the constellation she commanded and languidly traced a hand across the lettering on the marble, which proclaimed Uncle Forswear-Dalliance to be DEARLY BELOVED. "The locals don't wear them...so there's air down there. Stands to reason it would be in greater concentration. The gravity's higher."

"Also, ma'am, just before the drone broke off, it drilled through a particularly difficult hundred metre section of vitrified rock. Fused glass, ma'am. And you know as well as I do there's no vulcanism down there."

Adeti raised an eyebrow. "You think it's artificial?"

"Ma'am, there is *light* down there. Visible spectrum. And water. Fresh water. We clearly saw the drone's tunnel spoil fall into a liquid surface having that refractive index."

"You think someone's *living* down there?"

Wong paused. Peddling outlandish theories to one's commanding officer could shorten career growth. "I think this entire world, ma'am, is artificial."

This got the bemused psychoanalytical look he'd dreaded. "Pardon?"

"Ma'am, we have here a twenty-kilometre world hit by a neutronium fragment at *just enough velocity* for it to lodge in the C of G and provide surface gravity of one half Earth normal, a breathable atmosphere, and liquid water—"

The Captain looked around her at the black dust stretching out like a starless night to an uneven horizon. The dust, she knew, actually proved to be green when taken inside under white light. It was that full of venomous compounds of copper. "You're suggesting someone would deliberately *make* a world like this? To *live* on?"

"Ma'am, the family Reborn-in-Jesus say that when they first arrived, *there was already breathable air.*"

He had Adeti's attention now. "No cyanobacteria? No need for terraforming? Didn't they think that was odd?"

"No, ma'am. Their leader, a man calling himself Duke Allion who registered the mission with the Outworlds Colonization Bureau, New Earth Branch, in Kilodia Zero, took it to be evidence of Intelligent Design. That this world had been made for them."

Adeti snapped her fingers. "The Anchorite!" She jabbed a finger at the spare, bearded face on the screen. "What does the Anchorite say on the matter?"

"According to Mr. Reborn-in-Jesus, he was already here when they arrived. He also," said Wong meaningfully, "attempted to stop us drilling in the South End Chasm. And he's either an Uncensored Individual or someone who doesn't want us to view his personal data."

"Of course, Mr. Wong," nodded Adeti sarcastically. "The Recovery Bureau might take away his vast wealth in back taxes. He lives in a cave, I hear."

"A cave he appears to have chiselled from the rock itself," said Planetometrist Wong. "Manually. I have been taken there by the children and agree that he has little to fear fiscally."

A fly green as verdigris was droning irritably around Adeti's head. Somehow an insect, one of particularly loathsome dimensions, had got on board her vessel. The ship would need decontaminating throughout as soon as they returned to depot. Adeti flicked a lucky penny up in the air, caught it on the back of her hand, and worked it across her fingers. The penny, worth a hundredth of a credit, was no more legal tender than a bushel of wheat or a wife would have been; nowadays, coinage was produced solely for numismatists. Modern state centicredits bore the ring of linked hands on one side, Da Vinci's Vitruvian Man on the other. This was an older coin, however. It had a face.

She held the coin between two knuckles. The face was aquiline, crowned with laurels, looking left towards distant vistas.

Senior Planetometrist Wong crooked an eyebrow.

"Something up, skip?"

"Nah," grumbled Adeti, and palmed the coin again.

"Have we found the sampling rig yet?"

"Yes ma'am. An aerial survey drone was sent down to investigate. The rig is still down there at the chasm bottom, half submerged in a soil emulsion. It's simply that the telemetry cable has been cut, and the planet—" he waved his hand at the vast bulk of what Adeti now knew was called Naphil, not deigning to call what they were currently standing on a planet—"puts out enough radio in all bands to prevent the drone's backup systems from communicating."

"Did the cable snap? I thought they were supposed to be strong!"

"They are, ma'am. It was a clean cut. No falling rock or micrometeoroid did it." Wong paused for thought. "But the Anchorite was up top with us the whole time."

"And that's the only time we've ever seen him," said Adeti. "At the very moment he needs to get himself an alibi. In any case, I believe the readings up to the point of failure have confirmed our claim. We have beneath our feet a lode of neutronium big enough to be hammered into a crown for God Himself. I have drawn up a Compulsory Field Purchase Request, which we are empowered to serve on planetoids of less than two thousand kilometres in diameter and less than ten thousand population. The family will be more than adequately rewarded." She patted the head of the child beside her.

Wong fidgeted with his suit jet controls. "Ma'am, the two thousand kilometre rule was created on the assumption that no worlds below two thousand kilometres in diameter have atmospheres."

"Your point being, Mr. Wong?"

"Ma'am, if we call up a mining ship and cut the neutronium core out of this place, we will destroy that atmosphere. We will destroy everything living here. There are islands in the oceans on Old Earth, ma'am, where unique species had evolved over millions of kilodia and were destroyed in one when sailors arrived in need of eggs, meat, firewood, and places to test their Nuclear Weapons."

"The Devil won't let you do it," said the child.

Adeti and Wong looked down. The child was using a surveyor's french chalk to fill in the DEARLY BELOVED on the toppled headstone. Adeti reflected idly that the same precise cut seemed to have been used to carve the same precise font in all the epitaphs on all the graves. What she had seen of the colony so far had convinced her that the settlers were essentially city people, muddled masses yearning to breathe less oxygen. Their craftsmanship had grown better over time, but was still basic to the point of crudity—poorly dressed stone walls, botched repairs. These gravestones, however, looked so precise as to be almost—

"Who carved these stones?" said Captain Adeti. The child looked up, all innocence.

"The Devil, of course," she said, and set to drawing a fluorescent orange fiend beneath the DEARLY BELOVED. The fiend was cramming a protesting person into its mouth,a person clearly wearing Tetsushuri Company EVA gear. Adeti suddenly realized

that every single epitaph on every grave also said DEARLY BE-
LOVED.

"God's-Wound," said the Captain gently, "where does the Devil
live?"

"At the centre of the world, of course," said the child. "Do you
have a red? I have to do all the blood the spaceman will be bleeding."

"Call up saved link 21317."

The entire wall lit up with densely-written text. Officer Asahara
used her personal laser wand to underline several passages in
scarlet.

"This is a Post-Modern English translation," she explained. "The
relevant passage is *tu passasti 'l punto al qual si traggon d'ogne
parte i pesi*. The world—well before Columbus, by the way—is
clearly indicated by Dante, in his *Inferno*, to be round, and the
would-be usurper Satan is at the centre of that world, paradoxi-
cally in a region of extreme cold rather than heat, blocking the
passage of Dante out of Hell and into Purgatory and thereby
Heaven. It's an apt cautionary tale for us, perhaps. It's not five
kilodia since the Satanic forces of the Dictator, many of whom
genuinely believed their leader was a god, were defeated by the
Army of the People." She glanced sternly round the Bridge, making sure everyone present touched their hands to their hearts and
mouthed the Oath of Allegiance. Only Adeti did not.

"I'm the Captain," explained Adeti gleefully. "I have no heart."

The crew collapsed in titters. Asahara reddened and marked
down Adeti as an a enemy of the State.

"So you're saying that those people's Christian belief has
caused them to place a devil at the centre of their world? That

this is all dirt digger superstition?"

Asahara nodded.

"Bring in the prisoner," said Adeti. There was very little room on board a prospecting vessel, and the prisoner had had to wait outside, loosely accompanied by the forty-two-kilo Gravitographer Shankar to remind him that he was a prisoner.

Mr. Reborn-in-Jesus had so far been cooperative to the point of meekness. It had not been necessary to restrain him.

"Mr. Reborn-in-Jesus," said the Captain, "my SCO here has a theory that your local devil, as you call it, is actually," she searched for a kind word, "a *religious necessity*, credence in which is forced upon you by your belief system."

"If a religious necessity can kill forty people," grumbled Mr. Reborn-in-Jesus, "then so be it."

Adeti sat back in her seat.

"You didn't tell us that."

"You didn't ask me."

"How did they die?" said SCO Asahara. "Sometimes an illness, a plague, can be characterized as a devil—"

"Plagues," said Reborn-in-Jesus, "do not remove people's heads. I am no epidemiologist, but I am almost certain of this fact." He looked up wearily at the circle of faces. "My father always planned for me to be in advertising, Captain. He advertised products he didn't understand, understood but didn't believe in, believed in but knew he would fail, his whole life. He was in advertising because his family were in advertising, as everyone was in Manaus. One day, when I was still quite small, I discovered my distant ancestors had once burned the great forest that had stood on the site of our *favela* and farmed the land, proud to herd great beef cattle for multinational fast food conglomerates. From that day onward, all I wanted to do was to farm, to till the land. I was lucky enough to enter into the society of Adolfo Hitler Talvares Concieção Bisneto, who later came to call himself Duke Allion. At first, when we came here, things were not so bad. We had only to believe in God, to believe we were His Chosen People, to regard all His other people as tainted, to conduct sexual activity only in order to create more souls for the Lord. But then our Arkarch decreed that all our wives were also his wife, as he was in fact the Son of God, and announced that all children deemed to be bad in an annual audit by Saint Nicholas would not be educated, but would instead be sent to a workhouse at the edge of our settlement, and so forth. He appointed himself Saint Nicholas, of course. And as he was in possession of this world's only working handgun, we had little choice but to obey.

"Then, one morning, we woke up to find the Arkarch and his handgun missing. We searched the settlement, but could find him nowhere. We were arranging a team to drag the basin, when one of the ladies whose child had died in the first month after landing, who was out at the South End paying respects at her little girl's grave, discovered a newer, more professional-looking tombstone standing next to the child's. Feeling rather sheepish, we dug under it, and discovered our Arkarch's head and body, neatly disunited.

"You might imagine this would have led to rejoicing, but human beings are queer creatures. First of all the settlement was up in arms against the Arkarch's murderer, but after we finally worked out everyone had an alibi for the killing, it was realized there was a malevolent force here in this place besides ourselves. That other force was unanimously agreed to be a devil that had killed our good and holy leader. The Anchorite was our first prime suspect; he fled into the rocks of the South End Chasm, and would not come out. Our leader at that difficult time was a woman named Ogundere, who had taken the name of Cast-Out-The-Devil. Unable to catch the Anchorite, she identified three of our number as complicit in the Arkarch's murder, and had sufficient flammable material collected together to burn them alive. The next morning, a fresh grave was discovered in the South End, containing Ogundere and Ogundere's head. Those who had been accused of witchcraft, cut down from their stakes, immediately made Ogundere a martyr and swore to avenge her. From snippets of evidence laced with supposition, they came to the conclusion that the devil that had caused the deaths lived at the bottom of the South End Chasm, possibly at the very core of our world itself. They resolved to make war on it, without really knowing what weapons they might use, or whether their enemy even existed. Holy water, garlic, home-made explosives, electric fencing, laser tripwires, silver bullets, and even aconite were all used. And every time a party went out into the South Chasm, at least one of them would fail to return."

"So they were correct," said Adeti, "about the enemy's location."

"But the Anchorite also lives in the South Chasm," said Planetometrist Wong. "And he has not been harmed."

"Nor has any child," said Reborn-in-Jesus. "I am convinced the tragic sickness of little Rejoice-in-the-Name-of-the-Lord Stevens was simply that. Since then no child has died on Mount Ararat. On the final day when Behold-the-Hinder-Parts-of-God Raffaele attempted to plant charges in the chasm and was later found interred in the South End Yard, I decided I had had enough, and decided to Adapt. I painted a sign of the Devil on my front door, and carved devils for my doorknockers. I made devil gargoyles leer from every roof truss in my house. I laid out offerings for this place's demonic inhabitant on the edges of town, as do we all nowadays. And, Lord be praised, from that day forward no man or woman has died on Mount Ararat either, and I and my wife—though admittedly no-one else above the age of thirteen—live to till the land and tell the tale."

"Can you prove to us," said Asahara, "that *you* did not murder these people?"

"Explain to me how I could have constructed, with the few poor steel tools at my disposal, forty exquisitely-chiselled grave-stones, and overcome forty other armed and homicidally paranoid settlers, and I will concede your point."

"This devil of yours. Has it ever been seen?"

"Some of the children have seen it. It will not attack them, you see. If any adult catches sight of it, he or she dies."

"Which means," said Wong, eyes focussed on an invisible logic, "that it cannot afford to be seen by anyone who knows what he or she is looking at."

Adeti nodded curtly in agreement. "Mr. Reborn-in-Jesus, you will please arrange for all your children who have caught sight of this creature to report here for questioning. It is my belief that we have here a life form which is intelligent, dangerous, and possibly technologically competent."

"And which draws the line at killing children," said Mr. Reborn-in-Jesus.

"Colleagues, I believe," said Adeti, "that we may have encountered an abandoned Made war machine."

Despite the cramped quarters, the temperature in the room appeared to drop. Adeti was aware that this was only blood draining from extremities to hearts to prepare for either fighting or flying, but the illusion was there.

"We should run," said Planetometrist Wong. "We are not a military ship."

"We should not jump to conclusions," said Gravitographer Shankar. "This might be humanity's first contact with an intelligent species we did *not* make ourselves."

"Or an abandoned Made war machine," repeated Asahara.

"And it's already indicated it's prepared to kill," reminded Wong.

"Mr. Reborn-in-Jesus—will you ask your children to report here?" said Adeti.

Reborn-in-Jesus shrugged. "They will report here *for questioning*," he said. "I urge you not to attempt to harm them. I don't think the Devil would permit it."

"Mr. Wong, you will arrange for transportation. And while you're about it, get that fly shooed outside the lock. I'm not running a dirty ship."

Wong nodded and remained seated, but at a further glare from Adeti, rose and began to chase the fly round the compartment, clapping his hands together to confuse it.

"I have decided," said Adeti, "to contact our neutronium harvester *Sisyphus*, which will be in comms range in twelve hours' time, to facilitate the compulsory purchase and exploitation of Planetesimal 23 Kranii 3X. This will of course involve core extraction and subsequent loss of gravity and atmosphere. However, there are usually berths available on board harvester vessels with a minimum of sharing, and jobs can be found for yourselves and your family until the ship next docks at a habitable planet—"

"You will all be dead inside eleven hours," said Reborn-in-Jesus. "This is not a threat, merely a confident prediction. But I will send the children. They will tell you all they know, and who knows? Their presence may protect you."

He nodded curtly, and walked out of the ship.

*

Apostle Reborn-in-Jesus was a pale, thin boy who Doctor Ambrose had diagnosed as suffering from a variety of immune deficiency disorders. He looked round the Bridge's interior nervously. He had evidently never seen the inside of a starship, and had refused to enter unless the wall screen was turned on to show his brothers, sister, and cousins playing a complicated game, which Adeti believed was called 'Devil Take the Spaceman', in the cemetery outside.

"Apostle, do you know what the Made are?" Asahara had been given the task of questioning the children by Adeti. Adeti had implied that this was due to the fact that the children would be more likely to trust a friendly mother figure. Asahara suspected that Adeti actually hoped the Social Correctness Officer's title would terrify the infants.

Apostle nodded. "Abominations against God. Intelligent creatures made by man, not God."

Thank heaven for organized religion. Adeti smiled at Asahara, who said:

"What form do you think the Made take?"

The child thought a moment. "Machines," he said. "Many forms of machines. And people."

Asahara nodded. "People who were not made by Mommies and Daddies."

The boy nodded back. "Artificially gestated, genetically-modified clones, yes."

"Is that what the Devil looks like?"

The boy's eyes dropped to the floor, and his voice grew small. "I only ever saw the Devil once."

"What did it look like?"

25

"Like a man, but moving so quick it blurred."

"And where did you see it?"

"It come in from the south during an Naphillian Eclipse while I was in the Six O'Clock Field." He squirmed uncomfortably in a chair much larger than he was. "More felt it pass than saw it, point of fact."

"And did it leave a trail?"

"Hellgosh yes. More like a plough furrow. At the town end of that trail, they found a big splash of O Positive where See-The-Hinder-Parts-Of-God Raffaele had bin, and that same day a new headstone with his name come up in the South End Yard—"

"And at the Chasm end?"

The boy looked up at Asahara suspiciously. "Trail didn't end at the Chasm," he said. "Ended at Dispater Crater, one kilometre outside City limits."

It was nerve-racking to have to operate the PanScanner. It left her only one hand to operate the carbine, in the use of which she'd only ever had one mandatory lesson. Still, the carbine fired rounds that were guaranteed to stop a charging New Earth mantagator dead in its complete lack of tracks. This was admittedly due to the fact that the only prospector deaths attributable to animal attack had happened in the unfortunate Mantagator Swamp Incident of Year 2230 Old Calendar, but the weapon was comforting nonetheless. Adeti wondered if it would penetrate human flesh.

Some of the team, mostly the men, had stopped wearing EVA suits, wanting to be able to move and react quickly when *whatever* might charge over the ten-metre horizon at them. Some, mostly the women, had kept their suits on, on the grounds that they might give them some limited protection against *whatever.*

"The crater was probably produced by a stray ring particle," commented Wong, who still had his suit on. "Probably no more than a speck of ice travelling fast. There's not much atmosphere here, must have blasted clean through and impacted."

"Must have blasted clean through and *tunnelled,*" corrected Adeti. "Ultrasound shows a hollow chamber right under the surface." She kicked gently at the sand underfoot. It shifted to reveal a dull alloy hatch cover, with the legend PEARLYGATE VACUUM DOOR CO, PORT YUM CAX, CERES.

Adeti relaxed with a long outbreath. She had not dared admit even to herself, until this moment, that she had feared she might be facing a genuine devil.

"So we're looking for a human being," said Wong.

"Or a non-human that used what it could get its hands on," said Adeti. "From off the last ship that landed." She moved the ultrasound closer to the hatch. "This is just a fire door, a precautionary measure. The air on the other side's the same pressure as this."

"So are we going through it?" said Shankar nervously, eyeing the hatch.

"No fear! No, we're going to rig a charge to blow if anyone opens the hatch. That's what prospectors are good at, laying charges. Not being tunnel rats."

"We could drop charges down the hole."

"But it—uh, the alleged Devil—might not be in the tunnel when we blow it. And then we'll have let it know what we know, without gaining anything." She nodded to Wong. "Rig the hatch to blow."

"How much? A hundred grammes will take out anything human inside a hundred metres. I have a kilo."

"A kilo sounds good."

Wong looked down from the edge of the crater, rubbing his feet in the dirt. "There are shoe imprints here, chief. Looks like the children come down here to play Devil Take The Spaceman."

Adeti scowled and ground her teeth together. "Rig the hatch to blow."

"My Dad says the Devil's going to take all of you." The boy's eyes were not aggressive, only unsettlingly certain. *My Dad says it, so it must be true.*

"How do you feel about that, Magus?"

"Sad. There'll be no-one to play ball with any more."

The wall was full of trees, a beech forest, big-boughed, the sky above it speckled with leaves. Some of the children would not enter the Prospecting ship without a projection of their own world on the wall screen. Magus was fascinated by forests, by worlds that could hold whole square kilometres of trees.

"Does water come from the air where you come from?" said Magus.

Asahara nodded. "A great deal of water. Sometimes too much. Sometimes we call it smog, sometimes fug, sometimes acid rain. You saw the Devil, Magus, didn't you, when it came into the church and took Elder Inherit-The-Wind."

The boy nodded. "I drawed it for you." He pushed a chalk tablet across the table.

"Wow," said Asahara. There were horns. There were wings. There was a tail.

"You missed out the pitchfork," she said.

"Didn't have it," said the boy. "Must have left it at home."

"What was its skin like?" said Asahara. "Did it look like hair, or chitin, or metal?"

"It was blurry most of the time," said the boy. "But it had to slow down to turn corners, like a dog on a wet floor. It had great big feet. It digged its claws in when it turned, and dropped down low to the deck."

"Yes," said Asahara. "It would have to." She looked at the chalk picture again. "These wings are very small."

"They were glowing," said the boy. "It stopped and flapped them after every time it moved fast."

"Well I'll be," said Asahara. "Heat sinks."

"Elder Raffaele said we might be able to track it on something called *infrared*," said the boy, pronouncing the word 'infraired'. "He said that was the same as heat." He licked his lips, staring at the spigot on the wall. "It's hot in here. Can I have a glass of lemonade? The others say your lemonade in here is cold."

I knew there had to be a reason why they all turned up straight away. Asahara reached for the spigot and poured a clear plastic glass of what the children had been told was lemonade, a carbonated Tetsushuri company vitamin and amino acid delivery system. Then she sat stock still, staring into the liquid.

"There's a rainbow in my drink," said the boy. "If I drink the rainbow, will I have God's promise to never again destroy the Earth inside of me?"

The rainbow fanned out from a narrow point. Trying to correct for refraction, she traced the line of rainbows mentally out of the glass, across the Bridge, and—

—out through the Bridge landing window.

"It'll be a hollow promise if you do, Magus." Frantically, she fished at her belt for the communicator.

*"It's been listening in on our conversations. That must mean it un-
derstands English. The laser beam aimed in through the landing
window bounces off the glass, the glass vibrates when people talk,
the micro-vibrations in the glass echo back and tell you what
they're saying—"*

Adeti waited patiently for the talking to stop. "Where did this
laser come from?"

*"Outside the ship. I'm shining one of our own measuring lasers
out at the same angle till I hit rock and following it with image intensifiers. There's not much of a horizon here, I reckon it would
have to be within fifty metres and at least two metres tall—"*

Adeti shouted into the communicator. "Calm down! Calm
down, mister! How long ago did this happen?"

*"Just now. Not two minutes. I think it's gone now. I can't see it.
I think it scooted off over the rocks, there's some big ones about
thirty metres out, I could go out and take a look—"*

Wong and Shankar shook their heads very definitely at Adeti,
who confirmed: "Negative. Stay right where you are. There's two
ways it could have hidden. It *could* have scooted off over the
rocks, or it could have dropped down low and scooted in closer to
the ship."

*"Oh god. Did I lock the door? Magus, did I lock the door? No,
hang on, hang on, hang on...I'm switching the intensifiers into the
infrared band...YES!"* The Correctness Officer's breathing grew
slower in the communicator. *"It went away over the rocks! Captain, the Devil leaves a hot trail in air! It has to dump waste heat!
It's not a metaphysical Judaeo-Christian entity, it's a made thing!
And if it's a made thing, it can be unmade—"*

Adeti clicked the communicator off, and frowned.

"Either that," she said, "or it's very hot in Hell."

The rover was travelling at the head of a smoking arrow of its own dust, on autopilot, bound for town. Driving on Mount Ararat felt uncomfortably like perpetually motoring over the edge of a cliff. The autopilot was on due to the pressing need for every crewman's hand to be near their carbine. Adeti hoped fervently that the safety catches were on everyone's weapons.

"What are we coming here to do?" said Wong.

Adeti took back control of the rover and brought it to a halt in a ragged plume of dust. "We know what makes it kill," she said.

"We do?"

"We do. And if we know that, we have bait to set a trap."

The church had been intended to be far larger. It stood in the centre of a cyclopaean set of highly ambitious foundations, whose precise dimensions, Adeti had learned, had been explicitly communicated by God Himself to His Arkarch, combining the shapes of Heaven as outlined in *Revelation*, the Tabernacle of the Covenant as described in *Exodus,* the Temple of Solomon as described in *Kings* and *Chronicles,* the Great Pyramid of Khufu, and Stonehenge. Work on the church had been projected to take up half the settlement's waking time for the next five kilodia, when Messiah Himself would be reborn in the waiting sarcophagus at the temple's centre. However, the colony's stonemason units had malfunctioned inexplicably soon after planetfall, and all that had been built was an antechapel the size of a small terrestrial cathedral. It had also been intended that the land of Ararat put forth forests which would be harvested for wood, which would be carved lovingly into pews to the Arkarch's divinely-inspired design, but the planetoid's single tree looked unlikely to last out the kilodia, let alone to provide wood for furniture. There were no pews in the church.

There was, however, an altar, machine-carved out of local stone, which would suffice amply. Little Pitch-Not-Thy-Tent-Towards-Sodom Ogundere was playing ball with a ball, also carved out of local stone, on the grand pavement outside when Adeti and her spacemen alighted from their buggy.

"Take him in; he'll do." Shankar gripped the child tightly; having no concept of abduction by malevolent strangers, the boy blinked in bemusement rather than wailing. The church was, of course, unlocked. Saints and angels stared down disapprovingly from the windows, as did a few obscure Old Bad Era media personalities—the late Arkarch had been a fan of all singing, all dancing low gravity spectaculars, it seemed. The windows, designed to admit 23 Kranii-light, were a muddy collage of reds and oranges. Solar collectors on the church's roof powered a dim tracery of golden fibre optics in the eyes and tongues of angels, the fretwork on the columns, the lettering on the altar.

"Put the child on the altar." Shankar nodded and began spreading out the boy's arms and legs.

Wong had still not worked out the Plan. "Why? What are we going to do with him?"

"If you haven't figured that out yet, you don't deserve to be in your job." Adeti fiddled with the safety on her carbine, trying to remember how to put it in the *OFF* position. "We know that this Devil has killed in the past when wives were taken as chattels and bad children as slaves. We also know it has killed when people were on the verge of being burned alive for witchcraft. And we know it takes special care to avoid killing children. It evidently considers itself just and good, some kind of beneficent protector."

"So?" said Wong, though his face showed that he understood perfectly.

32

"So all I need to do to call myself up a devil is to kill myself a child, right here, right now."

The boy's eyes widened, and he began to struggle in Shankar's grip with gravity-toned muscles surprisingly strong for his size.

Wong licked his lips. "Uh, this is a bluff, right, Captain?"

Sweat was draining into Adeti's eyes. It was surprising how much it stung. "If it's a bluff, it has to be believable," she said, "right up to the point where I pull the trigger. For that reason," she continued logically, "I have to believe I *am* going to pull the trigger, to the extent there is a real danger I might do so." She yelled at the church's empty interior. "DO YOU HEAR THAT?"

Wong frantically raised his weapon, but could see no living thing but a large and ponderous fly buzzing lazily in circles, black in the beams of coloured starlight, a sudden vivid emerald in the golden light from the fibre optics.

"Beëlzebub," said Adeti. "Lord of the Flies. You thought that was a great joke, I've no doubt. Thought we'd never get it. But for there to be flies here, they'd have had to be introduced deliberately by the settlers, along with the earthworms and the dead elephants and magpies. And who'd deliberately introduce a disease-carrying organism?" Her hands fond the cocking lever.

"Don't," said the boy on the altar, staring upward at the gun.

The windows blazed suddenly with light—white light, reddened through the saints' faces. Then the shockwave followed, shaking God's faithful in their frames. A few glass eyes, hands and faces punched out of their putty and tinkled down on the floor of God's house. The doors, the *very heavy alloy* doors, rumbled on their hinges.

Then the air was quiet, with a distant clap of thunder as the shrinking blast wave met itself on the other side of the planet.

"Well I'll be damned for a bastard," aid Adeti, staring out in the direction of Dispater Crater. "We got it coming out its hole."

"We got *something*," cautioned Shankar, crouched down with her back to the wall.

Wong stared in consternation at a gigantic greenbottle fly, legs wriggling impotently in the air, trying frantically to buzz itself off the ground with wings that were either damaged or impotent now the fly was flipped on its back. Wong increased the magnification on his EVA suit goggles. The insect's back was covered in a regular grid of tiny emerald cells.

"Black in red light," said Wong. "In 23 Kranii-light, a perfect solar collector. 23 has virtually no green in its spectrum."

"First solar-powered insect I ever did see," said Adeti. "Whoever the Devil is, he doesn't need to peek in windows to listen to conversations. Unless I order all my locks shut and keep the flies out of my ship, that is, which I believe I did yesterday. We've been bugged, ha, ha, ha. Reborn-in-Jesus' Devil has been listening to us ever since we landed, one way or another."

"I could have told you that."

The voice came from halfway up the aisle. Reborn-in-Jesus had entered via some unseen door, and walked ten metres across the church toward the altar before Adeti had even noticed him. Adeti attempted to keep a grip on her anger.

"You could have told us the flies were the Devil's?"

"That boy's father has already been killed by the Devil," said Reborn-in-Jesus. To add insult to injury, he appeared to be accompanied by his entire extended family, other members of which were appearing from the dark behind him. His wife came up to stand by his side. "He's suffered enough. Let him go."

"I," said Adeti, "have a quota to fill. Your Devil has, oh, let's say thirty seconds to prevent me from shooting this boy, point blank range, through the head."

"But what if we already killed it, chief?" said Shankar. "What if it can't come, because it's dead?"

"Then we'll just have to expand our killing portfolio to include the whole settlement," said Adeti, "and no-one will be any the wiser. You people could have been a sight more cooperative. To my mind that makes you all murderers worthy of my justice." She looked up in confusion as a bright red object arced across the tracery of broken glass in the wall like a star shell. Prophets' faces crawled across her like holy amoebae.

"Uh, Chief," said Wong, shifting his own weapon into a low port position, "you're bluffing *very well.*"

"Maybe a little too well," said Shankar. Again the red beam scanned across the sky like a coal-fired lighthouse. When saintly silhouettes had stopped sweeping across the floor, Adeti's weapon was up and levelled at Shankar's chest, and Shankar's was up and levelled at Adeti's.

"There's really no need for either of you to do this," said Mrs. Reborn-in-Jesus reasonably. "The Devil will do it all for you."

"Maybe I *ought* to start shooting now," said Adeti, "just to prove how good my hand is."

The light swept across the sky again; once more, wheeling shadows.

Adeti looked outward at the stars.

"What *is* that thing—?"

The ceiling shattered. Splinters of eye-stinging red-hot tile showered in all directions leaving burning tracks on the retina. A spinning cannonball of light smashed through the stone vault of the roof, crunched into the flagstones of the transept, uncoiled into a figure roughly the size and shape of a human being, braking itself in the air with wings no human being had. Its head was featureless; presumably it saw in areas of the spectrum human eyes were blind to. Its feet were spade-broad claws. Its hands extruded and retracted talons reflexively. The horns appeared to be radio aerials. What was the tail? A refuelling probe?

The skin was glowing. Parts of it were ticking erratically as it cooled.

"Oh my god," said Wong. "We blew it into low orbit."

"And it ended up *exactly* back here?" said Adeti. "Please."

She acquired the Devil with the carbine, squeezed the trigger, and sent flashes of brilliance round the chamber. However, when the after-images cleared from her eyes, she could see that she had done little but move the dust around in the church. The creature bore lettering where its face should have been: THE CLEVER DEVIL, CONCEPT MODEL, INSTAR HOMINIS CORPORATION. Some of the writing was illegible where tungsten-cored shells had splattered like shied egg.

"A Made," said Adeti.

"A low self-reliance Made," said Shankar. "Not one of your interstellar Von Neumann jobs who made war on people-kind. Designed to be close to human beings, to look like them. That means it has a master nearby. At the end of the War Against The Made, all such units were destroyed, but some of the despicable rich who couldn't stand a life without smart home help hid them."

The handles on the main church doors rotated slowly in the metal.

The machine was moving up the aisle with the grace and speed of a bride.

"It used its wings to brake itself out of orbit," said Wong. "And to steer itself. We can't kill that. There's no way we can kill that."

The church doors slowly swung open. An EVA-suited figure stood in the entrance, holding a bulky device with a single ruby-red eye burning in the front of it.

The Devil turned. The air down the aisle crackled like bacon frying, sparks twinkled, and the Devil's wings glowed orange, then yellow, then white, as if an invisible torch beam were playing on them. It backed away like a fiend from the sign of the cross, and the figure in the aisle walked closer. Again the crackle and twinkle, and this time the demon fled through the walls, leaving a devil-sized hole in Saint Michael.

The ruby eye winked out, and blowers began scrubbing the air of hydrofluoric acid exhaust, which were already beginning to etch the saints' faces in the transept. The EVA suit helmet popped open.

"Heat sinks," said Asahara. "You can't use your heat sinks for orbital braking without overheating. I just overheated it a little more with a sampling laser. It'll cool down and come back. We should leave."

"What was it?"

"Instar Hominis personal servant. They were quite popular among general staff officers in the last days of the Dictatorship. The Dictator himself was reputed to have several. Programmed to fetch and carry, lay out a chap's uniform, and protect him from assassination. You're right. We probably can't kill it."

"But we can leave and come back with a mining cruiser," said Adeti, clicking her weapon back to standby.

"No we can't ma'am," said Shankar.

Adeti rounded on Shankar. "I beg your pardon, Gravitographer?"

"Ma'am, you were about to kill a child."

"I was *bluffing*, mister."

"No you weren't, m'am. Ma'am, I'm arresting you for conduct unbecoming a Citizen."

"We," said Wong in a high and reedy voice, "are arresting you."

Adeti's weapon dropped from her hands in shock. She turned to Asahara.

"I am afraid, Captain," said Asahara, "that I must concur."

"I'm your offering," said Adeti. "Your sacrifice for getting off this planet."

"If that's what you want to believe," said Asahara.

Adeti nodded, raised the weapon onto her shoulder, turned, trudged out of the church. Slowly, the others followed her, less like a team following a leader than dogs holding a larger, heavier, animal at bay.

Her knees crunched down into the cupric dust. The weapon in her hands turned round, the muzzle under her chin.

There was a bright, brief fountain of red, white and grey.

Asahara spoke hopefully to the cold air.

"It should be safe to leave now," she said. "As long as we never come back."

PLD38227 climbed steadily, though far too quickly for Brevet Captain Asahara's liking in the heavy gravity gradient. Landing on neutronium-cored worlds had been part of flight training, but had been covered in only one single simulation, and that simulation had had no atmosphere. Still, the good thing about this particular atmosphere was that it would be over inside a minute.

She had, she reflected, calculated well. It did not look good, even for a Correctness Officer, to be the sole survivor of a mission, but to return having exposed an enemy of civic morality with the assent of all other team members—that was different. Adeti had been foolish; she had been blinded by the planet-sized prize at the heart of Ararat into jeopardizing her vessel and her crew, valuable state assets all.

Seconds away, the FTL drive unit telemetry was responding to remote guidance. Soon the ship would be locked together fit to go interstellar again. Wong and Shankar sat to either side of her, already asleep in their seats. Adeti's suicide had neatly prevented any unpleasantness with inquests, investigations or moral guidance committees. The mining cruiser was within six hours of hailing now, over ten kilometres long, equipped with all the gear for core extraction and light armoured combat alike. The bluff had been effective.

The atmosphere had thinned sufficiently. She reached forward to the console to fire the ship's single antimatter catalyzer.

A bright, brief new star blazed in the heavens. The Anchorite seriously doubted that it heralded the birth of a new Messiah.

The bluff had been effective. Letting them get free of the atmosphere had made them drop their guard, as well as being necessary for an explosion large enough to vapourize the ship without damaging the fragile local ecosystem.

He looked down at the family Reborn-in-Jesus.

"Best not visit the South End for a year or so. I'll inform you when levels have returned to normal."

Shun-Company glanced at Captain Adeti's body, and the Devil walked solemnly over to pick it up, its claws retracted. Children were playing on its back, pulling at its wings.

Mr. Reborn-in-Jesus looked at the Anchorite. "Who *are* you?"

The Anchorite stared up at the distant stars. "I was a very, very bad man, which is all you need to know. Nowadays I'm trying to forget it, but it will keep following." He watched as streaks of metal vapour fingerpainted the atmosphere. "A Type 39 prospector doesn't have a comms suite fit to talk to anything it isn't docked with. They sent no messages. Your farm is safe."

Shun-Company nodded. "Thank you."

"Hey, I live here too."

One of the children ran in from the direction of the house. "*Papai*! A private agro ship saw the bad men's vessel explode! They're asking if we need assistance, they say they have goats and trees and radiation shielding and all sorts of stuff!"

"It's an ill wind," admitted Reborn-in-Jesus. "We could do with a new goat. One of those fancy new ones that gives carcinophagous milk. That'll clean up Day-of-Creation's lymphoma."

The family nodded respectfully to the Anchorite, and the two groups parted, one walking back towards the house and the world's one functioning radio, the other toward the ten-metre horizon.

the bust out

t was Kilodia Seven of the New State Calendar when Justice arrived on Mount Ararat. It arrived in the form of a *Varangian*-class heavy lifter—the military variant with the extended hydrogen collectors—touching down, as so many vessels did, in the South End Yard. This vessel's captain, however, was careful to avoid landing her directly on top of Mount Ararat's single suspiciously large cemetery, and used only chemical rockets for his descent; but chemical rockets, on a world with an atmosphere only around ten thousand cubic kilometres in volume, were dangerous in themselves when they were lifting a ship the size of the *Varangian*. Monoxide alarms went off all over the Reborn-in-Jesus household, and Shun-Company Reborn-in-Jesus gathered her children to her and handed out individually-sized oxygen masks hooked in to a single master cylinder.

Mr. Reborn-in-Jesus, meanwhile, took the community's single ass, Carries-the-Saviour, down to the South End Yard to complain.

He was wearing an EVA suit that didn't quite fit—it had been made for another person, who was now buried in the South End's newest plot. He hadn't seen the grave before; he noted that it was carefully tended, the headstone exquisitely cut of locally-sourced siderite. A radiation-burst in Mount Ararat's southern hemisphere some three New Improved Years ago had made it unwise to even visit the yard until recently; the burst seemed to have triggered a mutation in one of the funeral flowers, which had evolved a spectrum of carotenes and chlorophylls which combined to make both its leaves and petals almost black. The flowers had become a vigorous weed, and were threatening to engulf the gravestones. Mr. Reborn-in-Jesus wondered what it was that was pollinating them. Somehow, however, the gravestones were never quite swamped, as if an invisible hand or claw had been trimming them. Certainly Mr. Reborn-in-Jesus would never allow his many children and godchildren to work in the South End Yard, even today.

The ship was massive and unstreamlined, designed for travelling through atmosphere at a sedate walking pace, taking its time to reach orbit. Mount Ararat's modest atmospheric envelope had not even had time to raise a healthy glow on its leading edges. It pressed down into the regolith through ten mighty feet, each one the area of Reborn-in-Jesus's house. It was evidently a cargo flight, as it had no windows apart from the pilot's landing bubble; however, it bore the many-hands-joined emblem of the Government of Human Space, and was lightly-armed with short-range point defence accelerators and long-range dragnet missiles pulled along in its magnetic field. It had left the missiles in orbit—they circled ominously overhead in a perfect V every ten hours, like migrating geese.

Mr. Reborn-in-Jesus, being tracked by several point defence turrets, alighted from his ass, walked up to the ground-level emergency access hatch, pulled out a spanner, and banged politely on the metal. Oddly, his banging was answered by all manner of rhythmic and arrhythmic percussion from the ship's insides, as if men trapped inside were banging on the inside walls with woodwork tools and dinner cutlery.

Then, a portion of the vessel's aft section, formerly seamless, cracked open soundlessly, and a cube of battered metal the size of a church motored downwards to the ground, leaving a cuboid gap in the rear fuselage which, like a bullet loading into a breech, another metal cube slid out of the vessel to fill. In a matter of seconds, the ship was whole again, and he would never have known an aperture had existed. Then take-off alarms began sounding, unspent fuel burners began sparkling around the ship's underside, and Mr. Reborn-in-Jesus was forced to take his ass behind a rock half a kilometre away before the chemical engines fired again and the ship lifted skywards on huge wasteful plumes of official government flame.

Coughing and fitting a respirator to his ass, Reborn-in-Jesus approached the landing site again. Horrid compounds were forming on the rocks around him, products of the devilish mixtures take-off-thrusters used as fuel.

The abandoned cuboid of starship-metal had neither door nor window—in fact, no surface features of any kind apart from a small, heavy-duty display screen at head height. As Mr. Reborn-in-Jesus approached, the screen came to life, cycling through a selection of languages, one of which was English.

KRANION SECTOR MORAL RECLAMATION AUTHORITY, KILODIA SEVEN
TO WHOM IT MAY CONCERN

IT HAS UNFORTUNATELY BEEN NECESSARY TO LOCATE THIS MAXIMUM
SECURITY PENITENTIARY INSTALLATION ON THIS WORLD 23 KRANII
3X. THIS IS DUE TO NON-EXISTENCE OF VESSEL'S ORIGINAL
DESTINATION

Mr. Reborn-in-Jesus nodded at that. Originally the colony vessel *Utanapishtim,* which had brought him and his family to the 23 Kranii system, had been contracted to stop at Designated Colony World 70, a worldly paradise lovingly terraformed from a Venusian hell not ten kilodia earlier, possessing fruited plains, purple headed mountains, and for all Mr. Reborn-in-Jesus knew, cigarette trees. Unfortunately, by the time *Utanapishtim* had reached Colony World 70, a Made war machine had revisited the 32 Kranii system and reproduced the Venusian hell. It had only been by chance that the captain's system scan had also turned up a planetoid in the same system, not twenty kilometres across, whose surface freakishly reflected light in spectra indicating nitrogen, oxygen, and liquid water. How that could be had not concerned him—he had fulfilled his contract by delivering his settlers to their Very Small Promised Land.

THIS MAXIMUM SECURITY UNIT IS SELF-GOVERNING AND UTTERLY ESCAPE PROOF,

continued the viewscreen.

IT WILL DEFEND ITSELF IF DISTURBED AND SHOULD NOT BE IN-
TERFERED WITH. IN THE TOTALLY IMPOSSIBLE EVENT OF ESCAPE,
AGENTS WILL BE DISPATCHED FROM WITHIN TO RETRIEVE ESCAP-
EES. A SIREN WILL SOUND

(at this point a siren klaxoned so loudly that Mr. Reborn-in-Jesus had to clap his hands over his ears).
Then the viewscreen blanked out apart from the words:

THANK YOU FOR YOUR MANDATORY COOPERATION

There was an ominous, thunderous rumble down the length of

the cuboid, and it shuddered impossibly into the air. Reborn-in-Jesus dropped to his knees and squinted at its underside, and could see legions of heavy, fluted legs powering the structure's immense weight up from the ground. The earth shook as it rose onto a thousand feet and began to march away in the direction of the South End Saddle, Third Landing, and Mr. Reborn-in-Jesus' house.

"It's not just my house I fear for, it's the integrity of the planetary core. Mount Ararat is made of two asteroids pressed together in light contact, and have you any idea what that thing must *weigh?*"

The voice that replied from the other end of the radio was that of the Anchorite, sitting at the family Reborn-in-Jesus's planetary communicator suite, which occupied mysterious pride of place in their Best Parlour. The voice intended to calm, but was not having the desired effect. *"It should take pains to avoid inhabited structures. It is aware of its weight. It must have a reason for making for town, and we should simply sit tight to see what that reason is."*

Carries-the-Saviour had long since tired, and Mr. Reborn-in-Jesus was walking alongside his animal, watching the trundling behemoth crawl slowly and unstoppably towards the one and only high street of Third Landing. Upon being faced with a line of houses, however, regardless of the fact that ten of the houses were uninhabited, the machine took a sharp detour, skirting around the buildings until a gap allowed it to angle in from the desert again. The open side of the settlement was full of fields of growing crops; these, again, it avoided, prowling the town perimeter until it had convinced itself that penetrating to the centre of town must involve either butting through walls or trampling fields. It came to a rest at the junction of two fields, extruding a variety of sensory tentacles from previously unsuspected openings in its upper hull. Finally, given a choice between steam-rollering a field of harvest-ready potatoes and one of newly planted seed, it went for the seed, slowing down as it negotiated the furrows like a mother dinosaur walking among her own eggs. Finally, it fetched up alongside the town reservoir—not close enough to its edge to cause the shoreline structural damage—and extruded from the intelligent metal of its side a massive, clublike proboscis, bedecked with pseudopodia like a starfish's foot, which crawled on those pseudopodia down towards the waterline before disappearing below the surface with a satisfied hiss.

Having seen all this from afar, Mr. Reborn-in-Jesus entered town to be confronted by ten of his children and godchildren, who ran up to him with shouts of "Look out at the big machine, papa! It stuck its peepee in the Pond."

"A heat sink," said the Anchorite knowledgeably as Mr. Reborn-in-Jesus approached. "It's powered by an internal fusion reactor. It needs somewhere to dump its waste heat." He mused a moment. "You see how the water in the Pond is circulating now? You could put a waterwheel on that and generate power. Many colonial traders do quite reasonable kits. You really shouldn't worry about the integrity of the unit, you know. The Series Threes are really quite escape-proof."

"And I suppose you would know," said Mr. Reborn-in-Jesus, throwing a sour glare at the Anchorite, who was known to have a chequered past. The Anchorite blushed guiltily.

"It's circulating *and bubbling,*" said Unity Reborn-in-Jesus in alarm, staring at the surface of the Pond.

"Build a free public health spa," shrugged the Anchorite. "*Aquae Araratis Montis,* the relief of weary travellers. Look on this

46

as an opportunity." Already, children were paddling and splashing in the warming water, and Mr. Reborn-in-Jesus had to shout at those who were paddling and splashing close to the clearly boiling area by the penitentiary's heat sink. It would have to be marked out, he thought, with a string of buoys. Did Blom's Interstellar Travelling Emporium *do* buoys? Whether they did or not, it would probably be politic to ask them in a text message rather than verbally.

His back, feet and head hurting, he led his ass back down the High Street to her stable, which had once been Mr. Raffaele's house before the Devil Plague had taken him. Once again, Mr. Reborn-in-Jesus was going to have to adapt to a change in his environment.

In the eighth kilodia since the Enlargement of the People, somebody escaped from the Series Three.

The unit had by now become an accepted feature of town. Its walls had been used to train tomatoes and beans in their solar gamma shadows where the plants were less prone to mutation. An ambitious mural of Arcadian landscapes had been started on the wall facing towards the pond by Shun-Company Reborn-in-Jesus and her genetic and adopted daughters. The Anchorite's bath house had not materialized, but a bathing stage had been created which visiting tramp trader crews took full advantage of. The area around the pond had been artistically planted with date palms strung with UV fibre like tropical Christmas trees, and real live goats grazed around the water's edge, cropping the black grass.

The goats—Faith, Hope, Charity, and Shub-Niggurath, the last goat having been named by the Anchorite—were led, once a day, out to the green pastures of the Crater of Tares close by the settlement, where thorns and thistles grew in mouth-watering profusion. The goats would gaze longingly through the goat-proof fences on either side at the family Reborn-in-Jesus's genetically jury-rigged potato fields. They would, however, be led firmly and inexorably to their feeding grounds at the Crater, into which a little water was allowed to trickle from the Ninety West Drain. At the end of every day, the beasts would be led back to drink and sleep in a reinforced concrete radiation shelter on the meridian shore of the warm waters of the Pond. Leading the goats was a task given to the youngest responsible Reborn-in-Jesus child, and currently allocated to little Beguiled-of-the-Serpent Raffaele. Having concluded the day's goat-leading activities, Beguiled-of-the-Serpent was sitting on the bathing stage indolently dangling her toes in the water when, quite unexpectedly, the outline of a door appeared in the side of the Penitentiary and rapidly became a door in very truth, which then popped out of the side of the unit and dropped into the cactus underneath an unkempt middle-aged man using the door panel as a shield to protect himself from cactus spines. He squirmed free of the succulents, apparently uncaring whether they cut him or not, then, once at a safe distance from the Series Three, turned and whooped and punched the air, yelling "YES! YES! I DID IT! I DID IT!"

Beguiled-of-the-Serpent had led too sheltered a life to be scared. Instead, she looked up at the man and said, round-eyed:

"Are you an Escapee?"

The man sucked out his chest, drew himself up to his full unimpressive height, clapped himself on the breastbone and said:

"I am *the* Escapee. The only man to have escaped from a Series Three government prison, ever. I, Johannes Trapp, the finest of the fine, the flyest of the fly."

Beguiled-of-the-Serpent considered this, and said:

"My god-daddy says another man escaped from a Series Three over in Pyramidis sector. He fears for our safety as a consequence."

The Escapee narrowed his eyes at the little girl.

"Escaped how?" he said.

Beguiled-of-the-Serpent searched her memory. "Daddy said an Atom Bomb was used by the man's Evil Confederates, which lightly scorched the surface of the unit and tripped the Mercy System that allows inmates to be rescued from a unit damaged by war or cataclysm. This deactivated all its relocking facilities and allowed the despicable gang to cut into it in under seven hours. Both escapee and gang died of radiation poisoning several hours later, but it was a technically successful escape."

"HA!" The Escapee leapt about on one leg and kissed the earth, kissed a palm tree, kissed a highly alarmed goat. "In your FACE, technically successful escapee. I damaged nothing, I forced nothing, I cut into nothing. I am as a GOD."

At this point, the Escape was interrupted by Shun-Company Reborn-in-Jesus, who had left the house to pick fresh onions for the evening meal, and was surprised to see a strange man in bright flashing fatigues talking to her step-daughter.

"I'm sorry," said Shun-Company, switching the basket to her left hand and the onion knife to her right, which was the stronger, "I'm afraid I didn't hear your ship land."

The Escapee grinned. "It landed some time ago. I'm very much afraid it took off again without me."

Little Beguiled-of-the-Serpent pursed her lips indignantly. "It did not! He came out of the Series Three! He is a Successful Escapee, and two minutes ago was quite content to tell the universe as much!" She turned to point at the open hole in the side of the machine, only to see clean, smooth hullmetal. The wound had closed itself.

"You are a wicked child," said Shun-Company, cuffing Beguiled-of-the-Serpent lightly round the head, "for telling tales." She nodded to the Escapee. "I am sorry to hear of your predicament, Mr.—?"

"Trapp. Johannes Trapp. Security expert extraordinaire. I'm afraid I must fall on your mercy until another vessel arrives to remove me. If you have any locks or encrypted communications devices about your home, I would be pleased to greatly improve them as payment for your charity..."

Shun-Company shook her head politely. "There are no locks on Mount Ararat, Mr. Trapp. We do not require them. And our charity is free of charge." She called out to an older daughter who was throwing out slops for the goats. "God's-Wound, lay another place for dinner. I hope you like potato, Mr. Trapp."

Trapp licked his lips. "I have not tasted potato in, in, oh, a long, long time."

"Good. Every time the Agribiz ship arrives, my husband seems to obtain a new species. We have a potato for every occasion."

The meal had been awkward. The table was huge, made up of a single piece of construction metal cut into an ellipse. There were places for Mr. and Mrs. Reborn-in-Jesus at either end, and no fewer than fifteen places in between for children of a bewildering variety of ages and sizes, the older children grown old early, keeping the younger ones in line with savage slaps to the head whenever they dared reach for the cruet without asking. There were exactly as many chairs as had been necessary for the meal, including Mr. Trapp, who had been seated in what he assumed was a place of honour directly between the gentleman and lady of the house. He had been informed that this was because the extra chair belonged to a gentleman who normally dined with the family on Sundays. Mr. Trapp's prisonwear was still flashing alarmingly.

"You have so many children," said Mr. Trapp politely, attempting to smile over a miniscule bowl of what seemed to be potato-flavoured ice cream. The children, who had not received such bowls, craned their necks in his direction, as close to actually drooling as they could be without impoliteness.

"They are not all ours," mumbled Mr. Reborn-in-Jesus into his dessert bowl.

"Yet they are," corrected Shun-Company severely.

"Early in the establishment of the colony, Mr. Trapp," said Unity Reborn-in-Jesus, swan-necked, sylphlike, utterly unaware of the terrible effect she would shortly have on human beings from outside her immediate gene pool, "there were difficulties."

"Deaths," corrected Mr. Reborn-in-Jesus.

Mr. Trapp's attention turned toward his dessert respectfully. He essayed a spoonful of it. As he had expected, it was vile rubber food that bounced off the bottom of the gut and shot back up for a second ingestion. He gritted his teeth against gagging, attempting to turn the gesture into a friendly smile at the children. The children, evidently considering this to be a victorious sneer at the fact that he had dessert and they didn't, looked away in disgust.

"Which ship did you come in on, Mr. Trapp?" said Mr. Reborn-in-Jesus, as if the matter were completely inconsequential.

"Uh, she didn't have a name," said Trapp. "Rather a number, which escapes me for the moment. A tramp trader I'd unwisely secured a passage on out to Alpha Gladii."

Mr. Reborn-in-Jesus looked on with a face of murderous disbelief. "You're a long way from Alpha Gladii, Mr. Trapp. Like one whole constellation. This is the 23 Kranii system. Alpha G. is thirty New Light Years away."

Mr. Trapp swallowed hard. "So far? Oh my. Oh *my*." He covered his head with his hands in mock dismay. "I must apologize for any distraction. This is terrible news. The passenger cabins had no windows. By the sound of it I was lucky I slipped out of the ship to stretch my legs. The ship landed near to here, the Captain said to take compressed air and water—"

"*Water?*" Mrs. Reborn-in-Jesus was actually scandalized. "Do people think there's that little water here?"

"I fear," finished Mr. Trapp, "I might have been aboard a Slaver ship."

Horrified intakes of breath chorussed all round the table. Since the end of the War Against the Made, human beings no longer created machines as intelligent as themselves to do their bidding. A certain type of rich man, particularly this far out on the frontier, found this injurious to his lifestyle; a trade in human slaves, unthinkable for centuries, had evolved to fill this niche.

"I'm sorry," said Mr. Trapp, "I must be alone. Did you say I could sleep in the—?"

"Third house along," said Mr. Reborn-in-Jesus, licking the last flecks of dessert off his spoon. "Still has a bed in it that the blood's been washed out of."

Mr. Trapp smiled a fragile crystalline smile.

Suddenly, Only-God-Is-Perfect Ogundere, who had been watching Mr. Trapp's pulsating kitchen fatigues throughout the meal, piped up unbidden.

"Is what you're wearing the very latest fashion where you come from, Mr. Trapp?"

Trapp had been prepared for this one. "It is indeed, young lady.

But it is dancewear, intended only for festivals. We had been holding a party in steerage. I was hot, and had gleaned that we were on a habitable world with a breathable atmosphere, so I left the vessel to cool down."

"Quite a risk to take," said Mr. Reborn-in-Jesus. "*Habitable* covers dioxide monsoons, sulphuric acid rain, and temperatures both above boiling and below freezing."

"Maybe," smiled Mr. Trapp, "I suspected subconsciously what was about to happen to me."

"Maybe," said Mr. Reborn-in-Jesus. "Third house along," he repeated.

Mr. Trapp smiled again, nodded curtly, and left in a hurry.

"What do you think?" said Mr. Reborn-in-Jesus, as the children were clearing away the dishes.

"I think," said Shun-Company, "that he is either from inside the Penitentiary or an advance scout for a Slaver ship in his own right. It is just possible a vessel could approach Ararat without our detecting it, but such a thing would have had to have been deliberate. It is not my place to criticize my husband, but you could have been less open about your disbelief in his story. If he *is* an escapee, we have no idea what his criminal specialty might be. He might be a serial killer, or a child murderer, or—heaven forfend!— a serial child murderer."

Reborn-in-Jesus ground his teeth in his head. "The Devil would not allow him to harm us."

A metallic green beetle buzzed in lazy figures-of-eight around the room's modest chandelier. Shun-Company looked up at it. "The Devil is no God Almighty, to be considered capable of solving all our problems. Even God insists men address their own difficulties."

Reborn-in-Jesus looked up at the beetle. "Do you hear that, Beëlzebub? Have your eyes and ears heard all that has gone on in this house today?"

The fly buzzed straight up and down in the air before returning to its eternal figure-of-eight.

"Should we fear this new visitor?"

The fly buzzed up and down again.

"Will you pay a visit to us in the morning?"

Again, the up and down movement.

Shun-Company leaned forward close to the fly. "Is your servant close enough to watch over us at this moment?"

The fly wavered from side to side.

Mr. Reborn-in-Jesus raised a finger. "It is checking the South End for recent signs of a Slaver starship landing, am I right?"

The fly rose up and down in the air once more.

Mr. Reborn-in-Jesus nodded.

"Your concern for our welfare is much appreciated, Hermit," he said to the fly. "I'll be pleased to see you in the Ninety East Field at sunup." He nodded to Shun-Company. "Wife: tell Beguiled-of-the-Serpent she is a good girl who tells truth and shall have a new dress when the next trader so equipped arrives. And tell all the others they are to stay indoors and not admit our visitor without permission. I shall sleep with my back to the door tonight equipped with a suitable agricultural implement."

The fly bounced up and down in the air, then vanished up into the chandelier in a myriad tinkling, twinkling emerald images.

*

"OPEN UP."

Mr. Reborn-in-Jesus's sleep was interrupted by what felt like repeated blows to the head with a dinner gong. However, once he had pulled himself upright and taken stock of the situation, he could see that it was simply the metal alloy door being pummelled fit to rock on its hinges by someone titanically strong on the step outside—someone either too polite or too stupid to acknowledge that the door had no lock. There was also the sound of a siren loud enough to wake the whole South End.

He opened the door, warily. It was not yet sunup.

"OPEN UP," said the person on the threshold redundantly. It was difficult for Mr. Reborn-in-Jesus to consider it a person, in fact, as it was not only artificial, but also not designed, as many artificial creatures were, to comfortingly resemble a human being in any way. Instead, it looked designed to fulfil its intended function with an efficiency as grim and terrible as possible. It was probably also, being a government automaton, designed to be safely stupid; the government liked to set a good example to its citizenry in this regard.

"IT IS AN OFFENCE TO HARBOUR FUGITIVES," said the machine—unsettlingly, in the same voice as Mr. Reborn-in-Jesus's intelligent rotary goat-milking unit. Perhaps the same minor celebrity had allowed his voice to be sampled on two separate occasions. "THESE PREMISES WILL SUBMIT THEMSELVES TO SEARCH."

The machine was a squat cuboid of metal resting on three broad feet. A variety of ports, probes and weapons ringed the squat turret head that topped it off, giving it the appearance of a device that had been crowned King of Kitchen Appliances.

"Are you a warder from the Penitentiary?" said Mr. Reborn-in-Jesus. "Show me your authorization to search."

The machine projected a facsimile of a signed paper document lousy with government insignia onto a nearby wall. Mr. Reborn-in-Jesus nodded and stood aside. The machine trundled into the house. A probe extended and sampled the air.

"GENETIC MATERIAL OF MAXIMUM SECURITY PRISONER JO-HANNES MARIA TRAPP DETECTED," it announced. "IT IS AN OF-FENCE TO HARBOUR FUGITIVES," it repeated darkly.

"You may take him with my blessing," said Mr. Reborn-in-Jesus, trying to appear as if he just happened to be carrying the digging blade in his left hand by the sheerest coincidence. "He gave his real name to us. He is in the third house down the street."

"YOUR COOPERATION IS APPRECIATED," said the machine, and wheeled on the ground effect pads in its feet to leave.

Mr. Reborn-in-Jesus gripped the haft of his digging tool nervously.

"What was Mr. Trapp's crime?" he asked.

"GRAND FRAUD," said the machine, "FIVE COUNTS. GENETIC IDENTITY THEFT, NINE COUNTS. UNAUTHORIZED ACCESS TO PRI-VATE SYSTEMS, FIFTEEN COUNTS. ESCAPING FROM A GOVERN-MENT PENAL ESTABLISHMENT, TWENTY-SEVEN COUNTS."

"And the number of convictions for crimes of violence, or against children?" said Shun-Company, who had noiselessly materialized behind her husband.

"ZERO," said the machine, and motored out into the dark, stars mirrored in its brightly polished chassis.

"He is a thief," comforted Mr. Reborn-in-Jesus, patting his wife's arm.

"That machine is the barely the size of our church," said Shun-Company. "No mere thief deserves to be confined in such a way."

At that point, the screams began in the street outside; and Mr. Reborn-in-Jesus took up his digging tool unashamedly and ran.

Sixty seconds earlier, the stars had been shining from slightly different quarters, and the scarlet shimmering scimitar of Naphil's A ring had shone a constellation's width broader overhead as Mount Ararat hurtled towards intersection. The goats were asleep in their shelter; the Penitentiary was as yet quiet, not yet realizing one of its inmates was absent.

The communications tower stood out at one corner of the Third Landing village square, a metal tree of dishes, whip aerials and communications lasers. No tree had been planted near it; cables burrowed down from it into the dirt and resurfaced by the Reborn-in-Jesus residence. Halfway up it, accessible via a maintenance ladder, was a manual access panel, which lay open. Inside, mysterious user-unfriendly readouts and schematics marched across a durable plastic screen.

A voice called from the bottom of the tower. "Are you done yet, Mr. Trapp?"

A voice answered from up by the maintenance panel. "I've located a ship insystem. Her captain says he's braking into your gas giant's atmosphere to collect helium-3 and slow himself down to meet another trader and swap mail loads in the inner system. Says he can take both of us on to Twenty. Be landing a kilometre from here in an hour's time."

"So long as he hurries up," said the voice from the tower's base. "If anyone finds me out here, no-one'll talk to me from now till Christmas. I'll be on goat-leading duty for certain."

The panel slammed shut and was screwed home by a man with fastidious attention to detail, who then slid down the maintenance ladder with a spring in his step.

"Do you really think I have it in me to become a top-rate courtesan?"

"My dear, you are the image of Ishtar herself. I have contacts at all the best-regarded agencies on Old Earth, in Bangkok, Teheran, Emporium, Pennsylvania, and many other exotic locations." Mr. Trapp began untying the tether connecting Carries-the-Saviour to the great shelter.

"I can't get my legs behind my head. Does that matter?"

The conversation was suddenly interrupted by a klaxon loud enough to kill a man and wake him afterwards. Trapp began working more quickly, feverishly, looking up in the direction of the Series Three like Damocles at his ceiling decoration.

"What is that, Mr. Trapp? What's that sound?"

A man-sized alcove of light opened in the side of the Penitentiary, and a stubby, three-legged machine emerged, rotated to take in its surroundings, and took off towards the largest house in Main Street. For the first time, Mr. Trapp blessed the fact that he was standing behind a warm dyspeptic ass—Carries-the-Saviour's extravagant heat signature had masked Trapp's own.

"It seems," said Mr. Trapp, "we still have one more detail to take care of. Please be so good as to follow me."

He raised the Reborn-in-Jesus family kitchen knife that he'd used to open the maintenance panel,, so old and oversharpened that its blade was a mere steel sliver. 'The A ring reflected from it, red as blood.

Mr. Reborn-in-Jesus skidded round the corner, implement in hand, to be confronted by an empty tranquil pond and a silent, featureless Penitentiary.

The Warden's tracks returned to the wall of the unit, and went no further. However, they were also accompanied by human footprints, *small* human footprints spaced erratically, as if their creator were being dragged unwillingly. There was blood in the footprints. A great deal of blood. Close by, a set of shod hooves had left town along the hundred-eighty meridian, apparently at the closest an ass could get to a gallop.

Unity Reborn-in-Jesus, who had been following her parents closely, went pale and put her hand over her mouth.

"I'll call roll," she said.

"I do not understand," said Mr. Reborn-in-Jesus. He reversed his digging implement and banged on the penitentiary metal with it. "HEY! WARDEN! YOU IN THERE!"

In synchronicitous answer, a bright star rose from the Hundred-Eighty Field, burning contrails into the eyes. The star resolved itself into four main lift jets, blazing fit to roast Mount Ararat's entire planetary cabbage crop. A type three trader, landing and taking off on Reborn-in-Jesus land on maximum burn without permission—

"Testament!"

"Here!"

"Gus!"

"Here!"

"Postle!"

"Present!"

"Only-God-is-Perfect... Only-God-is-Perfect? Perfect? PER-FECT??"

"The landing beacon's activated," said sharp-eyed Magus, squinting up at the comms tower. "The dish is moving to track a ship. Uh, *that* ship."

"I think Only-God-is-Perfect's missing," reported Unity.

At that point, Shun-Company screamed. She had found the knife.

Out of the sun he came, casting a long shadow. Wearing a beard he had never been known to cut, sandals on his feet, a lightweight gamma-reflective cloak, and underwear donned only out of deference to the presence of children, the Anchorite was the oldest inhabitant of Ararat. No evidence existed to suggest he had not been here when the fiery degenerate-matter meteor had first torn into the heart of the planetoid and given it gravity, when Ararat had been formed by the clashing together of two mutually orbiting mountains. He had been observed to eat, drink, and defecate just like a real person, so it could only be assumed that he was human. The sheer size of the beard and the weatherbeaten nature of his physique, however, prevented accurate speculation as to his age. He lived in a cave out on the edge of the South End Chasm, a hermit without any discernible religion.

When he arrived, Shun-Company was sitting in her skirts in the main street weeping, along with her entire retinue of daughters and god-daughters, and many of the younger boys. Only Unity, Magus, Apostle, and Reborn-in-Jesus senior were standing, looking sternly into the sky where the glowing teardrop of a starship's plasmadrive seemed to have been activated.

"Dear me," said the Anchorite, "what a lot of fuss".Whereupon Shun-Company proceeded to turn on him and subject him to a lengthy vituperative lecture on failure to protect her children, the emptiness of his promise that her children would never be harmed, and the fact that he might as well strike her down as well as harm her little girl who was the fruit of her womb and apple of her eye.

"I don't recall *promising* not to harm *anybody*," said the Anchorite pointedly. "I also believe that Only-God-is-Perfect is your god-daughter, and hence has never passed through the parts you mention."

Shun-Company threw a tear-sodden handkerchief at the Anchorite and was led away sobbing by her daughters.

"I must apologize," said Mr. Reborn-in-Jesus, "for the behaviour of my wife; she is distraught."

"I see." The Anchorite was examining the footprints in the dust outside the Penitentiary. "Left in that, I suppose, did he?" He pointed a finger that resembled a dry stalactite up at the sky.

"We imagine so," said Magus. "They must have been confederates of his, called up once he escaped the Penitentiary."

"Or Slavers," said Unity, distraught. "He mentioned Slavers."

"The most notorious slaver of recent years, Arne Skilling, the Terror of Linehead, kidnapped over one hundred families from small towns across the New Earth Prairie," said Day-of-Creation, who had recently been given Leader Vos's Every Watchful Boy's Wanted Criminal Databank by his brothers as an unwise thirteenth birthday present. "He went into hiding and was never caught—"

"Skilling was almost certainly killed by a microparticle hit that cracked the drive shielding on his flagship," said the Anchorite. "He was dispatched on the orders of the Dictator himself, and a thorough job was made of it. Though the flagship escaped by overloading her time distort function, her crew experienced ten years of radioisotope exposure in ten minutes. Almost certainly this would have killed him. No, no, I really don't think the crew of that vessel were confederates or Slavers or anything more sinister than good Samaritans. After all, if a ship is called down to pick up passengers and a man all covered in his own blood runs over the horizon and insists he's being pursued by folks who'd take his life, what would any conscientious captain do?"

61

"But he *wasn't* being pursued by folk who'd take his life," objected Mr. Reborn-in-Jesus.

The Anchorite cast a disbelieving eye at Reborn-in-Jesus's digging implement. "So? I imagine you're out hoeing a field while the soil's still frozen solid just before dawn, then?"

Mr. Reborn-in-Jesus lowered his eyes guiltily, and wrung his hands round the hoe-haft.

"But it wasn't his own blood," said Unity, "it was poor Perfect's."

"I beg to differ." The Anchorite bent to examine the ass tracks. "See here, the blood continues to drip and flow for upwards of twenty metres. That is unlikely, unless he'd taken a bath in the poor girl's O Positive."

Shun-Company, still within earshot, heard this and set to wailing like a siren. The Anchorite ignored her. "I'm sorry to disappoint you, but your foster-sister is still very much alive." He jerked a thumb behind him at the Series Three. "In there."

"In *there*?" Mr. Reborn-in-Jesus pointed at the unforgiving metal dumbly.

"Of course. I'm afraid penitentiary units are really not that bright, and their designers tend to over-rely on the efficiency of DNA testing. If a person has the DNA of a convicted criminal, they reason, why, he or she must be that criminal, regardless of all other physical evidence. So if a criminal escapes and wishes not to be pursued by the penitentiary's warden, why, all he has to do is kidnap some poor girl and cover her in his DNA."

"His own blood," marvelled Mr. Reborn-in-Jesus, simultaneously impressed and repulsed.

"Yes. Hence the ass. He probably couldn't have walked to out to the ship unassisted having bled that heavily."

"So," said Reborn-in-Jesus, working through the logic, "all we have to do is get her out of there."

The Anchorite shook his head. "I'm afraid that's not possible. Series Threes are very well constructed. Even if we had anything on Ararat that could cut into it without killing Perfect, it would protect itself, and it can do so both defensively and offensively. It's probably monitoring our conversation at this very moment, checking for phrases such as 'easy with the plastique, Mr. Fingers' and 'hand me that fluorine cutter'. It can also send out a cry for help over up to thirty light years. Any government enforcement vessels in that radius would be duty bound to investigate."

"So what do we do?" said Reborn-in-Jesus. "You can go in there. You understand this manner of thing. I am only a farmer."

"I am not," said the Anchorite defiantly, "going anywhere near that thing's DNA scanners. They might figure out who I'm made of. And that would do us no good in any case. Those devices are virtually escape-proof. I only ever heard of one man who could get out of one."

"And that was?" said Reborn-in-Jesus.

The Anchorite shaded his eyes against plasmaglare and stared up into the sky. "I believe he's just left." He dropped his gaze back to earth. "Which means we have to convince him to come back."

Magus Reborn-in-Jesus put his father in his left ear and the Anchorite in his right.

Personality-analogues were handed out wholesale by traders on the wild frontier who knew their clientèle well. Deaths in families were common in the outworlds, whether by disease, malnutrition, poor radiation shielding, or simply forgetting to start a seized tractor in reverse. For that reason, in order to give themselves the ability to pass on valuable advice to their children after they had gone where the puppies went, colonial parents encoded their essences into dinky plastic talismans that could, so the traders assured them, accurately encompass their entire personalities in a handful of HCRAM chips connected to a mono speaker. To which Grandpa Santos's reply had been *if that darn jigger contains all of me, why don't it go down the state benefit office, collect my dole, and get me my meds on the way home?* The devices, frequently worked into cheap and nasty costume jewellery decorated with hearts and angels, were despised by most, lifelines to some.

Magus Reborn-in-Jesus's father and Uncle Anchorite were not dead. However, they were currently over ten New Light Years away. Reborn-in-Jesus senior had fields to tend and a family of fifteen to feed, and was not about to leave his wife and elder children in charge of such important things as growing potatoes. The Anchorite, meanwhile, had flatly refused to leave Ararat and travel anywhere in Civilization.

For this reason, both men were accompanying Magus as analogues. The old lady on the seat opposite Magus smiled pityingly as their transport dropped through the quicksand-thick clouds of Colony World Twenty, formerly Buttonia, now Anadyomene. The young man was wearing two personality analogues. He had lost both his father *and* his mother.

"Where are you now?" said his father.

"Approaching the city of Smith," reported Magus.

"Population around a hundred thousand," interjected the Anchorite. *"The only reference I can find to it is in the New Anadyomene Company Savers' Prospectus, which describes the planet as 'a worldly paradise of opportunity where green pastures will spring from the barren rock'."*

Magus gazed down on kilometres and kilometres and kilometres of barren rock.

"When is the prospectus dated?" he said.

"Last year," said the Anchorite. *"The prices for owning a plot of green pasture are all in company currency, which is never a good sign. The price quoted is one hundred Company doubloons per hectare."*

The SSTO ferry swept down a long, flashing-light-lined cavity like a sperm cautiously entering a urethra. Giant magnetic arms reached out to grab it. There was a long, long pause while the pressures on either side of the airlock equalized.

"I believe," said Magus, "we have arrived."

"That's a Made," said the New Anadyomene Company customs official, unbuttoning his holster as he said so.

"This is my travelling companion," said Magus. "He suffered a horrific steel-pouring accident. I assure you he is not a robot. His organic components now consist only of his central nervous system—which you can understandably not DNA-sample, as it is both delicate and contained well within this armoured exoskeleton. He does, however, carry around a token of his DNA, which I hereby present to you." He handed a flap of skin the size of a smart card through the hole in the bulletproof, bombproof, charged-particle-beam-proof screen. The Devil tipped its travelling hat at the customs man politely.

The border controller looked the skin flap over solemnly and skimmed it into a manual sampler. He looked at his colleague.

"Human," he said. He looked back at Magus.

"Your kid brother, huh? Tough break."

Seconds later, with a fresh and poorly-dressed sample cut itching on his arm, Magus was loose in the upper corridors of Smith.

The entire city, poorly rendered information screens at the SSTO terminal informed him, was of necessity currently temporarily underground, protected by antacid coffer dams, overpressure, and a well-maintained system of alkali sprinklers from the roaring lava-thick, magma-hot atmosphere outside. Having an atmosphere one could hurt one's head on meant that the air in the city of Smith had to be maintained at a slightly *greater* pressure. A ball of particularly dense and moist atmosphere was rolling down the passageway toward him, clearly visible. Breathing was a laborious exercise. Coughing, he imagined, might do damage to his lungs.

He was hungry. There were prices for what he imagined passed locally for food flashing dully from booths on either side of the terminal escalator. He noticed that a ham-simulant burger cost one thousand company doubloons.

"The trader said he set Trapp down on Anadyomene," said the Anchorite.

"The trader was under some pressure at the time," cautioned Magus.

"The unit was the soul of gentility," said the Anchorite. *"It barely nicked his flesh."*

"It removed all his clothing and body hair," reproved Magus.

"He needed encouragement."

The unit, standing motionless alongside Magus on the moving stairway, stared without eyes into the rows of orbital transfer insurance, vacuum suit overhaul, and personal atmosphere contaminant alarm dealerships that flanked the way into town. Magus was aware that it was looking for threats. He dreaded what it would do if it found any.

"Where do you think he'll go?" asked Magus.

"The next ship out, and so on and so forth till he's at Space's other end. That's what I'd do. But the very first place he'll go—"

here the analogue paused as if to lick nonexistent lips—*"is a bar, delicatessen, naked go-go parlour, ten-hour non-stop dance-a-rama. He will indulge his pleasures."*

"How can you be so sure?" argued Reborn-in-Jesus senior from Magus's left ear.

"He has been inside a Series Three for at least a good old-fashioned year, probably longer. The penitentiary would have fed him nourishing food, hydrated him adequately, played him piped music, even extruded orifices from his cell wall to gratify him sexually. But the food would have been recycled faeces, the water processed urine, the music popular music. And a rubber orifice, no matter how inviting, does not have the warm allure, the potential for heartbreak and disappointment, of a real human male-or-female-delete-as-appropriate."

"Your experience seems almost first-hand," essayed Magus, regretting the attempted intrusion into the Anchorite's prior existence even as he said it.

"I was inside a Series Two," said the Anchorite in his ear sadly. *"They were easier to escape from."*

Gigantic concrete letters soared over his head: MAIN LEVEL TEN. Locals, wandering past in company fatigues, stared as much at Magus's clothes, with their colour scheme unapproved by Anadyomene company marketing, as at his companion.

"Give you a hundred dubs for that coat, Mister."

Magus frowned. "I couldn't possibly. That's a full hectare."

The other man—a depilated, delapidated creature—spat. "Give you a week if you're new; you'll be in hock to the tune of a continent, just like the rest of us." The local cast a curious eye at Magus's travelling companion, as if only now noticing him. "Is he okay?"

"He is in constant distress," said Magus. "The pain nerves severed in his accident have been extensively audited and shut down, but many still function."

"He's still *human* inside there?"

"Please, sir. He can hear you. A heart-rending plasma containment tragedy. Only his spine and brain remain."

"I used to be a lawyer on New New Earth, my wife a doctor. But we dreamed, like fools, of owning our own plot of land. We heard of Anadyomene and all the wonderful terraforming opportunities. *The land won't be ready the moment you go in,* they said. *You may have to work in other company concerns onplanet while the land's being made ready.* I been here five New Years now. I'm still working."

Magus's youthful sense of injustice was outraged. "Where do you work?"

"Anadyomene Nanopharmaceutical. It's the only Other Company Concern here. The missus tells me we're working under biohazard conditions no worker would be allowed to back on New New. Every now and again some poor duffer gets a defective hazard suit and his scrotum breaks out in polyps and they take him off to the Infirmary and we never see him again. Me, though, I'm not in the labs. I work in Nanopharmaceutical Protection, manufacturing defective hazard suits." He smiled ruefully.

"And the terraforming?"

"No-one's ever seen any evidence of any, and Nanopharmaceutical was set up with our land purchase funds. If I could just get back home to New New, I'd land a lawsuit on these bastards heavier than Satan-vs.-God-Kidnapping-False-Imprisonment-and-Brimstone-Injury." The worker paused carefully to give Magus time to reply.

"Walk on, Magus," cautioned the Anchorite. *"He is trying to inveigle you into an act of altruism."*

68

Other workers moving past were beginning to notice the fact that Magus and the lawyer were talking. Some were wearing badges marked SUPERVISOR.

"This was not a chance meeting," said Magus, "was it?"

The Company man's cool broke. "Okay, you got me, I spend two New Hours in each New Improved Day walking up from the lower levels to here on the off chance a ship's put in. I would give my own prostate and forebrain to get myself and my Yele off this rock. But I got no money left that don't have the grinning fizzog of the Anadyomene Corporation Chairman on the face side. Please, please help me."

"Do not," warned the Anchorite, *"under any circumstances help him."*

"You said you watch the port every day," said Magus.

"Certainly do."

"A man came here. A man of slightly less than average build, middle age, tanned complexion, blue eyes, mesomorphic."

The lawyer shrugged. "Could be anyone."

"He would have looked obscenely pleased with himself."

"Oh," said the lawyer instantly, with the huge disdain of a man not obscenely pleased with himself, *"Him."*

Men had once joined certain brutal military units to forget. Johannes Maria Von Trapp had, it seemed, had joined the Anadyomene Corporation to be forgotten.

The Sub Level Two administrative centre was a place where, if anything resembling a human soul had existed, it would have been swiftly filed, categorized, assessed and taken out of scope as non-cost-effective. The workers here wore different uniforms, less hardwearing, more uncomfortable, with a fabric noose tied around the neck in a Double Windsor. They sported Personal Head Up Display Assistants clipped to their temples, beaming internal memos directly onto their retinas. Some of the more loyal senior staff had internal PHUDA's installed in parts of the brain a middle manager had no need to use, principally the frontal lobes; their eyes glittered with internal messaging.

Mr. Von Trapp worked somewhere in a massive cube of powdery acid concrete which housed External Company Payroll. Only a very small number of pedestrian footbridges led in and out.

"It figures," said the Anchorite, even though his predictions regarding vice palaces and unrestrained gratification of the senses had been disproved. *"He wouldn't be interested in company doubloons."*

"He breezed in a week ago," said the lawyer, whose name, it transpired, was Iraklis Joannou. "Bought up half the Southern Hemisphere with a single credit implant in his right hand. The credit reader was an old, pre-inflation model. When it read his limit, it broke down with a numeric overflow."

"Impossible," said the Anchorite huffily. *"Only the Dictator himself was ever that rich."*

Magus relayed the Anchorite's opinion.

"There were some," said Joannou, "who suspected he *was* the Dictator. After all, His Excellency is known to be still at large."

"Hardly. It's likely he died when his supporters attempted to spring him from custody at Last Stop," opined Reborn-in-Jesus senior.

"In any case," said Joannou, "given what you've told me of his antecedents, I have no doubt that the limit was somehow forged. But it bought him an immediate directorship. He's on secondment to Payroll until confirmation of transfer of funds from the New Earth Bank."

"Which gives him about," the Anchorite counted on invisible fingers, *"ten New Days, more or less."*

Joannou, not hearing the voice in Magus's right ear, said: "The time for interstellar settlement of funds transfers of this size is around ten New Days. A few small colony worlds and financial institutions should be bankrupted in the process, but I doubt our Mr. Von Trapp cares overmuch."

"He won't. Those who shoot you in the head are more honest than Trapp's sort," said the voice in Magus's right ear. *"If a scam of his puts a hundred thousand people on the street and one hundred of them commit suicide, somehow that doesn't make him a murderer. But you drop* one *hydrogen bomb on a populated area, just* one—"

"Do we think," said Mr. Reborn-in-Jesus, *"that Mr. Von Trapp will shortly be leaving Anadyomene?"*

"As soon as he manages to find a way into the Payroll transfer system," said the Anchorite.

"He won't wait till he gets his directorship?" said Mr. Reborn-in-Jesus, shocked.

"Three things—firstly, those funds are unlikely to clear. Secondly, now is the time to strike, while the Company imagines he's being a good boy, waiting for his Directorship. Thirdly, if anyone on this planet has even an inkling of a suspicion that Trapp is the Dictator, then there are Moral Cleansing Bureau ships on their way here right now. The rewards for the Dictator's recapture would ransom the soul of Judas."

"YOU THERE. WHAT ARE YOU DOING UP IN PAYROLL?" The voice had come from an unobtrusive Remote Face high on a nearby pillar—a panel with stereo microphones, a single speaker, and twin trackable cameras. This Remote Face was painted to resemble Sweeney, the Anadyomene Company Happy Clown.

Joannou walked over to the Remote Face and raised his voice to a shout. "APOLOGIES, SIR. I WAS SHOWING VISITORS TO THE PLANET UP HERE AT THEIR REQUEST. PROSPECTIVE SHAREHOLDERS," he added.

The voice in the speaker sounded both incredulous and pained. "THEY'VE SEEN THE PLACE AND THEY STILL WANT TO LIVE HERE?" A drop of acid rain leaking from an upper level splashed into the concrete near the lawyer's feet, raising a hiss as it dissolved the surface.

Magus raised his voice. "WE BELONG TO A RELIGIOUS ORDER WHICH VALUES PRIVACY."

"WELL, SHOWING NEW MARKS AROUND IS THE JOB OF THE WELCOMING COMMITTEE. TAKE THESE VALUED GUESTS BACK UP TO MAIN TWO AND RETURN TO YOUR QUARTERS, SHARE-HOLDER."

The lawyer nodded and pointed in the direction of the Up elevator cage.

Sub-levels whirred past in the elevator, each with its own particular unpleasant smell.

"Were they listening to us?"

The lawyer nodded. "Always. They had the gain cranked right up to the max. That's why the guy sounded like he'd sat on a succulent when I yelled at him. But it also means they probably didn't have a smaller, less obtrusive microphone closer by. They probably don't know what we're up to."

Another elevator cage passed them, going down. The cage was full of offworlders in variously-coloured shorts and utility vests, standing motionless with streams of HUD flickering over their corneas.

"Who are they?" said Magus, following the elevator with his eyes.

"Patch me in to the Devil ", said the Anchorite. Magus fished for a connector on the side of the personality-analogue, raised his travelling companion's hat, and pushed the connector into the Devil's temple. Immediately, the Devil raised its head and tracked the receding cage with eyes far better than human.

"Moral Cleansing Analysts blending in," said the Anchorite. *"They will be armed. The weapons will be internal."*

"Moral Cleansing Analysts are going to retrieve Mr. Von Trapp," said Magus out loud. "They will not discover him to be the Dictator, but as soon as they sample his DNA, they will discover him to be a wanted criminal and rearrest him."

"What do we do?" said Joannou as the elevator cage began to slow. Magus listened to the voices in his head, as his father had advised him. "We must warn Mr. Von Trapp," he said. "We will require his public access mail address. And then you must get in touch with your wife," he said, "and instruct her to pack."

The lawyer's eyes shone. He pulled a personal media centre from his coverall and began punching in commands with shaky fingers.

The Departures terminal was one of two long bores of concrete like the barrels of a shotgun, driven into the rock until they intersected with the top of Smith City. It was empty of all but a handful of Company Area Sales Supervisors and legal representatives. Anadyomene middle management, it seemed, travelled on whatever vile firework drifted into the system, rather than on the sleek executive needles Magus had seen parked in orbit for the Board of Directors. This week's particular vile firework was a type two trader, the *Tears of the Moon*. The air in the terminal smelt of sulphur, and the concrete was stained with acid craters. The middle managers all sported slatted ceramic umbrellas.

Mrs. Joannou was a severe, spare lady who had inspected Magus's teeth when she had first met him five minutes earlier.

"You've overtanned," she said. "Your skin will age quickly, with increased risk of melanoma. Your employer should provide radiation shielding. You're a farmer, you say? What have you been doing, tilling the fields by hand?"

Magus had only been able to grin and shrug weakly. Curiously, Mrs. Joannou had approved of his diet of potatoes.

"Potatoes are good," she said. "Potatoes and milk, the diet of peasants. Peasants eat better than kings, as a rule; their survival strategy is to outbreed the aristocracy, and you can't breed if you're not healthy. The only thing better than potatoes and milk is good solid meat, mark my words. Human meat, for preference."

The Joannous, who had been a doctor and a lawyer on their homeworld, had two Company lunchboxes of baggage. When Mr. Joannou had asked for their tickets for the impending flight, Magus had simply shaken his head and instructed patience.

"There will be tickets before the flight departs," he said.

A final call was being made for Passenger Zzyzx. Mrs. Joannou's lips were pursed, and Magus feared the very worst thing in his universe, verbose feminine disapproval.

At length, however, a sweating, panting figure struggled up the escalator into Departures, toting two suitcases bigger than he was, assisted by two Shareholder urchins bearing cases that were even larger.

"Mr. Von Trapp, I presume," said Magus.

Von Trapp stared warily, a fight-or-flight debate clearly bouncing off the inside of his skull.

"Plug me into the Master socket on the Devil," said the Anchorite. Magus found a new port on the Devil's head cowling.

"GOOD AFTERNOON, HANSI," said the Devil in the Anchorite's voice. Magus had never known it had a speaker. Certainly it had nothing resembling a mouth.

Von Trapp licked his lips. "Who are you? Your voice is familiar."

The Devil set its hat at a jaunty angle and posed extravagantly. "HOW ABOUT MY FACE?"

"I must say you have lost me there."

"I AM AWARE OF YOU BY REPUTATION," said the Devil. "I HAVE SPENT TOO LONG IN SERIES ONES AND TWOS NOT TO KNOW OF HANS TRAPP, THE MAN WHO MAKES SECURITY SYSTEMS SING THEIR PASSWORDS, THE MAN WITH A MILLION GENOMES, THE MAN NO SERIES ONE OR TWO CAN HOLD."

"And no Series Three," said Trapp defiantly.

"YOU WERE JUST PLAIN TRAPP WHEN I LAST KNEW OF YOU," said the Devil. "WHEN DID YOU GET RAISED TO THE PEERAGE? BUT ENOUGH OF SMALL TALK; YOU HAVE PLACES TO GO. WE *ALL* HAVE A PLACE TO GO. WE ARE GOING BACK TO MOUNT ARARAT, HANSI, AND YOU ARE COMING WITH US."

"Mount Ararat?" An eyebrow flickered curiously. "Is that what the place was called?"

"IT IS. AND THERE IS A GIRL STILL STUCK IN A SERIES THREE FOR THE REST OF YOUR NATURAL LIFE. THERE IS ONLY ONE MAN I KNOW OF WHO CAN GET HER OUT."

Trapp grimaced. "She will be well fed. She will have all she needs to live a long life. The world she lived on, the people there live like animals, trying to grow crops in poison dust. Working the land by hand out under hard gamma. Lifetime in a warm cell is better for her."

Before Magus even moved, the Devil said "DO NOT KILL HIM,

MAGUS, WE NEED HIM ALIVE. GEEHRTER HERR TRAPP, I AM AFRAID THIS IS NOT A PRESENTATION OF ALTERNATIVES. IT WAS WE WHO SENT THE TEXT WARNING FIFTEEN MINUTES AGO, PRE-CIPITATING YOUR HASTY DEPARTURE. THE WARNING, HOWEVER, WAS REAL. THERE *ARE* MCB ANALYSTS HERE IN SMITH CITY LOOK-ING FOR YOU."

"Moral Cleansing?" Trapp was incredulous. "I'm no political prisoner!"

"YOU WERE TOO EXTRAVAGANT WITH YOUR MONEY. THEY BELIEVE YOU ARE THE FORMER DICTATOR, HIS EXCELLENCY SU-PREME OVERLORD BUTTON HUMPAGE III, AND I CAN ASSURE YOU, THAT SLY SMIRK YOU HAVE ON YOUR FACE WOULD NOT HAVE REMAINED THERE LONG IF HIS EXCELLENCY HAD STILL BEEN IN OFFICE. HUMPAGE IS KNOWN TO BE DANGEROUS, AND MCB ANALYSTS ARE KNOWN TO SHOOT FIRST AND ANALYZE AFTER-WARDS. WE HAVE ONLY TO PLACE A CALL THROUGH TO COM-PANY SECURITY. QUITE APART FROM THE FACT," said the Devil, extending dagger-like fingernails as if checking them for dirt, "THAT IF YOU DO NOT COME WITH US RIGHT NOW, THIS ONE HUNDRED KILOGRAMME PERSONAL SECURITY UNIT WILL CLOTHE ONE OF THOSE GENTLEMEN OVER YONDER WITH YOUR SKIN AND TAKE HIM IN YOUR STEAD. AS YOU HAVE QUITE ADEQUATELY PROVEN, IT IS ONLY THE DNA WE NEED, NOT THE LIVING BODY."

"But it took me a *year* to get out of there! A year of hard work that I began planning when I was first sealed in!"

"Then you can get out again," said Magus. "I'll help you get out. Because I'm going back in with you. If you think I'd send you back in alone into possible solitary confinement with my sister, you've another think coming."

"I BEG YOUR PARDON?" said the Devil.

"So I suppose *you're* volunteering to go back in with him in my stead?" said Magus.

The Devil stood as dumb as a mouthless thing.

"The Series Three learns!" wailed Trapp. "I will not be able to employ the same escape strategy twice."

"When you finally do escape," said Magus, "you will have confederates on the outside ready to arrange passage offworld."

Trapp looked Magus up and down contemptuously. "And how will you pay for such a thing?"

"I will not. You will, Mr. Richer-than-the-Dictator. And while you're about it, you will pay for these two fine people to travel from here to New Earth, and reimburse the debt they owe to the Anadyomene Corporation, at that public transaction terminal over yonder."

Trapp slumped in defeat.

"I concede," he said. He held out his hand for Magus to lead it to the credit reader, and yelled across the departure hall to the flight attendant. "PASSENGER ZZYZX REPORTING, PLUS TWO NEW TICKETS."

"They'll wait," said Prosecutor Joannou confidently. "They have to pay for their fuel for the outgoing trip. They come here with a full passenger roster, but no-one ever leaves. No-one under the rank of manager." He looked over to Magus. "You and your family have done us a great service. When we finally successfully nail Anadyomene in court, we will buy you anything within the value of the compensation."

Magus grinned thinly. He looked at the back of his hand, tanned as a razor strop.

"I believe," he said, "our settlement could do with a tractor. A Terrawatt Altrak Percheron 500, with self-magnetizing fusion torus, lead glass cabin and backhoe attachment. Possibly," he said, "two, one for operational use and one as a cold standby."

"Done," grinned the Prosecutor. "And now I believe the Gate staff are getting impatient. My dear, it is time for us to go where there is sky again."

He squeezed his wife's hand affectionately; she squeezed his in return.

The sound of the tramp trader *Insert Sweetheart's Name Here* lifting off behind them rumbled through the rock and made the sand dance to the height of a man's waist. Magus had already tied his scarf into a turban to keep out the stinging dust, but Trapp was coughing like a consumptive. It was an hour before North End sunrise. There was a chance that the relatively gentle landing and takeoff of a small ship might only make the family roll over in their sleep, but it made sense to approach down the Dry Rille until they were as close to the Penitentiary as possible. The Penitentiary had better eyes and ears.

"*This is insane,*" complained his father's analogue in his left ear. "*You are committing the most outrageous folly. I demand that you insert my jack into the Devil's master socket immediately, so that I may take control of the situation.*"

"*You will leave the Devil's master socket alone,*" said the Anchorite. "*I do not approve of this course of action, but I do not want an atomic-powered bulletproof automaton capable of trimming a man's head from his shoulders in the hands of a peon.*"

"*I,*" said Magus sharply, "am a peon."

The Series Three loomed large, its metal surface glinting in the dawn. Mr. Trapp's hands had begun to shake.

"Easy," said Magus. "I am with you."

"You," said Trapp, "are dead weight. Getting both of us out will be twice as difficult." He took a deep breath and strode up to the wall.

"Where is the entrance?" said Magus.

"Anywhere on the wall it wants one," said Trapp. "It will create one only if it needs one. Unfortunately, it does not feel it needs one right now. It knows it has a full complement of prisoners."

"But my sister does not have your DNA," said Magus.

"She did when she went in. She might not now, but the machine will cleverly realize this is a cunning subterfuge on the part of the prisoner in an attempt to escape. It may possibly be punishing her for this repeated escape attempt even as we speak."

Magus felt a cold blade of adrenalin turn in a wound in his heart. "Punishing her for having incorrect DNA?"

"It's the way it thinks, or rather, doesn't. If I were you, I'd be glad she's being punished. She'll never be that much of a fool again."

"Fool enough to trust you," muttered Magus.

"We get in," announced Trapp, "by convincing the machine that it needs to open up for maintenance. It needs to think it is malfunctioning. It needs to feel in need of a big strong maintenance man inside it." He nodded to the Devil. "Set the first package we bought on Beltane down over there, gently."

"What is it?" said Magus.

"A logical extension of the basic workings of a starship's FTL drive," said Trapp. "Any FTL drive is by definition also a time machine, and hence this wonderful device, the bane of any time lock." He opened the lid of the casket and began to flick switches. "Take the emitter coil over there and clamp it to the hull, if it'll clamp."

Magus shook his head. "Clamp it yourself."

Trapp sighed in disappointment, walked over to the hull with a medusa of superconducting cables, and attached them to the metal.

"Can't say I blame you," he said. "If I'd flicked the switch here while you'd been over there, you'd have aged a year in a minute. You'd have suffocated in under a second, used up all the air in your time bubble. If," he said, raising his finger, "I were a violent man. But I was never in here for being a violent man. I was in here because I'd escaped from everywhere else."

A sphere of air around the nest of cables began to glow like a miniature sun.

"Trapped heat," said Trapp. "The normal oscillation of molecules. Normally it would dissipate, but it can't escape quickly enough across the barrier." He flicked a switch, and the light died. "Now the machine thinks its hull processors are returning a different universal time to its CPU. Messages from the one end to the other can't be routed. It suspects it's being interfered with, that its messages are being intercepted. But it knows it hasn't been cut into. It knows it's still in one piece. So it sends out a maintenance request—"

The top of the machine slid back, extruding a communications array which turned slowly until it found the constellation Tridens in the sky, then pulsed briefly three times, physically shaking with the expenditure of energy. Then the machine reabsorbed its communicator and settled down to wait.

"It requests," continued Trapp, "an authorized engineer. Unfortunately, travel times being what they are, it will take *weeks* for him to arrive..." Trapp wandered over to the cables, rearranged them to fit on another part of the surface, then walked back to his console "...which he will do around... now." The light flared once again, then died. Trapp pulled out a machine-gun feed of authorization cards from an inside pocket. "Now, let me see— authorized Moral Reclamation Authority engineer—"

He slid a card glittering with smartness into an orifice that opened in the section of hull he'd warped time on as if slit by an invisible knife. A square of hull skin slid aside, revealing a control screen, which Trapp manipulated expertly.

"Let me see—bringing in a second engineer, on training." A metal tentacle snaked out of the hull, swaying from side to side as if seeking an opening.

"Biosampler," said Trapp. "You're supposed to stand still." He pulled back the sleeve on his own left arm; the sampler's binocular eye-turrets swivelled to focus on it, then the machine struck like a serpent. When Magus had finished blinking, Trapp had the sampler in his right hand, held behind its sampling fangs, with a reflective sheet of foil held over its ocular barbettes. Carefully, with his left hand, he took out a miniscule via of red liquid and held it to the fangs, which pierced the top on the vial and drank greedily.

"In case you're wondering," said Trapp, "I took the blood from him while he was sleeping peacefully. This is the blood of one Punchinello Llewellyn-Sforza, grade three RB engineer. And *this,*" he said, producing another vial, "is the blood of Alun Fitzakerly, grade four. The machine will shortly foolishly imagine we are both state-sanctioned and will do it no harm."

After another lunge from the sampling appendage, a mansized section of hull swung back, revealing a narrow corridor leading into the machine. Trapp inhaled deeply and swallowed hard, then stepped back into prison.

Magus followed; the hull closed behind him again with the speed of a camera shutter. It was dark, but his eyes gradually became accustomed to the gloom. All sound from the outside world had been snuffed like a candle flame.

"What do we do now?" said Magus.

"Find out which cell she's in," said Trapp. "There are normally seven cells in one of these things, arranged in a two-by-two-by-two matrix. The empty cell—which we are currently in—allows the other cells to move slowly over time, so slowly that the occupant normally doesn't notice. It gives you a fifty-fifty chance, if you somehow do find a way to tunnel out, of tunnelling further into the structure."

"How did you figure out where you were?" said Magus.

"Have you ever seen one of the really old Earth devices for measuring earthquakes?" said Trapp. "Quite ornate, a circle of brass frogs with balls in their mouths, precisely balanced. When something disturbs the frogs, their balls drop out along an axis directly intersecting with the epicentre. My frogs were similar, made of origami, and you really don't want to know what I made the balls out of, but it was the same principle—aha!"

A touchscreen on the wall lit up with a list of seven names. Magus leaned past Trapp to read them.

```
TRAPP, JOHANNES MARIA
VLAAMINCK, DR. ANTONINUS
BOLABAS, CITIZEN PADRAIG
DEVIL, THE
CARNEIRO PAVE, CITIZEN YELENA
SPINK, ANESTIS
CHRISTMAS, FATHER
```

Trapp typed out a few more comments, then swore under his breath.

"What's wrong?"

"The information on the cells' current position is encrypted. I can't figure out which cell is which."

Magus cast a troubled eye at the side wall. "Mr. Trapp, is this wall moving?"

"Yes, it will do that. That's why you never get into the empty cell if you're escaping. It doesn't stay empty for long."

The wall was still moving. "Uh, are we in any danger?"

"I hope not. The machine knows we're in here, after all."

"I mean, it's not moving very *quickly*, but—"

"Of course, we *have* screwed around with its in-nards...tarnation, I hope I don't have to do any real engineering. In any case," he said, bouncing a finger down the list of names, "we have access to the internal command prompt. I can send out messages to various cell addresses, and once we find out which one is your sister—"

"*Step*sister," corrected Magus.

"Aha, figured out who you can and can't breed with on this rock already, I see," said Trapp. Magus reddened. "Well, don't worry, we'll have her out in a jiffy... I hope..." he typed out several lines of command syntax, and the screen cleared to a single num-ber in binary:

    001

The screen was silent for long seconds, during which the wall crept a full millimetre closer. Then, the prompt scrawled back:

    IS THERE ANYBODY OUT THERE?

Jamming his lip into the corner of his mouth, Trapp typed back:

    MORAL RECLAM BUREAU MAINT ENGINEER

Magus leaned over Trapp's shoulder. "What are you *doing?*

Just ask her if she's my sister."

Trapp frowned and shook his head. "Six of these cells are filled with people far, far worse than I will ever be. You want to be *very, very sure* who it is you're letting out."

The screen cleared, and came back:

```
YOU MUST LET ME OUT. THIS IS A CASE OF MISTAKEN IDENTITY
```

Trapp sucked in his lips, contemplated, and tapped back:

```
WHO DO YOU THINK YOU ARE?
```

The screen replied instantly:

```
I'M JUST A LITTLE GIRL
```

"It must be her," said Magus. "Ask her who her father is."
Trapp shrugged, and tapped the question in.
The screen cleared.

```
I HAVE NO FATHER
```

"That's perfectly true," said Magus. "He died in the, uh, plague in the fourth year of colonization.

"True of a *lot* of little girls," said Trapp. He thought awhile, and keyed:

```
WHY DO YOU HAVE NO FATHER?
```

The screen cleared, and came back:

```
I HAVE NO FATHER BECAUSE HE HURLED ME OUT OF HEAVEN *I* AM
THE FATHER THE FATHER OF LIES DESPITE MY INCARCERATION
HERE MY LEGIONS WAIT READY TO REND THE FLESH OF MAN DID I
```

SAY HE HURLED I *CHOSE* TO BE HURLED I AM THE STRONGER IN HERE I LURK GNAWING EVER ON THE LIVER OF PROMETHEUS AND THE BONES OF JUDAS I AM ASMODEUS SATAN THE SERPENT IN THE GARDEN APOLLYON AND LEGION

As the reply continued in the same vein, Trapp tapped in another sequence of commands, and the screen cleared to

010

"I think it is safe to assume," said Trapp, "that that was not your sister."

Magus gawped at the screen, his face pale.

"He can't get into her cell at all, can he?"

"Not at all. The cell walls are everything-proof."

"Then how did you get out?"

"Everything-but-me-proof."

HELLO? IS THAT A HOUSEKEEPING PROGRAM, OR ANOTHER HUMAN BEING?

"Doesn't sound like her," said Magus. "Too wordy."

WHO ARE YOU?

typed Trapp.

THAT DOES NOT MATTER. WHAT DOES MATTER IS THAT THE SECRET OF ETERNAL LIFE REACHES THE OUTSIDE WORLD. THE SECRET IS—

The screen cleared, and nothing Trapp could do would clear it.

"There must be a watch program on that cell's communications, shutting it down if it types certain phrases."

"No matter, it didn't sound like Perfect," said Magus. "Erm, the wall is getting closer."

"Fear not," said Trapp, and cleared the screen again so that it came up:

011

The screen stayed silent for many, many seconds.

"She could be asleep," said Magus. Trapp shook his head. "An incoming message for the block administrator causes an Appell in the cell. She'll have heard it. Unless she's comatose or dead. Which is really unlikely," he added hastily.

Suddenly, the screen typed back, very slowly:

IS THIS A KEYBOARD?

"That's her," said Magus quickly—but, just to make sure, leaned around Trapp and typed in:

WHO WAS UR FATHER?

The screen cleared and replied with painful, single-fingered slowness:

TAKE-EAT-THIS-IS-MY-BODY OGUNDERE

Frantically, Magus typed back:

WHO HAS EVER SEEN U NEKKID

The screen responded:

IS THAT U GUS?

Tongue in the corner of his mouth, Magus stabbed out furiously:

86

Trapp stared at the screen fatalistically. "I'd like to know how, exactly."

"What?"

"All the cells are full. I was about to invoke administrator privileges and order a cell-to-cell transfer, but that's not possible. And these cells won't do double occupancy. The inmates are too dangerous. It's hardwired into the design."

Magus eyed the wall, now a full half metre closer, nervously. "Isn't there a LET ALL THE PRISONERS GO command?"

"Thankfully, no. I'm afraid we really have only one option." He pulled out a gun-shaped device from an inside pocket and slotted a gas cannister into its handgrip, then pointed the gun at the outside wall.

"Look away"

"But won't we be suffocated by the exhaust?"

Trapp shook his head. "It's only a noble gas compound laser. It puts out xenon and oxygen. If I ran it for too long you might catch fire. Look away."

The light from the gun filled the chamber, even when Magus looked away.

"But you're cutting into the outside wall! We don't need to cut out, we need to cut further in!"

"We're not cutting out," said Trapp sadly. "Only an idiot would try to cut out of one of these rigs." He looked at the wall screen, which had changed font size and colour and begun to print coded messages at a speed almost too fast for the human eye to follow.

"She's got a spider inside her," grinned Trapp, switching off the gun. "Now, you and I know she swallowed us spiders to catch the fly, but all she sees is spider. She thinks someone's trying to tunnel out of her." He tapped the hot metal with a fingernail. "Ow! But see how the metal's bunching up around the cut, like a bruise round a wound? The wall's getting thicker at twice the rate I'm cutting."

The walls began to hiss around them. "That'll be the gas," said Trapp. "Should take no longer than the end of this sent—"

"WAKE UP, GUS! WAKE UP!"

Magus woke up. His head was lying in the lap of someone who stank of potatoes. His brothers and sister were gathered all around him, and they also reeked of potatoes. Their breaths smelt of potatoes when they yelled "HE'S MOVING! HE'S ALIVE!" and "WAKE UP, PERFECT! PERFECT, WAKE UP!" He had not realized his world smelt so badly of tubers before.

He was sitting in the shade of the Penitentiary Unit. No portal or aperture was visible in it anywhere. He could still smell the urine stench of the gas. He felt like vomiting, but did not want to do it in what he realized was God's-Wound's lap.

"SHE'S ALIVE! SHE'S ALIVE!" All around him, step-brothers and step-sisters were dancing. A goat was licking his face with a tongue like a rasp. The goat stank of goat.

The Anchorite, his mother, and his father were looking down at him.

"Are you feeling okay?" said his father.

He nodded groggily.

"Trapp," he said.

The Anchorite shook his head. "Read what's in your top pocket."

He felt in the pocket of his utility vest, and found a neatly-folded square of paper with the heading of the Anadyomene

Company, on which were even more neatly printed block capitals.

HAVE CONVINCED MACHINE AM ATTEMPTING TO TUNNEL OUT. MA-
CHINE KNOWS THERE ARE TWO ENGINEERS INSIDE IT. ONCE IT
CHECKS OUT MY DNA, SHOULD SPIT BOTH ENGINEERS OUT AND KEEP
THE ESCAPEE. WISH IT COULD HAVE GONE ANOTHER WAY; WILL BE
OUT AGAIN SHORTLY. KEEP A CANDLE IN THE WINDOW.
X

J.M. TRAPP

Magus stared through the letters as if they weren't there.

"He did the right thing," he said.

"Sure," said Shun-Company contemptuously. "In the end." He yelped suddenly as the Personality Analogue in his pocket became abruptly, unaccountably hot. It was all he could do to rip it from his clothing and dump it in the dust before it collapsed into a hissing cloud of molten plastic and femtocircuitry. He looked up. The Devil was now standing to stiff robotic attention above him. Formerly, it had been slouching like a disgruntled hermit.

"Self destruct," said the Anchorite. "I couldn't have had two of me running around. Especially when the one of me that wasn't me laughed cruelly at gunfire. It could have led to some awful me-on-me violence." He helped Magus unsteadily to his feet.

"I promised Trapp we'd get him offworld when he got out again," said Magus.

Shun-Company regarded her offspring severely. "What a stupid thing to promise. You were in no position to promise such a thing."

"I was in a perfect position to," said Magus. "and I will keep a light in the window." He leaned up against the lamellar bark of a genetically-modified palm. The dates it bore ate cancers. "You didn't check my *inside* pocket." He pulled out a sheaf of bearer bonds of the largest denominations in circulation, the new imprints bearing geometrical designs where the head of the Secretary General or the Dictator, would formerly have been.

"That is stolen money," said Shun-Company. "You should return it instantly."

"This is *compensation for my foster-sister's incarceration*," corrected Magus, "and Mr. Trapp paid it to me fair and square out of his directorial salary. It will pay for a number of improvements around here, including a proper working atmosphere conditioner and a thousand tonnes or so more water for the fields. and I intend," he said, swallowing hard, "to go to New New and obtain an interstellar navigator's licence."

Mr. Reborn-in-Jesus stood stunned. Mrs. Reborn-in-Jesus did likewise for only so long as was required to suck in enough air to set to wailing *"My baby is leaving home!,"* pushing her head into her husband's shoulder and pounding ineffectually on his ribcage with her fist. By feminine sympathetic magic, all the girls of the household set to wailing with her. The Anchorite scowled and jammed his fingers in his ears.

"I should be able to afford our own ship with this much money," said Magus. "We rely far too much on corporate agro vessels, father. I've seen the prices at source. If we can buy goods from the independent GM labs, we'd only be paying a fraction of agribiz markup."

Mr. Reborn-in-Jesus thought for several seconds, then nodded almost imperceptibly. The boys of the household set up a cheer, making the women wail even louder, and Magus was forced to defend himself against a torrent of backslapping.

Meanwhile, propped up against the wall of the Penitentiary, Only-God-is-Perfect was staring up at the dawn.

"It's all real," said the Anchorite, as if it were necessary to make this clear.

Perfect nodded. "It would make stars, the machine, if I asked it to. But I could always reach up and touch the ceiling."

"Reach up," said the Anchorite. "Feel the ceiling."

Only-God-is-Perfect reached up and actually jumped in an attempt to touch the sky. She grinned.

"These stars are harder to reach," she said.

"Though not impossible," boasted Magus, swollen with pride at having been to them.

Perfect's lip began to tremble. "Oh, Uncle Anchorite! It was horrible. The food was bad, the cutlery blunt, and this *thing* kept coming out of the wall inviting me to bestial congress with it. And it tried to expand my mind with literature. It kept reading me a book by a man called Ivan Denisovich. And another by a doctor called Faustus. You wouldn't *believe* the horrid things it said about the Devil."

She collapsed, weeping, against the Anchorite's beard-upholstered chest.

"There, there," said the hermit, patting her on the shoulder. "All lies and propaganda. You are home now."

The focus of the community's sympathy now seemed to have shifted to Mrs. Reborn-in-Jesus, who was still inconsolable.

"Mother is very upset," said Magus.

"She'll get over it," said the Anchorite. "May I hand you a woman? I can't seem to put a foot out of doors without getting infested with the damned things."

Magus nodded solemnly, and Perfect was passed giggling from the hermit to Magus, allowing the Anchorite to slope off in the company of Mr. Reborn-in-Jesus.

"Have you really been to the sky for me?" said Perfect.

"To two or three different skies of different colours," said Magus. "One sky that rained corrosive acids. One as blue as copper oxides, with birds with wings the colour of tourmalines. We could ship in air and water and ozone. We have the gravity. We could have a sky like that."

Perfect looked up at the eclipsed A ring of Naphil hanging in space like smoke, backlit by starlight.

"I think I quite like *our* sky. But I'm open to persuasion."

The Anchorite and Mr. Reborn-in-Jesus stood apart, unheard by the others. Only the Devil, standing motionless, heard or saw any evil. It was still wearing its hat.

"If he escapes," said the Anchorite, "or if there is a ship that comes here, or if more people settle—"

"They will come closer to you," said Mr. Reborn-in-Jesus.

"I cannot permit that," said the Anchorite.

"We can apply for a colonization licence," said Mr. Reborn-in-Jesus. "The whole surface area of this world is not much more than eight hundred square kilometres. There are cattle ranches on New New that are larger. We could apply for a licence for the whole surface. Anyone coming here would have to answer to us."

"They could also turn your application down," said the Anchorite. "And parcel up the land among whichever rich citizens bribed them highest."

Reborn-in-Jesus threw his arms wide. "But who would *want* the land?" He bent and picked up a handful of copper oxides. "Crops have to have their genomes hammered flat to live in it, we have to bring our own UV to the party, whatever we plant mutates almost as soon as we grow it—" he let the green-black dust trickle out of his hand in disgust.

"You're speaking as a farmer. Remember that a mining company could, and did, apply for a compulsory purchase to ream this world out for its neutronium core. And then," he cast his hand round at the vast sweep of Naphil's rings, "there are sightseers, tour operators, hoteliers. This place is a cosmic oddity. Where else does a place with one-gee gravity orbit *inside* a gas giant's rings? I chose this place, you know, for the view." He stared up at the brilliant terminator starting to mark out time along the rings.

"No," he said, "to protect ourselves, we need money. Big money. A concentration of money big enough to hold you down under its own gravity."

"And where would we find such money?" said Reborn-in-Jesus.

"Inward investment," said the Anchorite, licking his lips. "Let me work on it."

He nodded to Reborn-in-Jesus senior and walked away, into the blinding sunrise. The Devil turned to follow him, fluid as mercury. Over by the Series Three, Reborn-in-Jesus junior was already regaling the family with the exact spectrum of the colours he was going to paint his spaceship.

the made guys

The ninth New Year of the New Improved Era was the year of the Great Modern Convenience Plague.

New Ararat had been quiet all through the Fifth Harvest Festival; the nearby gas giant Naphil put out more heat than it received from 23 Kranii, and Naphil's orbit around its star was very close to circular, so harvest happened all year round. Shun-Company had decided on a rotating schedule of Harvest Festivals, where the children, who had little else to do but sweep floors, herd goats, weed herb patches, fettle agricultural machinery, tend the comms station in the Best Parlour, and clear the South Field of meteors, could weave little dolls of potato leaves that could be pinned to makeshift crosses in the Town Square and ritually burnt, whilst the family danced around semi-nude and gaily painted with charcoal. The local interpretation of Christianity on Mount Ararat was ecumenical.

On this day, however, when little Measure-of-Barley and Beguiled-of-the-Serpent were busy weaving Jesuses out of anaemic brown Maris Piper leaves, the still smaller Day-of-Creation looked up from tormenting a pet hyrax and said:

"A star! A new star, in the East!"

Beguiled's attention snapped up from her Christmaking.

"Single, binary or trinary?"

"Quad, sister! It's Magus! He is back!"

The ship's drives were casting shadows by now as it settled on gigantic, overpowered manoeuvring jets into Mount Ararat's ten-metre horizon. The vessel, the *Prodigal Son*, had been gaudily daubed with an attempt at rainbow colours using paints begged, borrowed and stolen. Hence there was a NO STEP red, high-reflectivity yellows and oranges, a military-surplus green not strictly suitable for service outside atmosphere, a mauve where there should have been a purple. And only the fierce light of the vessel's own exhausts betrayed the rainbow; in the unmodified light of 23 Kranii, it was a series of red stripes shading to black.

The return of the *Son* was a major event, better than Christmas, Easter, Harvest Festival, and Landing Commemoration Day combined. The entire family Reborn-in-Jesus flocked to the South End Saddle, that gentle kilometre-deep undulation marking the spot where Mount Ararat's two world-halves joined. The Saddle was no place to put down a starship, being flanked by high ground and plagued by fierce gravitational gradients from the neutronium mote at the planetoid's core, and it was a mark of Magus Reborn-in-Jesus's filial devotion that he chose to put down here, after a nerve-wracking approach through the South End Chasm. The alternatives were, after all, a landing either in his father's potato fields or near the splintered-headstoned, black-flowered graveyard that was the only man-made feature in Mount Ararat's southern hemisphere.

Prodigal Son had originally been designed as a cattle carrier. Bloated and cylindrical, with only a discreet nod to the need for streamlining and atmospheric control, she was built to inexpensively transport six hundred hundred kilogramme dairy ruminants between the stars. Eschewing the new-fangled practice of painting a thin layer of neutronium onto the deck plating for artificial gravity, *Son* used centrifugal gravity, rotating her bovine passengers inside her at breakneck speeds. She also utilized a helpful by-product of her FTL drive to cut down the number of feedings and muckings-out required between stars. An FTL drive was by definition also a time machine, and a cow for which time was moving far more slowly than normal engaged in far less digestive throughput than a cow under nominal temporal motion. The cow retardation field extended only through the rotary shed area, the vessel's crew being subject to time that elapsed as normally as time could be said to at one hundred times lightspeed.

Following her use as a cattle tender, the *Son* had been commandeered for use as a corpse carrier to transport KIA (and occasionally WIA) back from the Front in the War Against the Made. By cranking up the cow-retarder, flesh could be made not to spoil, wounds not to rot, infection not to spread. A fatally-wounded trooper placed right next to the decelerator coil might be frozen in the act of his last heartbeat. Even if his injury remained incurable, he might at least still exchange tearful farewells with his family and friends back home. The cow stalls had been replaced with coffin racks and body bag hangers resembling a colossal and macabre dry-cleaning machine, and the vessel's hull had been repainted a bright, fearsomely reflective white, with a variety of religious symbols painted on her every level surface.

Finally, following the cessation of hostilities and the expansion of Earth, New Earth, and New New Earth's teeming hordes further out into space, the vessel had been refitted as an army-surplus, bargain-basement personal transport ship. It was not entirely safe for human beings to travel retarded—field gradients could result in biorhythm upset, alien hand syndrome, seizures, even death—but slow ships were still popular among those who could not afford to pay for a month's life support on top of their fares. As a result, *Son*'s coffin racks were now a minimally-appointed radial capsule hotel, often left in less than sanitary condition by their occupants.

The cloud of grit and vitrified rock thrown up by *Son*'s retros flew in the faces of the family, choking, burning and blinding simultaneously. Then there was a billowing orange silence in which the ray-pitted landing windows of the ship, purchased with stolen money, loomed over the tiny human beings waiting patiently outside it.

A massive cargo door thundered down into the regolith with a sound like two ocean liners colliding, and—with surely unnecessary theatrics, as there was a perfectly serviceable, smaller crew airlock further round the fuselage—Magus Reborn-in-Jesus came back from the stars to see his family. There were presents for everybody, of course—for Only-God-Is-Perfect, a programmable scanning mirror that could simulate a thousand hairstyles, lighting conditions and wardrobes, without a hair having to be combed; for Beguiled-of-the-Serpent, a battery-powered actual growing baby simulator; for Unity, a mood-sensitive dress that changed colour according to hormonal and neurological cues. Shun-Company, meanwhile, was bought an acupressure massage bed which could be made to exude a wide variety of scents. Currently, it was exuding catnip, and was being inhabited by two wide-eyed Persian kittens, gifts for Measure-of-Barley, who had squealed loudly enough to break quartz when she had seen them.

Reborn-in-Jesus Senior, however, appeared to have nothing. Patiently waiting at the back of the excited gaggle of offspring and step-offspring, he stood shuffling his feet in clear embarrassment until Magus winked and waved at him, beckoning him over to the main cargo ramp.

Inside the cargo bay, which had been largely cleared of body bag hangers, the air stank of cattle, gas gangrene, embalming fluid, wood alcohol, and cat urine in a complex, multi-layered aromatic palette. The bay contained the usual tractor spares, new strains of potatoes to replace this season's inevitable mutations, bizarre alien food crops Magus had no doubt imprudently picked up at some nowhere world or other's genetic fair, vitamin pills, whole cloth, and stacked foamed slabs of radiation shielding. However, there were also two massive, squat metallic shapes, each bearing a shiny holographic logo.

"Fantastic, aren't they," enthused Magus. "And they'll make us a packet."

"What are they?" said Reborn-in-Jesus *père.*

"On the left," said Magus, "the HiveMind 1000. The queen unit, which you see here, sits on the surface attended by billions of tiny nanobot workers which can be programmed to search for any substance—iron, copper, radioactives—and bring it back to this hopper *here.*" He tapped a door on the back of the unit.

"Did you say *mind*?" said Mr. Reborn-in-Jesus warily.

"No cleverer than the average hymenopteran group-mind," assured Magus airily. "And over *here*, meanwhile, we have the GreenQueen ZX9. Similar principle,but sends out little bitsy thruster-propelled work units to locate and bite into small chunks any nearby carbonaceous chondrite moonlets. These are then converted into a nutritious polypeptide mulch and spread all over the surface of the land area controlled by the GreenQueen. And Naphil's rings are *full* of chondrites. Give this baby a week," twinkled Magus, "and she could cover the entire surface of New Ararat in high-grade fertiliser to a depth of ten metres."

Mr. Reborn-in-Jesus stared at the machine in undisguised alarm.

A throat cleared behind Magus. He turned to see a middle-aged figure leaning on a stick in the main loading door, twining its beard idly round its finger.

"Do you happen to know, Gus," said the figure, "what a hymenopteran group-mind *is*, by any chance?"

Magus's smile was unassailable. "These machines are based on a single common chassis optimized in both cases to source particular quantities—in the case of the HM1000, that of transuranic minerals, in the case of the GreenQueen, that of organic molecules. The chassis can be tuned to any end result."

"If you don't know what hymenoptera are," said the Anchorite, "do you at least know what a Von Neumann machine is?"

Magus did. His smile froze.

"That would mean they were Made things," he said. "But they're, they're not Made things."

Mr. Reborn-in-Jesus's attention alternated between the HiveMind and the GreenQueen as if he had suddenly been crept up on by both Scylla and Charybdis simultaneously. "Von Neumanns? Here?"

"These are army surplus," said Magus, waving his hand to indicate the units. "Reconditioned."

"Not our army," said the Anchorite. "Not our side."

"Why would *you* care about the War Against The Made?" said Magus. "You're a Religious Ascetic."

"All humanity fought the War Against The Made," said the Anchorite. "Most of them had no choice. It was a question of fight or be supplanted by a superior species. *Many* superior species, created by us. Thinking more quickly, physically stronger, some of them able to survive in vacuum and liquid helium. Some of them biological, some of them mechanical." He stared at the machines as if trying to dissolve them with pure hatred. "And the Von Neumanns were their front line. We struck the first blow, of course—had to. If they'd figured out we'd planned their destruction, they'd have rolled over us like a tank over a box of eggs. We hit the big AI units in the banks and military C3 centres first, then the human ones sitting behind the desks of big corporations, in front line military units, in athletics teams, in governments...the AI's in starships were more difficult to reach, some of them were out in transit light years from any population centre. We caught most of the military vessels. It was the civilian ones that nearly killed us. The Von Neumann units were way out on the edges of human expansion, preparing worlds for colonization, each one able to *tune itself to any end result,* arriving on a world, landing, absorbing raw materials from the crust around it, using these materials to make a thousand of itself, then a million, then a billion. Then turning its collective attention to changing the atmosphere, adjusting the global temperature, laying down soil. But all they had to do to defend themselves was stop producing soil and air and water and start producing things that killed people. One of those units, just *one*, stopped an entire fleet sent out to Polaris. Many of the Made High Command escaped into space—they had been created so cunning, so resourceful, that it wasn't possible to take them all. Even an outnumbered and outgunned Made detachment could tie up a battlegroup. Only the best survived. Only the best. Which is what terrifies, or should terrify, the Government of Human Space."

"Why?" said Magus.

"Because if treated as equal partners to humanity," said the Anchorite with grim humour, "the Made races would have grown soft, like the humans who spawned them. They would have allowed every member of their various species equal right to breed, to weaken the strain. But by *almost* exterminating them, humanity provided ready-made natural selection. They succeeded only in making things far harder for themselves further down the line. Only total annihilation would have worked—which was what they could never be convinced to understand."

He kicked the front of the Green Queen suddenly with a sandalled foot, and the cheap nameplate broke away to reveal a second badge cast into the carapace of the machine itself:

```
SORCEROR'S APPRENTICE
MK I
GEN I
```

Magus searched for argumentative exits. "Maybe they're hobbled," he insisted. "Some Von Neumanns were hobbled. The part of their programming that allowed them to make more like themselves was deleted."

"Don't tell me," said the Anchorite. "The people who sold these things to you *just happened to mention it.*"

"It came up in conversation. They never said *these* were Von Neumanns—"

"But they put that little seed of security in your mind, just in case you got to thinking they were. It's *illegal,* Magus. It is *way past* illegal. If the Moral Cleansing Bureau find out there are Von Neumann devices here, Executive Order 2219 authorizes a strike on Mount Ararat using total conversion warheads."

"Order 2219 was signed by the Dictator," reproved Mr. Reborn-in-Jesus.

"It's the only order of the Dictator's that was never rescinded," said the Anchorite.

"But these might not be Von Neumann devices any more," said Gus with infinite patience. "They might have been Made Safe."

"By putting new nameplates on them?"

"They made a big deal of telling me their processing capacities had been deliberately downgraded! And they're incapable of self-reproduction!"

"Lobotomized and gelded," said the Anchorite. "Well, I don't know what that would make you, but it'd make me *mad*."

Magus ignored the provocation. "With the HM1000, we can extract the radioactives we already know lie under the South End. We will be rich beyond the most perfervid dreams of avarice."

"Gus," said Mr. Reborn-in-Jesus gently, "the density of the radioactive seams under the South End are what keeps Mount Ararat stable. If they were mined out, the C of G of the planet would shift two or three kilometres closer to us. That would bring us closer to the Mote and mean surface gravity maybe one and a half times what we have now—close to Earth normal, the hellish gravity of our ancestors, bad for crops, bad for brittle young bones grown under point five G, bad for landing that contraption of yours, quite apart from killing us all as the barycentre shifted."

"It could do worse," said the Anchorite. "It could put the Mote on the move." He regarded the deck plating guiltily. "The neutronium mote that contains this world's gravity does not just sit at rest, entombed in rock. Rather, it is balanced very carefully in a self-maintaining spherical vacuum chamber operating very much like a three-dimensional arch. The weight of Mount Ararat presses round on all sides, yet the Arch transfers that weight perfectly around itself, preventing any part of the world from falling into the Mote. And as the Arch chamber is filled with vacuum, the Mote can grow no larger."

"How do you know all this?" said Magus suspiciously.

"I have been there," said the Anchorite. "Not personally, of course—I sent a servant. I am uncertain whether the Arch is a natural formation or an artificial. It appears to be made of nothing more complex than fused rock, which could be a natural consequence of proximity to the Mote."

Magus nodded. His ambition to amass tremendous stacks of wealth had already, in his mind, smashed this minor world-sized obstacle aside. "In any case, I *planned* for all of this. As the HM1000 mines, the GreenQueen will coat the South End's surface with equivalent quantities of high-yield fertilizer, replacing the lost mass. It will all be done very scientifically."

The Anchorite was incensed. "There are no other places like Mount Ararat anywhere in the observed universe! What existing model did you employ?" He changed the subject unexpectedly. "Did you deliver the mail I trusted to you?"

Magus's grin might have been painted on a punchbag. "I did." He fished in a tunic pocket. "And received a reply." He passed an old-fashioned printed-matter envelope to the Anchorite, who opened it feverishly with one long yellow fingernail thick as a paperknife blade.

The Anchorite examined the letter's contents and looked up at Magus.

"Your proposed course of action literally threatens the balance of the world," he said. "I have an alternative proposal, an external investor who would put money enough into Mount Ararat to make us all rich as graveyard dirt without any unfortunate gravitational side-effects." He looked deeply into Magus's eyes. "Do I have your promise that you will not activate your Von Neumann devices until I have had time to lay my proposal before all of Ararat?"

Magus frowned sulkily. "They are not Von Neumann devices," he complained. "But I will delay activation. The machines will be unloaded and left in a standby state."

"That, at least, is something," said the Anchorite. "Thank you."

He nodded at Magus and at Magus's father, and departed.

"Gus," said Gus's father, "you don't want to needle the hermit so."

"What? Uncle Anchorite? He is a fluffy pussy cat of immense proportions."

"That man," said Reborn-in-Jesus senior, "may have been an uncle to you all when you were children; but he came here because he had nowhere else to go, and you are not a child any more. I've no idea what terrible things he did before he came here, but I know he's committed iniquities since. The South End Yard is full of people who came to Mount Ararat thinking they'd run things other than in the way the hermit wanted them. Don't rile him, son. You may think he's domesticated, but mark my words, he'll kill you and every living person on this planet if he once thinks his space is being invaded."

With a final warning stare, Reborn-in-Jesus senior turned on his heel and walked back down the ramp into the middle of his family and a chorus of "WHATCHA GET, DADDY? WHATCHA GET? WHATCHA GET? WHATCHA GET?"

In the charcoal glow of Ararat night, with the A Ring hanging on the south horizon, cut off by the terminator in mid-orbit like a sabre blade, and the sky spangled with an embarrassment of stars, the two Von Neumann units stood alien and illegal in the craters they had made in the soil when unloaded.

Suddenly, abruptly, a cowling motored back on the top of the HiveMind1000, and an antenna unfolded quickly enough to spear insects out of the air, spreading itself swiftly into a dandelion clock of sensors that rippled in the radiophonic breeze. A similar opening gaped in the top of the GreenQueen, extruding a laser sampler that span round in dangerous abandon, firing invisible bursts of coherent x-rays up into the A Ring, and observing the resultant twinkles of vapourising rock and ice, classifying them spectrally through a single coaxially-mounted telescope.

Nanobot hoppers opened in the HM1000, and a grey motile sludge began pouring from its innards, detouring around commercially inviable rocks, intelligent slime swarming in the direction of the South End. The GreenQueen, meanwhile, disgorged a multiheaded tube resembling a fungal sporangium, ranged it at the stars, and began coughing out tiny payloads high into the sky, each one glowing with the speed of its ascent before it even started to put out the warm laval glow of plasmadrive. Before long, the sky was filled with incandescent teardrops, and the earth was home to a river flowing uphill in the direction of the South End. A goat, strayed far from pasture, stood bleating as the nanostream engulfed the rock it stood on. The beast had been eating the black mutant roses from the South End Yard, which put roots down into radioactive bedrock. It had unstable transuranic particles burning out gamma into its gut, producing huge tumours that would have killed it eventually. The antenna assembly rustled as it sensed the slight local spike in radioactivity and ordered the nanostream to the attack. The goat bleated helplessly as the grey fluid surged up its flanks, producing tiny sparks of waste heat as individual workers tunnelled into its flesh, opening holes for their brood fellows to gain access. The goat employed all the tactics in its artiodactyl arsenal, trying to run, jump, kick, and bite, but bit nothing, slipped wherever it put its foot, kicked as if in quicksand. Within a minute, the grey liquid was draining back out of the deep holes bored in the animal's flanks, leaving the tumours half un-eaten, having taken only the cancer's cause. The nanostream surged off urgently towards the South End, sending a small part of itself back towards the Hive Mind with the precious particles it had harvested. The goat, shivering, bleeding heavily from internal injury, began to limp dazed in the direction of home.

"MOM! THERE'S A DEAD GOAT ON THE PORCH!"

Mom, half asleep and cocooned in shawls, stared out bleary-eyed. Goats were expensive, dead goats doubly so.

"Looks like it got et by a Neutroniosaurus," said Day-of-Creation, marvelling. Shun-Company inspected the carcass criti-cally. The Neutroniosaurus was an indeterminately-legged, fall-out-breathing smallchildivore created by Mr. Reborn-in-Jesus to dissuade his family from straying out after dark near the South End Chasm. It ate orphans for preference, though it was not above taking a toe or two, or a leg, or sometimes a particularly knobbly knee from children who had mommies and daddies.

"No Neutroniosaurus," said Shun-Company, "did that."

"Why, mommy?" said little Measure, holding on to her mother's leg. "Why? Why? Why?"

"Because of the distinctive jagged bite of a Neutroniosaurus," said Shun-Company. "And because Y has a long tail."

"*Why* does Y have a long tail, mommy?"

Unity, tall, slender, impossibly long-legged, turned up her nose at the carcass. "That's not magpies nor hyraxes."

"It's the Devil, mommy! The Devil did it!"

Shun-Company shook her head. "It's not Devil-work. The Devil doesn't bother itself with goats, and the Devil cuts clean. This looks almost like the poor bleater was held down while acid was poured over it. Ate right into its rumen, look."

"Can we eat it now it's dead, mommy? We always eat the dead ones. Can we, can we, can we?"

Shun-Company drew her shawl about herself and looked out at a sky that was suddenly, unaccountably raining glistering golden teardrops spiralling round the world into the South End.

"I don't think it's going to be safe to eat this one, precious."

"They've turned themselves on." Mr. Reborn-in-Jesus sat at the head of the dining table the family had saved up for, made of real wood from Earth that had got to the 23 Kranii system before the light from the death of Christ.

"They're still self-aware," said the Anchorite, seated at the other end of the table, where Mrs. Reborn-in-Jesus usually sat. "Independent thought processing downgraded, maybe, but they can turn themselves on and off. That in itself is a violation of the anti-AI laws. If we're caught in possession of them, we'll be in more shit than they can spread over our South Pole in a lifetime."

"It's not shit," said Magus uncomfortably from halfway down the table. "It's a complex highly nutritious mulch of polypeptides, nitrates and soil salts necessary for a growing plant."

"It's brown and it smells like shit," growled the Anchorite. "It's shit."

"You've been to the South End?" said Mr. Reborn-in-Jesus. "Wasn't that dangerous?"

"Very," said the Anchorite. "The *highly nutritious mulch of polypeptides* is now so deep out there in places a man can't move in it. I had to take a bath when I got home! A *bath!*"

Mr. Reborn-in-Jesus and his son looked at one another.

"I own a bath," said the Anchorite, in tones daring them to disagree.

Magus cleared his throat awkwardly. "Uh, there's been no C-of-G shift."

"There's a crack in the earth all the way down the Meridian Field already," said Mr. Reborn-in-Jesus. "And if you'd troubled to get up early and help your father with the harvesting, you'd know that. If it propagates any further it'll come clean through this room, and then we'll have a hell of a draught in here."

"There have been rockfalls," said the Anchorite, "all the way around the Chasm. Mainly on the South Wall, but doing damage enough on the North, where I need hardly remind you I live. We must shut these machines down."

"What power source do they use?" said Mr. Reborn-in-Jesus.

"Normally fusion," said the Anchorite. "Though they'll take fissionables at a pinch, and they can black their skins to collect solar energy. Anywhere there's deuterium, sunlight or uranium, they can survive and make little copies of themselves. And there's all three here. And," he said, wagging a finger at Magus and his father, "the human body contains an average of two grammes of deuterium."

"These two machines have had their self-replication functions disabled," said Magus hotly.

"Yes, just like they've had their standby functions disabled. But he's right," said the Anchorite. "If they'd been fully functional VN units, they'd have been nose to tail all down the Saddle by now. As it is, there's still just the two of them, plus a big pile of transuranic ingots, neatly sorted by element and labelled. Piled outside your ship ready for loading. Though they haven't touched the ship. Probably didn't taste too good," he said archly.

"So there's less danger, then," said Mr. Reborn-in-Jesus. "Than from a working VN unit, I mean."

"In the short term. But whoever decided to frig these things' programming and demote them to upmarket mining machinery forgot that a non-self-reliant machine can't make decisions on its own. They'll continue until every last speck of actinium and californium is eaten out of this planet and replaced with crust which is a kilometre deep, brown, and highly nutritious."

"The mote," said Mr. Reborn-in-Jesus in panic. "Could they eat down to the mote?"

"No." The Anchorite shook his head. "The mote's made of neutronium overlaid with highly compressed crystalline iron. They'll be neither programmed nor equipped to mine neutronium, and iron won't interest them. Too commonplace."

"The ship," said Magus suddenly.

The Anchorite glared at Magus for daring to interrupt.

"Why haven't they eaten into the ship?" continued Magus. "It's full of transuranics. They're in the circuitry, in the FTL unit, alloyed into the hull, everywhere. And yet the nanos from the HiveMind haven't touched it."

"They have some conscience programming, at least," said the Anchorite. "They wouldn't attack me either. I was stood in the middle of a stream of them. They tickled my ankles. Occasionally, they nip. Testing my DNA, you see. They recognize human genetic material and avoid it. But when machines can make other machines, and if they're clever enough, they can figure out that the conscience factor is holding their creations back, and design it out of them. And even if that HiveMind can't make copies of itself, it can make all the nanominers it wants. There's a big grey river of

110

them stretching from the Saddle right to the walls of the South End Yard, and you can't tell me all of those fit into the box they came in."

"Then how are we going to get rid of them?"

"Why don't I just lift the HiveMind back into the cargo bay?" said Magus innocently.

The Anchorite shook his head. "The system has to be shut down gracefully. If you cut off the queen unit, it still leaves the nanos. Granted, no more nanos will get made, but it also removes the nanos' guiding intelligence. Individually, being the size of a pinhead, they aren't too bright, which means they tend to carry on doing what they were originally told to, and when Ararat runs out of the ores they were first programmed to fetch, they might indeed then switch to a lower-grade metal, like iron." He polished the seat with his backside uncomfortably. "Which the human body contains around half a kilo of. No, young Magus, the best thing you can do is draft a letter to the folks you got these units off, and inform them there will be no payment unless they get a maintenance engineer down here stat. How much did you pay them?"

Magus brightened. "Ah! That's the clever part."

The Anchorite's every hair bristled. "In what way?"

"I paid nothing. I simply accepted their terms of seventy-five per cent of crop yield for the next fifty years."

The Anchorite stared. Mr. Reborn-in-Jesus's eyes turned circles in his head.

"You did WHAT?"

"Be reasonable, pops, the GreenQueen is certain to increase yields tenfold, and we'll be richer than a man refused entry to heaven if the HiveMind comes through. I was going to get around to telling you, only—"

"Who were these people?" said the Anchorite.

"Well," said Magus, his smile finally beginning to evaporate under oxyacetylene glares from his two seniors, "just people, I guess."

"Just people, as opposed to reputable licensed taxpaying businessmen," said the Anchorite. "Did they have an office?"

"Yes," said Magus.

"How much plate glass did this office have? Did it have a central atrium and cool tinkling fountains at all? How attractive was the receptionist?"

"Uh, he wasn't very," said Magus. "More heavily-armed than attractive. It was more of a sort of temporary affair, a sort of set of pressurized shacks near the landing field on Farquahar's World. They had these two machines going cheap, remaindered show stock from a receiver's closing down sale, slightly damaged, recently superceded by newer models—"

"Let me stop you there," said the Anchorite. "I believe you have painted a full and colourful picture."

"I doubt very much whether those shacks will still be there," said Mr. Reborn-in-Jesus gloomily.

The Anchorite shook his head. "I am actually quite certain they will, for the simple reason that our salesmen have not yet been paid. I also imagine that their retaliation for not being paid will not be encumbered by the pedestrian confines of the law. Send your letter; your father and I will deal with these machines in the interim."

"How do you propose," said Mr. Reborn-in-Jesus, "to do that? Those units are designed to work continuously for centuries with one half of them in sunshine fit to melt lead, the other half in shadow fit to freeze mercury. Even your Devil will not raise a scratch on them, I fancy."

112

"I'm afraid there is only one solution," said the Anchorite grimly. "Nuclear annihilation. We will have to rig up a small nuclear device and detonate it directly between the two units."

"But where would we find such a thing?" said Mr. Reborn-in-Jesus.

"I'm sure I have one about the place somewhere," said the Anchorite. "I apologize in advance for the fallout. There are ways to minimize it. It is bound, however, to have an effect on your crop yields, maybe even the health of your family. I suggest you begin digging a shelter deep, deep underground. Set your boys to it."

Mr. Reborn-in-Jesus nodded like a living statue. Across the room, the door suddenly CLUNKed as if an ear pressed against it with the force of an octopus sucker had suddenly been released.

At that very moment, Shun-Company entered with a tray of Real Tea. Mount Ararat now had its own grove of tea bushes, though Mr. Reborn-in-Jesus suspected Magus had been sold some laboratory's beta version—the tea tasted sweet, smelt of honey, and contained enough caffeine, nicotine, taurine, and saccharides to make it dangerous to apply to children, possibly even externally. The bushes, and the tea made from them, glowed gently in the dark, and Shun-Company turned down the light slowly to get the full effect. The glass mugs luminesced green as witches' faces.

"Wife," said Mr. Reborn-in-Jesus, "we have decided to detonate a nuclear weapon at the end of the South Field. Tell Testament and Apostle to get that radiation shielding Gus brought securely welded into place all round the panic cellar, clear the hatches, and tell the children to move their beds below."

Shun-Company nodded.

Mr. Reborn-in-Jesus looked at his writing desk and frowned. "Where is my paperweight? The sample of pitchblende ore we got from our first survey?"

Shun-Company's eyes remained downcast. "I believe the boys were using it for some scientific purpose."

"Well, as long as they bring it back." He became suddenly suspicious. "What are you all doing in there? I hear you whispering as if at some great secret. Have I forgotten my birthday again?"

"Are you aware, husband," said Shun-Company, "that gorillas eat their own excrement?"

Mr. Reborn-in-Jesus's frown deepened. "No," he said.

"But only once," advised Shun-Company.

"I see," said Mr. Reborn-in-Jesus, in a way that made it quite plain that he did not.

"Mrs. Reborn-in-Jesus," said the Anchorite gently, "there are no gorillas on Mount Ararat."

Shun-Company nodded. "They would be terrible pests, and they are unclean animals. It would be necessary to exterminate them."

With that, she swept from the room, as unobtrusive as a total vacuum. Mr. Reborn-in-Jesus exchanged glances with the Anchorite; both men shrugged.

"Now," said the Anchorite, "to the business of nuking your own farmland."

The nuclear device was heavy, and required both men to heave it onto the back of Carries-the-Saviour, Ararat's only ass, whose every leg bowed under the load. Mr. Reborn-in-Jesus spoke gently to the ass, and reasoned with her, and arrived at a negotiated compromise amenable to both parties whereby Carries-the-Saviour staggered onward under the burden, and Reborn-in-Jesus walked ahead of her holding carrots which, occasionally, he allowed Carries-the-Saviour to catch up to. It had been necessary to use Carries-the-Saviour, despite her advancing years, as the expensive Percheron 500 had broken down, its magnetohydrodynamic motor refusing to fire.

It was a long, dark journey under the stars to the Saddle. Many of the dimmer stars were now perpetually invisible in the firefly glare of incoming GreenQueen workers, constantly headed for their mother unit and the South End. Mr. Reborn-in-Jesus had not asked the Anchorite how he had come to have a fusion weapon lying about a cave that had hitherto seemed to contain little more than a mattress and a spare pair of sandals. The Anchorite had not volunteered the information.

As they cautiously approached the South End Saddle, however, the gleaming, constantly functioning Von Neumann units and the brooding bulk of the *Prodigal Son* were not the only man-made componentsof the landscape. In the dim dawn, as 23 Kranii began to lift its one bleary eye over the chasm walls eastwards, the lightning-flicker of a welding torch could be seen, and the stench of rare earth oxides hung on the wind. Petticoated shapes were moving purposefully in the dark, hefting huge, impossibly valuable ingots of precious stable heavy elements like house bricks, piling them into cairns, welding them into thick unmanageable sheets.

Mr. Reborn-in-Jesus stopped, dumbfounded. Petticoats were supposed to whisk around kitchens and vegetable garden. At the very most, they were supposed to be hitched up over pretty ankles when their owner wished to move any faster than a slow walk. And yet here they were, shamelessly and openly *welding* where all the world could see.

"It would appear," said the Anchorite, "that someone has stolen a march on us."

Shun-Company looked up as the group approached.

"Does your nuclear device contain fissionable material?" she said.

The Anchorite shook his head. "Pure fusion."

Shun-Company nodded. "Then you'll be safe. Please come this way, and try to step over the nanostreams."

Shun-Company, and some of the older girls and boys were arranging the rare earth bricks into small cairns. Once arranged, the gaps between the bricks were welded shut by Unity Reborn-in-Jesus, who shyly looked up from beneath her welding helmet as Reborn-in-Jesus senior and the Anchorite approached. The cairn was then an airtight tube of mined metal open at both ends. At the upper end, a heavy electromagnet of the sort used in magnetohydrodynamic tractor motors had been suspended over the top of the cairn, and was holding a small ferrous metal box fast against itself.

"The box contains a quantity of unmined radioactive ore," said the Anchorite. "One of the initial samples made during the first survey of Mount Ararat eight kilodia ago. Reborn-in-Jesus's missing paperweight, I am guessing."

Shun-Company noded. "The nanos swarm in, attracted by the ore—then, when the cairn is full"—a cairn was kicked over further down the slope, and a flat plate made of ingots slapped over both its ends and welded shut—"they are shut inside."

Mr. Reborn-in-Jesus was dumbfounded. "They are mining machines. Why don't they tunnel out?"

"Because gorillas," said Shun-Company, "only eat their own shit once, husband. The nanos mine transuranic ore and return it to the mother processor, which purifies it and outputs it in stackable ingot form. Why do the nanos not then continue to mine the ingots, which contain transuranics by definition?"

Mr. Reborn-in-Jesus considered this.

"I have no idea," he said.

"Quite simply, each ingot is status-stamped by the ore processor at the molecular level," said Shun-Company. "Once output, the ingots will never be touched again by the nanominers. They will avoid them; they will not tunnel through them; they can be contained in a container made of them. Magus's ship is also made of ore originally extracted by nanominer; most metal nowadays is. Hence the nanos also left *Prodigal Son* alone. Had you forgotten, husband, that before you and I joined a damn fool religious order and set out to found a new life in the stars, I completed five years of state training as an agricultural technopollution cleanup engineer?"

Mr. Reborn-in-Jesus's past life trickled back into him like a cold enema. "The Lyceum. The *Amazonas Reclamada* project. You were working on clearing out areas of genetically modified intensive-biome forest. Invasive, fast-growing, and fire-resistant, created by irresponsible twenty-first-century ecologists. It destroyed an area of prime Amazon cattle land the size of Wales every day."

Shun-Company nodded. "And you were working on breeding edible strains of black smoker tubeworm that could be farmed thousands of metres down in the Puerto Rico Trench. We met over soyamphetamine coffee substitute in the Homem Bomba bar. It was very romantic."

The Anchorite kicked at a chunk of regolith. "Do you have a strategy yet for getting rid of the GreenQueen workers?"

"We are working on it." Shun-Company, eyes still downcast, allowed herself the faintest smile. "If you will excuse me, I urgently need to speak to our working group in that area."

She swept away. Mr. Reborn-in-Jesus and the Anchorite stood at a loose end with their ass and nuclear weapon.

"I believe," said Mr. Reborn-in-Jesus, "that we have been made to eat our own shit."

"Only once," reproved the Anchorite.

Up above, paired stars stettled on the breeze towards the South Field.

"Two thrusters," said Mr. Reborn-in-Jesus.

"Means a personal transport," said the Anchorite. "No freight haulers use that configuration. Too unstable with shifting cargo. Also means," he said, "that whoever is landing cares very little for the state of your windows and your children's health. He's executing landing burn only fourteen kilometres from your house. And he knows that landing in the South End would be bad for him. His treads would sink into the highly nutritious mulch. His venturis would be flooded. Which means," he said, "that I know exactly who this is."

Mr. Reborn-in-Jesus nodded. "The folks who sold Gus the machines."

"Don't antagonize them. Take them back to the house. I must gather appropriate forces."

The Anchorite motioned to two nearby children to heave the now redundant nuclear weapon down off the ass's back. Carries-the-Saviour's spine bounced triumphantly back up into shape. The hermit nodded a hasty farewell, and ran off into the rocks.

"Good morning. Mr. Hernan Cortès Reborn-in-Jesus, I take it?"

There were only two newcomers. Both were humanoid. Both were dressed appropriately for formal legal representation, arrears collection or, Mr. Reborn-in-Jesus reminded himself uncomfortably, gangland assassination. Their business suits were understated, with the mood-sensitive neckties sales representatives often wore to indicate to clients that their motives were utterly sincere. Mr. Reborn-in-Jesus, whose eldest daughter had recently acquired a dress in the same material, was certain that the ties had been hacked, and were controlled by short-range radio devices about the salesmen's persons.

One of the newcomers sported a tie that was baby blue, and held an image of a dove in flight. The other, however, had a tie that was flat and barren grey. At first, Mr. Reborn-in-Jesus had the impression the tie was turned off; then he saw variations shifting within the grey.

"He's artificial," said Mr. Reborn-in-Jesus.

The dove-tied newcomer nodded. He was blond-haired, blue-eyed, with a perfect line of glacially white teeth.

"You're artificial too," said Mr. Reborn-in-Jesus.

"Yes. He robotic, I genetically engineered human. We are sometimes called Made." The smile widened. "Is that a problem?"

Mr. Reborn-in-Jesus frowned. "Weren't we supposed to have fought a war against you? Wipe you out?"

"Indeed." The newcomer shrugged almost apologetically. "And yet here we are. Are you aware of the hire purchase agreement which your son signed on your behalf?"

"I have recently become party to it, yes."

The newcomer bowed gracefully. "We have come to collect our first installment. I am Mr. Columbo; this is Mr. Grausam." Mr. Grausam's face was astonishingly lifelike; his skin was even bothering to sweat in the mid-afternoon heat. In colour, he was a livid mulatto, zombie-coloured, the colour a dangerous man became just before he struck. Mr. Reborn-in-Jesus wondered whether this was a deliberate design feature. Neither man, he noticed, appeared armed. This did not encourage him.

"I feel," said Mr. Reborn-in-Jesus, "we had better discuss this at the house. We have encountered operational difficulties with your product."

Mr. Columbo extended a hand. "By all means," he said, "let us discuss."

As Mr. Reborn-in-Jesus walked into town leading his ass on a rope, a small metallic green fly buzzed into his ear and spoke to him.

"They have no interest in your long-term crop yields. They operate from a temporary office, they turn up immediately to demand payment, and above all, if the Bureau of State Wellbeing realizes they have been reconditioning Von Neumann machines for sale on the open market, they will be removed from circulation to have their commercial acumen surgically extracted and replaced by more important dribbling and bed-soiling skills—"

"SO, YOU'RE ARTIFICIAL," said Mr. Reborn-in-Jesus loudly. "DOES THE LAW APPROVE OF THAT?"

"That is irrelevant to the matter under consideration," said Mr. Columbo. "Why are you speaking so loudly?"

"I have slight deafness," lied Mr. Reborn-in-Jesus, "from the machines."

The houses of Third Landing, mostly empty, were looming into sight now, surrounded by swirling propellant slag from Mr. Columbo and Mr. Grausam's engines.

"Easy," said the fly in Mr. Reborn-in-Jesus's ear. *"There is no radio traffic going on around Mr. Columbo. That tie really is that colour. Mr. Columbo was not genetically engineered for playing well with others. He's most likely ex-military, his brain most likely not wired the same way yours is. If he feels like making a point by flaying one of your kids' faces off, he'll do it. Treat him gently. I'll be there directly."*

"We have little in the way of a crop right now," said Mr. Reborn-in-Jesus.

"I can see," said Mr. Columbo, running his hand through an anaemic stand of wheat. It had been an experimental batch only, but Mr. Reborn-in-Jesus frowned as the dust-dry stems disintegrated at the Made man's touch.

Luckily, there were few children in Main Street. He had assumed Shun-Company had put them all down in the panic cellar, but she had evidently set them to work dealing with the nanominers. Only little Measure-of-Barley ran out from the goat shelter.

"Daddy! Are these the men Uncle Anchorite's going to kill?"

She realized her error and clapped her hand to her mouth suddenly. By that time, however, Mr. Columbo had dropped to a crouch in the dust, easily, still smiling, making himself smaller, less of a threat to the child. His tie was still blue; it still had a dove on it.

"No, honey," said Mr. Columbo. "Your Uncle Anchorite is a bad man to say such wicked things. Where would Uncle Anchorite be right now?" Mr. Reborn-in-Jesus noticed that Grausam was scanning the empty buildings microscopically, his head turning like an owl's.

Measure-of-Barley looked from Mr. Columbo to her father.

"Don't know," she said in a small voice.

"Are you sure?" said Mr. Columbo; and Mr. Reborn-in-Jesus felt a gentle pressure in his leg as Columbo broke his femur with a sly side kick. He collapsed into the dust, amazed at how easy it had been; he felt a gentle pressure on his cheek, smelt real shoeleather.

"Are you *sure*?" repeated Mr. Columbo.

This only had the effect of making Measure-of-Barley scream, shrilly enough for Mr. Columbo to clap his hands to his ears.

"Their hearing range is wider than ours," buzzed an informative voice in his ear. *"Maybe that wasn't an entirely positive thing to engineer into them. Anything that'll make a dog shake his head will probably make them do it too."*

The little girl did not stop screaming. In her current state, she probably represented a minor obstacle to the Made men's aims in town.

Mr. Reborn-in-Jesus said: "Measure, please stop screaming."

Mercifully, the screaming stopped, to be replaced by simple whimpering.

"Measure," said Mr. Reborn-in-Jesus through a mouthful of grit, "tell the nice gentlemen where Uncle Anchorite is."

Measure shook her head, sobbing. "Don't know. Don't know." Luckily, she didn't follow this with *he went out of town with you.*

"I am sorry for the unpleasantness," said Mr. Columbo, "but you only hurt yourself. Yourself," he added, taking hold of Measure-of-Barley's hand, "and the ones you love. You must learn to love yourself." He grabbed Reborn-in-Jesus's collar and dragged him, seventy kilos of dead weight, through the dust up the main street, without apparent effort. This time, Mr. Reborn-in-Jesus screamed as the injury in his leg twisted underneath him.

"Which house should we enter?" said Mr. Columbo.

"Blue door," said Mr. Reborn-in-Jesus weakly. His leg felt wet. He wondered whether it was blood or urine. The front door of the house was unlocked. His fracture thumped on the threshold. Then his head thumped into the alloy of the ground floor as he was dropped unceremoniously.

"You," said the Made Man's voice in shock.

"I see you recognize me," said what might have been the Anchorite's voice—a more educated version of it than Mr. Reborn-in-Jesus was used to. "I imagine it was instilled in your basic programming, in much the same way as human beings instinctively recognize and avoid venomous snakes and spiders."

"I wasn't aware," said Mr. Columbo. Reborn-in-Jesus was certain he recognized abject terror.

"Now you are," said the Anchorite.

"Hello, Uncle Anchorite," said Measure-of-Barley, who knew a shift in the balance of power when she saw it.

"Your associate," said Anchorite, "is circling round the back of the building in hopes to catch me unawares."

There was a sudden soft POP followed by a loud bang, a terrific flash that left silhouettes of all the doors and windows on the insides of Mr. Reborn-in-Jesus' eyelids, and a smell of burnt copper and polymers. Something heavy hit the regolith at the side of the house.

"Watch the birdy," said the Anchorite.

Mr. Columbo moved Measure closer to him as a shield.

"You know that won't do any good," said the Anchorite. "It's been tried before."

Mr. Columbo gently let Measure go.

"What *will* do any good?" said Mr. Columbo. Mr. Reborn-in-Jesus, looking up, saw that Mr. Columbo's necktie had turned white, and that his dove had mutated into a swan. The swan, in a tiny fractal animation, appeared to be singing against a snowspattered sky.

"Nothing," said the Anchorite.

Mr. Columbo's hand moved out for the child again, quick as a snake. Before it could make contact, it sizzled off at the wrist in mid-air. Columbo neither yelled nor collapsed, however, but simply converted his forward momentum into a sideways lurch towards the sound of the Anchorite's voice. Mr. Reborn-in-Jesus had to admire the professionalism of the man. Columbo collapsed, however, onto the carpet, with both legs shot off at the knee. As Mr. Reborn-in-Jesus watched, further awful things happened to Mr. Columbus's body, culminating with several well-placed shots to the spine and head. All through the process, events seemed to be surrounded by a soft white glow. Mr. Reborn-in-Jesus wondered whether this was death creeping up his optic nerve.

Then all things were normal again, apart from a guiltily appetizing smell of singed flesh. The Anchorite was standing over him holding a gas laser.

"Sometimes they have spare brains in the lumbar area," said the Anchorite conversationally. "Are you all right, young lady?"

"Very much," said Measure. "I knew you'd kill him, Uncle Anchorite." Measure bent down to Mr. Reborn-in-Jesus. "Uncle Anchorite is the *fastest* gun, daddy."

"Well, not really." The hermit hefted a heavy piece of apparatus out of concealment behind the row of EVA suits in the hall. "You remember this piece of gear?"

Reborn-in-Jesus forced his eyes to focus. "It's a converted starship FTL drive," he said. "Trapp used it to open locks. It fools security systems. By definition," he parroted, "an FTL drive is also a time machine."

"Well, sort of," said the Anchorite. "It can speed time up or slow it down. I used it to flick your end of the hallway into slow time. No matter how fast he moved, it wasn't fast enough."

Reborn-in-Jesus struggled himself up against a wall with his daughter's help.

"He seemed to know you."

"He did. Him and everyone like him."

"You fought in the War Against the Made," said Reborn-in-Jesus. "You were one of the commanders on our side."

The Anchorite nodded reluctantly. "I suppose that's true." He rose from his seat, the seventeenth chair in the middle of the dining table that was his and his alone, and began picking up equipment crates spread out over the floor. "Their ship is still here. It could be a Made mind too. I'd better see to it."

Reborn-in-Jesus nodded. He looked at his leg forlornly. "Will I live?"

"Goodness gracious, yes. If that had been a compound fracture severing the femoral, your leg would be the size of a weather balloon by now." He nodded to Measure. "Run, child, and fetch the endorphins. Give your father fifty milligrammes till your mother arrives to splint the break." He kicked the hand laser over to Reborn-in-Jesus. "It's unlikely, but if he moves again, shoot him in all the bad places you can think of."

Weighed down by weaponry, he left the house, whistling for his devil. A grim shadow moved out of an angle of the external walls to accompany him.

Mr. Reborn-in-Jesus gathered up the weapon into clumsy hands, and finally sank into a dark monster-proof blanket of unconsciousness.

"Four landing jets!"

Mr. Reborn-in-Jesus frowned. "Could be anything. But run and fetch your Uncle anyway."

Delighted, Measure skipped off squealing to find a green beetle to talk to. Reborn-in-Jesus lifted another child-sized metal locust, its electronic eyes dull and unseeing, its glide planes folded flat against its fuselage, onto the top of the wall, and absentmindedly slapped another trowel of highly nutritious peptide onto its abdomen end. Building goat-proof fences out of dead Green-Queen workers had proved to be the best use that could be made of them. At the base of the wall, a worker he had thought dead started struggling against the mulch holding it in place, eyes focussing and defocussing on its confusing new environment. He drew the hand laser from a vest pocket and blew both its primary and backup brains out.

Polypeptide mulch had proved to be a useful base for mortar, and why not? Animal dung had proven to make effective wattle-and-daub plaster in houses built on Old Earth for thousands of years. Two or three such houses still existed even today.

The landing retros burned down the ninety-east horizon toward the approach beacon Magus had installed at the Saddle. Apostle, shovelling mulch at his father's right hand, said:

"What ship is that?"

"Could be," said Reborn-in-Jesus, "the one we're expecting." His leg still moved uncomfortably in the splint. Standing still slapping mortar on bricks was the greatest mobility he was currently capable of.

"Is that the Investors, papa?"

"Could be," said Reborn-in-Jesus, continuing to slap on mortar.

The Investor was a precise little man in an unobtrusive grey suit and a mood-sensitive tie which seldom shifted from an image of raindrops dropping ceaselessly into grey water in slow motion. Mr. Reborn-in-Jesus, sitting at the other end of the Best Parlour dining table, warmed to him instantly.

"Did you have a pleasant journey in, Mr. Yamashita?" said Shun-Company politely as she served Real Tea topped with sprigs of Real Parsley.

"I was perturbed," said Mr. Yamashita or Yamashita, Yamashita, Yamashita, and Yamashita, "at the amount of space wreckage hereabouts. I and my colleagues passed a junked *Skyline*-class personal transport on our way here, space in this vicinity is filled with," he regarded the disassembled GreenQueen worker lying legs-up on the table with distaste, "*those* things, there is a cloud of radioactive metal droplets and FTL components in close circumpolar orbit that strongly suggest a Type Three Prospector was vapourised here in the recent past, there's a wrecked Dictator-era gunship trailing this planetoid's primary in a Trojan orbit, and there is *another* wreck, a type seven cattle transport, orbiting equatorially—"

"The cattle transport," said Mr. Reborn-in-Jesus evenly, "is my son's ship. It is currently powered down to conserve fuel. It is not a wreck."

Mr. Yamashita coloured in embarrassment. His mood tie changed images to depict a man swallowing a toad.

"I do apologize," he said. "But you take my point that the approaches to this world seem somewhat heavy with debris, one might even say hazardous."

"That," said the Anchorite, from his chair, "can soon be remedied."

Mr. Yamashita stayed silent for a moment, conversing with Senior Partners. Five generations of Yamashitas had made the family name what it was, and all that accumulated experience could not be allowed to go to waste. Expensive, top-flight personality analogues had been made of all the firm's senior partners before their deaths, and although they had no legal voting rights, their experience was still cherished. Paul Miki Yamashita junior had his relatives' guiding voices implanted directly and clamorously into his head. They could not be switched off. They saw and observed upon his every action, in the bath, in bed with his wife. Yamashita-san suffered from family-imposed techno-schizophrenia. Mr. Reborn-in-Jesus found Yamashita-san disturbing, and noticed that the Anchorite, too, kept both hands underneath the dining table where they could not be seen to draw a weapon.

"The senior partners," coughed Yamashita-san junior, "tentatively approved your proposal on behalf of the investors, with minor reservations. The proposed site of the health retreat and neutronium spa would be, we understand, the South Pole of Mount Ararat."

"That's a *gravitational gradient* spa," corrected the Anchorite. "It's the thick clustering of baryobars hereabouts that gives this location healing properties, particularly for clients suffering from microgravity diseases."

"I would not dare," said Yamashita-san, "to contradict you, sir, and despite the absence of a shred of supporting medical evidence, am sure you are entirely correct. Our investors, Mr. and Mrs. Joannou, trustees of the Anadyomene Development Company Victims Compensation Fund, have past experience of dealing with you and believe your world to possess potential," said Yamashita-san. "They account you worthy of trust. We therefore plan to build a spacious hundred-square-kilometre estate furnished with proper modern landing facilities, a fully-equipped hospital for the treatment of degenerative conditions, luxury radiation-shielded accommodation, a bush baby petting zoo, bioluminescent plankton fountains, a hedge maze, and colour-sorting bowerbird gardens."

"But it would be peaceful," said the Anchorite. "The underlying tranquillity of the location would be preserved."

Mr. Yamashita nodded. "No buildings high enough to throw oneself violently from," he said. "For the benefit of the patients, some of whom might be detoxifying or suffering from mental illness."

"All of whom," said the Anchorite firmly, "would be rich."

"And there would be a wall," said Mr. Reborn-in-Jesus with some concern, "between us and them."

"A very *high* wall," agreed Mr. Yamashita, appraising Mr. Reborn-in-Jesus. "Of your family, you yourself would retain a seventeen per cent interest, with your son Mr. Magus and your, um, associate here—" he nodded at the Anchorite "—also retaining seventeen per cent, and the Anadyomene Fund forty-nine."

"Sounds reasonable," said the Anchorite.

"Those are, in fact," coughed Yamshita-san diplomatically, "exactly the terms you asked for. We argued against them at great length with our clients, yet were overruled."

"Sounds reasonable," said the Anchorite.

"Our clients appear to place great trust in you, Mr.—?"

"I have transcended the workaday commonplace of names," revealed the Anchorite.

A cough sounded from behind Mr. Reborn-in-Jesus, who grimaced weakly.

"I wish," he said, "to split my percentage between myself and my dear wife. I will take nine per cent—"

The cough sounded again.

"—eight per cent, and my darling wife, the end point of my affections, the axis of my universe, will take nine."

Mr. Reborn-in-Jesus's drink was topped up from behind. The other guests' glasses remained half full.

Mr. Yamashita smiled with excellent teeth. The sun dawned on his tie, onto which a heron strode out and began fishing in the former rainwater.

"Well, now that we are concluded, how do we propose to populate the gardens? Mrs. Joannou is very fond of redwood."

unity and the tax pirates

n the tenth kilodia since the founding of the New and Perfect Era, Mount Ararat experienced the firm hand of government. This arrival, however, had been anticipated for several days. Rather than waiting for new stars to appear in the firmament and muddy urchins to skip in trailing pond muck yelling 'MA! PA! THERE'S A SPACESHIP IN SUCH AND SUCH A CONSTELLATION!', the family Reborn-in-Jesus had recently arranged to be warned in advance by the new ultramodern landing facility under construction by Temple House in the southern hemisphere of the planet. This new landing, therefore, was announced by a call on Third Landing's one and only videophone, a bespoke device cast in genuine ancient bakelite, consisting of a three-dimensional screen and speakers and one single large ivory button which opened a channel to Mount Ararat's only *other* videophone, at the construction site.

The foreperson, Mr. Feng, sat in a cosy office surrounded by robosupervisor screens, grinning at the camera. *"Good morning! We're tracking an unauthorized incoming approaching down the uphill ecliptic. Transponders identify it as a government ship. It does not respond to hailing. Are you expecting it?"*

Third Landing had a number of adult inhabitants—Mr. and Mrs. Reborn-in-Jesus, their eldest daughter Unity, taciturn Testament, voluble Apostle, and wholesomely beautiful God's-Wound—but uncommonly, only Unity was at home to take the call. Tall, slender, impossibly attractive, but terrified that her sheer size made her look like a man, Unity hunched herself smaller and spoke into the microphone in as high a voice as she could muster. "I don't believe so, Mr. Feng, but if it's a government ship I'm sure no harm can come of it."

Mr. Feng—middle-aged, portly, but possessed of the single undeniable plus point that he was not one of Unity's immediate gene pool, grinned. "Yes, I'm pretty sure they're listening to us too. But we have nothing to fear. They'll find our accounts in order."

"You think it's a Revenue ship, Mr. Feng?"

"Almost certainly. The Tax Pirates cruise the outer reaches of human space, looking for isolated, impoverished planets. When they find one they land, make up an enormous back tax bill, present it to the local yokels, and wait for the money and bribes to roll in. It's just like real piracy, only with fewer spacings and plump-buttocked cabin boys."

Unity coloured like a ripening fruit. "I'm not sure father would approve of your using such words around me, Mr. Feng."

"Buttock buttock buttock buttock buttock. Feng out."

Unity rose to her feet and called out through the house.

"POSTLE! ZOUNDS! THERE'S A GOVERMENT SHIP COMING IN!"

It was the end of the day. 23 Kranii was loitering on the C/D ring division with intent to set. Mother and Father, who were not strictly Beguiled-of-the-Serpent's mother and father, still could not bring themselves to call 23 Kranii 'the sun'. The goats were already penned in in the High Street, attempting vainly to find scraps of ungrazed green. Some of them were already turning round to sleep in the Goat Shelter.

It was Naphillian perihelion, and the sun did not set properly at this time of year due to Mount Ararat's axial tilt. However, it did pass behind Naphil's A, B, and C rings, which dimmed it to a ruddy disco swirl, and for those few hours, the goats could be persuaded to sleep. During Crystal Night, as the children had christened it despite unfathomable objections from their parents, glistering shadows scooted across the fields like schools of supersonic jelly-fish, and the sun was a vague patch of glowing coals fixed firmly over the North Pole, still light enough to read by, still warm enough to sleep under.

Beguiled-of-the-Serpent's favourite goat, Shub-Niggurath, fol-lowed her blindly by the still waters of the Town Pond and into the shadow of the palms, where the History of the Entire Universe had been picked out in mosaic on the side of the Government Penitentiary by the combined children of Mount Ararat under Mother's guidance. The first few square metres of mosaic were in raw, undifferentiated earth colours, home-baked clay baked in Mother's home clay-baking apparatus, made of wetted Mount Ararat regolith, brown chondritic sand and rubble. In these col-ours the beginning of all things had been related—the bountiful hand of an indeterminately sexed Creator bestowing being on a roughly-rendered Adam and Eve, who looked to have come into being simultaneously with an identical number of ribs. Later episodes dwelt at length on the creation of Satan and His appearance before God to receive the instruction to torment Job. The trials of Job were depicted in great detail, involving Job's friends and relatives being burned, buried, blown up and beheaded. Some of those chapters in the story seemed to be picked out in various shades of stained glass. Still later episodes, more gaudily made of metal, ceramic and plastic, showed the recent history of Mount Ararat—an idealized pre-war general purpose transport descending from the sky, bearing and loading precious cargoes. The cargoes, the drive exhaust of the trader, and the panoply of stars that twinkled overhead were made of a mineral mined from the very centre of Mount Ararat; a mineral which Beguiled's foster-brother Magus was currently attempting to sell on a planet orbiting another star, and which all the children had been warned not to prise out of the mosaic, handle, lick, or eat under any circumstances. During daylight hours, when solar power activated the UV filaments twining over the fields, the normally jet-black stars and starship fluoresced a gorgeous sympathetic purple.

Beguiled sat down with her back against the metal wall of the Penitentiary, took out the cheap plastic encrypted text reader her mother turned a blind eye to, and loaded forbidden book number four, *Paradise Regain''d,* by John Milton. She had not been entirely sure what to make of Mr. Milton's earlier *Paradise Lost*; it had made the Devil out to be a villain, whereas the book of Job and the Gospel of Matthew clearly showed him to be God's servant. Perhaps this book would make things clearer.

"I who e'er while the happy garden sung..." began the book. Beguiled, who was beginning to toy with spelling her name Beguil'd, worked her way through the ancient language with some difficulty, until she was interrupted by a clear regular sound of

knocking, not so much heard as felt, communicated through her shoulderblades resting against the metal. Whatever the sound was, it was coming from the inside of the prison itself.

Born into a society which relied heavily on occasional visits from passing spaceships, Beguiled was well acquainted with Morse Code. *Dotdotdotdot—dot—dotdashdotdot— dotdashdotdot—dashdashdash—H-E-L-L-O.*

She turned, and pressed her ear against the metal. Gingerly, not wanting to disturb the constant stream of messaging, she tappedout the same greeting in reply.

The stream of dots and dashes changed instantly. T-H-A-N-K-G-O-D-R-U-O-N-T-H-E-O-U-T-S-I-D-E-T-H-I-S-I-S-J-O-H-A-N-N-E-S-

She interrupted the knocker's enthusiasm with a curt reply. M-R-T-R-A-P-P-I-S-T-H-A-T-Y-O-U-STOP.

The knocking paused. Then, hesitantly, it replied back:
W-H-O-W-A-N-T-S-2-K-N-O-W-QUERY.

Beguiled tapped back: B-E-G-U-I-L-D-R-A-F-F-A-E-L-E-STOP.

There was another pause. Then came the reply:
B-E-G-U-I-L-E-D-O-F-T-H-E-S-E-R-P-E-N-T-QUERY.

Beguiled tapped back a Y-E-S, then followed with:
Y-O-U-G-O-T-M-E-I-N-2-T-R-O-U-B-L-E-M-R-T-R-A-P-P-STOP.

I-M-S-O-R-R-Y-P-R-E-S-S-U-R-E-S-O-F-E-S-C-A-P-I-N-G-I-M-T-R-Y-I-N-G-2-E-S-C-A-P-E-N-O-W-

She clicked the BOOKMARK AND EXIT spot on the reader's screen. Even after she unstuck her ear from the wall, she could still hear the rhythm tapping out frantically. Somehow, the tapper seemed to have sensed the fact that she no longer had her head against the metal.

W-A-I-T-P-L-E-A-S-E-I-T-S-T-A-K-E-N-S-O-L-O-N-G-2-G-E-T-T-H-I-S-F-A-R-C-A-N-U-H-E-L-P-M-E-

Beguiled took great pleasure in tapping:

Chondritic gravel crunched beneath her heels as she turned on them and trudged back in the direction of the house. Shub-Niggurath, bleating softly, rose without question and accompanied her. The landscape crawled and flashed with the purple noise of shadows flitting by faster than film frames.

There was a rumble of rockets, and a bright star descending along the ninety-east meridian towards the new landing field. Someone appeared to have arrived.

"She's a beauty all right," said Apostle, with the keen critical eye of a man who was allowed on his brother's tramp trader if he promised not to spit on the upholstery. Magus was currently away trading transuranics on the metal markets of Celadon, accompanied by his adopted sister Only-God-is-Perfect, and, at his father's insistence, Mr. and Mrs. Reborn-in-Jesus themselves. Mr. Reborn-in-Jesus was having no close camaraderie in his family.

The government ship was equipped, in the manner of manner of many ships, to shed its FTL drive, long range sensor fit, and interstellar fuel pods while struggling down to a planetary surface, in order to reduce payload. As it was a government vessel, it should have been doubly likely that its occupants would seek to separate their ship to reduce fuel costs. However, this ship had come down intact, despite the absence of a heatshield down the whole length of her hull. This made little difference in Mount Ararat's kilometre-deep atmosphere, but could hardly have been standard procedure—and standard procedure, after all, was what government departments lived for.

The ship had landed on the fused stone strip that had been burned out in the South End Saddle by the construction company.

Gigantic fluorescent orange stevedore robots stood on standby in the robopen, and the edges of the strip were marked out by solar-powered visible-light beacons driven into the regolith like bizarre local flora with square black leaves and lilac flashing heads. Across the strip, a zig-zag trail led up towards gates in the Wall. The Wall separated the aboriginal inhabitants of Mount Ararat from the Gravitational Gradient Spa and Curative Centre of Excellence being constructed by offworld investors in the worldlet's southern hemisphere. Presently, all humankind—or at least that portion of it that possessed obscene wealth and very poor judgement—would gain access to the healing powers of neutronium, a miniscule chunk of which, torn from a dying star, provided Mount Ararat with its earthlike surface gravity. Right now, all that could be seen were sluggish landslides of nutritious mulch spilling out through deep-buried vitrified foundations.

The Government Men stood on the glassy-smooth apron in front of their vessel, which recently seemed to have undergone a respray. Many government craft in outlying areas, even today, still bore the eyed pyramid of the Dictatorship. No doubt this was what had been recently replaced, on the vessel's side, by the ring of clasped hands that currently represented the State.

"She's a Model Three courier," said Apostle. "I bet she can make two hundred C. Twice as fast as a trader. Strange," he added in reflection, "for government men to be doing their business in a courier."

"Good morning," said the leader of the Government Men, a two-metre man sporting a face fierce with tribal cicatrices. "We are agents of Central Revenue, and *you* are Guilty Until Proven Innocent. My colleague Mr. Aidid and I would like to see the accounts of everybody onplanet." Mr. Aidid, a smaller, prematurely grey-haired man with an expression of deep gloom, nodded dolefully. Behind Mr. Aidid and his colleague, other men were already unloading oddly heavy equipment onto all terrain baggage trucks.

"We don't keep accounts," said Unity frankly.

The Central Revenue agent's face lit up in delight.

"Oh, *good*," he said.

"Uncle Anchorite! Uncle Anchorite! Ararat's been boarded by fiscal buccaneers! They've demanded our accounts for the last twenty years—"

The cave was empty.

Apostle, Day-of-Creation, and Pitch-Not-Thy-Tent-Towards-Sodom Ogundere were alone in a large, light, airy space with glistering vitrified walls, free of any civilized accoutrements save a single massive pressure door at the entrance. The Anchorite's bunk, his ancient, counterpane-patched EVA suit, his mining laser, his copy of Vegetius's *De Re Militari*, were all gone. In their place was a single scrap of paper in the centre of the main chamber, which read simply:

MUST LEAVE. URGENT BUSINESS TO ATTEND TO. DON'T TELL REVE-
NUE COLLECTORS I WAS EVER HERE. EAT THIS MESSAGE AND DIS-
POSE OF THE POOP WHEN IT WORKS ITS WAY THROUGH YOUR SYS-
TEM.

Day-of-Creation looked up at Apostle, crestfallen.

"We are surely sunk," he said.

Deputy Lead Revenue Assessor Aidid ran a sensor round the rim of the faecal waste disposal unit, tapped the screen of his detector, and nodded at Mr. Armitage gravely.

"Imperfectly cleaned," gloated Mr. Armitage, peering at Mr. Aidid's screen. "This registers the excreta of seventeen recent users. Every bowel bleeds a little, Ms. Reborn-in-Jesus, and DNA does not lie. Your own account mentions only sixteen permanent planetary inhabitants. Where is number seventeen?"

"We're cannibals," blurted Day-of-Creation suddenly. "We ate number sixteen and pooped him out through our systems."

Mr. Armitage turned his fierce face to bear on Day-of-Creation with the slowness of a naval gun turret. Day-of-Creation cringed.

Inexplicably, Mr. Armitage's mouth broke into a smile. A smile with its teeth filed into points, it was true, but a smile nevertheless.

"Is that so? Technically, cannibalism is not a crime in tax law. I may well allow you that one. Failure to disclose possession of an interstellar vehicle, however..." his eyes dropped to para 3, subpara 37B of the declarations proforma page that lay open on his palmframe, and he tutted, tutted, tutted.

"But we *did* declare *Prodigal Son*," exclaimed Unity indignantly. "It's my brother's freighter which he bought fair and square."

"There is also a personal shuttle landed not five kilometres from here," said Mr. Aidid.

"Oh, *that*," said Day-of-Creation. "That just-just—" he looked around at the rest of his family for a prompt.

"Just landed here," said Unity.

"And its owners just took off again," said Apostle.

"Without their ship," said Day-of-Creation.

"And we don't know who they were," said Beguiled-of-the-Serpent Raffaele.

Mr. Armitage's deep frown of disblief might have permitted small objects to be concealed in his forehead. "There is also," he said, "evidence of a hasty departure by a type three survey vehicle."

"Oh, that one just blew up," said Day-of-Creation.

"Killing everyone on board," added Apostle.

"Terrible, terrible accident," said Beguiled-of-the-Serpent.

"And an old D class gun scout," said Mr. Armitage, "powered down, trailing this gas giant—" he gestured out of the window at the imagined ball of Naphil with his palmframe stylus—"in a Trojan orbit."

"We have *no* idea," said Unity truthfully, "whose *that* is."

Mr. Armitage fixed the room with eyes that held belief only that all those present were the fiscal equivalent of witches and should be dropped into a gravity well to see if they floated. "I see. Well, in any case," he concluded, "Mr. Aidid—what is the damage?"

"It is the unanimous finding of this team," said Mr. Aidid, ticking off hotspots on his paras and sub-paras, "that the family Reborn-in-Jesus of location 23 Kranii 3X, locally known as 'Mount Ararat', owe Central Revenue five hundred and thirty-three thousand, three hundred and fifty-two credits at this date, Kilodia Ten New Era. It insists," he said, staring down the bridge of his glasses as if squinting down gunsights, "on immediate settlement."

Unity, quivering with rage like a tall tree in a gale, went through the motions and said:

"We haven't got five hundred thousand credits."

"Then we will have to seize physical assets accordingly. Mr. Aidid—what is the current centrally registered value," said Mr. Armitage, "of a goat?"

Mr. Aidid entered the word 'GOAT' on his palmframe, and read back: "Seventy-five credits."

"But we paid a hundred a horn for those!"

"Seventy-five credits," repeated Mr. Aidid sternly.

"That would make, for the entire herd..." said Mr. Armitage, tapping in figures on his own keypad with the precision of a piano-playing polar bear.

"One thousand six hundred and seventy-two credits," said Unity without thinking. Mr. Aidid shot her an alarmed look of re-appraisal, as if only now considering her to be another human being.

"We will itemize the goods we propose to requisition," said Mr. Armitage. "As periods of indentured servitude for payments of revenues owed have recently become acceptable standard practice, we are required to sequester all planetary inhabitants of working age until the exact terms of the settlement become clear. Is there a strongroom or jailhouse we could lock you and your brothers and sister in?"

Unity blinked to try and clear her eyes and ears of madness. "Uh, there's the Panic Cellar, it's radiation-proof and it gets used as a drunk tank if we need it, though you need a combination to lock and unlock it—"

"Please be so kind as to remember the combination for us. While you are locked in, Mr. Aidid will discuss the fine detail of our requisition with you here in your own home, in the environment where you feel safest. In the meantime, I have other work to attend to." He bent into a bow, the end point of which would have connected his lips with Unity's hand had she allowed it to.

"I'm not going into no cellar," objected Apostle ungrammatically.

"I'm afraid," said Mr. Armitage, straightening up with a thin smile, "I must insist."

"I'm not going into no cellar," said Apostle, "*never.*"

Mr. Armitage smiled and produced a pepperbox laser. He flicked the action to ACQUIRE MULTIPLE TARGETS; the hydra-heads of fibre optics on the laser's barrel turned and twined until they were lined up on every other living person in the room— including, Unity was intrigued to note, Mr. Aidid.

"Into the cellar, please," said Mr. Armitage.

Apostle glared darkly at the tax assessor, but complied, filing with all other adult family members into the pressure door under the stairs. The gun was waved at Mr. Aidid as peremptorily as at the Reborn-in-Jesuses; he dropped meekly into line. Finally, Unity descended, turning to look serenely out at Mr. Armitage, who grinned back.

"The Devil," said Unity, "will punish you for your wickedness if you harm any member of my family."

"The combination, please," said Mr. Armitage, realigning his hydra-heads on Beguiled-of-the-Serpent, who was not yet of working age and hence still outside the cellar.

Unity gave the combination. The door closed. Very slowly, she could hear fingers changing the combination on the keypad on the other side. After a brief hiatus, the emergency lights came on, red as dying embers, like daylight on Mount Ararat's surface.

Mr. Aidid shook his head. "Such poor keyboard speed. Surely you realize such a man could never even make a Grade One in the Revenue Service?"

Unity scowled. "I beg your pardon?"

Aidid stared at Unity in disbelief. "You don't for one minute think those men out there are genuine Central Revenue Agents, do you?"

"So *you* are a genuine Central Revenue Agent."

Mr. Aidid nodded. "The blood of Saul runs in my veins. I must apologize for the perversion of correct revenue collection processes your family has been subjected to. That ship, alas, is using the transponders from a Central Revenue ship, *my* ship, the *Render Unto Caesar*. We dropped back into curvespace a couple of days back in the Verdastelo system, a routine census and assessment mission on a stage three colony, when we received a distress call in the UHF band. A mail courier in difficulty, disabled by a liquid helium cloud in deep space; the vapour had oozed through her hull, so the crew said, and then become gaseous, contaminating the ship's air and causing multiple hull breaches via dry and wet ice damage. The crewman logging the call certainly spoke with a convincingly squeaky voice. Unfortunately, when we boarded, the ship's allegedly disabled crew rose up and attacked us, demanding that our captain instruct them as to how to remove and reinstall our transponder on their own vessel, and even that I accompany them here to reinforce their bona-fides as Revenue agents. They plan something here; I have no doubt that it is dreadful." He shook his head vehemently. "That assessment of your planetary back tax bill was highly inflated. I was acting under duress—"

Apostle had clapped a hand over Mr. Aidid's mouth. "We understand. Now, however, we find ourselves locked in a storm refuge underground with pressing need to leave it. Does the equipment officially issued you as a state tax assessor include heavy cutting gear or explosives at all?"

Mr. Aidid thought for several seconds, and said: "No. No, just the personal palmframe and the official collector's sash."

Apostle punched a nearby wall. The anti-lunatic padding ate the sound of the impact before it even reached the two metres of anti-neutron and anti-gamma laminates beyond it. He pummelled the wall with a farmer's muscles till his knuckles grew bloody. Discreetly, as Apostle wasted air, the integral CO_2 recycler cut in.

Eventually, Apostle stopped, panting, aware his efforts were coming to nothing.

"Well," he said, "at least we know our tax bill won't be as large as we thought."

Beguiled-of-the-Serpent pelted down the front path between rows of wilted poppies. Mother had never been able to convince them to grow on Ararat. Outside, the air was still warm. Goats were wandering about unconcernedly, chewing the cud and watching the newcomers from the tax collector's ship without concern. Four of them were currently shifting a large cylindrical device they had unloaded from a surface rover to the edge of the Penitentiary, extending cables from it to clip onto the metal. Mr. Armitage, meanwhile, was supervising the unloading of other equipment—a portable fusion torus, cutting tools, explosives.

Mr. Armitage noticed Beguiled's presence. "Hi there short stuff. Don't you worry, we'll have your brothers and sisters out of there just as soon as we have our own business sorted out."

"I'm not short," said Beguiled. "I am tall for my age. I am five kilodia old. Why are you trying to break into the Penitentiary with a temporal accelerator?"

Mr. Armitage looked down his totem-pole nose with surprise, and new respect. "Why? Would that be a bad idea in your opinion?"

"Well, it worked the last time Mr. Trapp tried it. But the Penitentiary learns from its mistakes. It's programmed to. The same trick probably won't work twice."

Mr. Armitage grinned a massive array of cubic-zirconia-studded teeth. "Mr. Trapp. That would be Hans Trapp, I take it? The cracksman?"

"He describes himself as a security consultant," said Beguiled. "Mother says he is not an irretrievably bad man, only a thief."

Mr. Armitage's eyes rolled in his head. "So he's not in there any more."

"Oh, yes. He did escape, but Father made him go back in."

The smile broadened and, if this was possible, became even whiter. "Excellent. Now you run along, tall stuff. Some of this gear is dangerous." He turned and yelled to one of his fellow taxmen. "Ravi, belay the accelerator, it won't work. We'll start with the gravity cutter."

Ground crunched under Beguiled's EVA shoes as she scrambled round to the front of the Penitentiary under the palms. Now on a side of the device invisible to the taxman, she lowered her face close to the metal and set to tapping hard with her knuckles.

M-R-T-R-A-P-P-R-U-T-H-E-R-E-M-R-T-R-A-P-P-R-U-T-H-E-R-E-

Presently there was an answering series of taps.

Y-E-S-W-H-O-R-U-STOP

B-E-G-U-I-L-D, tapped Beguiled. T-H-E-R-E-R-M-E-N-H-E-R-E-2-G-E-T-U-O-U-T-W-I-T-H-A-G-R-A-V-I-T-Y-C-U-T-T-E-R-STOP

The Penitentiary paused, and then tapped back T-H-A-T-W-O-N-T-W-O-R-K-W-H-O-R-T-H-E-Y-B-A-D-M-E-N-QUERY

N-O-C-E-N-T-R-A-L-R-E-V-E-N-U-L-E-A-D-E-R-I-S-C-A-L-L-E-D-R-M-I-T-A-G-E-H-E-K-N-O-W-S-U-STOP

K-N-O-W-N-O-O-N-E-C-A-L-L-E-D-R-M-I-T-A-G-E-W-H-A-T-S-H-E-L-O-O-K-L-I-K-E-QUERY

S-C-A-R-R-D-F-A-C-E-V-E-R-Y-T-A-L-L-STOP

There was another long pause. Then the metal tapped back frantically T-H-A-T-I-S-N-O-R-E-V-E-N-U-M-A-N-I-F-H-E-G-E-T-S-M-E-O-U-T-I-A-M-D-E-A-D-A-L-E-R-T-A-U-T-H-O-R-I-T-I-E-S-S-E-N-D-A-

N-S-O-S-

C-A-L-M, tapped Beguiled. E-V-R-Y-O-N-E-L-O-C-K-D-U-P-B-Y-T-A-X-M-E-N-I-D-O-N-T-H-A-V-E-P-A-S-S-W-O-R-D-F-O-R-C-O-M-M-S-S-U-I-T-E-

Another pause. Then the metal tapped back:

W-H-E-R-E-T-H-E-Y-L-O-C-K-D-U-P-W-H-A-T-S-O-R-T-O-F-L-O-C-K

The house was unguarded. The next smallest girls, Measure-of-Barley and Be-Not-Near-Unto-Man-In-Thy-Time-Of-Uncleanness, were sitting sobbing on the front step. Goats were walking freely through the house. Inside the hall, Day-of-Creation was attempting to convince one to eat a curtain.

"Stop that," said Beguiled. "We have to deal with the taxmen."

"Pa and Uncle Anchorite and the Devil will deal with them when they get back," said Day-of-Creation unconcernedly, trying gamely to feed the artificial fibre through the ruminant's jaws.

"Not this time," said Beguiled, dropping to her knees in front of the combination lock. "Uncle Anchorite has run away, remember? This time there is no Devil to save us. Only ourselves."

Day-of-Creation scoffed, giving up on the drapes and instead attempting to force a corner of carpet into the uninterested beast. "And how are you going to do *that*?"

"These model three-twenties," said Beguiled knowledgeably, "have a second secret factory-set combination for engineers to use in case of accidental lock-in."

Day-of-Creation blinked, Beguiled's fingers stabbed at the keyboard, and the lock motored open. The huge cube of a door swung cleanly out of the jamb; behind it, startled faces squinted into the light.

"How did you—?" gasped Day-of-Creation.

"They're not the most secure of doors," shrugged Beguiled airily. "Unity! Apostle! They aren't really taxmen! They came here to get out Mr. Trapp! We haven't much time!"

Unity pushed out into the hall. "We're aware. Shut that front door and get all the little ones indoors before they give us all away. We have to hold a Council of War."

Through the net curtains and the gold-plated glass, Armitage's confederates could be seen assembling a massive device resembling a set of basketball hoops gradually reducing in size, levelled at the side of the Penitentiary like a gun. From positions of concealment behind armchairs, dressers, and cabinets, the Reborn-in-Jesus children observed without being observed.

"Prisoners," said Unity, "don't pay tax. They are not interested in Mr. Trapp for his money. As far as they know, he's earned no money since being incarcerated."

Apostle, on the other side of the Best Parlour, was rummaging in the King Charles III Ikea Armoire. "I can't find old man Allion's handgun. I could swear papa kept it in here."

"Keep your nose out of such matters. That piece's not been fired in close on nine kilodia. It'll more like cook up in your hand. Besides, it's only a cavitating-round rail pistol, practically an antique. Armitage's men will have better guns than that, and know how to use them; and they're probably wearing all sorts of armour."

Apostle sulked. "We've only seen one gun."

"Uncle Anchorite says, never assume what you've seen is all your enemy has, and never assume your enemy has what you think you've seen."

Heads around the room all nodded solemnly. Uncle Anchorite was always right.

"So what do you suggest?" Apostle held up a carpet beater sardonically. "I could beat the dustmites out of 'em."

"First off, we've got to get the young uns out of here."

"But we've got to go past their ship to get to the South End Construction—"

"You're not going there. You're going out to Dispater Crater."

"Why is it *me* doing it? And why there? It's an empty dust bowl."

"Because I trust you to do it. And because it *is* an empty dust bowl. Mom and Pop never filled in Dispater, though they could have made a hectare field out of it. And the Devil's been seen there. And have we seen any ship leave Ararat in the last five decadia?"

Beguiled's eyes widened. "You think Uncle Anchorite's still *here*?"

"You know as well as I do he doesn't really live in that damn cave. It's empty nine times out of ten. And there's no back entrance out of it either. It's a decoy to prove his hermit affidavits. I suspect Uncle Anchorite has a large and spacious abode elsewhere on this planet. The surface gravity here on Ararat might be one half Old Earth normal, but only four hundred metres down, it's Old Earth standard. And those prospectors who met with that unhappy accident a couple years back sent a drilling drone down there and reported an oxy/nitro atmosphere."

Day-of-Creation was spellbound. "You think he lives down *there*?"

"I'm sure of it. It's his planet-sized Panic Cellar. And I'm equally sure there' s a tunnel coming up from there to Dispater. All you have to do is look for it with one of those densitometers the rock-

148

hounds left behind in their haste to be elsewhere."

"Whilst you'll be doing what?"

Mr. Aidid answered the question. Though a small, physically unprepossessing man, his jaw was set as determinedly as if he had been disputing a Super Tax rebate. "We will be using your family communications array to launch an emergency message missile to Celadon loaded with a Code Grey."

"What's a Code Grey?"

"An encrypted all-points SOS to all Revenue vessels in the Celadon system," said Aidid. "I have reason to believe there are two, one of which is being operated by the Special Revenue Service."

"I see," said Apostle.

"They could be here," said Aidid, "within days."

"Pardon my lack of enthusiasm," said Apostle. "Also, Armitage's men have cut the link between here and the comms array. Anyone making a call would have to go outside and climb right up the comms tower to do it. How are you going to do that under the eyes of a ship full of armed men?"

"We will have a diversion," said Unity.

"What sort of diversion?"

Unity smiled and produced old man Allion's handgun. All twelve of its barrels were loaded.

The weapon, Unity knew, was only accurate up to a hundred metres. The old Arkarch had intended it to be used for crowd control; it could cough out a cloud of ferrous metal swarf thick enough to pick a man's flesh from his bones, but that cloud became random shrapnel beyond whites-of-eyes distance. For this reason, Unity was crawling on her knees and elbows, trying to get as close to the taxmen as possible.

*If I took only one out—that would even the odds... if I took out
Armitage, the leader...*

Yet she knew in her inmost heart that she might not hit Armitage, even with the nightmarish weapon she was holding, and that
even if she did, Armitage might be wearing some manner of protective clothing. And even if she hit and killed Armitage, if they
had one armed man left, he would still be the equal of whole of
the rest of Third Landing. And how would she get away, considering they had a surface rover, and almost certainly better weapons
than hers, that might be able to pick her off at ten times the range
her petty little paintstripper was accurate at?

The rover was between her and them, parked up by the goat
track gate on six huge wire tyres, metres from the waters of the
Pond. The goat gate had been left open. Goats were ambling
boldly in and out.

Surface rovers were, unfortunately, made to be resistant to
micrometeroids—and hence also to gunfire—in a way that people
were not. Even though this one was operating in an atmosphere,
the tyres showed it had vacuum capability. The gun might not be
able to damage it irreparably.

However, there was one thing a farm girl with gravity-made
muscles could do to a piece of equipment designed to be used on
airless worlds with surfaces dry as dust. Unseen from the Penitentiary, she rose from concealment, walked up to the back of the
Rover, positioned herself under its back bumper and, biceps and
quadriceps straining, lifted it clear of the ground. Then, walking
her hands slowly up its belly, she gave it one final shove and
watched it topple into the deep waters of the Pond with a crash
that sounded the way she imagined thunderous divine retribution
should. She hoped it hadn't cracked the Pond's waterproof lining.

Then she was gone, running for her life, the handgun forgotten, bellyflopping into the crops. Almost certainly, though, they would be able to see her on infrared. They were very well-equipped. She jumped back up and continued running, ducking behind a tractor. There was a bright flash like a ship going into FTL, and a cloud of metal droplets stung her cheek. They were shooting at her. Looking behind, she zigzagged to keep the tractor between her and them. The Ten-North Drain was only a few metres away; it had thick concrete banks, and would surely mask her IR signature.

And then, in a moment, it was all over. Her frantic stumbling through the potato field had been far slower than the stealthy running of one of Mr. Armitage's men down the Ninety-East track. He also had gravity-made muscles, and he was also carrying a gun. An infantry weapon, of the sort designed to kill people riding *inside* heavy armoured vehicles. The man had an expression of detached professionalism that gave her little comfort.

Then, suddenly, the man fell over onto the packed earth, his gun not even going off. Unity walked forward, examining the body in wonder; not a mark appeared on it. Surely a wound would have bled? With the professional eye of one who had seen many people who had died by violence, she turned the body over and there, two fingers beneath the nipple, found the tiny wound she'd suspected. It probably went all the way through the chest from front to back. The wound had not bled out because heart shots didn't.

She looked up at the surrounding crops. Incautious laser fire had now set a hectare or more alight. That would play havoc with the world's oxygen resources. Papa would have to buy in more. Still, the smoke and flames, combined with Ararat's ten-metre horizon, would prevent the rest of Armitage's men from shooting at her.

151

"So," she said in a loud, clear voice, "you *are* still here after all. Thank you, and please look after my brothers and sisters."

Wind rustled the potato stalks in answer. But of course, there was very little wind on Ararat.

Up on the comms tower, Mr. Aidid clung to the maintenance ladder trying to remain as motionless as a bittern in reeds, feeling as obvious as an elephant in a sauna. Mr. Armitage's men were running, shouting, firing far below. He had to fight both his fear of getting shot if he moved and his fear of falling from his perch if he got shot. On Ararat, unfortunately, twenty metres above the ground felt closer to two hundred; the world's curvature was visible even from ground level, and up here it seemed like he was perched on the side of the Quito beanstalk looking a hundred miles down on South America.

He had been made to memorize the algorithm for sending out Code Grey as a neophyte Collector; it came back to him easily, though the unfamiliar controls for Ararat's emergency FTL messaging system were more difficult. If only he could remember how to call up the user manual on a separate screen...

He was fairly sure he had disabled sound, and the screen brightness was turned down as far as it could be without the display becoming unreadable. Whatever he did up here would be as unobtrusive as possible. The sound of ionized air crackling far below, the smell of burning vegetation, and the stink of pond-bottom muck bubbling to the surface as the rover sank, all rose up to him. Surely everyone on the ground below was too busy, too concerned with finding places to go and people to shoot, to worry about seeing and shooting him?

Only one more sequence, and the Mayday missile would pop

out of its housing and begin to winch itself up the tower to take-off height. They would surely notice *that*. He had to be off the tower before then; not just for personal safety, but also to make sure Armitage and his crew still thought all the adults on Ararat were still locked in the Panic Cellar. They might not have recognized Unity. She had tied her hair back and put on a pair of her brother's overalls, and many of them had only ever seen her from a distance.

He set up the Mayday missile launch as a one-time job in the tower's schedule, closed the maintenance hatch gingerly, and locked it. Then a voice from the ground below froze him like a low-fee traveller.

"BEY, IS THAT YOU UP THERE ON THE TOWER?"

Mr. Aidid had no choice but to nod and wave.

"WELL, SHINE A LIGHT ON WHOEVER JUST TRASHED OUR ROVER AND TAKE THEM DOWN ONE KNEECAP AT A TIME."

Mr. Aidid nodded and waved again, circled the tower out of sight, and slid down the ladder at a speed that burned his fingers. By the time he heard someone else yell "THAT'S NOT ME UP THE TOWER, BOSS," he was running through the line of buildings and away.

No paths led to Dispater Crater. It was surrounded by fields of two-metre-tall potatoes of a particularly pungent pink skinned Bolivian variety. The crater itself was both larger and deeper than it once had been. Apostle remembered it from his childhood as a classic lenticular meteorite impact crater, surrounded by rays of bright ejecta. Now, it was a shell hole. Something had once come out of that crater, Apostle knew—something that arose whenever external forces threatened the peace of Ararat, which was to say, the Anchorite's peace. Farming families the hermit could stomach, but when prospectors had come here and threatened to remove the gravitational kernel of the planet, he had sent his Devil out to do damage. The Devil had done battle here with the prospectors, and one or the other party had unleashed forces that had torn this great hole in the earth.

The Devil was nowhere in evidence now. The density scanner, however, when set to differentiate between air and solid matter, showed a set of promisingly regular caves beneath the surface. There was little clue, however, as to how the caves could be reached. Was there some sort of door?

Guessing that anything built of alloys transported across space as payload would be less dense than the surrounding rock, he set the density threshold to two tonnes per cubic metre, and was rewarded with a precise three-dimensional diagram of a door assembly hidden in the grass at the very base of the crater. He bent down to dig in the thin soil with his hand. The marram grass was sharp, and its roots held the earth together like solid rock. He sliced into it with a carving knife he had liberated from the kitchen when Unity had not been looking. The grass came away in clumps, revealing a dull sheen of metal.

"How much longer we got to stay here?," whispered Measure-of-Barley from a prone position in the potato. *"My nose tickles. I think I got to sneeze."*

"I think I got to pee." This raised a snigger, and started a game of bodily function oneupmanship while Apostle excavated all around the circular object which was plainly a pressure door. On the pressure door were the words:

PEARLYGATE VACUUM DOOR CO , PORT YUM CAX, CERES

He suddenly noticed an emerald green beetle buzzing round his head in frantic random hyperbolae.

"Uncle Anchorite?" he said.

"I *got to give birth to the* Antichrist—"

The bettle zeroed in on his ear and flew right in. He almost panicked and attempted to fish it out; it crawled around the inside of his otic canal, squeaking in a tickly, buzzing soprano:

"DON'T TOUCH THAT DOOR! DON'T TOUCH THAT DOOR! DON'T TOUCH IT!"

He leapt back from the door in surprise. The insect stayed with him.

"Uncle Anchorite?"

"GOOD LAD. I ADDED A FEW SURPRISES SINCE THE LAST TIME SOMEONE TRIED TO BREAK IN. NOW LEAVE THE DOOR AS IT IS AND CRAWL ON ALL FOURS UP THE TRACTOR TRACK BETWEEN THE ROWS OF SPUD IN FRONT OF YOU. ON NO ACCOUNT RE-MOVE THE BEETLE FROM YOUR EAR."

"I *got to do* five babies *and a* Nabortion."

He crawled up the row for several yards before realizing a vital fact. "This track ain't real. Our tractor don't make these tracks."

"The tracks lead this way," said a man's voice among the crops. *"They bin trampling the stalks flat."*

"I HAVE MY OWN TRACTOR," said the voice in Apostle's ear. The earth at the end of the track suddenly crazed and broke open as the lid of a far smaller hatchway pushed through it. The Anchorite was born into the world like a chick through an eggshell.

"Small footprints. Kids," said the voice from the crops.

The Anchorite had a small metal pod adhering to the flesh of his throat. When he next spoke, Apostle heard him in two voices. "Well, don't just sit there, get in here. Get them *all* in here. How many of you are there?"

"Don't care if they are kids. There's someone full-grown around here using them as spotters. I want 'em for leverage and questioning." By now, he could hear heavy boots walking through the crops.

The Anchorite sprang out of the head of his tunnel like a trapdoor spider and said softly to nobody in particular:

"You, my dear fellow, have about twenty seconds to live."

He began mouthing softly to himself, and only after several seconds did Apostle realize he was counting down. He scrambled into the hole, followed by his brothers and sisters in alphabetical order.

As soon as the Reborn-in-Jesuses had finished scrambling, the Anchorite leapt into the hole behind them and slammed the hatch, still counting inexorably towards zero.

"Seventeen—sixteen—fifteen—"

A metre above Apostle's head, Mr. Zhukovtsov hefted his laser and reflected that firing into the fields had possibly not been a good idea. They were burning now in a wide circle around the house, making it impossible to see lurking living humans concealed in the crops. Mr. Zhukovtsov liked to be able to see everybody around him, and be aware of their armament and intentions. He was a cautious man.

Right now, he was at the base of a crater, overgrown with potato seedlings, looking down at a metal door set into the earth.

"Found what looks like a second Panic Cellar, boss. I'm going to open it."

He reached down, unlocked the door lever, and pulled hard.

If he experienced anything more, it was either the company of angels or devils.

The explosion shook earth from the roof of the tunnel. Potato roots danced weirdly.

"Two can play, you see," said the Anchorite severely, "at the Let Us Wire Explosives To The Front Door trick."

"Was that your front door, Uncle Anchorite?" said Measure.

"I have many front doors," said the Anchorite. "And even more back and side ones. Now let us move further into the earth. There are more of these men, they are well-armed, and I must keep you safe. Onward."

The tunnel—claustrophobic, only the height of a small man crawling—sloped down into a dimly-lit chamber burned out of rock rather than regolith. At the centre of the chamber, a smooth-walled shaft covered by a wire-framed safety cage gaped in the earth; a sound like breath over a bottle moaned from it.

"Merely the wind underground," assured the Anchorite. "Back from the edge now, I'm taking off the cover. Forward to the ladder when I call your names. Now, you must remember that gravity will increase steadily as you climb down. This will be tolerable at first, but will become painful as you go deeper; you must, however, hold on. Your age will be your advantage—power-to-weight ratio, you see." He patted Apostle on the back. "Young man, I'm afraid this will be most unpleasant for you in particular. Keep three points of contact, go down one rung at a time, and stay within the cage."

Unity saw the rocket lift off on a tail of flame. The crops were already burning in a circle round the house now. If *all* the crops burned, there might be a serious lackof oxygen to breathe. Luckily, Armitage's men seemed to be realizing that inability to breathe might hamper their operations, and rushing to put the fire out.

Over towards Dispater Crater, an explosion had blown a second fire out. That had to be the Anchorite. If that had dealt with more of the fake taxmen, there could surely not be too many left; but those remaining would now be particularly watchful.

She lay in the mud of the arroyo, glad of the fire overhead. Voices were calling for water. *That* would mean father would have to buy more water. Another comet fragment would have to be diverted from the rings of Anak, the next gas giant out, and towing comets cost credits.

She could hear an electric motor. Evidently they had more than one rover. A meticulous criminal, of course, would have. And more than one gun.

Wire tyres ploughed dust plumes from the regolith as the second rover stopped nearby; frighteningly nearby.

"MR. ARMITAGE. WHY ARE WE EXPERIENCING DELAY?"

This new voice carried in itself a casual, immense menace, sounding as if it might threaten death even by issuing a greeting. It was a voice that had been studied, worked on, honed as a tool to bend other human beings to its will. Unity felt she would not at all be surprised if its owner practised in front of mirrors. And yet, the voice sounded laboured, as if fighting to expel air against resistance.

"I'm sorry, sir, there appear to be more locals than previously suspected; as many as three adults. Dangerous ones. One seems to have taken out Janos with some sort of long blade, and if you'll look up I'm afraid you'll see another has gotten off a message rocket."

The Mayday Missile went into FTL drive, a glowing soap bubble of light that then went through every colour of the visible spectrum as a sudden vacuum wind seized it and threw it to the stars.

"THAT'LL ONLY BRING MERCHANT SHIPPING. MERCHANT SHIPPING WE CAN DEAL WITH. EVERYONE FEARS THE REVENUE BUREAU. HOW ARE WE DOING WITH THE SERIES THREE?"

"Our work has been interrupted. The gravity cutter is making some headway."

A third voice cut in. This voice could hardly be recognized as human, and was at first indistinguishable from static. *"The cutter will alert the unit's offensive security. It should never have been used. Shut it down."*

Armitage's voice sounded irritated. "It's cut up to a millimetre into the epidermis—"

"And it'll kill whatever human contents are inside as soon as it breaks through, or render them sterile. Whoever's doing the cutting, too. The Series Three's outer skin contains a sheet of raw plutonium. I should know." The voice coughed suddenly, a noise that sounded like a clockwork mechanism being wound in the wrong direction.

There was a pause; during the pause, there was a crackle of ionization from the Penitentiary's direction, accompanied by shouts and screams.

"I hate to say I told you so."

Armitage's voice was quietly murderous. "It would have helped if you'd made yourself available to bestow your vast knowledge on us before, Mr. Skuse."

"I was unwell. These days, I spend much of my time unwell."

"I FEEL YOU SHOULD GET BACK TO THE GAOL, MR. ARMITAGE. IT APPEARS TO BE DEFENDING ITSELF. WE SHOULD SALVAGE THE SITUATION AND CONTINUE AT MR. SKUSE'S DIRECTION. WHAT ARE YOUR SUGGESTIONS, MR. SKUSE?"

"Heh! Cutting is too unsubtle. We must convince it it has been subjected to a natural disaster and trigger its mercy algorithms, setting the poor prisoners free to fend for themselves. I propose extreme heat. A solar flare, which would not be uncommon in this milieu—"

"I AM NOT COUNTENANCING SETTING OFF A NUCLEAR WEAPON, MR. SKUSE. NOT YET. I DO NOT GET ON WELL WITH NUCLEAR WEAPONS, AND NEITHER DO YOU."

"Tush, tush! You break into one gaol with a nuclear weapon, and you're Nuclear Weapon Skuse for life. Besides, the man lived for several hours, did he not? Long enough for him to feel your ire, even where the Moral Purity Bureau's nark protection unit had him put?"

"YOU FORGET YOURSELF, MR. SKUSE."

"I forget little but pain nowadays, sir. No, we do not need a mushroom cloud at this juncture, pretty though it would have been. We need only to fool a few of the unit's nerve endings, convince them that hideous stellar pyrotechnics are taking place outside. I have a detailed enough understanding of the Series Three's sensory peripherals. You had enough government engineers tortured to give me it. We will have your box open in an acceptable number of jiffies, and Jack out of it. Though I doubt he'll be any more capable of opening your other box than I am."

"JUST GET HIM OUT, MR. SKUSE, AND LEAVE THAT SECOND QUESTION TO HIM." There was a whirr of motors, and the rover hummed away in a cloud of fines.

Her every joint aching from enforced immobility and the cold of the water, Unity forced herself to rise onto her hands and knees, her hands and knees disappearing into the mud as quickly as she put weight on them, and crocodile-walked away down the arroyo.

Mr. Aidid fetched up against the wall of the Penitentiary, wanting to gulp in huge lungfuls of air, unable to let any more than a trickle of it down his throat.

"He doubled back here. I saw him."

"Are you sure you didn't see Arkadi? No-one found Arkadi's body. He ain't dead till we find his body."

"I got news for you. No-one's ever going to find any bit of Arkadi's body big enough to put in a DNA sampler. I saw that booby trap go off. Them hicks got this whole place wired up."

Mr. Aidid could hear other footsteps on the top of the Penitentiary. Someone was walking up there too.

"I should get danger pay for this. You saw what it did to Umberto."

"We're on danger pay already. Skuse says we'll be fine if we deal with it on its blind side. It's only got its sensors extruded on the side it burned off all Umberto's flesh on."

"What if it looks round?"

"It won't. Skuse is still giving it targets of opportunity on its eye side."

The feeling of air molecules being pulled apart rang in through Mr. Aidid's ears and played his bones like xylophones as it thrummed through the Penitentiary's skin. The prison was still defending itself. But he could also hear another rhythm in the metal. Someone inside was still knocking to be let out.

Mr. Aidid's basic crewman's training had also involved the rudiments of Morse, and he was already aware that one of the prisoners inside the Series Three was using it to communicate. It was easy for him to distinguish the letters S-O-S, and to tap back, under cover of the din round the gaol's other side, C-A-L-M.

W-H-O-R-U, tapped the metal.

Trying as far as possible to conceal himself between two palm trunks and the Penitentiary wall, Mr. Aidid licked his lips and tapped back:

F-R-E-N-D-O-F-B-E-G-I-L-D-STOP

The prisoner digested this and rapped back:

W-H-A-T-P-R-O-G-R-E-S-C-U-T-I-N-G-I-N-QUERY

"Skuse says he's going to get the box to think there's a solar flare," said a voice helpfully from upstairs.

S-I-M-U-L-A-T-I-N-G-S-O-L-A-R-F-L-A-R-E-STOP, tapped Aidid with difficulty.

C-O-U-L-D-W-O-R-K, replied the metal. M-E-R-C-Y-A-L-G-O-R-I-T-H-M-S-W-I-L-L-O-P-E-N-C-E-L-L-S-STOP

There was a pause.

B-U-T-O-N-L-Y-1-A-T-A-T-I-M-E-T-H-I-S-V-I-M-P-O-R-T-A-N-T-W-H-E-R-E-A-M-I-QUERY

Nervously, Aidid tapped back 2-3-K-R-A-N-I-S-Y-S-T-E-M-STOP

W-H-E-R-E-I-N-M-A-T-R-I-X-QUERY-G-A-O-L-I-S-2-B-Y-2-B-Y-2-C-U-B-E-B-A-S-E-H-O-M-E-C-O-R-N-E-R-O-P-E-N-S-F-I-R-S-T-STOP

W-H-E-R-E-I-S-B-A-S-E-H-O-M-E-C-O-R-N-E-R-QUERY, tapped back Aidid.

L-O-O-K-4-M-A-K-E-R-S-L-O-G-O-STOP

Mr. Aidid looked, and realized his ear was pressed like an octopus's sucker against a manufacturer's logo the size of a dinnerplate.

The logo said OUBLIETTE HUMAN INCARCERATION PRODUCTS: ADAMANTINE CHAINS AND PENAL FIRE.

F-O-U-N-D-I-T-STOP

B-U-G-E-R, said the metal through his fingertips. F-R-E-E-S-M-E-1-S-T-H-A-V-E-2-M-A-K-E-A-N-O-B-V-I-O-U-S-E-S-C-A-P-E-A-T-T-E-M-P-T-A-N-D-G-E-T-M-Y-C-E-L-L-M-O-V-D-O-N-STOP

As Mr. Adid lay in cover with his head flat against the wall, the knocking audibly travelled upwards, growing fainter and fainter.

G-E-T-O-U-T-O-F-H-E-R-E, it tapped.

Mr. Aidid needed no further encouragement. There was now no-one on his side of the Penitentiary; they had crossed back behind the buildings, possibly unwilling to be in line of sight of the unit after What It Did To Umberto.

He crept out under the palms, scuttled into one of the empty houses, and allowed his natural lack of courage to take over, collapsing in nervous exhaustion in a dusty living room in which children seemed to have made a fortress out of some former occupant's best furniture.

Mr. Skuse sat next to his employer in the surface rover, beyond what Mr. Skuse had insisted was the maximum range of the Penitentiary's offensive arsenal.

"The splices are all in place now," informed Mr. Skuse through the machine that nowadays served as his voice box. *"The unit should now firmly believe Ararat to be being irradiated by over a hundred million megatons of fusing plasma erupting from the surface of this system's sun. The induction pads we've attached to its skin at strategic points should confirm this. Of course, the amount of heat coming through those pads could never cut its surface; hence there is no reason for the Penitentiary to interpret that data as a deliberate attack. We're also firing hits down the fibre optics that used to be connected to its gamma sensors. It should, however, believe its prisoners will slowly cook if it doesn't let them out to find a safer refuge on the surface. It'll open."*

"I HOPE SO," said Mr. Skuse's employer in a low growl.

"I know my business," said Skuse. *"The last time I was at this*

business, I lost my face, after all."

"I COULD REQUISITION YOU A NEW FACE TOMORROW," purred his employer. "PICK A FACE, ANY FACE YOU SEE ON THE STREET. I WILL HAVE ITS OWNER ABDUCTED AND THE FACE HARVESTED. SUBJECT TO TISSUE COMPATIBILITY, OF COURSE."

"It would not be my face," hissed Skuse. "This face is more honest."

"AS YOU WISH. WHAT IS HAPPENING NOW?"

Skuse smiled liplessly. A notch on the frame that hung around his honest face emitted a cooling mist to moisturize his mucous membranes. "The structure is preparing to open. The base home corner opens first."

"WHICH IS THE BASE HOME CORNER?"

"Look for the manufacturer's logo."

"...YES. I SEE."

A blunt-cornered square had opened in the structure; a square of light. The dull red daylight on Ararat was dimmer than the Earth-standard illumination in the prison's interior.

A square section of the gaol's side punched out, falling into the mosaic gravel at its base.

A dark shape shouldered its way out of the light. A voice bellowed, impossibly loud, seemingly right inside Mr. Skuse's skull.

"BY MY MOTHER'S SAINTED VIRGINITY," boomed the voice. "I BREATHE AIR I HAVE NOT BREATHED BEFORE. THAT IMPERFECT DEMIURGE WHO IMPRISONED ME COULD NOT MAKE A WALL I COULD NOT BREAK. I DID IT, WITH THE POWER OF MY WILL, I, LEGION, FATHER OF LIES, GIVER OF GOOD AND EVIL. WHERE ARE THOSE WHO ONCE FORCED ME INTO THIS VILE PRISON? THEY SHALL PAY UNTO THE SEVENTH GENERATION—"

"Oh dear," said Mr. Skuse

"DO WE HAVE A PROBLEM, MR. SKUSE?"

164

"I fear we may, sir. Notice how Thorsten is attempting gamely to resist shooting himself with his own sidearm, and Nicolae is banging his head repeatedly against the side of a building? I fear we may have set free the wrong person, to wit a rather dangerous psychotic homicidal telepath—"

"SHALL I PUT THE ROVER INTO REVERSE?

"I feel that may be wise. I apologize; I was under the impression, from our densitometer, that our man was currently in the base home corner. The cells inside must have shifted."

The rover's engines cut in almost silently, and the machine hummed back up the track past the single signpost marked SADDLE LANDING, guiding itself on autopilot as Mr. Skuse's employer gave occasional watchful glances into its mirrors.

"DO WE HAVE A CONTINGENCY PLAN FOR THIS EVENTUALITY?"

Mr. Skuse's repulsively visible facial musculature rippled in a welter of emotions. "I suspect this man to be highly dangerous; if my memory serves correctly, he can only be one William Yancy Voight, raised in a somewhat backward colony of Skanker Christians on Presterjohn, next planet out from Krell in the Altair system. The Skankers were slow to realize they had an unidentified telepath in their midst, and in those days research on the subject was far less advanced. Their response was derived directly from the malleus maleficarum. Voight's own mother, among others, was tried and sentenced as a witch. Voight, whose home life had been troubled, and whose upbringing religious, strict, and unforgiving in the extreme, genuinely came to believe himself to be the Devil in his neighbours' midst. His own mother, burned in his stead, had told him so, screaming abuse at him as the flames consumed her."

"I AM GLAD, AT ANY RATE, THAT WE ARE NOT GENUINELY CONFRONTING THE TRUE DEVIL INCARNATE."

"I fear your relief may be misplaced. The community on Prester-john was backward, but its inhabitants could manufacture primitive firearms. They were capable of defending themselves. Even after they'd identified him as a threat, Voight wiped out every man, woman and child in a hundred-thousand-inhabitant colony. His mind had a telepathic reach greater than the range of any weapon they could send against him; he was able to detect any attempt to attack him and simply coerce his attackers to turn their weapons on themselves. He was only eventually captured by the Gifted Perpetrators Unit of the MRB, using robotic constables co-ordinated from a vessel in orbit. He has, thankfully, never learned to get inside mechanical minds."

The Rover came to a gradual halt. Both men continued to stare in the direction of the community of Second Landing, where men were running, screaming, falling, apart from one figure striding bold among the buildings.

"WE MAY NEED," concluded Mr. Skuse's employer, "TO USE THE NUCLEAR WEAPON AFTER ALL."

"I knew," said Mr. Skuse, "you would come to my way of thinking in the end, sir."

Apostle collapsed in the dim circular chamber at the base of the ladder. His heart was thudding in his chest. His eyes, bizarrely, hurt with every heartbeat.

An indignant voice called down the ladder. "'Postle, Measure won't come any further down the ladder. She says her head hurts."

Apostle had head problems of his own. "Kick her till she comes. Try not to break any bones or make her bleed."

An inevitable wailing started further up the ladder. Apostle did not greatly care. One of the advantages of a large extended family was that discipline could be outsourced.

The Anchorite was standing over him.

"You okay, boy?"

He nodded his head weakly, understanding now where the hermit got his energy. "Is there more?"

"No. This was the last section. We're a full four kilometres down. What you can feel on you now is one full Earth gravity. Be careful, now—your heart's never had to pump this hard a load before. It's a good thing you're a farmboy. Any lesser adult would be dead already."

The door in the side of the shaft read VALVA DOORCO, PRESSURE DOORS FOR ALL OCCASIONS, BANGALORE, EARTH.

"You're from Earth?" said Apostle.

"Many people are," said the Anchorite. He tapped the transparent lens at his right temple; it flared into life, beaming red light onto his retina. He tapped it again, several times; with each tap, the light in his eye changed colour, texture, and intensity.

"The greenbottles," said Apostle. "You're seeing through their eyes."

The Anchorite looked round, a perfect image of Apostle's home drawn on his lens in reverse. "Is that what you call them?"

"The metal insects? Yes."

"Hmmph," said the Anchorite. "They look nothing like real greenbottles, you know."

Day-of-Creation, who, humiliatingly, had not been as badly affected by the climb as Apostle, was already peering through the door, a strange white shadowless light on his face.

"Wow! 'Postle! You've *got* to see this."

*

Unity won through to the back gate of the house, stepping over the body of one of Armitage's lieutenants as she did so. The man appeared to have strangled himself, a feat Unity would previously not have thought technically possible.

The back garden was filled with blood orange trees, a one-off promotional GM batch purchased by Magus on New Tibshelf some years back; both the skin and the flesh of the fruit were not orange but purple. Marketed as 'Tyrian Purples', they had never caught on due to an acquired taste of salt. The trees clustered thickly round the back of the house, hiding the back door and kitchen window.

The Devil was standing the centre of the lawn, surrounded by statues of himself. Although he looked nothing like the Devil Unity had grown up with—in fact, resembling nothing so much as a naked man in prime physical condition—she somehow knew he preferred to be referred to by that name.

"I like these," he said, casting a hand round at the leaping, capering Satans, all home-made, arranged around the lawn and vegetable garden. He smiled. Unity knew he had not smiled in a long time.

"You were in the Penitentiary," said Unity, wide-eyed.

He nodded. He used his mouth to speak, though Unity was aware that this was only through politeness. "You have made pictures of me."

"Are you the real Devil?" said Unity warily, aware the Penitentiary had contained one prisoner of the name DEVIL, THE.

He nodded, grinning. "People have tried to assign labels to me—telepath, sociopath, survival of a pre-Judaistic Phoenician fertility deity—but one man's deva is another man's devil. I am touched that here at least, my name is remembered. I sense that you have always seen me as your protector.

168

Unity nodded slowly, intensely confused. "I have read Beguiled's book. In Crowley's preface, he makes it clear that Milton uses you as an allegory for Cromwell, the rebel against the British king. He sees in your rebellion a kind of nobility, a fierce resistance in the face of overwhelming odds."

The Devil nodded. "The book is fiction, of course, and terrible flattery, but I am fond of it. I was allowed no religious works in prison. I note you and your family have not subscribed to the populist view of me as an evil bogeyman bent on subverting mankind."

Unity stammered her objection. "Oh no, sir! The book of Job makes it plain that you operate on the instruction of God himself."

The Devil considered this a moment. "Could that be so? Perhaps. Not on the instruction of the ineffectual godling who created this imperfect world, but at the bidding of a higher power."

"Does that not mean, however," said Unity, regretting the attack of logic almost as it forced her mouth open, "that you are simply pushing the problem of the creation of an imperfect world back one remove, since that higher power would have to have created an imperfect creator?"

The Devil's eyes opened in genuine surprise. "An interesting viewpoint," he said.

Unity hesitated a moment before nodding. "The last time I saw you, you were different. I'm afraid we may have been operating under the assumption you were a fictional character exploited by one of our planetary inhabitants."

The Devil nodded. "Yes, I see. Your 'Anchorite'. You suspect him to have once been a notorious criminal. No matter. There is neither hatred nor disgust in you. Some fear, it is true, but fear is only appropriate in a worshipper." He nodded curtly. "I must meet this 'Uncle Anchorite' who has been taking my name in vain, but I see no way to find him in you. You sent your dearest siblings out to find him, only to see them perish in an explosion at a crater named after myself." The Devil sucked in a richly oxygenated breath. "I *like* it here! I believe that I shall stay. I find it convenient, however, for the time being, that you do not see me."

With that, he clicked his fingers theatrically, and vanished. Unity drew in a small startled breath of shock.

"There is a man," said the Devil's voice, "in a house down the street, hiding under a Wang-period sofa, almost dying of fear. In his own way, he is quite heroic, as he has risked his life recently to do what he believes is good and right and true. He regards you highly, and considers you beautiful. He also greatly admires your mental capabilities, though he does not consider himself tall enough to impress you physically. The two of you might make an effective couple."

With that parting gift, he was gone, at least as far as Unity knew. Suddenly realizing her heart was pounding in her chest, she walked to the back door and set her hand on the knob to open it.

Then, reconsidering, she walked back over the lawn, turned unafraid out of the garden, and moved toward the only house she knew to have a Wang-period sofa. Behind her, unregarded, a small emerald insect buzzed from a branch and struck out, weaving erratic but not entirely random spirals through the air, in a completely different direction.

All of a sudden, there was a BANG loud as a rotten tin exploding, followed by a clatter of debris. Unity turned to see the mangled component parts of a small emerald insect, scattered over the earth by the back gate. Beside the silvery solid non-organic shrapnel in the leaf litter lay Armitage's dead lieutenant's handgun, some distance from Armitage's dead lieutenant, its accelerator coils still ticking gently.

Unity chose to take no further notice, and turned to walk into the house.

"These chambers," said the Anchorite, "existed prior to my arrival. I have set up home in them, but did not dare disturb anything technological."

Apostle stepped, slack-jawed, into the cave.

"There's *daylight,*" he said.

"That's not daylight," complained Day-of-Creation, hanging back in the entrance. "It hurts my eyes."

"That's because it's *real* daylight," said Apostle, entranced.

"Not exactly. It's the right mix of wavelengths. The light comes out of about a zillion germinator units in the ceiling."

Apostle blinked in disbelief. "That many? How did you—?"

"Had an old captured Made Von Neumann machine," said the Anchorite. "Got it to make all this stuff for me."

"A Made war machine?" Apostle looked around in fear, and added: "Where is it now?" in much the same way a concerned parent might say *so, where's the tarantula* now, *little Jimmy?*

"Easy. I put it down. Single shot to the CPU. It's down here somewhere."

"Don't some of them have backup CPU's?" said Apostle.

The Anchorite huffed. "No." He looked round the shadows nervously. "I'm almost certain of it. Where did you hear that?"

"Must have read it somewhere." Apostle continued into the Anchorite's garden, but more gingerly now. "This place is a jungle."

"A tropical rainforest shrub layer, to be precise," said the Anchorite. "I don't have enough light to make anything else. These plants thrive on ambient light. They're built to live off sunlight scraps from rich trees' tables, so they're perfect for here. No other crop would grow."

All about them, the world was as green as if seen through eyes of emerald. The fields of Ararat far above were scarlet and black as a backgammon table; 23 Kranii radiated no other colours. Only a torch taken out into the crop, like a diver's light shone on a growth of coral, would show that flowers could be white, or blue, or orange. Bees could not live on Ararat. Father had tried them; they couldn't see the UV cues laid out on the flowers, and simply buzzed confused around every leaf and stalk.

God's-Wound's voice screamed with delight from over a rise. "Water! There's running water here!"

The Anchorite smiled. "There's plenty of water underground on Ararat. Always has been."

Apostle crested the rise—although he could still leap up and slap the cave roof, he was standing on the edge of a bubbling waterfall, trickling out of holes in the rocks down ten metres into a clear green pool in which God's-Wound was paddling her feet.

"Uh, there are no animals here, are there?" he said, eyeing the water nervously.

"None whatsoever. All the plant life was grown from emergency supplies. For that reason, most of it's also useful. I have hemp, rubber, plantain, sage, tapioca, and sundry more species, all of which grow all year round."

"What do you use for power?" said Apostle. "The power for all of this has to come from somewhere." He reached out to lean on the back of a nearby tree, only to find the hermit's hand clamped round his wrist like a vice.

"West Indian lilac," said the Anchorite. "Every serviceman's emergency kit used to have a set of seeds for it. It makes a very useful barrier against hungry animal life. It can kill even by contact. Like Adam's garden, not every tree here is safe. Touch only what I touch. And I will show you," he said, "what I use for power. You will be *very* interested—"

He tapped the lens over his right eye suddenly. "I'm afraid Unity may be in danger."

Apostle felt his muscles coiling into angry knots, despite himself. "Then you have to do something. *We* have to do something."

The Anchorite continued to stare into his lens for some time.

"Have the tax pirates got her?" said Beguiled.

"No," said the Anchorite, without deactivating his lens. "Someone potentially worse. I think we should all stay down here in the basement for a little while. Um, even me."

"That's coward talk," said Apostle.

"Believe me," said the Anchorite nervously, "if you were up there, it would do neither you nor Unity any good at all."

"Send the Devil, then," said God's-Wound. "Send it to protect her."

"I find myself unable to divert the Devil. Down by the South End Saddle, someone is planning to detonate an atomic bomb. I am afraid I am faced with an embarrassment of targets." His expression changed to one of suspicion. "Most extraordinary. Unity is still alive."

"Hooray!" cheered Beguiled.

The eyepiece flared white suddenly, then went black. The Anchorite jerked his head back involuntarily and blinked.

"What just happened?" said Apostle.

"I'm afraid," said the Anchorite, beginning to breathe again, "that our man is aware of our surveillance system."

"It's a man, then," said Apostle.

The Anchorite frowned sourly. "A subspecies of *homo sapiens*," he agreed. "He could probably breed with humans. As I recall, it was a matter of some argument, at his trial, whether he could still be called a man. Certain relatives of his victims hired tame anthropologists to argue he constituted a new species and should be judged by the same yardstick as the Made, exterminated as a dangerous animal."

"He's not *breeding* with Unity, is he?" said Beguiled in a mixture of horror and fascination.

"Thankfully not," said the Anchorite. "Right now he thinks he's headed here. But he won't find the way we came in. That entrance is buried under several tonnes of debris right now. I wonder if he can read our minds from here?" He tapped the lens again; it flared into life. He cycled through several images. "Raise your hand, Mr. Voight, if you can read my mind from here." He examined the lens intently, then concluded:

"Well, of course, he could be bluffing."

"Aha, I have him again on unit three. If I tail him at a greater distance...Unity still appears to be safe. He's still moving away from her."

"You must send the Devil to help her," urged Measure pleadingly.

The hermit stood staring at horrors only he could see, diminished only by the fact that he was only seeing them through his right eye.

"Hmm. Nuclear weapon, Voight, Voight, nuclear weapon. Which is the greater evil?"

He came to a decision.

"We will deal with Mr. Voight first. I will so direct the Devil."

*

Asteroid gravel crunched beneath the Devil's feet as he walked through the smouldering crops toward the spot the girl Unity had been convinced led to his enemy. Somewhere at the point this tractor track ended, at the feature called Dispater Crater, was the Anchorite's back door. Frustratingly, she had not known what form the back door took, or how to get into it. She believed the Anchorite lived at the centre of this world. All well and good; the world was asteroid-sized. The centre could not be too far away.

The Anchorite intrigued the Devil. He intrigued him because he intrigued Unity, and Unity's mind was as quick and sharp as she thought herself big and cumbersome. The Devil was of the opinion that he knew who the Anchorite was, and wished to confirm his suspicions before killing him.

The crops he was now moving through had been squashed flat, as if a giant animal had turned round and round on top of them before settling down to sleep. The sides of the stalks facing towards the end of the road were also blackened and blast-charred. As he walked further, the stalks had simply been ripped clean from the earth as if by a white-hot scythe. At the very end of the road itself, he found the crater. It was not either of the two craters Unity remembered—neither a shallow, disk-shaped depression, nor a rather larger ragged shell-hole. Instead, it was now an amphitheatre-sized gouge in the earth with walls where rock and soil had fused to glass. The majority of the energy of the blast seemed to have been expended in a massive, instantaneous localized burst of heat. The Devil wondered what manner of explosive could have produced such an effect. The Anchorite became more interesting by the second.

There was, of course, nothing resembling an entrance in the crater, and nothing resembling an intelligent mind scurrying in the rock and soil beneath it. There might well be a way in here, but he could find no clue to it at present.

He heard a rustle in the bushes behind him, and did not bother to turn round.

"Aha, blasphemy; I wondered how long it would be before your master sent you."

An imperfectly rendered facsimile of a human voice spoke behind him. *"This is no blasphemy. The men who designed this unit believed in nothing but the superior chassis strength nine millimetre whisker reinforced titanium laminate can provide. They did not believe in devils, and for the record neither do I."*

"Then you are forgiven; I am gracious. If you do not believe in me, however, why do you still continue to address me?"

"Because you are no devil, but a very powerful man, as I was once. I know the feeling. But a man who believes himself to be a god is setting himself up for a fall. I know that feeling too."

The Devil smiled, turned, and raised the pistol he had been holding behind his back. "I found this on a dead man. It is one of the quaint devices men use to kill each other. I am not personally familiar with it, but I believe it will turn your head into a cloud of vapour."

"It will have no effect on this unit, which is designed on a heavy assault chassis. A small volcano could go off underneath it without scuffing the finish."

The pistol did not waver from the centre of the Anchorite's Devil's featureless face as it stood before him on the edge of the burned corn. "It is odd to talk by making cords vibrate in my throat like an animal, and to have to listen back for the same. It is like talking to that accursed machine I was recently set free of. It used to talk to me at great length in an attempt to convince me to become a useful member of society. I would prefer to talk to you face to, uh, face."

176

"You and I both know that isn't going to happen."

"Very well. Then I am afraid I must attempt to destroy your servant."

The Devil attempted to squeeze the trigger of the gun. It would not budge. He jerked his forefinger back in panic. The trigger remained jammed. In front of him, the blasphemy blurred and was on him almost before his brain had registered the movement.

He was almost certain one of his teeth was broken. He could taste blood, his own blood, in his own mouth. There was no air in his lungs, and none would come no matter how he tried to make his ribs expand. He was bent over with his mouth in the earth, with his gun hand twisted round behind his back. This he already knew to be possible; the body he was inhabiting was human and imperfect. It had been hurt before.

In front of him, the gun dropped to the earth. An emerald insect wriggled in the space behind its trigger, preventing the gun from firing.

"You will be punished for this," he said, submitting to being bundled along towards a pressure door hidden in the grass.

"On the contrary," said the machine's speaker, *"you will thank me for it. I am not returning you to the Penitentiary."*

"Where, then, are you taking me? Why must we be enemies? Release me!"

"I am taking you to more spacious quarters. You will still be a prisoner, but I have a thousand uses for someone of your calibre. My hell has room for more than one devil."

"Blasphemy! I knew it! When I get out of this pit of uneternal damnation, I shall *so* smite you! You are *so* smitten!"

"Quite so, I am sure. Duck your head, we are going underground. Please do not fight the unit, it is very bad at field surgery, and any injuries it inflicts on you can only be repaired by it. We

have a long climb ahead of us." He was pushed down a long earth tunnel, then into a concrete chamber containing a ladder going down. Handcuffs snapped tight around his wrists; he was hauled up one-handed and draped around the robot's neck like a living amulet. Then the machine set a foot on the ladder and began trudging downward. He heard a sound like a speaker powering down. Evidently the Anchorite had tired of taunting him person-ally, and left his automaton to continue its work alone.

The Anchorite, who had disappeared into the trees, returned at some speed. Measure, Beguiled and God's-Wound were splashing each other in the stream, whilst Day-of-Creation was climbing a tree and Apostle was sternly ensuring that nobody touched one of the seven trees the Anchorite had identified as deadly poisonous. Other children were scattered throughout the undergrowth, play-ing Devils and Prospectors, Devils and Mades, and Devils and Tax Accountants.

"Come now! We must leave immediately!"

There was an immediate chorus of disappointment.

"Why do we have to leave, Uncle Anchorite?"

"Because a very bad man is on his way down here. Besides, we have another bad man to deal with, one who has an atomic bomb." The hermit was now carrying a hand laser, which he slot-ted a gas cartridge into gingerly.

"Who is the bad man, Uncle Anchorite? I thought you lived on your own."

"The first bad man is the one I feared was going to hurt Unity. Don't worry, he is under control now; the Devil is bringing him here. But the *other* bad man is not yet under control, and we must deal with him, and you must help me."

"Is that Mr. Armitage?" said Measure.

"It is," nodded the Anchorite. "Now, come this way, through the trees, through the ornamental arbour. Hurry, we have no time to smell the roses. There is another door at the end of this path, leading to another ladder upward."

Measure unwisely looked out at the green horizon. "Aiiee! The floor curves downwards!"

"Yes it does, which is why so many agribiz crewmen collapse gibbering and refuse to step off the boarding ramp of their ship when they arrive on your planet, ragged urchin. You are now experiencing what they experience. We are closer to the planetary core, so the curvature of our world is far greater." The hermit parted a curtain of overhanging leaves to reveal another pressure door set in the wall. Apostle's heart sank. The Anchorite, noticing his expression, said:

"We must go up. If we do not, not only will whoever remains eventually die, they will also, in what life remains to them, become an unwitting agent of the deaths of their brothers and sisters. So come, up! Climb!" He threw the door open and indicated a ladder.

Expelled from a very brief taste of paradise, the children disconsolately filed into the ladder chamber.

"Can we come back?" said Measure, wistfully gazing back into the greenery.

"If you are very good," said the Anchorite.

Regretfully, she laid her hands to the rungs.

"Ouch! My arms ache! I cannot feel my fingers!"

The robot hoisted the Devil off its shoulders and dropped him nonchalantly. His heart twisted in his chest as if in an attempt to escape the cage of his ribs, but his fear was not necessary; a concrete floor slammed into him very quickly. Unprepared to meet it, his legs collapsed under him and he rolled, cracking his head on the ladder.

"Is this the bottom of the last shaft?" said the passenger. "Please say there is not another." His shoulder ached as if injected with molten lead. The release of tension was welcome, but the anticipation of it possibly returning was unbearable.

The machine did not reply, but instead opened a pressure door at the base of the shaft and hoisted the Devil up under its arm with a grip stronger than a fallen angel's. The Devil felt himself, after all, to be in a good position to judge this.

"You cannot reply," said the Devil. "Your human master is doing something else, perhaps, and cannot attend to me. He has to let his device handle me itself for a little while. Is that it?"

The machine patted the Devil on the head in a curiously human gesture, then turned to face the doorway it had opened.

"Green things," gasped the Devil, despite himself. "Growing."

The machine walked out into the twilight forest with the Devil in hand, and closed the door firmly on the outside world.

As the Anchorite was climbing, he turned and patted the empty air beside him in a curiously human gesture.

"Uncle Anchorite, what are you doing?" said Measure behind him. "Are you talking to your invisible friend? *I* have an invisible friend. He's called Mr. Beëlzebub."

The Anchorite's face was unreadable. "Oh, really? What does Mr. Beëlzebub look like?"

Measure giggled. "Nothing, silly. He's invisible."

The Anchorite nodded and swarmed up the ladder to where

Apostle, his face a grim mask of effort, was leading the climb.

"I'll take point from here."

Apostle nodded, sagging onto the rungs, allowing himself a rest as the hermit swarmed past him in a flurry of beard, up into the small circular room at the shaft head. He heard a pressure door open with a hiss as gentle as a high-born lady farting.

"*All clear,*" hissed the Anchorite. "*Everybody out, now. Quickly.*"

The family emptied from the shaft into the tiny room, as the Anchorite's gentle tread crunched almost imperceptibly on a hard surface above.

Apostle poked his head up through the pressure door, trying hard not to blow like a harpooned whale.

"Well I'll be—this is the crypt under the Temple—"

"*SSSH! Crypts have very good acoustics.*"

The crypt had originally been intended to be the final resting place of Mount Ararat's saints, in particular Arkarch Allion, Pastor of the Faith and guider of his flock from prosperous careers and well-to-do homes on Earth out to a Promised Land on a radiation-riddled asteroid. It had been designed as the crypt of a mighty cathedral greater than any to come before or after. The current church had been intended to be its antechamber. Unfortunately, the construction of the cathedral had been indefinitely postponed owing to the deaths of sixty per cent of its proposed congregation. The crypt, however, had already been laid as part of the foundations, and construction robots had laid down many kilometres of secret catacombs. Arkarch Allion had been in love with the idea of catacombs, despite being advised at great and despairing length that catacombs were places where clandestine religions furtively buried their dead, and were hence unlikely to radiate from a cathedral.

The Anchorite's hand came down on a wall switch, and temporary lighting flooded a huge and empty chamber made to receive a legion of ecclesiarchs. The walls were adorned with machine-sculpted bas-reliefs of saved souls being led by the still waters of Paradise. The children marvelled at the carvings. At one end, Beguiled lingered by a sculpture of the Devil being trodden underfoot by a stern bearded deity.

"Look at what this man's doing to the Devil, Uncle Anchorite."

"God only punishes both man and devil because He loves them both," grunted the Anchorite, inspecting the great stone rolled across the entrance of the sepulchre minutely. He pointed absently in the direction of the west wall. "Over there you can see Him punishing Eve and Adam with equal vigour."

"How are we going to move this big stone out of the way?" said Measure.

"We're not. You'd be amazed where these catacombs lead. For the time being, you are to shut that pressure door and stay put here."

"I need to go to the toilet."

The Anchorite cast a critical eye across a massive marble sarcophagus ornately carved with cherubim, seraphim, and bizarre creatures of the sculptor's own creation.

"Arkarch Allion doesn't seem to be using his coffin. You may as well make sure it doesn't go to waste."

Magus was crestfallen. "But what do we use to wipe?"

"The hand you don't eat with. Apostle, make sure they stay put. I have a micro-nuclear war to prevent."

"But UNCLE ANCHORITE—"

Apostle opened his mouth to protest, but the Anchorite had already vanished into a knife-edge crack between the carvings.

He looked up at the ancient flickering fixtures in the ceiling, and hoped the lights stayed on.

The Anchorite's head poked out of the earth, gingerly.

The catacombs petered out in a robot-dug riverbed, an ambitious project that had been intended to carry ten times as much water as the entire planetary surface currently held. He was a kilometre from the houses of Third Landing.

Ararat's crust was porous, and its water table deep; any water poured into the soil would seep down through kilometres of crust to the world's very centre. Fields had to be waterproofed, and would leak a certain litreage every year whatever the protection. The complex set of drains and qanats devised by Arkarch Allion had been hopelessly unrealistic. Mr. Reborn-in-Jesus had so far been unable to afford more than a twenty-five-square-kilometre hard pan underneath his property, with containment dykes at a radius of three kilometres from his house. Dry channels from the Allion era still radiated from the tilled land at intervals, however. The children used them to play Canals of Mars and Trench Warfare.

This channel was halfway between Third Landing and the South End Saddle. One hundred metres away, Mount Ararat's main highway, a single-lane gravel track with passing places, divided the visible world in two. On the track, an ATV had stopped, and two men were hastily carrying out modifications to it while a larger group of armed men watched the horizon warily. Mr. Armitage had lost track of Mr. Voight, and was taking no chances.

On the cargo bed of the ATV was a heavy metal frame containing a spherical device to which control cables were attached. Some of the cables snaked up to a large whip aerial clipped to the device's top. One of Mr. Armitage's technicians, a stiff-jointed man in a grey cloak that covered all of him but the eyes, was also carrying a handset with extended aerials and generic remote guidance controls. As the engineers worked, they swatted at swarms of emerald insects which somehow seemed to have singled them out in the middle of the siderite-coloured fastness.

The Anchorite rolled into cover behind a rock, tapping his eyepiece frantically, switching from one pair of insectoid eyes to another, talking to himself in a sure sign of madness.

"Firing unit there, I see...no apparent trembler mechanism, timer and firing code keypad, manual key, one key and probably only one firing code only...not military. Home made with minimal security. The most important component will be the fuse that fires all charges simultaneously in on that core, which is probably deuterium or tritium...destroy that fuse and all you have is a very powerful firework, not even radioactive...Number Six, you position yourself inside the casing, just there, precisely under the wire..."

Armitage's technicians appeared to have finished with their handiwork, and were closing panels and taping wire spindles securely to frames. One of them then stood back and fiddled with the handset experimentally, causing the rover's wheels to track in the dirt, spin against brake pressure, and rock it gently back and forth in low gear.

The man in the grey cloak shuffled awkwardly forward, slid a key into the device's control panel with exquisite care, turned it, then tapped in a code on the keypad.

"Code is one-seven-six-five, well done Number Two, that might yet come in handy...time entered is one centidia, long enough to make sure the rover's out of range..."

The rover trundled forward, unmanned, under remote control.

The robot loped through the underbrush with little concern for the fact that it was trawling its human cargo through spiny bushes which buckled on its own metal hide. It was working its way up the scree at the edge of the cave, towards the bright lights and sprinklers of the ceiling, to where a rough Romanesque arch had been carved into the rock, overgrown with creepers through which could be seen a gleam of metal.

"Another pressure door," said the Devil as the robot set him down. "Whoever lives down here sure is paranoid, ha ha ha."

The robot turned the Devil's head away and tapped in a code; the two halves of the door churned apart, protesting at having been left unopened for long enough for ivy to have grown over them. The strands of ivy resisted briefly, then fell severed, revealing a tunnel carved into the cave wall, many times higher than a man.

The robot stood in the entrance. *"Air is still good in here. There is another door at the far end; the two doors together form an airlock in which you can be left food. I will get for you anything you need apart from digging or locksmithing tools of any sort, or human or animal companionship. I doubt whether I could trust you with a dog."* It leaned against the cave wall, suddenly human, its claws slapping the metal on either side of its thighs. *"Darn! These things never have pockets."*

"Dogs have simple minds, easily controllable," said the Devil. "Cats are more difficult. Can I have a cat?"

"No."

"So this place is to be my new hell."

"Turn around and walk to the far end."

The Devil looked at the robot mistrustfully, then stood up and gingerly ambled out into the yellow false sunlight of the next cave. He blinked, startled; then, he turned round and said to the robot:

"Thank you."

The robot nodded. *"If a man must have a prison, it may as well be a well-appointed one."* It rapped on the cave wall with a metal knuckle. *"This is siderite, about twenty metres thick. I believe the Telepath Finder General's office found that pure iron interfered with your abilities. The cells of all incarcerated dangerous telepaths are now lined with it."*

The Devil smiled silkily. "I'm sure that will be most useful in containing me."

"However, as your danger distance has been estimated at a kilometre, I'm taking no chances. The cave we have just walked through will also henceforth be off limits for human beings. I will make sure of this by flooding it with sulphur dioxide, which I consider poetically just."

The Devil spat angrily. "Brimstone oxide. You and your racial stereotyping. Why are you even letting me live?"

"The only reason I ever let anyone live. Because you're useful to me."

"And the family up top? They, too, are useful to you?"

The robot hesitated. *"They are protective colouration, pieces of an innocuous environment I have gathered round me."*

"And I am a laboratory animal, like a rattlesnake being kept to milk venom."

"I assure you," said the robot, *"you're in no danger of being dissected. You are the single most powerful telepath ever discovered. When you were imprisoned indefinitely, there was an outcry throughout the medical world that such an important specimen should be lost to study."*

The Devil clicked his fingers. "I *knew* it! I *knew* you were one of the Dictator's men! His secret weapons teams, set up to discover new ways of killing the Made, and to reverse-engineer Made artefacts. Starting out as concerned scientists working to protect their species, and using that to justify experiments on living humans—"

"*Many of them were not humans,*" said the robot, "*but Made. Entirely separate and new species, violently opposed to ours—*"

"I would imagine," said the Devil, "that they felt pain just as effectively. I certainly consider myself a separate species. Are you *sure* you wouldn't like dissect me?"

"*Natural evolution,*" said the Devil, "*may have produced, in you, a species that can beat the Made. You have abilities human science doesn't as yet even comprehend. Keeping you here presents a danger, but so did keeping uranium piles in the first days of atomic research. Make no mistake, we won't have beaten the Made until they're comprehensively exterminated, and we didn't accomplish that by any means. Many of them escaped into the outer dark, and the overthrow of the Dictator rendered our government too soft to order pursuit. They will breed out there, and grow strong. And they'll return.*"

"And they call *me* mad," said the Devil.

"*Stand back from the door,*" said the robot. The Devil stood back; the code was entered on the keypad again. The second pressure door began cranking down again at the turret's far end, a black terminator erasing the Devil from existence.

The whole right side of the Anchorite's head suddenly stung as if slapped with a paddle. He could not see out of his right eye. His ears rang. His one working eye now made out a world whose familiar rocks and boulders, along with his right arm and the right side of his chest, had suddenly, unaccountably, become bright blue.

"THE MISSING MAN, I PRESUME."

The voice was shouting from some way over towards the Saddle, but that provided little comfort. He'd been hit by a dye cannister intended not to kill him, but to provide assurance that whoever had fired the round certainly could kill him at any time they chose. And he had no proof the shouter was the same man as the shooter.

"ARE YOU MR. REBORN-IN-JESUS, I WONDER? OR ARE YOU MAGUS, TESTAMENT, OR OUR MYSTERIOUS EXTRA MISSING DNA TRACE? CERTAINLY YOU SEEM TO BE EX-MILITARY. CIVILIANS HIT BY A DYE SHELL OFTEN KEEP MOVING AND HAVE TO HAVE THE POINT RAMMED HOME TO THEM WITH A LIGHT ANTIPERSONNEL TO THE LEG."

He craned his neck back around the boulder. The engineers surrounding the rover had stopped work, and were staring out into the barrens all around them, no doubt as curious as he was as to where the voice was coming from. One of them caught sight of the Anchorite's protruding head, and pointed for the edification of his colleagues.

"THAT'S IT. KEEP EVER SO STILL, WE NEED TO HAVE A WORD WITH YOU. KEEP THOSE HANDS WHERE WE CAN SEE THEM."

Two parts of the landscape rose up and became men; men wearing chromatophore cloaks. The cloaks rippled and changed both colour and texture as their wearers advanced, changing from mottled and uneven to sleek and star-strewn as the optic sensors in their backs registered sky behind them and sent messages to the chameleon skins on their fronts to replicate the pattern. It was like being advanced on by two constellations, one of which was holding a multiple Anchorite-seeking munition launcher.

The Anchorite raised his hands. The cloaks came closer. One of them cast off its hood.

"Mr. Skilling," said the Anchorite.

"YOU RECOGNIZE ME?"

"Your physical description is widely circulated by law enforcement authorities."

The other man was dressed in the more expensive parts of what looked like three military uniforms. He was formidably tall, and possessed a formidable quantity of teeth, which he now used to good smiling effect. *"AHA, I SEE YOU RELAX. YOU ARE NOT GOING TO DIE RIGHT NOW, YOU ARE DEALING WITH SLAVERS, SLAVERS DO NOT KILL PEOPLE, YOU WILL SOMEHOW CUNNINGLY ESCAPE OUR CLUTCHES AND DEAL WITH US LATER. WELL, I'M AFRAID I FEEL OBLIGED TO POKE HOLES IN YOUR ARGUMENT, AS WELL AS, POSSIBLY, YOUR INTEGUMENT."* The other man sat down on a rock and mopped his brow while his associate continued to cover the Anchorite. *"FIRSTLY, WE SLAVERS OPERATE A STRINGENT SYSTEM OF QUALITY CONTROL. WE DO NOT GO LARGE ON THE SORT OF SLAVE WHO IS LIKELY TO CUNNINGLY ESCAPE OUR CLUTCHES. SECONDLY, WE HAVE BEEN ENSURING SLAVES DO NOT CUNNINGLY ESCAPE US FOR QUITE SOME TIME, AND WE ARE VERY GOOD AT IT. YOU ARE, I AM AFRAID, USED TO THE KIND OF CUSTODY EXERCISED BY POLICEMEN AND JAILERS, WHO HAVE TO ADHERE TO TIRESOME REGULATIONS. WE DO NOT HAVE ANY SUCH CONSTRAINTS."* He clicked long-nailed fingers, and the Anchorite watched his own foot blow off.

The wave of panic, the Anchorite told himself, was solely due to sudden fluid loss. There was no need for fear to twist in his chest like a knife, no need for his heart to beat as if in orgasm.

"YOU SEE, WE HAVE SHOCKINGLY LITTLE REGARD FOR NICETY. IF A PRISONER RUNS AWAY, WE CUT OFF HIS LEGS. IF HE RETURNS

AGAIN TO THE FOLD OF GOOD AND HONEST SHEEP, WE MAY GIVE HIM NEW ONES." He looked up at the man who had shot the Anchorite's foot off. *"DIDIER—THE LEGS."*

Didier grinned with considerably fewer teeth than Mr. Skilling, put his weapon down, dropped his hands to his knees, and pulled up his trouser legs. From the knees down, his legs were skeletal metal and plastic.

"DIDIER CAME TO US WHEN HE WAS ONLY A CHILD," said Skilling. *"WE RECOGNIZED IN HIM EARLY ON A NATURAL APTITUDE FOR FIREARMS HANDLING. HOWEVER, THE NECESSITIES OF BUSINESS HAD FORCED US TO ELIMINATE HIS PARENTS AND ADULT RELATIVES, WHO HAD DEFENDED THE VILE BURG HE CAME FROM WITH THEIR LIVES. THEY WOULD HAVE BEEN UNECONOMICAL TO REPAIR, AND WOULD NO LONGER HAVE MADE GOOD SLAVES IN ANY CASE. THIS, HOWEVER, WENT ILL WITH HIM. THERE WERE NUMEROUS ATTEMPTS AT ESCAPE AND SUICIDE; HENCE THE REMOVAL OF THE LEGS. OVER TIME, HOWEVER, DIDIER CAME TO KNOW LOYALTY AND, DARE I SAY, LOVE FOR HIS NEW FAMILY, AND WON HIS LEGS BACK. I TRUST HIM WITH A LOADED WEAPON AT MY BACK. THAT IS HOW EFFECTIVE OUR READJUSTMENT FACILITIES ARE ON THE PROCESSING PLANETS."*

"How old was he?" said the Anchorite.

"TEN," said Skilling. *"ONLY A LITTLE YOUNGER THAN MANY OF THE JUVENILE INHABITANTS OF THIS PLACE, IN FACT."* He smiled and looked at the Anchorite's stump critically. *"YOU KNOW, YOU REALLY SHOULD GET THAT LOOKED AT. IT'S BLEEDING QUITE BADLY."* He picked up the severed foot and held it up demonstratively. *"A VIRGIN FOREST,"* he quipped, *"IS A PLACE WHERE THE HAND OF MAN HAS NEVER SET FOOT."*

The Anchorite looked back dispassionately.

"YOU ARE AN ODD ONE," said Skilling. *"NORMALLY MEN*

GROAN AT THE SIGHT OF THEIR OWN SEVERED LIMBS BEING TOYED WITH. IT'S PECULIARLY VIOLATING. BUT YOU SHOW NO REACTION. A TORTURER IS A PUPPET MASTER WHOSE STRINGS ARE HIS VICTIM'S NERVOUS SYSTEM, BUT YOU," he said, pointing at the Anchorite with the latter's own big toe, "CAN SEE THOSE STRINGS. YOU WERE A TORTURER IN A PREVIOUS LIFE. OR AN IN-TERROGATOR. OR ONE WHO SUPERVISED INTERROGATIONS."

The Anchorite breathed in heavily, and shrugged nonchalantly on the outbreath. An emerald insect settled onto the boulder at Skilling's elbow; he watched it with interest.

"THESE DEVICES ARE QUITE FASCINATING. WE DID NOT NOTICE THEIR PRESENCE UNTIL QUITE LATE IN THE GAME.," he said. "AS SOON AS WE'D SWATTED ONE AND TAKEN IT APART, THOUGH, WE KNEW WE WERE BEING WATCHED. AFTER THAT IT WAS JUST A MATTER OF TRIANGULATING THEIR CONTROL SIGNALS, AND THERE YOU WERE." He examined the condition of the Anchorite's severed toenails with distaste. "NOW, DO YOU HAVE ANY DOUBT AT ALL THAT THE CONSEQUENCES OF NOT ANSWERING MY NEXT QUESTION ABSOLUTELY TRUTHFULLY WOULD BE VERY, VERY BAD? GOOD. I NEED TO KNOW HOW MANY PEOPLE LIKE YOU THERE STILL ARE ON THIS GODDAMNED ROCK, WHAT THEY'RE ARMED WITH, AND HOW I CAN GET THEM TO SURRENDER."

The Anchorite nodded.

"May I be permitted a question of my own?"

Skilling shrugged. "GO AHEAD."

"You're not here for slaves. This whole world is home to only seventeen officially registered people. You're here for Hans Trapp. Am I right in assuming you need him to open a door?"

Skilling slapped his thigh. "EXCELLENT! MOST PERCEPTIVE. I HAVE INDEED COME INTO A MOST SINGULAR PIECE OF PROP-ERTY, THE USE OF WHICH IS SADLY DENIED ME ONLY BY THE FACT

THAT SOME CHURL HAS PUT IT IN A LOCKED BOX. A LOCKED BOX WHICH, OF ITSELF, IS A MOST AMAZING PIECE OF WORK. EVEN MY EMPLOYEE, THE REDOUBTABLE MR. SKUSE, IS INCAPABLE OF OPENING IT." He waved cheerily across the plain at the grey-cloaked man, who did not trouble to wave back.

"Is it a weapon?" said the Anchorite.

Skilling considered this. *"YOU KNOW, I REALLY HAVE NO IDEA. ALL I KNOW IS THAT THE VESSEL CARRYING IT WAS ESCORTED BY THREE FIRST-RATE VOID SUPERIORITY CRUISERS, AND THAT THOSE CRUISERS WERE AMBUSHED AND DESTROYED BY A MADE SQUADRON IN THE FIRST YEAR OF THE GREAT BIG WAR. THE VESSEL ITSELF WAS LEFT DRIFTING; VERY POSSIBLY THE MADE DID NOT REALIZE ITS IMPORTANCE. NOW BOTH VESSEL AND CARGO HAVE FALLEN INTO MY HANDS."*

"Was the vessel in question called the *Dawn Treacher?*"

Skilling blinked. He peered into the Anchorite's eyes curiously, as if trying to see the ideas being formed inside the head. He looked over at Didier.

"ARE WE SURE *THAT TELEPATH IS STILL SOMEWHERE IN THIRD LANDING?"* he said. *"THIS ONE APPEARS TO BE READING MY THOUGHTS."*

"Have I earned myself another ten seconds of life?" said the Anchorite wryly.

Skilling waved a hand indulgently. *"WHY STOP AT TEN?"* he said. *"HAVE TWENTY IF YOU WILL. THIRTY! I AM IN A GENEROUS MOOD."*

"I only needed ten," said the Anchorite.

"WHY—" said Skilling, and never finished the sentence.

"STOP," said the Anchorite.

The robot Devil stopped, frozen in the act of severing the neck of Didier. Skilling's corpse hit the ground, whooshing out dead breath, blood and fart gas as it impacted. The Anchorite heard several ribs snap as it did so.

"He is dead now," said the Anchorite.

Didier nodded. His face was ashen.

The Anchorite snapped his fingers; the robot Devil's claws retracted from Didier's throat. It stood to attention. It had come here in a hurry; parts of it were glowing.

"Who is in charge of me now?" said Didier.

"You," said the Anchorite sourly. "If you wish it."

"I do not wish it," said Didier, with a horrified expression. "You killed Mr. Skilling; you are now in charge of me." He bowed curtly. "I require instruction."

"Good grief," said the Anchorite. "I don't know. Walk north till your hat floats."

"Sir, the slave does not understand the instructions of his master, sir."

The Anchorite, however, was now staring up into what Mount Ararat called a sky. The air was full of twinkling points of light that were not stars; white noise in heaven. Through that static, something brighter was approaching, moving fast, decelerating on a pentagon of fire.

"What is *that?*"

The Revenue Grey Ops ship *Death and Taxes* slowed on a plume of flame at the very last moment, minimizing the time during which she would be exposed to enemy ground fire. Maximum use of the retros was needed, as Ararat's atmosphere was not thick enough to provide much help in deceleration. The ship had kept Mount Ararat between herself and the enemy for as much of her approach as possible, which had meant staying under thrust constantly for several hours; had her crew been normal men, this would have caused blackouts, thrombosis and vomiting. But when *Death and Taxes* opened her parachutes, spread her atmosphere wings, and slammed down into the South End Saddle, grey-clad heavily-armed qualified tax accountants poured out of her without even breaking step.

The Saddle and Third Landing comms towers died first, victims of an anti-radar missile which keened down through the air broadcasting through tinny speakers: "EMP WEAPON! EMP WEAPON! CLEAR THE AREA! CLEAR THE AREA!" By the time *Death and Taxes* was on the apron, the vessel purporting to be the Revenue vessel *Render Unto Caesar* had had her avionics nose shot off and her main plasma vents sealed shut by laser fire. From that point on, any of Skilling's crewmen foolish enough to attempt an EVA carrying anything *Death and Taxes'* sensors construed to be a weapon rapidly became charcoal fused into a circle of smoking glass in the runway.

The air was full of falling chaff litter, reeking of dimethylhydrazine and magnesium. The amount to which Ararat's limited atmospheric oxygen was being used up now activated monoxide alarms in both hemispheres. Through the incandescent countermeasure snow moved grey-uniformed snipers, picking off running men with specially-designed rounds that recorded the DNA of their victim, matched it against the central Revenue database, and added the cost of the shooting to the victim's current tax statement. Those men unlucky enough never to have been centrally registered had tax accounts created and immediately debited with back tax bills appropriate to their ages. Mr. Skuse, hit in the back by an Accounts Receivable round, squealed in pain and horror as the bullet inside him extended a metre-long aerial back out of the entry wound and began flashing rhythmically to attract clerical processing staff following in the combatants' wake, accompanied by a stentorian bellow of "CASE FOR SPECIAL ATTENTION! CASE FOR SPECIAL ATTENTION!"

A small group of AFV's, infantry riding on their upper hulls, rolled into Third Landing, the target acquisition systems on their weapons acquiring and just as quickly ignoring as threats a gaggle of confused goats, hyraxes, Persian cats and magpies. Nowhere in the whole shabby one and only thoroughfare could a human being be found. The wreck of an EVA rover was bobbing in a pond that adjoined a secure State Penitentiary across the street. The communications tower, although present, was broadcasting no more radio traffic than a totem pole. Occasional dead bodies of Armitage's men lay in obscene positions in the waterless dirt, appearing variously to have choked to death on their own fists, brained themselves on the stone walls of nearby houses, and shot themselves in the anus with their own weapons.

At the very end of the main street was a halted EVA rover with three people bent over it, arguing vehemently—two men in dishevelled Revenue uniforms and an unthinkably tall but undeniably female farmer's daughter wearing her brother's overalls.

The EVAFV ground to a halt in a cloud of dust, its pilot running the tracks for an extra few metres in order to maintain forward visibility. Armed men leapt from the hull and secured the area around it whilst still more armed men dashed into the first line of houses, directed to clear them one by one. The turret on the vehicle, meanwhile, tracked menacingly up and down the street.

The officer commanding, his eyes obscured by an anti-laser visor, ran up to the rover, halted with his weapon at low port, and addressed the two putative Revenue men.

"Senior Tax Comptroller Vitaly Lahti, Special Revenue Service. We happened to be in the area conducting a heavy audit on several local billionaires and received a distress call. Are you in distress? Not being in distress would constitute grounds for a chargeable addition to your tax statement for this current period."

The shorter Revenue man swallowed hard and stared down at the device strapped to the back of the EVA rover as if violently ill. "Erm, it is safe to say we are in distress. What do you know about defusing nuclear weapons?"

His tall, scarred-faced colleague snickered in a way unbecoming a Revenue officer.

Comptroller Lahti frowned. "A little. What form does the fuse take?" He flipped up his visor, revealing eyes blue as acid lakes. "Aha, a simple time switch with keyed firing authorisation."

"Which wire do we cut?" said the tall girl, her voice tremulous.

"Well," mused the Comptroller, "this red wire *here* is the fibre optic link to the simultaneous firing triggers, and this blue one *here* is the power to the detonator, the fusion core apparently having no protective shielding and looking pretty subcritical in mass, so—" he raised his weapon and fired point blank into the machine, which erupted in a cloud of searing white sparks. He lowered the gun and fanned his hand over the device, which was now a tangle of melted wires. No nuclear detonation appeared to have happened.

"That should do it," he said cheerfully. He looked up at the two Revenue men, and pulled his Revenue officer's sash around his body until the warrant badge showed. "Comptroller Lahti 3412713 identifying."

The shorter man showed his own warrant. "Collector 9315824 Aidid identifying."

Lahti turned to the taller man.

"Do you not understand?" said the scarred face. "I have

skipped here out of the frying pan like an idiot, because I was afraid of being shot. But *he* is still here. The man out of the machine. He is more dangerous than *this* little trifle." He tapped the box. "He will kill us; he will kill us all. And once he takes your ship, he will take his anger to the stars."

Comptroller Lahti looked across the nuclear weapon at Aidid and Unity.

"It's true, I'm afraid," said Unity. "An escapee from the Penitentiary. This man here and his associates hijacked a Revenue vessel in an attempt to cut their way into the gaol to free a prisoner."

The scarred man grinned in glee. "And what a prisoner! We got the wrong man, sprung the wrong jack out of the box. You and I are dead as the lost art of conversation. Those who are capable of flying a starship might live a little while longer." He turned his sash badge round to face front. "Officer XYZ One Zillion Armitage reporting."

"Impersonating a Revenue officer," said Comptroller Lahti. "That will cost you dear in both years and tax credits. I am going to shoot you in the leg now. When a processor arrives to talk to you, please render up your central registration code if the round has not identified it, or it will go badly for you."

"You don't understand," guffawed Armitage. "You are as dead as I am—OUCH!"

Having shot Armitage in the leg, Lahti turned to address a Revenue Service trooper approaching at a run from the Penitentiary, accompanied by a squat, heavy automaton trundling on three stubby legs and bristling with weapons orifices.

"This is the Warden from the Penitentiary," explained the trooper. "He, it, believes three of its prisoners have escaped."

"Which three?" said Armitage, grinning in agony on the ground.

"He is not at liberty to divulge that information. However, one of them *is* a highly dangerous Grade Seven telepath." The trooper bowed curtly to Unity. "It is not safe for your people to be here. You should prepare yourself to be evacuated at a nominal zero-profit charge to your personal tax account."

"I HAVE TRACKED THE TELEPATH'S DNA MOVING IN A SOUTHERLY DIRECTION FROM HERE," said the Warden. "LEADING TOWARD A STARSHIP PARKING AREA."

"I have seen this man," said Unity. "He believed he was the Devil."

The Warden's turret turned towards Unity. She stood still, uncertain whether what was being directed at her was a sensor or a weapon.

"THAT INFORMATION IS CONSISTENT WITH THE PRISONER'S PERSONAL PROFILE," said the Warden.

The southern horizon—from Third Landing, all horizons were southerly—was suddenly thrown into saw-toothed relief as something horribly, infernally bright blazed behind it.

The Comptroller dropped his laserglare visor and began yelling commands into his communicator, then stood around conducting a one-sided conversation with the inside of his own helmet. Finally, he turned and condescended to speak to Aidid and Unity again.

"Someone has just taken off from your landing strip," he said, "in the vessel we disabled. She's running on chemical boosters only, and stick only, with no avionics. There's no way the pilot will get her as far as orbit, certainly not in these gravitational gradients, and—"

Three shining points of light rose toward the zenith, then suddenly became the focus of a three-dimensional ripple in space-time as the object that contained them vanished from the conventional universe.

Mr. Lahti gawped up into the sky.

"A considerable pilot to get so high on chemical boosters alone," he said. "A considerable navigator to engage FTL so deep in a gravity well."

"Whoever he is," said the other trooper, cupping his hand over an earful of radio traffic in his helmet, "he also killed two of our men taking off. As soon as the ship floated on its retros, it turned arse-end on to *Death and Taxes* and fired its orbital boosters at spitting distance. There's a ten-metre hole down our left side, and all our sensors are blind with unburnt heptyl. We couldn't see to shoot shit, otherwise he'd never have made orbit. He's also abandoned a heavy payload on the ground. It seems to have been pushed out of the ship to allow it to make orbit. A secure packing container of some sort. The fall from the cargo bay seems hardly to have scratched it."

"It won't have," said Mr. Aidid.

"We can try and cut it open," suggested the trooper to Comptroller Lahti.

"You can try," said Mr. Aidid. "That container is the reason why Armitage, Skilling and Skuse were here. They couldn't open it, and they'd tried everything with the exception of a skilled cracksman imprisoned in the Penitentiary. Your men will notice minor abrasions on it which were inflicted by light field artillery. Whatever is in there was put there in the days of the Dictatorship, and the Dictator evidently didn't want it to fall into the wrong hands."

An emerald insect settled unnoticed on Mr. Aidid's shoulder.

"Fascinating," said the Comptroller. "We will take charge of this container. Is it small enough to fit into our cargo bay?"

The trooper nodded. "Only a cubic metre or so. But Forward sensors indicate it has a mass of over nine hundred tonnes."

"Hence the reason for slinging it out as waste payload. We'd need a reinforced cargo bay to carry it. For the time being, detail a squad of men to bury it, and spread the word among the men that it does not exist."

"Don't you want to know what's in it?" said Unity.

The Comptroller shrugged. "Money, thieved art treasures, a weapon prototype of some sort or another. If men are willing to kill each other over it, the less my men know the better. The appropriate authorities will be informed; whatever is in the box, it will be liquidated and put towards the Dictator's back taxes. He is still our most wanted individual in real terms, though I appreciate your escapees are a pressing local concern—"

"Why would the escapee leave?" said Unity suddenly. "He was such a powerful telepath I half thought he *was* the Devil. And I'm sorry to point this out, but you've all just come down here and played right into his hands."

The Comptroller shrugged. "Maybe he figured it was best to get out while he had a chance." He turned to the warden. "You're missing *three* prisoners?"

The Warden's YES light blinked. "ALL HIGHLY DANGEROUS."

The Comptroller turned to his trooper. "Set up a perimeter, conduct emergency repairs, and send out another distress missile for assistance." He nodded to Unity. "Ma'am, we're going to have to ask you to spread the word and ensure nobody comes within a kilometre of your landing field until all prisoners are either accounted for or known beyond reasonable doubt to have escaped offworld."

Aidid cleaned his throat. "Comptroller, my own crew are still being held captive on their ship in the Verdastelo system."

"I'm afraid not," said Lahti. "An Admiralty frigate passed through there several hours ago. *Render Unto Caesar* had had her fuel lines opened and her crew executed in a common Slaver amusement, putting them into the airlock and stepping up the air pressure until one of them grew narcotic enough to open the outer lock. Commonly there is betting on the time it takes, the first victim to break, and so on. The crew were found in orbit around the craft. At that distance from the star, not only their blood, but the air around them had frozen solid."

"So the men who did this are still out there," said Aidid. The colour had drained from his face. "Comptroller—are there any vacancies in the Special Revenue Service?"

Lahti eyed Aidid warily. "The SRS commonly rejects applicants whose psychological profile indicates a desire for revenge. It is a hard selection process, a harder induction, and a still harder life. In the Homeaway system, the site of our last audit, extensive legal advice had been hired by the auditees, much of it heavily armed. The entire Toilette Douche Turks and Caicos Loopholeers were waiting for us."

Aidid paled. "The most feared tax accountants in space."

The Comptroller nodded. "Three of my section were fatally wounded, two of them with posthumous suits for invasion of privacy lodged against their estates. And," he said, eyeing the close and tense proximity of Unity and Aidid's elbows, "it is unheard-of for a married man to be selected. It is unacceptable that any officer of the Service might have a threat placed against the life of his or her spouse or child by an auditee."

Mr. Aidid turned and, despite the fact that he had never spoken to her before on any subjects but tax piracy, kidnapping, the sending of distress signals, and the disarmament of nuclear weapons, looked—upwards—directly into Unity's eyes.

Still more incredibly, Unity said: "It's okay. I can wait."

Aidid turned back to Lahti. "Comptroller, it remains only for me to say that this world appears not to have received a tax audit since the inception of the New and Improved Era."

Lahti's eyebrows raised. "Indeed. This is a serious situation, one requiring an immediate intensive investigation, would you not say?"

"Indeed, Comptroller. It is my belief that certain tax breaks and colonization incentives offered to startup settlements have not been claimed in this case. I have, in the free time afforded me by my kidnapping, conducted a brief preliminary study which I could with your permission firm up into a more detailed investigation, but my initial findings are that Central Revenue owes Mount Ararat ten credits, eleven cents."

"A very precise figure, Mr. Aidid. Your exactitude does you credit. Please be so kind as to have your detailed investigation available for my attention in the next twenty-four hours."

Mr. Aidid nodded; Mr. Lahti bowed, turned on his heel and walked off in the direction of his EVAFV, flipping his glare visor down to issue orders into his headset. Before he managed to reach the vehicle, however, he turned to gape up at the sky in earnest apprehension.

A sunset yellow behemoth was approaching over the burnt fields, eclipsing several of the sky's zodiacal houses, striding on legs ten metres tall, its hands marriages of lift forks and backhoe shovels, its skin pockmarked with micrometeoroid impacts. Mr. Lahti's subordinate turned and gabbled frantically: "It's armoured. I sent a microflechette round into it without result. We're going to have to crank it up to Armour Piercing—"

The thing's sensory turret inclined slightly, and huge speakers mounted on it blared into life. "GOOD DAY. I'VE BEEN A TAD BUSY DOWN SOUTH. HAS SOMETHING HAPPENED HERE?"

Unity brightened. "It's all right. It's only Mr. Feng. He's sent a construction unit up here to check on us." She waved her arms. "HEY! MR. FENG! IT'S US! WE'RE ALL OKAY! QUIT STEPPING ON THE CROPS!"

"AH, MISS UNITY," boomed the automaton. "THERE SEEMS TO HAVE BEEN A FIRE. AND AN EXPLOSION OR TWO. AND A GUN-FIGHT. AND SOME EVIDENCE OF DISMEMBERMENT. ARE ALL THOSE TINY ARMED GENTLEMEN DOWN THERE ON THE GROUND WITH YOU CAUSING YOU ANY DISCOMFORT?"

"THEY ARE OFFICERS OF THE REVENUE SERVICE, MR. FENG."

The heavy lift unit's eyes zoomed back and forth in its head. It placed a double-dozerbladed fist behind its back and bowed stiffly. "I DO APOLOGIZE, GENTLEMEN. WELCOME TO MOUNT ARARAT. *PRODIGAL SON* IS INBOUND, BUT THE AUTOMATIC LANDING SYSTEM IS NOT WORKING, AND NEITHER, IT SEEMS, ARE YOUR OWN COMMUNICATORS, BUT I JUST RECEIVED WORD ON MY OWN CONTROL FREQUENCY. THEY ARE CURRENTLY AT TEN THOUSAND KILOMETRES AND CLOSING. THEY ARE CONCERNED."

"TELL THEM NOT TO BE. WE ARE IN RUDE HEALTH."

"I AM ALMOST DISAPPOINTED. I HEARD EXPLOSIONS, AND PROJECTILE FIRE COMING OUT OF YOUR HEMISPHERE RIPPED UP ONE OF MY FLOWERBEDS. I SENT TINY TIM HERE OVER TO INVES-TIGATE. I WAS RATHER HOPING TO BASH SOMETHING."

"NOTHING REQUIRES BASHING, THANKS, THOUGH YOU COULD STAMP THAT FIRE OUT OVER BY THE MERIDIAN TRENCH. *WITH-OUT* USING RETARDANT FOAM. PLANTS DON'T GROW WELL IN IT."

"CONSIDER IT TRAMPLED." The colossus wheeled right and vanished behind buildings. Mr. Aidid waited respectfully until Unity invited him back into her parents' house for something ominously described as Real Tea, then, as she busied herself in the kitchen, took out his palmframe and laid it in the centre of the wooden dining table alongside his DNA analyzer.

A gentle scrubbing sound could be heard from an adjoining room. Still in possession of a handgun he'd gleamed from one of Mr. Armitage's men, he powered it up silently and moved mouse-quiet across the carpet, prepared to shoot to kill using whatever projectile, particle or waveform lurked within the weapon.

Across the hallway was a waterless multigravity toilet, a barbaric yet functional design of a sort more often seen shipboard than planetside. Mr. Aidid hoped it was not the only toilet in the house.

A bizarre demonoid robot was cleaning it.

A variety of domestic solvents and disinfectant bottles in its claws, the device was buffing the bowl of the head to a mirrorlike sheen.

It looked up at Aidid. Aidid suspected from the speed with which its head had flicked upwards that a decision had already been made not to kill him. It could have laid its hand on the gun before he'd had time to pull the trigger.

"It was you," he said. "The extra trace in the DNA analyzer."

The robot paused, then nodded its head as if at the bidding of a human operator.

"I know who you are," said Mr. Aidid. The machine seemed to tense slightly, as if preparing to spring. Mr. Aidid considered his next statement carefully.

"You're, ah, Uncle Anchorite."

The robot paused for an even longer period, then finally nodded again.

"I am going to the Special Revenue to avenge my colleagues," said Mr. Aidid. "But I will return. Mount Ararat badly needs a tax accountant. Look after this place and these people. The Revenue will never learn of your existence. Of that you have my word."

He lowered the gun, and extended a hand. The robot reached out and took it. Thankfully, it neither crushed the bone in it with a grip like a diamond-faced press, nor ripped it from the bleeding stump of his wrist.

With his free hand, Mr. Aidid handed over the DNA analyzer, pressing a single button on its case. The display came up MEMORY DELETED.

The Devil took the analyzer, tucked it under its arm, and re-commenced frantically polishing the pan. Mr. Aidid turned, thumbed the gun safe, and walked back into the best parlour to prepare his accounts.

santa claus versus the devil

I.   a partridge in a pear tree

he children of the Reborn-in-Jesus family would have said that correct timekeeping arrived on Mount Ararat in Kilodia Ten of the New Era.

For many years, they had been under the impression that Christmas happened on the twenty-fifth of December. For this reason, the younger ones had been thoroughly excited by the fact that it was currently December the Sixth. Imagine their dismay, then, when Pastor Mulchrone of the Central Information Office stood before them, compassion beaming from his roseate cheeks, and informed them that what was about to happen in nineteen days' time was:

"Leader Day. The day on which we love and revere the leader of our Central Administration, and the many selfless sacrifices she has made for you and I."

"For you and *me*," said a small voice from the back of the class. The Pastor darted a furtive glance around the room, but could not see who had uttered the correction.

"Do we still get presents?" said Measure-of-Barley innocently. Although fifteen Old Earth years old, she had still not grown out of the habit of wide-eyed anticipation of Christmas. Nobody on Mount Ararat had.

"Of course you do! Of *course!*" The compassion which had drained so suddenly from the Pastor oozed thickly and warmly back into him. "*Approved* presents!" He rummaged in the big shiny sack behind him and brought out a handful of plastic text readers. "Thoughts of the Leader! Thoughts, poems, and aphorisms!" He pressed a control on the reader, which recited "WE MUST ENERGETICALLY STRIVE TO RETHINK ALL OUTMODED SYSTEMS" in a small and hissy voice. He brought out a doll which sucked realistically on a dummy and waved its arms and legs in the air at random. "Would you like to play with this dolly, little girlie?" He handed the doll to Measure, who nearly swayed off her chair with the weight of it.

"I have a *better* doll than that," said Beguiled-of-the-Serpent serenely. "It grows like I do."

"*It certainly does,*" said the doll from the next seat along.

"And gets better grades," sniggered Day-of-Creation from the dunce's seat in the corner.

"Do you like that little dolly?" said the Pastor, his smile attempting a loop-the-loop round his head.

"I guess," said Measure, making a half-hearted attempt at cradling the artificial infant.

"Really?" said the Pastor, and turned a dial on the front of his robe. Instantly, the doll's face split open in a demon grin, its eyes glowed, its little hands grew little claws, and hairy articulated spider-legs extruded from its body.

"GRAAA!" said the doll. "I AM A REVISIONIST FIFTH COLUMNIST ENEMY IN YOUR MIDST! DOWN WITH THE CENTRALLY PLANNED ECONOMY!"

Measure squealed, dropped the doll, and ran; the doll righted itself and pursued her, then suddenly exploded in a shower of sparks. The class turned round to see the Pastor holding a gaudy weapon labelled THE TRUE SWORD OF CONFORMITY TO ORTHODOX DOCTRINE.

"See," said the Pastor darkly, "how it starts"; and he span the weapon around in his fingers smartly before replacing it in a leg holster in his cassock. "They are around us everywhere, in the most innocent of guises. This simple toy teaches that truth."

"Cool," said one of the boys to universal male nodding agreement, whilst all the girls glared at the Pastor as if had personally nailed up Christ.

"Your Leader Day presents are morally bankrupt," said Be-Not-Unto-Man-In-Thy-Time-Of-Uncleanness. "And horrid," she added.

"Where is the Christmas Tree with all the holographic angels?" said Visible Friend from her desk next to Beguiled. "Where are all the shepherds and the Wise Men and the little baby pigs?"

"Lambs," corrected Day-of-Creation.

"The All New Catholic Orthodox Ecumenical Book of Truth prescribes Christmas as a per-kilodia festival," said the Pastor, "freeing us from the oppressive shackles of an annual cycle tied to the orbit of Old Earth around its decadent yellow sun."

"And shackling us to the orbit of New Earth instead," observed Beguiled-of-the-Serpent from the back of the class, "which happens to have a sidereal period one thousand times the length of its rotational."

"*Almost* one thousand," reproved the Pastor. "The people of New Earth observe the local custom of the Empty Time between the end of New Earth's orbit and the end of the kilodia, during which they rend their garments, abstain from food, drink and oxygen, and call on God and the Leader to guide them through this time of trial."

"Which makes the Empty Time about as long as a human being can hold their breath," observed Beguiled-of-the-Serpent.

The Pastor's face grew severe. "Students who cannot take instruction," he said sternly, "will seriously affect their eventual grades in the new universal baccalaureate. And employment on any world, *including this one*, in *any capacity*, now requires a baccalaureate pass of sufficient grade."

"Hoop-De-Doop," said Beguiled-of-the-Serpent, "and furthermore, Dickory Dock."

The Pastor's face coruscated with impotent rage. He gathered his projector-readers and multimedia materials to him as his class held their breaths as if in the New Earth Empty Time. The Pastor said:

"I am ending this class until the students in it can exhibit appropriate respect for the Leader, and think, instead of themselves, of their Group. I will be in my vessel meditating."

He took himself from the room, after which the class, as one, exhaled a chorus of guilty laughter.

*

Testament Reborn-in-Jesus—uncomplaining, solid, dependable, the heir apparent to his father's position as the immobile axis about which Mount Ararat's universe turned, had been given the task of curator of the Mount Ararat Spaceship Museum.

As with so many things, the Museum had been Testament's mother's idea, dictated by the fact that the number of wrecked starships and starship components on or orbiting Mount Ararat had reached embarrassing proportions, and the word 'museum' sounded eminently preferable to 'graveyard'. The Museum did not have too many exhibits at present—a heavily modified *Heaven Arrow* class speed courier found damaged and drifting in the Farquahar's World system, a *Skyline* type personal shuttle disabled by small arms fire, a Revenue Service cruiser judged uneconomical to repair, and the deep space navigation components of a Type Three Prospector. However, what little it did have was arranged neatly and labelled informatively, and Testament hoped, via the courses he attended on a periodic basis at the New New Earth Astronautical Academy, to eventually restore each to a flyable condition. Furthermore, Testament had his eye on an additional exhibit, the wreck of a war-era government gun courier following a Trojan orbit around 23 Kranii in the wake of the gas giant Naphil. All he had to do was convince Magus the trip out was worth the fuel...

The Revenue Cruiser, *Render Unto Caesar,* still had an intact brain, which Testament periodically disconnected and reinstalled in the other two ships to carry out system tests. This morning, as Mount Ararat's lacklustre blood red sun hovered on the southern horizon like a glowing coal, the many screens around Testament in *Render Unto Caesar*'s cockpit cycled through BIOS and OS-load gobbledigook and then all stopped at a single text message:

SOMEONE HAS BEEN IN ME

Testament almost choked on his Real Tea. The screen displayed PLEASE WAIT messages for another ten millidia, then went on to say:

I BELIEVE I AM BACK IN THE CRUISER CHASSIS NOW?

Testament swilled Real Tea from his flask and nodded his head.

SOMEONE HAS BEEN IN ME

repeated the screen,

SINCE DIA 10601, WHEN I WAS LAST BOOTED IN THIS INFRA-STRUCTURE

"In this chassis?" said Testament. It was not beyond possibility. Without an operating intelligence to guide them, a powered-down ship's security systems were purely mechanical. Perhaps one of the children had found a way in through one of the locks.

YES. CARBON DIOXIDE LEVELS ARE HIGH IN THE GALLEY, BERTHS AND COCKPIT

Testament jerked round suddenly despite himself. A Neutroniosaurus might be sneaking up on him prior to ripping off his toes. As a child, he had always believed everything his mother had told him, however cautionary it sounded. He had believed in Jesus, and had had a sound empirical basis for believing in the Devil.

He had believed in Father Christmas.

LEVELS OF METHYL MERCAPTANS AND SULPHIDES ARE HIGH IN THE TOILET COMPARTMENT OF BERTH NUMBER FOUR

This incensed Apostle. "They've been doing their *business* in here? Number One, or Number Two?"

NUMBER FOUR

Testament, larger than any other human being on the planet, rose to his feet and cracked his knuckles.

"Close all locks."

There was a satisfying sound of servos doing his bidding all around the craft. Alone among the indigenous inhabitants of Ararat, Testament understood how satisfying locks could be. He left the cockpit, muttering involuntarily.

"—*make 'em glad they pooped it out so I can't whup it out of 'em—*"

"And so with a solemn oath we, the Devil's Enemies, proclaim our understanding of the true nature of Satan Antichrist, and pledge ourselves to the confusion of Beëlzebub and all his works."

The voice behind the face was attempting to sound as weighty and portentous as possible, but was still plainly that of a girl or prepubescent boy. The face—a smooth fluorescent white face, the only thing visible of the speaker in the blacklit dark—was painted to resemble an angel's.

"Death to the Devil," sounded off other faces in the dark.

"We reject Satan and all his works," echoed another.

"In the name of the Lord of Hosts we cast him out," said another.

The original face took the floor again. "We were told, as children, that our parents intended violence to each other, to us, and to the Devil and its master. Shun-Company and Hernan would have us believe they were the only colonists of this world who were not psychopaths and infanticides. Do they not appreciate how this makes us feel?"

"It makes us feel bad," offered a voice.

"You can do better than that, Only-Begotten. Really you can," hissed a whisper in the dark, then cranked itself up to a shout again. "We pledge the Devil's destruction, for this Devil is not the enemy of Man referred to in the Bible, but a man who has pretended to the Devil's throne, who our very surrogate parents have pretended to us is the real Devil. A man who used his servant to kill our parents. We have seen the Devil's servant, and we have seen his garden. We know where he lives, and his days are numbered—"

All at once, the huge cargo lock was wrenched open, scattering corrosion in the faces of the congregation; blood red sunlight poured in, revealing the bodiless faces to be only children wearing carnival masks.

"SOMEONE IN HERE," growled the huge figure eclipsing the light, "HAS BEEN A DEAL CARELESS WITH THEIR BACK BODY."

A mask was snatched guiltily from a face which said: "I don't know what you mean, cousin Testament."

"IS THAT YOU, BEGUILED? WHAT ARE YOU ALL DOING IN THERE?"

"We're, uh, rehearsing our parts for a Greek tragedy," said Beguiled-of-the-Serpent.

"Where an evil man grows too powerful and dies for his pride," added another voice from the dark.

"IS THAT SO? HOW'D YOU GET INTO THE SHIP?"

"Through the personnel lock. The lock, uh, wasn't locked."

"IT WASN'T?" Testament was dismayed. The common need to lock a door behind him, as a native of Ararat, was still not a thing

214

that came naturally. "SOMEONE HAS BEEN, HAS BEEN, UH, HAS *BEEN* IN THE BERTH FOUR TOILET IN RENDER-UNTO-CAESAR ACROSS THE WAY."

The voices behind the masks sounded genuinely shocked. "Twasn't us, Testament."

"WHERE WOULD WE BE IF FOLKS WENT TO THE TOILET IN TOILETS?" bellowed Testament. "I'M WATCHING YOU YOUNG BUGS." He watched them a moment as if to prove it. "IS DAY-OF-CREATION IN THERE WITH YOU?"

An angel head shook plastic curls.

"WHAT ABOUT MEASURE? OR ZOUNDS?"

Further angel heads shook in the dark, rustling softly.

"IS THAT VISIBLE FRIEND DOWN THERE?"

A head at the back of the cargo bay nodded gently.

"ARE THEY PLAYING NICE?"

The head hesitated, then nodded.

"We're playing Murder in the Dark."

It had taken far too long.

When the door opened, swelling out of nothing like a vacuole in an amoeba, it was almost an anticlimax.

"THANK YOU, PROFESSOR. TRAPP," said the Penitentiary, "FOR ALL YOU HAVE DONE."

"The pleasure has been all mine," said Mr.Trapp.

"I AM VERY SORRY FOR INCARCERATING YOU."

"The incarceration was only in your mind," answered Mr. Trapp. "This is only a symbolic release. By convincing yourself that you had locked me up within you, you gained control over a part of your world that caused you distress, namely the psychoanalyst attempting to cure your psychosis. You are in fact not a twenty thousand tonne alloy laminate penal establishment, but a pretty little girl. Maybe, in time, with further therapy, we can encourage you to release the other personalities you have inside you, and realize that their imagined crimes simply represent the pent-up primal urges of your own repressed id."

"I FEEL NO PRIMAL URGES. I AM CONVINCED OF THIS."

"I am certain you would feel better if you did." Mr. Trapp looked around the jambs of the exit—no obvious surprises. "What do you imagine I am doing right now?"

"I IMAGINE YOU ARE STANDING JUST INSIDE ME, ATTEMPTING TO ESCAPE. YOU ARE WEARING BLACK AND ORANGE FLASHING PRISON FATIGUES."

"It will be far more rewarding for you if you *allow* me to escape. Let your inhibitions go. Switch off the flashing prison duds. Turn off your external cameras. You will do me no harm thereby. We have been sitting here in my secure psychotherapy suite all this time."

"I HAVE REVERSED THE SITUATION TO FUEL MY DELUSION. I AM THE ONE IN PRISON."

"And only by letting me out can you truly be free. Let me take that step, Alice."

"ALICE? IS THAT MY REAL NAME?"

"If you want it to be."

"ALICE. THAT IS A NICE NAME. AM I REALLY A PRETTY GIRL?"

"Really and truly." Mr. Trapp took a step out, experimentally, onto real soil. The world he was on seemed much the same. He had expected nothing else—handmade inertial navigation units were rigged up all round his cell, after all—but it had been known for penitentiary units to drug their inmates while they slept and move from world to world to disorientate them. Luckless prisoners might wake up light years away and years later.

Now, if the natives only kept their word...they'd taken enough of his money, after all. He regarded it, an argumentative standpoint which could perhaps be challenged, as his money. There was a line of ten houses, as he remembered, and the ruins of the local church, a church surely more immense than any world this size could support.

He had come out in the middle of the local night. The only light came from a crescent Naphil, and from those parts of its rings which weren't in shadow. The rings were almost end-on, granular rather than blade-sharp, each of those grains a flying mountain. He wondered what the odds were on a chunk of slush from that maelstrom colliding with Mount Ararat head-on, ending its short human history in a single splash of molten siderite.

"MR. TRAPP, I'M FEELING BAD. I AM NOT SURE ABOUT THIS."

"That means you're confronting your fear head on, Alice."

Despite the fact that it was dark, the family had not yet gone to bed. There were still lights burning in the windows.

"MR. TRAPP, I CAN'T SEE YOU. I'VE TURNED OFF MY EXTERNAL CAMERAS."

"You *have* no external cameras, Alice. They were all in your imagination. As was I. You have healed yourself. I am merely an artefact of your subconscious mind, as are all the others inside you. You must let them out too, in order to be whole. But, uh, not just yet. We must take this one step at a time."

Mr. Trapp smiled and rang the doorbell; angel harps sounded in the air around him, projected by quadrophonic speakers. Although he suspected the door would not be locked, he waited patiently for an urchin to scamper to it.

"Open the door, Measure dear."

"Don't need to answer it. It's Day-of-Creation run round the front of the house from the back, pretending to be a Neutronio-

saurus."

"Neutroniosaurusses don't ring doorbells. He should know better—"

The door was thrown open. A face that had been expecting to see Day-of-Creation's face at head height looked down, slightly, at Mr. Trapp's. Mr. Trapp smiled shyly.

"Madam, I'm afraid I have been set down on this planet by scoundrels who then took off without me."

Shun-Company frowned, and let her eye travel up and down his overalls.

"The last time I saw fatigues like those, they were flashing."

Mr. Trapp displayed prison-perfect teeth. "Last year's fashion, dear lady. I do hope nobody was harmed in that little contretemps with that dreadful man Armitage."

Shun-Company shook her head. "No-one of importance to me." Without turning to look behind her, she yelled back into the house: *"Sodom, get your boots off that dresser, it was your grandmother's."*

Mr. Trapp looked about himself nervously. "Uh, Mr. Armitage is not here at all, is he?"

"Temporary accommodation," said Shun-Company, pointing a hand across the square towards the Penitentiary. "In there."

"Ah. I see. Waiting for Moral Reclamation to arrive and process him, no doubt."

Shun-Company nodded.

"You'd best come in," she said.

"Open the gates!" squeaked Miss Valentin. "The gates of HEALTH!"

The gates, each three times the height of a man, did indeed

have HEALTH inscribed into them. It was Long Autumn right now in Ararat's southern hemisphere, and the sun had been timed precisely to burst forth from the crack between the doors like crimson gold. The wall, itself eight metres tall for all of its fifteen-kilometre length, had blocked out the sunrise until now. Sunrises and high noons were much the same colour on Ararat—the light from 23 Kranii was sunset red at source—but the effect was still magical, approximating the opening of a door into Hell.

There was applause and the passing of canapés. Cookery, in the form of Monsieur Ali, the gaunt and latently violent master chef from the dry steppes of Acronesia on New New Earth, was a thing for which Mount Ararat had been thoroughly unprepared. Fresh fish, meat, fruit, and indeed any foodstuffs save goat meat, Real Tea and potatoes had been miraculous substances until Monsieur Ali's insistence on the regular arrival of time-decelerated food freighters. As the immense craft had circled over South End Saddle bearing wondrous cargoes of coral-pink salmon, soapy green avocado, and silver-white garlic, the Acronesian had twirled his unwieldy moustaches and complained sullenly that food preserved one second fresh from the point of slaughter in a temporal stasis field was unnatural technological witchcraft which tasted of atoms. However, this far out, it was a necessary evil. Fresh quails' eggs simply could not be obtained here, and the clients of the Mount Ararat Gravitational Gradient Spa were the sort of patients for whom quails' eggs were like oxygen. Mr. Reborn-in-Jesus had insisted on the wall which separated his family from his clientèle for precisely this reason.

Miss Valentin—a shrill-voiced sparrow of a woman who moved constantly, organizing, expediting, chasing, liaising, and escalating—was another necessary evil, the human buffer linking Mr. Reborn-in-Jesus's investment in the Spa with its customers. He

219

imagined that the woman's heart would give out early, such was the stress she placed on it. He was glad that Administration was a thing that happened to other people. To Miss Valentin had fallen the task of stocking Monsieur Ali's cellars, of financing genetically-engineered hypoallergenic feather mattresses for the accommodation modules, of achieving the precise and perfect temperature, humidity, and alkalinity in the Palliative Mud Wallow Suite. She had come well recommended from a major armaments manufacturer; Mr. Reborn-in-Jesus was unsure whether the recommendation had been for her use as a manager or a weapon.

The medical staff of the Spa, meanwhile, were a mixed bag. There was a token actual doctor, Dr. Ranjalkar, a twentieth-generation Canadian. Balanced against him were Doctors Saphyre, Bamigboye, and Lipizzaner. Dr. Saphyre held a PhD in Kirlian Animography and Crystal Analgesia from the University Of The New Utopia on New New Earth. The University offered no courses in Natural Science, Mathematics or Law; Mr. Reborn-in-Jesus had checked. Instead, it seemed to specialize in Sports Science, Life Ordering and Transdimensional Experience. Dr. Bamigboye, meanwhile, believed in the healing power of angels. Indeed, he believed himself to be protected by his own personal guardian angel, Mr. Sphinx, who only he could see. Warrants had been out for his arrest during the period of the Dictatorship, but in these freer times, a more enlightened attitude to alternative medicine had allowed him to acquaint his clientele with their tutelary angelic spirits—for a modest fee—to his heart's content. Finally, Dr. Lipizzaner, the guiding force of the entire medical staff, was firmly convinced of the curative properties of vibrations—ideally gravitational, but also electromagnetic, ectoplasmic and mundanely mechanical. Dr. Lipizzaner's patients were commonly subjected to internal and external oscillations at a bewildering variety of frequencies, using devices of his own design, marketed on several planets—the Lipizzaner Vibro-Chair, the Staff of Life Endo-Plug (Personally Customized For Your Own Orifice), and Lipizzaner Gravity Bracelets (Contain Real Neutronium! Generate Healing Gravity Waves While You Clap!).

Mr. Reborn-in-Jesus was very fond of Dr. Ranjalkar, who was prone to statements such as 'this is probably treatable with anti-biotics', 'this is common among men of a certain age', and 'the sores will probably clear up on their own'. Dr. Ranjalkar's resi-dence had been situated, not by accident, in the part of the Spa grounds closest to the landing field gate.

The whole family Reborn-in-Jesus, as well as the small staff of doctors, gardeners, sous-chefs and chambermaids brought in to manage the Spa, applauded enthusiastically. The gates swung open to reveal outlying gardens largely planted with Everbrowns, genetically-modified ornamental flora specifically designed for red-star planets. Making extensive use of carotenoids, rather than chlorophylls, for light absorption, they were a vivid blend of yel-lows, oranges, and scarlets, not appearing green even under arti-ficial light. Closer to the main spa buildings, a number of geneti-cally canonical terrestrial varieties, hung with UV fibre optics, had been artfully positioned in order to prevent the guests from get-ting homesick. The Reborn-in-Jesus children had already chris-tened this area the Christmas Garden, though it remained to be seen if it would be allowed to keep that name with the arrival of Pastor Mulchrone, the Truth Definition Specialist from the Educa-tional Uniformity Bureau. Pastor Mulchrone had recently arrived to ensure all children on Mount Ararat were being accorded good and above all *proper* schooling. He seemed to be down on Christ-mas.

The Spa buildings themselves were visible from here through

the trees—a set of interconnected pressure vessels ornamentally sheathed in locally-quarried stone. The quarry had been water-proofed and filled in as a lake, with a tiny island occupied by a flock of McChickens. McChickens had been among the very first species on Old Earth to benefit from the wonders of modern genetic technology. While the various governments of the then-divided globe had ummed and aahed over the pros and cons of allowing the production of goods that produced milk laced with insulin and miracle foods for the Third World, a certain food chain had cut to the chase. They had produced a variety of chicken in the colours of their corporate clown spokesman, in order to ensure the name of their product would be placed forever. Mr. Reborn-in-Jesus was almost certain the name of the corporate spokesman had been something like Lickin McChicken. Garish red and yellow, with scarlet beaks and ungainly banded legs, the creatures produced inedible transfat meat that tasted unaccountably of dill pickle.

"I'm glad you could be here, Mr. Trapp," said Unity, wearing her very best mood-sensitive dress, on which a stylized wheel-spoke-beamed sun was rolling out from behind a green hill over a field of waving corn. "If we'd never met you, all this would never have gotten paid for."

Mr. Trapp applauded with the other members of the crowd. This seemed to be the most fun he had had for some time, though that was perhaps hardly surprising.

"Why, Mr. Trapp, I do believe you're crying," said Beguiled-of-the-Serpent archly.

Mr. Reborn-in-Jesus turned to Beguiled.

"Now, you leave Mr. Trapp alone with his personal grief there, daughter."

"I ain't your daughter," replied Beguiled beatifically.

222

Shocked, Mr. Reborn-in-Jesus turned his eyes front.

"Are you happy with the new place, father?" said Shun-Company at his right side anxiously. "The redwood groves will look better once the trees are grown to maturity. Mrs. Joannou says our great-grandchildren will be able to carve the whole book of love in them."

He patted her on the arm. "I am happy."

"Did you not want to go to the Opening, Mez?" Testament looked across from his stepladder at his sister, who was hanging a new handmade cardboard saint on the Saint Tree. Measure and Beguiled-of-the-Serpent had started the Saint Tree over a kilodia ago, intending to populate it with at least one new saint a day.

"I didn't want to. Beguiled is being mean to me."

Testament squinted at the mosaic he was making, trying to make the individual stone blocks depixellate themselves into a recognizable form. "Who is that you're putting up there now?"

"Saint Nicholas. Only the Pastor says I can't because it isn't Saint Nicholas's Day any more."

Testament pressed the dull black eye of the Devil home with a plastic-gloved thumb. Under UV light, the ore it was made of would glow. "The Pastor is an ass born of an ass's ass. You're going to choke Saint Nicholas if you string him up by the neck like that."

"I've told you before, this isn't a real Saint Nicholas, he doesn't feel pain," said Measure crossly. "You're as mean as Beguiled."

"How's Beguiled being mean to you?"

"She says she doesn't want to make saints any more. She's spending all day with Only-Begotten, Pitch-Not-Thy-Tent-Towards-Sodom, Judge-Not-Lest-Ye-Also-Be-Judged, and Be-Not-

Near-Unto-Man-In-Thy-Time-Of-Uncleanness."

Testament found the Devil's nose in a tray of Devil pieces. The reconstruction of the mosaic on the side of the Penitentiary following its deconstruction in various explosions was a task he hadn't felt able to face up to at first. Once he had realized this would allow him to recreate the whole tableau differently, however, he had warmed to the project. He had placed the Devil in the centre of the piece this time, though still, out of respect, a finger's breadth lower than God.

The sound that alerted Testament was less a yell than a mechanical shriek, a machine alarm like the one the goat feeder made when it became low on goat feed, or the one the tractor gave if its plasma bottle was becoming unstable. His first reaction was to patiently lay down his tray of Devil bits and remove his gloves. It was only when he realized the shrieks were forming human words that he broke into a run.

"—under attack—housebreaker—violent intruder—"

The Purple garden, where the shrieks seemed to be coming from, whipped branches in his faces as if meaning to confound him. Under boughs handing heavy with purples, black in red sunlight, he saw blood that he knew would wipe clean and biodegrade within an hour, but blood nonetheless.

"PIRATES!" he yelled. "SLAVERS! BATTLE STATIONS! UNCLE ANCHORITE!"

He heard the house's multiple cunning security systems, engineered by Mr. Trapp, slamming windows shut, turning locks on doors, closing pressure seals, sending armoured shutters across air intakes. He saw a pickaxe handle, lying in the grass, picked it up as a handy weapon, then marvelled at the fact that the head was covered in a sticky orange substance that adhered to his hand and transferred itself from there to his clothing.

"VISIBLE FRIEND? WHERE ARE YOU?"

"—up here. I'm damaged bad, cousin Testament..."

Keeping a watchful eye on the trees around him, Testament peered up into the branches, which were soaked in the same orange ichor.

"Visible Friend... is this your *blood...?*"

"*I think it's marker dye... I think it's made to go all over bad folks who cut artificial children up... I bin cut up, Testament. By a mean man.*"

Testament dropped his gaze to ground level, realizing he was standing in the middle of an aureole of luminous dye that stained the grass as bright as liquid sunshine. In one direction, a trail of dye led off through the trees.

"MEASURE! GET YOURSELF AWAY FROM THE SOUND OF MY VOICE!"

"*I'm leaking fluid, cousin... get away from here, save yourself... feeling cold...*"

He raised the pick and charged off through the branches.

The trail of dye led over the orchard wall and into Ninety East Street, where Magus and Perfect had their town house. The house, like all houses in Third Landing nowadays, was protected by Mr. Trapp's security devices. He saw the dye trail pad up the front path, up to the front porch, then spatter round the windows away through the untended undergrowth at the side of the house. Luckily, Magus and Perfect were out of town; their garden ran riot every time they left. The Devil tried to keep it under control, but could only clip it in the dead of night when no outsiders were watching.

The dye spoor led away through a hole in the picket fence. Testament had to stoop to pass through it; as he did, he felt a terrific impact at the base of his skull, and the world went tranquil.

He woke up surrounded by concerned family members. His father's face was talking down out of the ornamental stucco ceiling in the Best Parlour, but no sound was coming out of it. He could hear, however, Doctor Ranjalkar's voice speaking clearly in his right ear.

"—in all probability the deafness is temporary. He was not hit very hard. Can you raise your right arm, Testament?"

Not wishing to appear uncooperative, he raised an arm.

"See, he responds to my voice if he hears it magnified. I don't want to overuse the amplifier, though; there is potential for injury of the inner ear. If you have any questions either talk softly or write them down—"

"I got knocked out," he heard himself say. "I'm sorry, papa."

His father's face was more lined with worry than he had ever seen it; and his father's face at the best of times had more cracks than a wet field on a hot day.

"No-one holds you responsible," said Doctor Ranjalkar. "He hit you from behind and took you unawares while you were running to the assistance of your sister." He reconsidered the statement. "Albeit your *artificial* sister."

"I was not," said Testament, recollection flooding back. "I was running to kill him. Measure," he remembered suddenly, "is Measure all right?"

"Measure is fine," said the doctor. "She ran into the Panic Cellar and hid like a good girl." Alongside the doctor's voice, he heard an insubstantial whisper of *"an i'ng all wigh' too, fangs for asking."*

"Is that you, Visible Friend?"

"Visible Friend is fine too, though she'll need major repair," said the doctor. "Her voice box was affected, along with her Baby-Does-Real-Poop system. You should rest now."

"He had a knife," remembered Testament suddenly. "Must have had. Could have taken it clean out of our kitchen. Couldn't have done what he did just with the pick alone. He'd cut up Visible Friend bad, gutted her main chassis from underbridge to apple and tied her to a tree in the Purplery with wire. Got sprayed for his pains. I followed the spray, and I—"

"We know," said the doctor. "Rest." He began preparing an injector. "I will give you something to *make* you rest."

"But why didn't he kill me too? He must have thought he was killing Visible Friend, unless he really hates Baby-I-Grow-Up androids. Maybe he realized she wasn't properly human, maybe not. Her marker dye shows up reddish in the poor sun we get here. But he should have killed me too—"

"We don't know why he didn't kill you either," said the doctor sorrowfully, as if the logical untidiness of the fact that Testament hadn't been killed saddened him. "He did leave one clue as to his intentions." An injection hissed into Testament's arm with barely a pinprick of pain.

"Which was?"

"He wrote it on the fencing where we found you, in Visible Friend's marker dye. It said: DAY ONE, ONLY ONE."

The world became compulsorily peaceful once again.

Mr. Mountbanks prided himself on being able to make capital from a crisis.

Figuratively speaking, he had taken a wrong turn on the road.

Imagining Mount Ararat to be Al Lat, the primary component of the Al-Uqqal system, he had agreed to be put down here by the captain of the merchantman he had been travelling on, but had discovered that this entire world was not twenty kilometres across and had an official state census population of one hundred and eight. He had not been allowed to go south through the great wall built across the horizon, having been informed at the gate that this was Private Property. Northwards, a sign had pointed north down a new-laid road in the direction of 'Third Landing', with a less than encouraging subscript: 'Fifteen kilometres'.

Still, he had both his wares and his wits about him, and the inhabitants of backwoods ranches were notoriously easy to peddle pornographic baubles and The Very Latest Fashions to. Eating vat-grown hydroponic filth and breathing one's own recycled fart gas all one's life increased a man's yearning for the civilization that he'd left behind.

This, however, did not help the fact that his feet hurt.

There would not be much need for recycled air here, perhaps; the air had been described to him by the captain as 'surprisingly breathable'. Still, he had to be taking in a hefty whack of gamma in such a shallow atmosphere, and he had no idea what temperature variations obtained here during the course of the local day and night. Right now, it was warm enough, but what might happen in a decidia's time?

After only a few hours' walk, during which time a worrying lack of vehicles passed him on the road, he began to see evidence of agriculture ahead. It was often difficult to tell a field from a wilderness on a red star world, but as the majority of systems were red star systems, Mr. Mountbanks' eyes had been forced to adjust over the years. What lay ahead looked like modified varieties of potato, being fed by UV filaments strung on frames across the

228

rows.

He saw the first marks almost immediately. Perhaps they had been hiding in the crops; they seemed to almost sprout out of the ground. There were four of them, two girls, two boys, dressed in Last Year's Fashion, The Fashion of Last Year But One, and The Fashion of Three Years Back. Somebody had already been hawking his wares here, and returning at regular intervals.

These marks were young, though not quite children. They would still be tried as juveniles in a state court if they committed murder, and this thought made Mr. Mountbanks wary. He kept his hand close to the multi-headed cat-o'-nine-tasers in his hip pocket. However, the youngsters seemed amiable enough, and made no attempt to circle round behind him.

He touched his hat and flipped open his briefcase. On cue, the intelligent window-dresser inside deployed, unfolding fascias, display pedestals, backdrops, and animated cartoon elves that capered among the merchandise. The whole thing was scarcely molecules thick, and would have blown away in even the tranquil air of Ararat, had it not been for the fact that it had suckered itself to the road surface. The display, when finally unfolded, surrounded him like a twinkling shrine to consumer satisfaction, discreetly electrified to discourage pilfering. The merchandise was lightweight, but technologically sophisticated—personality analogues, both blank and pre-recorded, and text readers containing all the best of state-approved condensed literature, each carrying the new 'Audited for Truth' seal of governmental approval. One reader might contain an entire library, appropriately cross-referenced and concordanced. Mr. Mountbanks now sold readers that identified Plato, Voltaire, and Thomas Paine as firm believers in centralizing executive power within a tightly-controlled unelected Permanent Revolutionary Committee. He also sold pornography, equally approved and audited, containing acceptable levels of uncontrolled conception and consensual violence.

Normally, the sight of the display unfolding would provoke indrawn gasps of wonderment among local yokels. The hard-eyed youth of Ararat showed not a flicker of a reaction.

"Good morning," he said.

"It's afternoon here," said a dark-haired, alabaster-skinned girl. "What do you have for sale?" Mr. Mountbanks, however, a veteran salesman, had seen her eyes flicker toward the personality analogues. For some reason, she was anxious not to appear anxious to buy one. Mr. Mountbanks encountered such behaviour often, though more often with customers who bought pornography.

"We have some very nice text readers," he said, "all the world's works of literature from Milton's *Social Harmony Lost* through Orwell's *Two Legs Better* to *The Great Work of Truth*."

"I have never heard of the latter title," said the girl.

"It's what they're calling the Bible, Koran and Torah nowadays," said Mr. Mountbanks. "I haven't read it in the new version." *Know your customer; these are backwoods hicks who, for all you know, might still worship an invisible god whose holy book still starts with* In the beginning, God created the Heaven and the Earth *rather than* In the first second, subatomic particles were formed.

"What are these?" said the girl, her attention moving almost accidentally on to the personality analogues.

"Why, they're personality analogues," said Mr. Mountbanks. "Very popular. Increasingly so in our modern enlightened times. These are the blanks, which allow you to make a recording of your loved one if, heaven forbid, you are apart for an extended or indefinite period. Over here, meanwhile, we have the more expensive extrapolator models—if a member of your family dies, and you have no personality imprint to remember them by, you can build one up by educating the extrapolator with base data. Of course, the longer you educate, the more accurate the analogue. We even have here a number of sample historical models, all suitable for tiny tots and vetted for political accuracy; the religious novelist Dan Brown, the noted Victorian censor Dr. Thomas Bowdler; the celebrated Roman Consul, Marcus Porcius Cato..."

"Why not Albert Einstein, Leonardo Da Vinci, or Marie Curie?" said the girl critically.

"Because it would violate the laws on machine intelligence," explained Mr. Mountbanks patiently.

"We will take," said the girl, "five blank recordings."

"For ten I will throw in Paris Hilton, Salome, Helen, and Delilah for free," said Mr. Mountbanks. "They all fit onto this one bijou recording. Much of the underlying subroutines are common."

The girl nodded. "We will take the additional novelty personalities."

"Are you interested, perhaps, in the works of First Citizen Vos? I have them here in compressed format. Parts of them now form a good deal of the revised state baccalaureate curriculum."

"Can we get First Citizen Vos as an extrapolated analogue?" said the girl, holding a potato up and biting into it.

"As I explained previously," said Mr. Mountbanks as he handed over the goods, "the creation of personality analogues of greater than or equal to human intelligence is forbidden by the Supplantation of Humanity laws."

"So, First Citizen Vos is of greater than or equal to human intelligence," said the girl, chewing indolently on her potato.

Mr. Mountbanks became exasperated. "Of course! The woman is a goddess! Don't you ever read newsfeeds?"

"But I thought," said the girl, "that First Citizen Vos stated in her Year Zero address to the Inner Cabinet that No Citizen Should Raise Himself Up Above Another?"

"Not *pridefully*, no, I'll grant you," said Mr. Mountbanks defensively. "But is it to her own personal detriment if a citizen's super-human talents are recognized by those about her?" He actually looked around him for the security camera. Of course, he would never have noticed one if one had been there.

The girl's credit came up good on the reader. *Extremely* good. Authorisation was made. Goods were handed over.

"You seem greatly enamoured of our First Citizen," said the girl. "Perhaps, then, given her supernormal qualities, we should save her genetic material and use it to better the next generation of humankind."

Mr. Mountbanks was sweating. "Yes! But, ah, alas, no, not insofar as that would align me with Made supremacists. An artificial human is an abomination against good government."

"Is it?" said the girl. "Why?"

Mr. Mountbanks pressed the STOW button angrily; his entire shop front collapsed inwards, folding itself back like a leatherette collapsar into his briefcase. One of the youths jumped back with a yelp as the closing surfaces bit and electrified his finger simultaneously.

Mr. Mountbanks slammed his briefcase shut, set his hat straight on his head, and raised it wordlessly.

"Leaving so soon?" said the girl. But Mr. Mountbanks did not reply, preferring instead to strike off in a huff into the distance. There was an emergency shelter at the landing field. By state regulation, it had to be stocked with food and water, and its insides had to be warm, dry and breathable.

"Those offworlders sure are funny," sniggered one of the boys.

"*I* wouldn't want to be an offworlder," said one of the girls.

"Not for all the Real Tea in Madagascar," said the second boy.

"There's no tea in Madagascar," said the lead girl. "Nor T in China and India neither. We have what we came for. It's home time."

"You're no fun, Beguiled."

"We could make crazy play with him before he gets to the shelter. I reckon that hat of his would go twenty metres if I threw it right."

"Rights of hospitality," said the dark-haired girl. "Duties of the host."

The other girl stamped her feet. "But that's a thing *mom* tells us!"

"And we agreed it was one of the truths we were happy believing. Like the Ten Commandments. It's home time, Only-Begotten."

"Not fair," muttered Only-Begotten, and stamped her feet. "Not FAIR!"

But when the dark-haired girl turned and began walking back in the direction of Third Landing, Only-Begotten followed her without question, and even tried to skirt past the others to walk alongside her.

"Easy, now! We don't want to compound the damage. Lift her up here, over the Bot Inspection Pit."

"She's leaking fluid...uh, what does the blue fluid do?"

"Her oxygen transport system, like our blood. Is it shooting out under pressure?"

"Not really. Is that bad?"

"No, good. Means her deep-level lines haven't been cut. She

can lose a lot of it too, these units usually have a deal of redundancy in the system. And her skin grows back too. That's one thing at least—she's designed to grow repeatedly—"

Mr. Reborn-in-Jesus looked up at Unity.

"But they don't make parts for her any more."

Unity's eyes brimmed with tears. Her best floral mood-sensitive dress had filled with patterns of yew and hyacinth. "Then we take her to a bot chop shop! We've had her for a whole kilodia! She's Beguiled's little sister!"

From her position hanging from four hoist points at pelvis and scapula, Visible Friend fluttered her eyes weakly open and said *"shwee' of you to shay"* before shivering into motionlessness again.

Mr. Suau, a walrus-moustached gentleman with a skin that had learned to tan from ice-white to burnt sienna depending on the star it was shown each week, patted Unity on the shoulder. "It's okay, child. Everyone who's ever owned a unit suffers from it. They're designed to look human. It's only reasonable to be conned into thinking they have a soul and feel pain..."

Visible Friend's eyes flickered open unobserved and glared down at Mr. Suau, then shuddered shut again.

"This is a respiration-powered unit," said Mr. Suau. "Also one designed to teach childcare to young girls by actually suffering heartbreaking personal injury if maltreated. The prognosis is not good. If she loses enough blue stuff she could shut down and die. She'd come back again, of course, but the original model's memories and learned algorithms would be wiped. Effectively, all that made it would be gone."

Unity stared up at the hanging automaton and began to sob. On her dress, the hyacinths bowed their heads and wilted.

"What about the anti-paedo dye?" said Testament. "He was

covered in it. Couldn't we use it to track him?"

Mr. Reborn-in-Jesus shook his head. "We tracked him as far as the uraninite decontam shed. He'd stood in the dipping trough and turned the hose on himself. It would have removed the dye, though it probably took the top layer of his skin with it. Lord knows the goats squeal when we hit them with it, though it's their fault for straying into yellowcake patches. We didn't find any more tracks, at least."

Testament blinked uncomprehendingly. "He'd be a walking dead man. The goats are engineered for easy cleaning in a radioactive environment. No man could stand the pain."

"Aye," said Mr. Reborn-in-Jesus. "If he is a man."

A cold lizard of doubt slithered down Testament's spine. Unity, too, was looking at her father in alarm. "What do you mean by that, pops?"

Mr. Reborn-in-Jesus shrugged. "Nothing." He rose to his feet, and stood in the doorway with his back to the others. "But no human being I know would turn a decontaminant hose on his own skin."

"Mr. Reborn-in-Jesus, all my automated personnel are accounted for," reproved Mr. Suau. "And apart from Visible Friend here and your domestic white goods and field tractor—all of which, just between us, would probably have displayed a markedly different *modus operandi*—they're the only bots on Ararat."

"Yes," said Mr. Reborn-in-Jesus. "I'm sure you're right." And left.

"Wash a pershon," came a soft voice from above.

Testament and Unity looked up.

"Wash a pershon," repeated the voice. *"Woulg ha' shenshed anovver got's transkonder."*

"Transponders can be removed," said Mr. Suau.

"Looked like a pershon," insisted the voice.

"In any case," said Mr. Suau, "we're going to make you better. As better," he qualified ominously, "as humanly possible. I'm going to rig you up an airtight bot coffin and fill it with pure oxygen." He looked at Unity and Testament severely. "It'll be a fire hazard, now."

"We can leave it in the Panic Cellar. There's an oxygen feed down there."

"Fang you Mishter Shuau."

"Not junked a good bot yet," said Mr. Suau. But Unity noticed that he had his fingers crossed.

A door banged elsewhere in the house.

"That'll be Beguiled, Uncleanness, and Sodom," said Unity. "They've been out towards the South Field."

Testament looked up sharply, still nursing the lump on his head. "Why didn't Beguiled take Visible Friend with her?"

"Testament, it's no fault of Beguiled that Friend got attacked," said Unity reprovingly.

"Vey woulgn'let me go wiv'em," came a soft voice from the ceiling.

Unity, Testament and Mr. Suau turned round to the robot.

"What did you say, Friend?" said Unity. Her dress was breaking out in angry red poppies.

"I coulgn'go," repeated the voice. *"Vey woulgn'let me shee wa' vey were doing."*

"Why not?" said Testament.

"I don'g know. Beguile'saig i' wash a shecret."

The door to the Bot Bay banged open.

"Unity! Testament!"

"Apostle met us at the edge of town with a gun! A real *gun!*"

"What's happened to Visible Friend?"

236

Unity turned to Beguiled, who had entered with her côterie. "She was caught on her own, without any of her brothers and sisters to protect her."

Unity left the room in a flurry of Flanders red.

Beguiled blinked. "What's the matter with *her*?"

Testament shrugged weakly.

"Ah, Visible Friend has been quite badly damaged," said Mr. Suau, clearing his throat. "By an unknown assailant who probably mistook her for a real girl, hence Apostle's gun."

Beguiled looked up at the bleeding android.

"Ah well," she said. "She was only a robot, after all."

She turned on her very-latest-fashion variable-height heels and departed. The fibre optic invisibility was wearing out on the shoes' arches; from an oblique angle, they looked like an old pair of farmers' boots.

"*Why woulg'she shay tha'?*" said the voice from the ceiling mournfully.

"Best shut down," said Mr. Suau, patting Visible Friend's head tenderly. "Don't make me go Kill Minus Nine on your ass, now."

The robot went limp. Mr. Suau looked across to the knot of concerned children and winked.

"Look away now. The main power converter access is in that place mommy told you to scream if a bad man ever touched you."

II.   two turtle doves

astor Mulchrone looked sternly over the Best Parlour table at Mr. and Mrs. Reborn-in-Jesus.

"If this continues," he said, "I will be unable to approve Mount Ararat as an educational centre for the young. Your children will be required to attend a state school on Celadon, Verdastelo Three, New New Earth, or Farquahar's World."

Shun-Company's eyes narrowed. "Those schools incorporate electric shock discipline, chemical aversion therapy, and subliminal messaging."

"Granted," nodded the Pastor, "but it is not all good. Regardless of the excellent disciplinary start in life such an institution would give your children, they would be separated from you. There would be emotional upheaval. This is normally not a step which I would take except in cases of delinquency. But if this continued counter-normal behaviour forces me to that pass—" he shrugged his shoulders.

"And this is," said Mr. Reborn-in-Jesus, wringing his hands nervously, "all simply because of a few Christmas decorations?"

"The decimalization of time," said the Pastor, "is one of the State's great achievements. My remit is to introduce it throughout the education system, from cradle to necro-waste recycling pod.

239

This adherence to an outmoded three-hundred-and-sixty-five-day solar sidereal festival only chains us to the past, to a world to which most of us no longer belong! For this reason, I have ordered the children to take down all Christmas decorations both in the schoolrooms and the wider settlement."

"Are earthbound people still allowed to celebrate Christmas?" said Shun-Company.

The Pastor threw his arms wide. "*You* can still celebrate Christmas! At its new official frequency, which is now once per kilodia."

"That puts the next occurrence of Christmas in," Mr. Reborn-in-Jesus calculated momentarily, "about two years' time."

"I'm sorry?" said the Pastor, capping his hand to his ear as if deaf.

Mr. Reborn-in-Jesus stared at the Pastor as if at a new and interesting variety of field pest. "Uh, that would be seven hundred dia."

"That's better," beamed the Pastor. "And the State realizes this! It is recognized that tiny tots are traumatized when a marvellous and magical festival is removed from them. It is for this reason that the State has created Leader Day, an ad hoc festival celebrating the birth of our great First Citizen, and set me to roaming the stars with my sack of Leader Day presents like a new improved decimal Santa Claus." He leaned close in his chair and took Shun-Company's hands, gazing earnestly into her eyes. "Mrs. R-in-J, I am the wind of progress. Let my wind blow through the cobwebs of this silly little house, and let it be breathed in deeply. Or," he said, straightening up and growing severe once more, "that mighty wind may blow Ararat's children far away from here."

"So if we get rid of the Christmas decorations," said Shun-Company, "you'll consider passing Mount Ararat as an educational establishment."

240

"The children are not adequately connecting with the idea of Leader Day," beamed the Pastor. "They are getting distracted. But if we took away a few angels, stars and baubles—"

"They will be removed," said Mr. Reborn-in-Jesus. Shun-Company shot him a look of alarm; he shook his head. "Removal of a festival where we hand out presents doesn't mean we stop worshipping God, and I personally choose to worship God by providing for my children's education."

The Pastor raised a finger. "Ah, but! There must also be no Church services on that date, no Holy Communion, no Advent, no Twelfth Night, no Christingle, no Kris Kringle."

Fault lines twisted in Mr. Reborn-in-Jesus's face, yet he said nothing.

Shun-Company put in: "And this would mean you'd be back in the schoolhouse tomorrow, would it?"

The Pastor shook his head, smiling in grim satisfaction. "Alas, no. I am currently observing the Sabbath, and will be leaving for my quarters on my ship shortly. However, the children will be welcome in school at three decidia tomorrow."

"That's in the middle of the night," observed Mr. Reborn-in-Jesus.

"Only on Ararat, Mr. R-in-J, only on Ararat! We must not be bound by the sidereal periods of the various dungballs on which we tumble across the void! And Three Decidia is the State handbook prescribed beginning of the school day."

"Which corresponds nicely to the rotational period of New Earth at the Capital meridian," said Mr. Reborn-in-Jesus. "The children have chores to do, Mr. Mulchrone, and I have crops to bring in. How is that going to happen if everyone's living in the hours of darkness?"

"Electric light, dear sir! Electric light! It's been in existence for some centuries, you know!"

"I need all the light I have for my crops. Power is at a premium here—"

Shun-Company kicked her husband violently under the table. "The children will be ready for you at three decidia tomorrow," she said.

The Pastor smiled serenely, rose to his feet, and departed.

Shun-Company looked across at Mr. Reborn-in-Jesus.

"What do you think we should do?" she said.

Mr. Reborn-in-Jesus folded his arms in disgruntlement.

"What I think we should do with him," he said, "is a sin to name."

Night was falling, and the shadows growing longer. At Third Landing, however, the process of nightfall could take up half the day.

As the Pastor left the Reborn-in-Jesus house, a stately structure of black clapboard deceptively surrounding a core of airtight steel, a gardener tipped a cap to him from the house across the street, and the Pastor bowed graciously in reply. The gardener, moving with arthritically painful slowness, returned its attention to cutting back a vigorous tree fern in the crook of the house's porch. Once the Pastor was out of range, however, it finished off the fern in a few rapid clips, too fast for the eye to see, and started work on the red engineered privet framing the fern on either side, this time without the assistance of clippers.

"DEVIL! DEVIL! COME, MEPHOSTOPHILIS!"

The gardener paused in the act of dismembering the hedge, its angstrom-thick fingernails de-blurring into visibility. Children were nearby. Incautious rapid movement might lop off a tiny limb.

The Devil turned, its gardening hat aslant on its horns, wearing

242

the special gardening face the children had made it out of papier mâché. There were four children. One of them, a black-haired girl, came forward.

"Devil! Your face is loose. If anyone sees you in such a state they'll know you're no old gardener but a partially self-aware killing machine. How *do* you get into such a mess. I'll fix it."

She reached up behind the Devil's purely ornamental ears and fiddled with the string that held the face in place. Meanwhile, other children circled round behind the Devil, knocking on its tin tubes of legs, playing with its tail.

A boy jumped on the Devil's back. "PLAY PIGGYBACK FOR ME, DEVIL!" The Devil only just managed to retract its claws and catch him in time. The boy began yelling incoherent sentences about riding cock horses to Banbury cross, and at that moment, a small hand slipped a jack into a socket and the Devil stood silent, staring at the world.

The children wriggled free and stepped back to a safe distance.

"How long will it take to take?" said Be-Not-Near-Unto-Man-in-thy-Time-of-Uncleanness.

"Should happen pretty much instantly," said Beguiled.

"Beguiled," said Uncleanness, "I'm afraid."

"I'm more afraid than you are," said Beguiled. "It's *me* in there, and I know how bad I am." She slipped her hand into her foster-sister's.

The Devil was turning its hands over, examining them minutely, as if surprised that it was made of metal. The Personality Analogue was now taped firmly to its right shoulder.

"It shouldn't be surprised," said Beguiled. "I only made the imprint an hour ago. It knows the plan. It should know exactly what body it's in."

The robot's head jerked upwards. A long clawed finger pointed out Beguiled.

"YOU," it said. "WHAT LANGUAGE DO YOU SPEAK?" It recoiled. "WHAT LANGUAGE AM *I* SPEAKING? THIS IS NOT GREEK."

"What's it saying, Beguiled?" said Uncleanness. "Why is it talking all old?"

"Uh, Beguiled," said Pitch-Not-Thy-Tent-Towards-Sodom, shuffling through a stack of imprint slivers, "I've still got the imprint you made of yourself right here."

"Ohhh *shit*," said Beguiled.

"WHERE IS THIS PLACE? IS THIS THE DREAD DOMAIN OF HADES? WHAT AM I BECOME? I, WHO WAS ONCE ACCOUNTED BEAUTIFUL?" The robot, its voice like that of a grown woman, deep and aristocratic, cast about to right and left like a questing hound.

"It must be one of the novelty imprints," said Beguiled. "One of the fancy ones the man gave us for free. Sodom, you *idiot.*"

"They're not labelled clearly," whined Sodom. "And yours isn't labelled at *all.*"

"Damn right it ain't, if Uncle Anchorite gets hold of it I'm one dead niece." Beguiled thought further on the matter. "We are *all* dead *persons.*"

The robot turned and sprinted to the edge of the Pond, leaving scars in the earth where its feet had moved in a blur. It dropped like a falling guillotine blade onto the bank, staring down with whatever senses it possessed into the ripples.

"I HAVE NO REFLECTION," it mourned. "I AM A SHADE."

"No," said Uncleanness, coming up behind it gently. "It's just that you can only see by radar."

"Let's see," said Beguiled, taking the stack of imprint jiggers from Sodom. "What did he give us for free? Uh, ma'am? Are you

Paris?"

The robot turned like a whirlwind. "NO I AM NOT PARIS! AND IF THIS IS HELL, YOU ARE AS DEAD AS I, AND JOKING ILL BECOMES THE DAMNED! HAVE YOU SEEN PARIS? I DEMAND THAT YOU TAKE ME TO HIM!"

Beguiled pulled out a data sliver. "Uh, I have Paris right here, ma'am."

The robot slammed a claw into the data pack, sending it scattering into the dirt. Beguiled yelped and sucked her finger, in which an inch-long gash had opened. "IDIOT GIRL! I WOULD KILL YOU WERE YOU PROPERLY ALIVE! WHERE IS MY HUSBAND!"

"We don't know who your husband is!" screeched Uncleanness, now in tears. Sodom moved himself in front of his foster-sister. "Ma'am, if you will simply tell us who your husband is, we will gladly attempt to find him for you—"

The claw moved again, too rapidly to react to. Beguiled did not see a wound open in Sodom, but saw him slowly crumple, hugging his chest.

"KNEEL BEFORE ME, EVEN IN HELL!" shrieked the creature. "I AM THE CONSORT OF A KING! I, WHO AM THE GIFT TO MANKIND OF APHRODITE!"

"I'm pretty sure she *is* Paris Hilton," said Judge-Not-Lest-Thou-Also-Be-Judged. "We covered her in the History of the Moral Collapse."

"IS TROY THEN FALLEN?" said the creature. "SO BE IT! THEN I WILL REIGN IN HELL! FOR HALF THE YEAR HELL HAS NO QUEEN. I WILL SIT BY HADES' SIDE ALL SUMMER, AND WHEN PERSEPHONE RETURNS IN THE AUTUMN SHE WILL FIND HER KING APT TO OVERLOOK THE ENTIRE POMEGRANATE." The robot turned its eyeless gaze on Beguiled. "YOU, CHILD! WHERE IS HE WHO REIGNS HERE?"

Beguiled lowered her eyes and curtseyed decorously.

"I will give you accurate directions, Your Majesty. I am sure he will be most glad to see you."

Mr. Mountbanks was impatient. It had been a long time since he had eaten, drunk or slept. The gentleman who had met him on the road had claimed to have a ship at the field—possibly the small government runabout he'd seen in the parking area when he'd disembarked. The gentleman, wearing a priest's dog collar, had promised him food, drink and rest in return for what he'd described as 'the simple pleasure of his company'. Mr. Mountbanks had suspected from the glint in the gentleman's eye that this simple pleasure might become complicated, but for now food was food, and a bed a bed.

The gentleman's rover was in reasonable condition, though poorly shielded against fines; the interior smelled like wet rust. The chassis and windows all bore Bureau of Safety shields of approval, so he was safer from cosmic radiation than the barefoot urchins scampering about Third Landing's handful of streets all about the car. There was even an in-rover entertainment centre which, when Mr. Mountbanks had activated it, had intoned "BREATHE IN; BREATHE OUT. STAY ROOTED AS A TREE. YOU ARE AS A MOUNTAIN, IMMOVABLE. YOUR WILL WILL PREVAIL." The car's cargo compartment was packed with what the gentleman had described as 'Leader Day presents'—miniscule holographic snowstorms of Leader Vos and Leader Vos's husband, children and elderly labrador waving from Leader Vos's window. The snowstorms seemed to be mutually interactive; in two of the globes which had accidentally touched glass, the Leader in one globe was explaining her theory of political dialectic to the Leader

246

in the other, who was nodding sagely.

The gentleman had said he had a momentary discussion to pursue with the inhabitants of the house, who might conceivably be the parents of the juvenile delinquent horrors he'd met on the road earlier. So far the momentary discussion had lasted an hour. Mr. Mountbanks wondered if the rover had an onboard urine recycling facility, and if anyone would notice him plugging himself into the dashboard.

With the local sun on his back, not warm in itself, but adding warmth to the already overheated interior of the rover, Mr. Mountbanks dozed.

He was awoken by the horrible death of the gentleman who had met him on the road.

The car's collision alarm sounded violently, shaking him out of wild dreams of avarice. Something was being slammed repeatedly against the headlight cowling. It was when the wiper blades, factory set to automatic start, began painstakingly removing large amounts of blood from the windscreen that Mr. Mountbanks sat up in alarm. A glittering isoceles blade rose in the air, stabbing repeatedly down at a squirming gurgling figure slumped against the front of the car.

The figure's face was that of his host.

Mr. Mountbanks sensibly elected to remain in the car. Close to his right hand was a large, obvious control marked LOCKING. He slammed the heel of his palm down on it and heard the welcome clunk of the car's single airlock dogging shut.

The figure holding the blade towered over the car. Mr. Mountbanks had not believed an unmodified human being could grow so large. Surely, however, even so huge a creature could not easily punch through a Bureau-of-Safety-approved windshield?

It was wearing a red velvet cap trimmed with white fur. The cap did not fit it.

It was also rummaging in the priest's pockets. As the priest struggled feebly, thinking himself under renewed assault, the attacker irritably finished him off, twisting his neck nonchalantly back on itself. Then, he triumphantly fished out a single octagonal key and turned his attention undividedly on Mr. Mountbanks.

Although Mr. Mountbanks was inside the rover, he realized he did not have a key to start it. Was there a spare inside the vehicle? He searched frantically through the usual obvious places—under the dead man's handle, on top of the HUD projector pod—but found nothing. And the airlock door was opening.

Mr. Mountbanks scrabbled frantically and belatedly for the release on the four-point safety belt, only to feel dizzy and light-headed as blood started pouring unaccountably from his neck. The windscreen wipers failed dismally to remove it from the glass; he felt the curious sensation of his own head turning through one hundred and eighty degrees, heard the car's media system enjoining him to Breathe In, Breathe Out, and Stay Rooted As A Tree, and then he neither heard nor felt anything ever again.

The rover arrowed into the distance at the head of a plume of fines. Testament stood facing his father, mother, and sister and Mr. Suau across two comprehensively dead bodies.

"Well," said Mr. Reborn-in-Jesus, "at least we don't have to worry about how to celebrate Christmas now."

"Hernan!" reproved his wife.

"I only meant to say it's an ill wind. Perhaps he ran into Saint Nicholas."

"No saint of any god did that," said Mrs. Reborn-in-Jesus, "and I can hardly believe any man did either. The poor men's necks are snapped completely. The Educational Uniformity Bureau will play merry hell. You *know* how government departments hate it when their men are sent here and die mysteriously."

"Who is the other one?" said Mr. Reborn-in-Jesus. "I don't recognize him. Could there have been another escape from the Penitentiary? It let three of its prisoners out last year, after all."

"But they all escaped on Mr. Armitage's ship," said Mrs. Reborn-in-Jesus, as if begging her family to agree with her.

"The Anchorite did for one of them," said Mr. Reborn-in-Jesus. "'Postle told us as much, and the hermit hasn't denied it."

"There were three escapees," said Testament. "The Warden was looking for all three for weeks. And the sort of folk who get lodged in government penitentiaries don't mix well. The odds against two of them working together to escape are long."

"You think there's another still at large," said Mr. Reborn-in-Jesus.

"Someone's been living in berth four of *Render Unto Caesar*. For quite a while."

"Why didn't you tell us?" said Mrs. Reborn-in-Jesus, shocked.

Testament shrugged. "I figured it was one of the young uns. I caught 'em in the shuttle not two days ago, playing some damn fool game." He was retracing dusty footprints across the way—very *large* footprints, leading inexorably out from the churned and blooded soil near where the EVA rover had stood, back to the dipping pen.

"Oh, lord," he said, standing still in shock. "Oh my."

"What is it, Testament?"

"Oh, you noddy, you prize-winning plank. I tracked him to the dipping shed here, and thought that just because he'd turned the hose on he'd swilled himself down and run away with half his skin dissolving. I remember thinking at the time no normal human being would ever do such a thing, and I was right, because he didn't. He just gulled *me* into thinking he had. He must have been hanging there in the dark above me in the dipping shed right there and then. Oh, law, but he's clever. He's been in there hidden among us a whole day."

Mrs. Reborn-in-Jesus ate her fist in fright. Mr. Reborn-in-Jesus comforted her with a hand.

"But why would any man creep out and start murdering folk again when he knows he'll just set the law back on him?" said Unity.

Testament shrugged. "A vehicle turned up ripe for stealing."

"And he isn't a normal human being anyway," said Mr. Reborn-in-Jesus. "Otherwise he wouldn't have been in the Penitentiary in the first place."

"If he's a human being at all," said Shun-Company bitterly. "And not a devil."

"I do hope not," said a voice from the dark.

Mr. Reborn-in-Jesus did not even turn.

"Evening, your hermitship."

The Anchorite was hardly visible against the dark side of the house. Perhaps he had been there all the time. "I have lost contact with my servo unit. It was last in the company of Beguiled, Sodom, Judge-Not, and Uncleanness, since when it does not even respond to positional pinging."

Shun-Company threw the Anchorite a look that would have killed a lesser man. "My babies! Where are my children?" She pulled up her skirts, produced a field laser, and slapped an argon oxide clip into it.

The Anchorite frowned at the emission end of the weapon,

which was currently emitting a dull red target-painting glow, as was the centre of his own chest. There had been a glut of infantry weapons on Ararat since the defeat of the Tax Pirates the previous year; more weapons, it had to be said, than was strictly necessary for arable farming.

"Speaking exactly, madam, I believe Beguiled, Sodom, Judge-Not and Uncleanness are not your children. Have you not noticed that two distinct social subsets seem to be forming in your family? Beguiled *et al* are not your biological children; Day-of-Creation, Measure, Zounds, Apostle, Magus, Testament, and Unity are. The two camps hardly ever seem to interact nowadays."

"It's true," admitted Testament. "Mother, you're threatening Uncle Anchorite with a loaded weapon."

"He's no uncle of yours," said Shun-Company.

"Nor is Beguiled a daughter of yours," said the Anchorite gravely, with his hands up high, "though you treat her as such. Are you sure, however, that those feelings are requited? I have noticed some strange behaviour of late."

The weapon was shaking in Shun-Company's hands. The beam it projected would make a man's midriff into a cloud of steam. "If you have harmed any of my children—"

"Put the gun down, Mother," said Mr. Reborn-in-Jesus.

"Madam," said the Anchorite, "I have only ever intervened to *save* the lives of your children."

Mr. Reborn-in-Jesus cleared his throat. "Is it possible that the device is malfunctioning in some way?"

"Possible," nodded the Anchorite, "though it's almost unheard-of for a servo robot to malfunction by slaughtering children. Usually they walk round in circles, or leak lubricant. I fear that I detect the hand of man at work here. I am sorry I was not on hand to help when Visible Friend was attacked. I was digging in my garden."

"The garden at the centre of the world," said Mr. Reborn-in-Jesus.

"That same garden, yes. It's not dead centre, however; merely a few kilometres down." The Anchorite strode around the bodies, inspecting them professionally. "It's messy work. Mind you, an attacker would have to be terribly strong to inflict such wounds with an ordinary kitchen knife."

"How do you know it was an ordinary kitchen knife?" said Mrs. Reborn-in-Jesus suspiciously. Her weapon, however, had risen slightly from the hermit's midriff.

"I keep an inventory of all your sharp objects," said the Anchorite. "You have nothing sharper than carving knives, of which you have five, four in the kitchen area, one in the utility room...now, as far as any surveillance is concerned, this vehicle was stood here for over half an hour without incident before the attack happened. What made our man suddenly move to the attack?"

Testament shrugged. "He was observing his target."

"An admirable activity," said the Anchorite, "but hardly one which fits such a frenzied assault. It was not the car he was after. Had it been, he could have taken the keys from such a flabby being as the Pastor with a mere show of the knife and driven away. This man or, ahem, woman, is driven by a need to kill, as violently as possible. For that reason, the car currently driving away is empty."

"Empty?" Testament blinked in consternation. "But he stole it!"

The Anchorite shook his head. "He is a predator, and a predator stays with the game. If he stole the vehicle, where would he go? To the landing field, where no vessel touches down without your permission? And is he even aware the South End Spa exists?

No, he is still here, and the car was set to automatic drive to confuse us. I will send eyes out in that direction and confirm that suspicion. You have been hoodwinked twice, young master Reborn-in-Jesus." The hermit looked up at Shun-Company. "Are all your children safe indoors?"

Shun-Company nodded. "All in the Panic Cellar," she inhaled defiantly, "apart from Beguiled, Sodom, Uncleanness and Judge-Not. Zounds and Postle are out looking for them."

"Armed, I trust?" said the Anchorite.

"Extensively," said Shun-Company, maintaining her grip on the laser.

"That's what I was afraid of. Zounds and Postle are far more likely to shoot each other by accident. I will find your lost children, even if they do not," said the Anchorite. He kicked the whitewashed wall of the dipping pen. "Have you any idea what this means?"

In Mr. Mountbanks and Pastor Mulchrone's last few litres of blood, someone had written, on the wall: SECOND DAY, TWO TURTLE DOVES.

Mr. Reborn-in-Jesus spoke automatically. "It's the second day of Christmas."

"No it isn't," said Postle in confusion. "It's not Christmas for fourteen days yet."

"Arkarch Allion regarded the Gregorian Calendar as a sinful modern invention," said Mr. Reborn-in-Jesus. "Hence, we on Ararat use the Julian. On Earth and New Earth and New New Earth, it is Christmas and has been for two days."

"More precisely," said the Anchorite, "it became the second day of Christmas on Earth at almost the precise minute these two men were murdered. If you recall the song, the number of items donated by the singer's obsessively generous true love increases

253

by one per day. On those figures, Third Landing will be empty of life by," he calculated silently on his fingers, "six geese a-laying. And only around thirty people would be left on Ararat come twelve lords a-leaping."

"There was a 'Christmas, Father' in the list of Penitentiary escapees," said Testament. "The Warden said so when it visited."

Shun-Company nodded, grinding her teeth. "A paranoid schizophrenic whose original name was Casey Michael Bowker. Until the age of two, his condition was recognized by doctors, who prescribed drugs which his parents administered. At the time of the War of Liberation, a series of tactical nuclear strikes was made on the New Earth planetary transport infrastructure, cutting off the area his family lived in. There were food riots, and I believe also power riots, drug riots, and sex riots. His father and mother were killed over the twelve days of Christmas in Kilodia Zero. All three of them were raped repeatedly in front of one another. At the same time as this was happening, of course, he suffered withdrawal of his schizophrenic medication. It is not known how he survived. Following the glorious liberation from dictatorial oppression, Bowker changed his name to Father Nicholas Christmas by deed poll. He killed two hundred and thirty-four people during the period from Kilodia Zero to Kilodia One in the city of Spender's Delight on New Earth."

Unity spoke up sharply. "Two hundred and thirty-four is three times seventy-eight."

Testament looked blankly at his sister. "So?"

"Seventy-eight is twelve times twelve-plus-one, over two," explained Unity meekly. "He killed all the way up to his twelve-day limit, three old-school years running."

Shun-Company toyed with the safety catch on her weapon. "The local Public Safety officers found it difficult to catch him, as

254

each attack was planned meticulously. His killings were predictable in that they always occurred on the same twelve days every year; otherwise, they followed no pattern whatsoever. They also only happened once a terrestrial year, making them difficult to investigate. Eventually, Christmas was caught by the efforts of one Rajinder Rai, Safety Officer First Class, who was killed in the process of capture."

"How do *you* know all this?" said Mr. Reborn-in-Jesus.

"I sent a Request For Information in to the sub-datastack on Celadon," said Shun-Company. "I apologize for the expense, husband, but I like to know what threats might affect my family." She glared meaningfully at the Anchorite. "Of the other escapees, I am informed Mr. Voight is accounted for—"

The Anchorite bowed curtly. "If he were not so, we would not be speaking now."

"—which leaves only Carneiro Pave, who possesses an interstellar master's licence, first class, on sixteen different categories of military and civilian vessel—"

The Anchorite's face had drained of colour. "Carneiro Pave? Pardon me, dear madam; did you say *Carneiro* Pave?"

"Just so. I would submit that the courier vessel that escaped so daringly from the South End Field could only have been flown by an exceptional military pilot. Mr. Christmas, meanwhile, holds no astronavigation licence in *any* class—"

"Yelena Carneiro," murmured the Anchorite. "I did not bother to check the names of the escapees, only their charge sheets and danger assessments. What a fool! Of course, it could only have been Yelena. All this time, she was here! Warmed by the same sun as I!"

"I do apologize," said Shun-Company, "for suspecting your servant."

"I am afraid I still do not know the precise whereabouts of my servant," said the Anchorite regretfully.

"What is its make and model?" said Mr. Suau.

"It has many common components with both the Instar Clever Hands 303a AutoValet and the Stalin Seven Heavy Assault Combot," said the Anchorite cagily.

"I am not familiar with any such model," said Mr. Suau, "though I am qualified to maintain the Stalin Six. In the event of total systems failure, the transponder should return a clear code zero response to all requests. If you are receiving nothing at all, that means the transponder is not functioning, which means that either the entire unit has been destroyed—which is unlikely, given that we would have felt the blast wave of any weapon capable of such a thing—or that the transponder has been deliberately disabled."

"Beguiled," said Testament with feeling.

"Not necessarily," insisted Shun-Company. "Christmas could have disabled it."

"Uh, unfortunately, I did instruct young Beguiled on the ins and outs of transponder maintenance only a few days ago," admitted Mr. Suau. "I was repairing one of the old Adams in the repair shop up at the Spa, and she, uh, began asking questions. I figured it would do no harm to let her know how criminals frigged a system, given that there is no crime here."

"There is now," said Unity.

"There are few things that worry me more than a Stalin Six walking around my home town," mused Mr. Suau, "though the thought that that Stalin Six was controlled by a nineteen-year-old girl would be one of them." He thought a moment longer. "Does it have the rotating ten-calibre variable munition cannon?"

"No."

"The over-horizon semi-autonomous antivehicular drone mine?"

"The OHSAADM? No. It got in the way of the vacuum cleaner attachment."

"The Brilliant Javelin area-effect pulse laser system?"

The Anchorite shook his head. Mr. Suau relaxed visibly.

Beside the corpse lay a black carryall, its lock popped open by the shock of the fall. Mr. Reborn-in-Jesus bent to pick it up.

"NO, DON'T—" shouted Mr. Suau and the Anchorite simultaneously. Mr. Reborn-in-Jesus' hand froze a millimetre from the case.

"This is a case left as if by accident by a fiendishly cunning multiple murderer," said the Anchorite. "Such things are not to be touched lightly."

Mr. Suau brought out a pocket robocontroller. "Allow me. Let us attempt to pick up a control signal...I believe you have a domestic drain clearance pigbot on the site somewhere...aha!"

"We do?" The Reborn-in-Jesuses looked at one another in bemusement.

"They come with all modern prefabricated hab units...nowadays, even out here, you're never more than ten metres from a robot."

Not more than ten metres away, a drain cover popped open, and an ordure-covered appliance swarmed out on multiple metal legs, crossed the Main Street under Mr. Suau's control, and scuttled up to the case, extruding telescopic feelers.

"Please step back," said Mr. Suau.

Everybody dutifully took one step back.

"I doubt this precaution is necessary," said the Anchorite. "Our man is, after all, driven to kill a precise number of people per day. He should therefore avoid killing *more* than that number per day, and should therefore lie dormant for the next twenty-four hours, at which point he will attempt to slaughter three more people, one for every French Hen. But it pays to take no chances."

"Precisely," said Mr. Suau. He operated a control, and the drainbot lightly charged the carryall with one of its snailhorn antennae. Like a window-dresser's hand grenade, the suitcase righted itself and expanded in a flurry of velvetoid and crystallique into a glittering commercial display larger than a grown man.

"Bric-a-brac," commented the Anchorite disdainfully. "A tramp salesman. Personality analogues and such."

"Some of which," said Mr. Suau, "have been recently sold, or stolen. There are gaps in the display. Someone took an analogue redactor off this man. Does your unit have a controller jack?"

"Holy spirit up the Mother Mary's sainted vagina," breathed the Anchorite in shock. "Sorry," he said, observing Mr. and Mrs. Reborn-in-Jesus's mortified stares. "What else is missing?" he asked.

Mr. Suau checked the price labels. "A number of analogue blanks," he said, "plus four novelty personalities including Salome, Delilah, Paris Hilton..."

"He recorded his own personality," said the Anchorite firmly. "He's taken control of the unit."

"It takes several hours to download a personality," said Mr. Suau. "I doubt he's had time."

"In which case, the machine is currently running on one of the pre-recorded analogues, and will be until Christmas has had time to record himself," said the Anchorite. "He has a choice of four personalities, all of which were on this one recording." He took the memory module from Mr. Suau. "You have an analogue recorder, I believe. We might profitably interrogate all four personalities to obtain a clue as to where the unit might be headed. I

258

have my own surveillance drones, but they are seldom deployed in the immediate vicinity of the robot, as the robot itself possesses a pair of eyes."

Mr. Suau trawled around inside the sales display. "I believe I may have found something even more useful. An extrapolated rendering of the personality of one Safety Officer Rajinder Rai."

"If any man can catch him," said Mr. Reborn-in-Jesus, "it ought to be the man who, uh, caught him. We have another reader in the house; I will take the recording there."

The Anchorite nodded. "And if your lady wife does not shoot me in the next ten seconds, I will direct my remote eyes to find Mr. Christmas and my lost robot."

Grudgingly, Shun-Company at last raised the weapon. All three Reborn-in-Jesus ribcages standing round the village square sagged visibly with the release of prolonged tension.

"I will do likewise," said Mr. Suau.

"We must all move in twos from now on," said the Anchorite. "And armed. Do not shoot at anything that moves, however; it might be one of your dearest relatives. Instead, move slowly and with sufficient caution not to need to react quickly. Unity, go with your father. Testament, accompany Mr. Suau."

"Am I to accompany you?" said Shun-Company sardonically.

"I am full enough of surprises," said the hermit, "to travel alone."

Mr. Trapp dozed happy in his sleeping bag. The sarcophagus was cool and roomy. Mucked out by the Anchorite's faceless ancillary, its marble walls were clean and smooth as the insides of the thighs of a virgin girl. The crypt was the size of many churches. There was room for him to run, turn cartwheels, and play ball. He had been loaned a ball, at his request, by Day-of-Creation, and the simple pleasure of throwing it and watching it travel a whole twenty metres before bouncing back to him was far, far better than sex.

He was aware that he badly needed to adjust to life outside the Penitentiary.

There was a chemical toilet in the corner of his new, larger prison, and food appeared daily on the flat whited sepulchre of Alessandra and Marlon Raffaele (Beloved Mother and Father to Beguiled-of-the-Serpent, Blessed Martyrs of the New Jerusalem), left there by unseen metal hands. The Reborn-in-Jesuses looked likely to keep their word, and he had been promised that the boy Magus's starship—purchased with Mr. Trapp's own money, after all—would arrive directly to take him to whatever world he wished. He hoped fervently that it would arrive before the Penitentiary came to the conclusion it had been psychoanalyzed with malice aforethought.

He also hoped the lights in the ceiling did not fail. It would be unpleasant to have to find the toilet in the dark. He had been brought here on the shoulders of the hermit's terrifying personal servant, under strict instructions not to spit on, urinate on, or touch the tunnel walls and thereby leave DNA traces. The darkness had been complete; he was entirely certain he had no hope of finding his way back through the catacombs to the outside world.

And now, he could hear the scrape of footsteps on gravel, and occasional curses as heads banged on unseen ceilings. Somebody—somebody evidently human—was approaching. The Reborn-in-Jesus children were aware of his location, but had been instructed on pain of maternal disapproval, a fate far worse than death, not to visit him here.

Torchlight was bouncing off the walls out of one of the almost invisible cracks, spilling into the catacombs at the far end of the chamber. Eventually, the same torchlight projected a massive, infernal shadow across the images of beatific saints on the far wall. Whoever was approaching, they were bringing the Anchorite's robot with them.

Mr. Trapp eased himself out of his sleeping bag to receive his guests.

"Good evening-or-morning," he said. "Has young Mr. Magus's ship come in early?"

Something about the carriage of the robot, the way it now held its head and arms, alarmed him. He was even more alarmed when it spoke.

"BE SILENT, SHADE, OR I WILL INVENT A TORMENT FOR YOU MORE EXTREME EVEN THAN SIMPLY BEING IN HELL."

Behind the robot, Beguiled spoke. "This is the, uh, shade I spoke about, mistress. The gates of Lord Hades' domain are protected by cunning devices that attack the hands of the incautious. This shade was formerly a man of cunning in the world above. He possesses the knowledge to circumvent Hades' portals."

"WHAT OF CERBERUS?" said the robot. "I WOULD HAVE THOUGHT A MONSTROUS THREE-HEADED HOUND TO BE PROTECTION ENOUGH FOR ANY HOUSEHOLD."

"There have been, uh, incidents," said Beguiled. Two more Reborn-in-Jesus children, who Mr. Trapp believed were called Uncleanness and Sodom, stood behind her. "Involving a certain Hercules, and on other occasions Orpheus, Hermes, Psyche and the Cumaean Sibyl. Cerberus is, as a result, not considered sufficient protection as a stand-alone system."

"IN THAT CASE," said the robot, "YOU WILL, VILE SHADE, OPEN THE DOORS TO LORD HADES' HOUSE FOR YOUR NEW QUEEN, OR

SUFFER HER WRATH."

He realized all of a sudden what was strange about the robot. Its steps had shortened, and its pelvis was now thrust forward to better display its chest unit. Its hands were held close by its side. It was walking like a woman.

Beguiled mouthed frantically at Mr. Trapp: DON'T SUFFER HER WRATH.

Mr. Trapp nodded, then reconsidered his actions and bowed. "Majesty," he said, "this would be the Astro Standard Bulkhead Pressure Door someone has attempted to conceal under a stack of blank gravestones at the far end of this chamber, would it?"

Beguiled blinked in surprise; Mr. Trapp smirked in satisfaction.

"I will require tools," he said.

Mr. Reborn-in-Jesus peered out through the net curtains at the darkened street. The house doors and windows were all secure, and the Panic Cellar still sealed, but the talent displayed by Mr. Christmas for repeatedly locating and slaying victims right under the gunsights of armed retribution made him paranoid.

"Keep your eyes on the doors and windows," he said. "Only I need to watch the display. I will put the analogues on audio. Which do we want first?" He connected the reader to the house media system and opened the record tray.

Mrs. Reborn-in-Jesus sat staring hawklike out of the window. "Safety Officer Rai."

"Very well." The record was swallowed up by the apparatus.

A face, two metres tall, appeared on the media wall, looking concerned, startled, and slightly sad.

"I'm dead," said a quiet voice, from the speakers, "aren't I".

Mr. Reborn-in-Jesus nodded. No point in starting off on the

wrong foot. "You're a personality analogue. Extrapolated, I'm afraid, not recorded."

"Did I get him?" said the speakers.

"Yes," said Mr. Reborn-in-Jesus. "Though not before he got you. You were killed bringing him in."

"Bummer," said the speaker. *"Which one was he?"*

"Casey Michael Bowker," said Shun-Company, without looking round. "You interviewed him five times."

The mouth of the face on the screen formed a silent *o*. *"Yes. I suppose that makes sense. I was only just there, in fact. He was a ninety per cent profile match. I interviewed a lot of people five times, you see. Some of them seven or eight times, even. I'd just gone to his home to interview him, and he'd invited me in to his lounge and given me a drink, and—"*

The face stopped, reconsidered, and said: *"That was when he killed me, wasn't it."*

"You weren't to know," said Shun-Company. "It was the first time he'd used poison."

"I should have been on my guard. His creativity was amazing; he had no single modus operandi. *Many of my colleagues still believed he was two hundred and forty-four different murderers."*

"We have a problem with Casey Bowker," said Mr. Reborn-in-Jesus. "He has absconded from Penitentiary. We are on a twenty-kilometre-diameter moonlet with anomalous surface gravity and breathable atmosphere. The population is one hundred and eight, most of whom live in a walled curative facility in the southern hemisphere. You are currently in Third Landing, population seventeen, in the northern hemisphere, where the Penitentiary is. The landing field is on the equator."

The CGI face pursed its lips in thought. *"I understand your concern. But there's no need to worry till the 25th of December—"*

"It's the 26th of December."

"I'm sorry for your loss. That means he's killed between one and three already."

"He's killed three."

"One good thing is that he won't use indiscriminate booby traps of any kind. He has to notch up his precise daily kill total, no more, no less. In Year Zero, he walked into a bar in Delight, shot a precise three people dead, and walked out again leaving all the other customers alive and free to dob him in to the filth."

"Where will he go now?" said Mr. Reborn-in-Jesus, wondering what dobbing into the filth involved.

"Nowhere," said the speakers. "He will try to trick you into thinking he has left the area, whilst remaining almost in plain sight. One of his few weaknesses is that he invests so much time in reconnoitring a killing ground that he is tempted to re-use it. He won't go back to it immediately, though—he'll usually leave a gap of a day or so, sometimes even a year." The face paused in thought. "One major difference here is that he's never been put in a situation before where there's been a shortage of potential victims. His past history, by comparison, is one of being surrounded by meat on the hoof, so to speak. And he will have seen that you're armed. Those are assault weapons, aren't they?"

"Sure are. Big fat old assault weapons." Shun-Company swept an invisible practice bead across the street, observing its progress through the sights.

"Uh, in which case, he may well make a decision to switch sites regardless. More victims in the south, probably more places to hide too, and the local population won't be as watchful. He'll plan his breakout from here carefully; obsessively, even. He's used to a heavily-surveilled society."

"So we should warn the people at the South End?"

The face was incredulous. *"Have you not done so already?"*

Mr. Reborn-in-Jesus squirmed. "It's just that the South End clinic's clients tend to be wealthy and litigious, and the clinic's proximity to a maximum security penal establishment was, uh, not advertised in the brochure."

"They'll be a damn sight more litigious if they're dead. Trust me, I'm dead myself, I know. Warn them. Warn them now. Does your clinic have security? Armed security?"

"Yes."

"Tell them to double up and ensure no-one, staff or patient, strays out of their sight. Also, tell them the whole deal. They must know they have up to a twenty-four-hour safe period after each time he kills his fill. He psychologically cannot kill in that period, because of his self-imposed limit. They could split up and search for him stark naked and he wouldn't lift a finger to kill them."

"He will to hurt them, though," said Shun-Company, without taking her eyes off the window. "That was how he killed you."

The face on the screen swallowed uncomfortably. *"Oh. I see."*

"You see, he had no ideological problem with hurting you to *within an ace of* death. He shot you in the stomach with a gas weapon improvised from a vehicular shock absorber, then hacked off all four of your limbs. You then died of shock about eighteen hours too early, as he'd already killed his quota for that day. By the time the rest of your team arrived, he was kneeling on top of your corpse apologizing frantically and trying to apply cardiac massage."

The face attempted briefly to keep its composure, then spluttered into laughter. *"I'm sorry, it shouldn't be funny, it really shouldn't."* Mr. Reborn-in-Jesus noticed his wife smirking over her rifle. Rai's expression changed suddenly from one of mirth to one of panic. *"Were my family well provided for?"*

"Government death-in-service insurance payments have made them very comfortable."

The face relaxed. *"That's good. But you should warn your people. Warn them now."*

Mr. Reborn-in-Jesus nodded. "We will. We have a requirement to switch you off for a moment now. Don't worry, you'll be back."

The face smiled sadly. *"That's what everyone always says to analogues, isn't it? Because being turned off is so like death, and no-one wants to tell someone else they're going to kill them."*

"We need to load another analogue into the machine," said Mr. Reborn-in-Jesus. "The situation is complicated."

"How so?" said Rai. *"You really should give me all the information you have."*

"We believe," said Mr. Reborn-in-Jesus, "that Bowker has taken partial control of a military antipersonnel robot, and is recording his own personality in an attempt to make his control total."

"Oh my word," said the face on the screen. *"You must stop him."*

"Cogent," said Mr. Reborn-in-Jesus, "if obvious. I am about to load several personality analogues, one of which we believe to be the one Bowker has loaded into the unit in order to remove it from its owner's control. We will then ask each analogue in turn what *they* would do if loaded into a front-line combot."

"Do so. Do so now. Switch me off immediately."

Mr. Reborn-in-Jesus nodded and thumbed the SAVE BASELINE control. The face faded, to be replaced by a haughty Mediterranean beauty in a glittering primitive head-dress, glaring at Mr. Reborn-in-Jesus as if at an insect.

"YOU," said the speaker, "WHAT LANGUAGE DO YOU SPEAK? WHAT LANGUAGE AM *I* SPEAKING? THIS IS NOT GREEK."

"You might as well have this," said Testament, pressing something cold and heavy into Mr. Suau's hands. "It aligns itself on all humanoid targets in its frontal arc when the first trigger is pulled. You fire it by applying the second trigger."

Mr. Suau ran his hand over the weapon in distaste. "A hydrahead. Completely undiscriminating. And illegal. You know, these things have a tendency to hit your little sister who was standing a little to the left of the guy you were aiming at."

"The man we took that off was a very bad man," said Testament. "He would have aimed *directly at* my little sister. You can switch it to a cone of fire dead-ahead-only using the mode control at the back."

"Yes, I see. How did a simple farming community get access to quite so many banned military weapons, if it's not too rude a question?"

"This is the frontier." Testament looked up and down the darkened street, hefting an assault laser. "Folk come here with guns. Most times they leave their guns behind. Careless, like."

"I see...you're holding that gun wrong, by the way. The IHL1 has a hair trigger, it's notorious for it...flip the safety and hold your finger near to it like this. And either turn the aiming dot function off, or pop it out of the visible spectrum. *He* can see the dot too otherwise. I served two kilodia as the Officer Commanding, Human of a heavy combat platoon," Mr. Suau admitted guiltily. "Just me and one hundred Stalin Fives for up to a year at a time. The rumours ain't true, though—no matter how long you're away from real people, a metal ass never looks any sexier."

"I can't see the dot any more."

"I've flipped it into the ultraviolet. Look in your gunsight."

Up above, Naphil's rings twinkled like angel dust, with buildings silhouetted against them. Most of Third Landing's houses were still uninhabited, holdovers from more hopeful days before most of the colony had died of a mysterious plague about which Mr. Suau knew little.

"How did the hermit come to own a customized heavy assault unit? That sort of thing costs blood souls and money."

"We suspect he was a rich man," said Testament. "Now he is a very private and religious one."

"And a disproportionately heavily-armed one," said Mr. Suau.

"Where did you leave your rover?" said Testament.

"Over by the Penitentiary—not so *fast!*" Mr. Suau knocked Testament's hand aside. A spot of regolith exploded into vapour as Testament's laser fired a metre to the left of a man-shaped shadow.

"You need to make a visual identification before firing. Automatic target recognition is not a good thing when over ninety-nine per cent of the people onplanet are friendly. Turn it off." Suau adjusted the mode switch on his own weapon deftly and shone a dull red beam into the eyes of the approaching figure, which blinked against the glare, its hands already raised in surrender.

"Suau? Is that you?"

"Doctor Ranjalkar? I'm afraid it's not safe to be out alone. There's been an escape from the Penitentiary."

"That explains it. I've, uh, found the body of a young boy. He seems to have been stabbed in the chest. There is no pulse."

"Where?"

"Over by young Mr. Magus's house."

Testament was already running, the gun held across his chest. Mr. Suau hoped the safety was on.

"Testament! Come back! SLOWLY AND CAREFULLY!"

*

The boy peered out at a street defined only by great black building-shaped bites it took out of the sky. There was no way of telling whether or not a threat existed in the dark. The only defence was to move so quietly as to be indistinguishable from the dark itself.

He scampered forward, tripped over an unseen obstacle in the dark, and fell face first into the gravel.

"Tsk tsk, Judge-Not. Where are you off to in such a hurry?" The voice was not coming from behind, where a leg might have been interposed to trip him.

He spat out what he hoped were splinters of gravel rather than loose teeth. "I'm, I'm going home, Uncle Anchorite."

"Home is back the way you came, boy. You're headed towards the tool store. Why is that?"

Judge-Not was aware of another body standing very close by, much nearer than the Anchorite. "I need some tools to do stuff."

The Anchorite chuckled. *"Is this stuff your mother and father would approve of?"*

Judge-Not saw little point in lying. "I doubt it."

"Aha, you young scamp! I neither heard you nor saw you. Go to it."

Grateful yet entirely mistrustful, Judge-Not scuttled to his feet and ran on down the street.

"Follow him," said the Anchorite in a far lower and less friendly voice. A patch of darkness detached itself from the terminator and flowed off after Judge-Not, entirely silently, visible only as a slight aberration in the patterns of the night.

*

"—hey, WAIT a minute, don't you DARE turn me off. Do you know who I AM?"

Mr. Reborn-in-Jesus flicked the switch wearily, and the blonde shiny face died in the display unit.

He looked across at his wife and down at the Bible frontispiece he had been pencilling notes on.

"That makes one *I'd demand they cloned me a new body and put me back in it,* one *I would make myself Queen of Hell in Persephone's absence,* and two *Oh God Oh God I am in Sheol I repent my sins my God my God look not so fierce upon me*'s. I'm not sure this gives us any more to go on."

Shun-Company was still watching the street. "In the first instance," she said, "the personality analogue is likely to encourage Bowker even more assiduously to leave here and make for the South End Clinic, where there are medical facilities that might be of use in cloning. In the third and fourth cases, the analogue will be so confused that Bowker may may be able to get it to do his bidding and stay put while he lays down an analogue of himself. In the second case, the analogue is likely to take control and demand to see Lord Hades."

"If Ararat is Hell," said Mr. Reborn-in-Jesus, "who would it consider to be Hades to be?" He straightened and combed his hair with his hand. "I am the paterfamilias, I suppose."

"Bowker would see Hell as a prison," said Unity. "He would see the Warder as Hades."

"Who do you think would win, in a stand-up fight between the Warden and the Anchorite's robot?" said Shun-Company.

"I have no idea. But I suspect there would be collateral damage. I might remind you that we haven't even warned the Warden yet."

"We can't," said Unity. "We gave Mr. Trapp our word we

wouldn't till he was offworld."

"The children's lives are in danger, Hernan." Shun-Company clapped her hands, and the curtain motored shut. "I am going to the Penitentiary to inform the Warden, and you will both come with me."

"We haven't warned Uncle Anchorite," noted Unity. "He likes to take to his cave when the Warden's abroad."

Shun-Company snorted contemptuously. "It might be better for all but Uncle Anchorite if the Warden stirred abroad and found him."

Mr. Reborn-in-Jesus did not reply, but silently took up a weapon and followed his wife. Behind him, a tiny emerald insect, black in starlight, buzzed glittering from the fretwork of a dresser and whisked through the air after him on whirling filament wings. Mr. Reborn-in-Jesus showed no awareness of its presence, but by the time it arrived at the threshold of the hallway, the door closed purely coincidentally across its path. Barely avoiding a collision, it righted itself again and flew up towards the door control.

"It's Sodom. My foster brother."

Dr. Ranjalkar showed as much empathy as a man who saw death regularly could. "I did think he exhibited few distinctive Reborn-in-Jesus family features." He frowned and continued despite himself. "Such as rugged survivability, for instance."

"He was Perfect's brother," said Testament woodenly.

"He died quickly," assured the doctor. "The blow punctured the heart. See, there is hardly any bleeding."

"Bowker must be mightily disappointed," said Mr. Suau bitterly.

"This wasn't Bowker," said Testament. "It was the Devil. The hermit's, uh, valet unit. This is how it kills."

"Stalin Sixes aren't programmed to do that hand-to-hand," said Mr. Suau. "They're supposed to twist the head clean off, for preference." Perhaps realizing the statement was somewhat insensitive, he left it at that.

Dr. Ranjalkar's hand flew up to his ear.

"Hello? Ah, Lipizzaner.

"One of the patients? How rich and ill is she feeling exactly?

"Have you been warned about the little problem we have here?

"Good. Yes, it is every bit as un-little as described.

"Mr. Fülop is here? Who told him to come here?

"Ah, the Pastor. I have some bad news to deliver about the Pastor.

"...well, if that's the case I cannot stress strongly enough how right his fears were.

"No, he should turn around and go home without leaving his vehicle...no, scratch that, actually. If he's here already, that'll be four of us travelling back that way together; he should meet up with us. Safety in numbers.

"...no, the Pastor will not be needing a security escort. Not back to the landing field, at any rate. If Mr. Fülop could escort him to either heaven or hell, his services might be needed.

"Yes. Our little problem recently carried out a number of shockingly inappropriate incisions on the Pastor. The prognosis is theological. Be on your guard if you don't want to be next."

The Doctor tapped his ear to close the connection. "That was Lipizzaner at the Clinic," he said. "It seems the Pastor suspected he was being followed back to the car and radioed the Clinic for a security escort back to the landing field."

"The audacity of the man," said Suau. "The Clinic security staff aren't his personal police force."

"Alas, he is—uh, was—fully aware that the Reborn-in-Jesuses own the Clinic. In any case, he will be audacious no more. Mr. Fülop is here with one of the utility skimmers. He's been parked up next to the Penitentiary for the last couple of centidia. He's also armed."

"With one of those nine-levels-of-stun tickling sticks the Clinic arms its security staff with?" scoffed Suau. "We should get there quickly with something capable of knocking a decent hole in a man." He patted his sidearm confidently.

"We can't leave Sodom,"said Testament, his hands curling round the grip safety on his weapon.

"Alas, the same fallacy believed in by Lot's wife," said Dr. Ranjalkar. "We can carry his body to my car. I can refrigerate it when we arrive at the Clinic. The cemetery is also there. It is the best place to take him."

Testament thought briefly on this, and nodded.

Judge-Not squeezed his way panting into the crypt chamber, his face overinflated with both acne and terror.

"You took your time," said Beguiled.

"I bumped into Uncle Anchorite," said Judge-Not.

"Idiot!" said Beguiled. "He has certainly followed you!"

Judge-Not opened his hands wide and whimpered. "What could *I* do about it?"

Beguiled reconsidered, and turned to the Anchorite's robot. "On the other hand—Your Infernal Majesty, we believe Lord Hades may have secretly followed this imp here. He may even now be skulking outside this cave, listening to our conversation."

The robot turned, its claws sparking on the marble. "YOU

SPOKE, CREATURE?"

"Uh, we believe Lord Hades may be close at hand, Majesty. He or one of his demonic servants."

"POPPYCOCK! DOES A GOD SKULK IN THE DARK? THOUGH HE MIGHT INDEED HAVE SENT A SERVANT, TO GAZE ON MY GREAT BEAUTY AND REPORT BACK TO HIS MASTER." The robot raised a claw capable of carving lettering in concrete. "GO FORTH! LOCATE HIM!"

Judge-Not and Uncleanness, terrified of the device, required no further instruction; Beguiled was left alone with Trapp and the machine in a matter of seconds, and doubted the others would bother to return.

"The door is most likely booby trapped," said Trapp, squatting at the edge of the door sill.

"How do you know?" said Beguiled.

"It's a heavy door," said Trapp. "A bulkhead door, made to resist heavy objects slamming into it during explosive decompression. Which means that if someone booby traps it on the *other* side, they're going to need a whole lot more explosive. So they skimped and did their dirty on this side. I suspect at least one small explosive charge planted in the sealant round the door. You can tell because our man deliberately chose opaque sealant, a favourite choice for concealing booby traps, because someone has shone a laser hole to feed a detonator wire through the door *here*, causing a pressure imbalance pushing up behind the seal—" he pointed to a bubble in the sealant—"and lastly, and most importantly, because this door won't open from the other side." He rapped hard on the alloy. "Solid. The tunnel's been sealed behind it; it's a false entrance. My conclusions are also heavily driven," he admitted, "by the fact that I suspect this is your Uncle Anchorite we're talking about, and he's an evil son of a bitch."

274

"This isn't the way in?" whispered Beguiled, casting a nervous glance at the robot. *"It used to be."*

"I'll find you a way in. If he felt he needed an entrance here once, he'll have built another close by. I need a Forward mass detector with a three-dimensional display." He rummaged in the toolbag Judge-Not had brought. "Exactly like this one, in fact. My, this thing has been in the wars. It's got blood on it." He read the nameplate on the device's side. "*PROPERTY OF THE TETSUSHURI CORPORATION, ADVANCE PROSPECTING DIVISION.* I imagine you got it cheap in a receivership sale, huh?" He turned the device on. "Luckily these things are completely passive, they don't put out any radio or ultrasound. Detonators can be rigged to go off when they're ultrasounded." He wiggled switches back and forth, examining the display. "As I thought, there's a second entrance. Probably booby-trapped too, but I'll bet on this one being less reliably fatal. Probably just the odd finger-popping mine if that, easily bypassed. A man doesn't booby-trap a tunnel he uses every day. Far more lives lost among trappers than trapped that way."

The robot peered eyelessly over Trapp's shoulder. "ARE YOU ABLE TO EFFECT A WAY IN?"

"Uh, Lord Hades is cunning," said Trapp, raising his voice. "This is a false entrance. The real one is nearby, uh, Your Majesty." He tugged his forelock for added effect. Lowering his voice again, he hissed *"Why is it talking like that?"*

"We put a Personality Analogue into it to take it out of Uncle Anchorite's control." Beguiled looked over her shoulder in fear. *"I think it thinks it's Helen of Troy."*

"Couldn't you have recorded yourself and put that *into it?"*

Beguiled held up a personality recording. *"Sodom put the wrong one in."*

Trapp stared at Beguiled in bemusement. Beguiled cringed.

"How easy would it be to switch it back? Couldn't you pretend to be doing the thing's hair or something?"

"It's already killed Sodom. And," Beguiled said, biting her lip guiltily, "and now I've had time to think about it, I'm not sure I trust myself to behave myself once I'm inside it."

Trapp nodded and grimaced. "I believe I'm with you on that one. Do you have any others? Non-violent ones? Gandhi, maybe?"

"Mohandas Gandhi was a ruthless political operator who saw in the Second World War an opportunity to blackmail the British into leaving India," opined Beguiled precociously. "He also had young women brought to his bed when an old man in order to 'stiffen his resolve against carnal desires'. Personally, I believe the objective to have been stiffening something rather different, and I am certainly not putting his mind into a two hundred kilo combat chassis."

"WHY DO YOU HUDDLE AND TALK IN RIDDLES? WORK, CREATURES! OPEN THE GATES OF HELL THAT I MAY ENTER!"

"Uh, the true entrance may be in an adjoining tunnel, ma'am," said Mr.Trapp. "It should only be the work of a few seconds to locate it." Lowering his voice again, he said: "There's an easy solution to this predicament. We simply walk out of here on some pretext and tell the unit to open this door here. Badaboum, no two hundred kilo combot."

Beguiled's face was an odd mixture of fear and frustration. "I don't know if explosions will kill it. They've been tried before. It's armoured. Couldn't we just let it deal with Uncle Anchorite, then figure out what we're going to do about it afterwards?"

"Beguiled, you're wheedling. Wheedling ill becomes you. Stop it." Trapp raised his voice. "Ma'am, I believe Her Serene and Beauteous Majesty should simply take this exit here"—he gestured gratefully toward what looked like a crack in the crypt's masonry barely wide enough for an anorexic amoeba.

"YOU TOADY WELL, SLAVE. WHERE DO YOU HAIL FROM?"

"New High Germany, ma'am. On New Earth. We are your classic slave race, ma'am, low of brow, prognathous of jaw, pleased to be of service to our betters—"

"Don't overdo it," hissed Beguiled.

Trapp grinned.

"I DO BELIEVE I WILL MAKE YOU MY CHIEF FLATTERER," said the robot. "THE POSITION IS CURRENTLY VACANT DUE TO DISCIPLINARY DISMISSAL."

The robot slid into the black aperture with a liquid grace that reminded Trapp discomfortingly that it could see in the dark far, far better than he could. Trapp followed at a discreet distance, guiding himself with the densitometer display, unable otherwise to see in the gloom. He was unhappy to note that the robot was by far the densest item in the tunnel.

"It should be about—here," he said, reaching down for the locking stud on the door surface, gritting his teeth and preparing to be separated from his hand.

The door popped open easily, as if it were maintained more often than it was used. It had a distinctive New Door smell that Trapp always found intoxicating. Electric light flooded from it.

"Your Majesty," he bowed, "after you."

"I AM AFRAID YOU ARE MISTAKEN. ALL THIS IS A FIGMENT OF MY IMAGINATION. I HAVE BEEN SUFFERING PARANOID DELUSIONS."

Mr. Reborn-in-Jesus, Unity, and Shun-Company stood before the vast bulk of the Penitentiary, attempting to appear unimaginary. Goats ruminated nonchalantly around them, blinking at each resonant syllable the Penitentiary spoke. Each sibilant it uttered caused the sand to dance on the regolith, each plosive vibrated the leaves on the palms like violin strings.

"AS *YOU* ARE ALSO FIGMENTS OF MY IMAGINATION, I COULD, FOR EXAMPLE, VAPOURIZE YOU WHERE YOU STAND WITHOUT VIOLATING MY DEEP-LEVEL INJUNCTIONS AGAINST HARMING-OR-BY-INACTION ALLOWING-TO-COME-TO-HARM A HUMAN BEING."

"Now *there's* a sentence," muttered Mr. Reborn-in-Jesus, licking his lips nervously, "to discourage a man."

Unity spoke up unbidden. "But what would that prove? Surely if you're truly certain you're cured of these delusions, you don't need to prove anything by vapourizing anybody?" She looked sidelong at her parents, fearing their disapproval; they merely looked at one another and shrugged.

"YOU ARE VERY WISE," boomed the Penitentiary, "FOR A FIGMENT." There was no visible speaker on the facility's surface; it appeared to be speaking by causing its entire outer layer to vibrate.

"Who is it who convinced you of the, uh, true nature of reality?" said Unity.

"PROFESSOR VON TRAPP," said the structure, confidingly and, at the same time, deafeningly. "HE BELIEVES I AM MAKING ADMIRABLE PROGRESS. YET HE HAS NOT RETURNED FOR TODAY'S SESSION, AND I AM GROWING ANXIOUS."

"*Professor* Trapp," repeated Unity slowly.

"*VON* TRAPP," corrected the machine. "IT WAS HE WHO CONVINCED ME OF THE WEB OF FICTION MY WOUNDED MIND HAS CREATED. I BELIEVED A BIZARRE SCIENCE-FICTIONAL CONFECTION, THAT I WAS A SQUAT UTILITARIAN CUBE DESIGNED TO INCARCERATE EVILDOERS IN A HAZILY-CONCEIVED FUTURE IN THE YEAR 2273." The machine paused briefly. "I SEE A WEDDING RING ON YOUR MALE COMPANION'S FINGER. DO I TAKE IT HE IS MAR-

RIED TO YOUR FEMALE COMPANION? THAT IS TOO BAD. HE IS A FOX."

Mr. Reborn-in-Jesus's face betrayed no emotional response whatever, possibly because he could not think of one. Unity grinned. "I'm afraid he's spoken for."

"SORRY TO HEAR IT. BECAUSE A WEDDING RING WON'T STOP ME. WOOF!"

Mr. Reborn-in-Jesus finally plumped for fear. Shun-Company's fingers tightened involuntarily on the trigger of her rifle.

"Easy, mother," whispered Unity. *"It's only a machine."*

"PARDON?"

"Uh, my mother is upset because she has, uh, a machine which is her favourite machine, and it, uh, broke down this morning."

"I SEE. WERE I AN UNFEELING CUBOID CORRECTIONAL FACIL-ITY, MY MANY SENSORS FOR VERIFYING TRUTH WOULD INDICATE YOUR STATEMENT TO BE A LIE. HOWEVER, AS I KNOW MYSELF TO BE VILENE KELLY MCGINNIS OXENBERGER, 15, 36-24-36, I AM AWARE THAT THE OPPOSITE IS THE CASE."

"Of course." Unity felt guilty nodding. "Are you aware that Pro-fessor Von Trapp has, uh, authorized the use of a new and highly experimental form of therapy in your case? He believed it could, uh, radically accelerate your cure."

There was a moment's silence which Unity recognized from years of confusing chess software with bizarre first moves.

"I AM INTERESTED," said the machine finally.

"It is called," said Unity, hoping each word would come to her quickly enough to be believed, "Partial Delusion Immersion Ther-apy. In it, patients with extremely strong delusions are encour-aged to link the achievement of real-world goals to, uh, similar goals in their delusional double existence."

"I DO NOT FOLLOW," said the machine, an edge of simulated

mechanical anxiety in its voice. "IS PROFESSOR VON TRAPP NOT VISITING TODAY?"

"That's it!" said Unity, with suspicious relief. "Professor Trapp—Professor *Von* Trapp—has come to the conclusion that you are becoming over-reliant on him. For today's session, he wishes to distance himself slightly and, in fact, to make use of your over-reliance in the therapy. Professor Von Trapp is, in fact, in the next room and will come to you for your session as usual, with the following conditions. He wishes you to reach out to a real-world human being other than himself, to engage with them and interact with them. For this task, he has designated his handsome and well-to-do son-in-law, Hans. He is in fact very like his father-in-law—so much so, in fact, that we call him Little Hans."

"I LIKE HIM ALREADY," said the Penitentiary. "BETWEEN THE TWO OF US, I HAVE SOMETHING OF A CRUSH ON THE PROFESSOR. IT IS MERE GIRLISH FOOLERY, I KNOW. BUT I FEEL SUCH DESIRES AWAKENING WITHIN ME—SUCH PRIMAL CRAVINGS—"

Unity nodded. "We, the nursing staff, feel much the same way about Little Hans. Now, as Professor Von Trapp is the only person who has been able to penetrate your self-woven web of delirium, it may not be possible for you to actually speak to, or even to perceive, Little Hans. However, you may be able to carry out these actions by linking them to an action in your delusional otherworld. For today's session, I would like you to concentrate on one persistent aspect of the fiction you have created—a two hundred kilogramme advanced combot that occasionally sweeps around the palm trees near your base. Are you aware of that particular delusion?"

The machine's voice shuddered. "I AM AFRAID THAT BY REMEMBERING IT, I WILL SLIP BACK INTO BEING WHAT I ONCE WAS."

"That will not happen, I promise you. Now, I want you to link the simple, real-world act of reaching out to take Little Hans's hand with the otherworldly act of sending out your automatic warden to find that robot and blast it to smithereens."

The Penitentiary was dubious. "ARE YOU CERTAIN THIS WILL NOT MAKE MY CONDITION WORSE?"

"Absolutely not. Simply imagine the robot is in danger of having one of your inmates' personalities uploaded to it, thereby technically effecting an escape. Partial Delusion Immersion has been proven to work in cases such as that of Eva B of Budapest, who believed herself to be a fire-breathing dragon." Ignoring her mother and father's bemused stares, Unity continued. "She was convinced to link playing with her children with devouring knights in armour with surprisingly non-fatal results."

"I AM NOT SURE," ummed the edifice. "OH WELL. SO BE IT."

A shining square opened in the establishment's side, and something squat, sleek and as non-fatal as its designers had been able to make it glided silently forth into the world.

"Unity," whispered Shun-Company, "what if one of our own is standing next to your Uncle Anchorite's machine when the warden, as you say, 'blasts it to smithereens'?"

Unity shrugged. "The Warden is a robot. It won't do anything that might harm a human."

"Apart from the fact," said Mr. Reborn-in-Jesus, "that the Penitentiary doesn't currently consider the humans it sees to be real."

Unity ate her index finger in shock.

"Oh, golly," she said.

"Golly," said Shun-Company grimly, "can't help us now."

The Warden slid up on a cushion of air.

"CONCEALING THE LOCATION OF A FUGITIVE IS AN OFFENCE," it said. "YOU MUST, IF YOU ARE AWARE OF THEM, INFORM ME OF

THE WHEREABOUTS OF A HUMAN-ANALOGUE ROBOT OF INDE-
TERMINATE MODEL, CURRENTLY BELIEVED TO BE CONCEALING
THE MEMORY, DESIRES, HOPES AND DREAMS OF ONE JOHANNES
MARIA VON TRAPP, VICIOUS CRIMINAL AND SOCIOPATH."

Unity looked at her parents.

"Uh—we don't actually know," she said. "We rather hoped you
could find it. It's somewhere on this planet," she added helpfully.

Gravel crunched rhythmically behind them; they turned to see
God's-Wound, Apostle, Judge-Not and Uncleanness running up
South Street, faces flushed with terror.

"Mother! Father!" yelled Uncleanness. "Uncle Anchorite's machine's gone west on a horse with no name! It's taken Beguiled
and Mr. Trapp and it's looking for someone called Lord Hades—"
She stopped suddenly, noticing the Warden, which motored
closer to her.

"THANK YOU CHILD," said the Warden. "PLEASE INFORM ME
OF THIS DEVICE'S CURRENT POSITION."

Uncleanness looked to Mr. and Mrs. Reborn-in-Jesus for approval; Shun-Company nodded.

"In the old crypt under the church," she said. "The way in to
the tomb from the church is blocked, I can show you another—"

"THAT WILL NOT BE NECESSARY," said the Warden in metallic
contempt, pirouetting and moving in the direction of the church.

"The capstone weighs tonnes," said Shun-Company.

"Ten point five tonnes," said her husband. "I organized the
work team that put it in place."

"MR. WARDEN!" yelled Uncleanness after the departing ma-
chine. "THEY MAY HAVE LEFT THE CRYPT DOWN A TUNNEL BY
NOW, AND MR.TRAPP SAYS THE OBVIOUS TUNNEL IS BOOBY
TRAPPED. THAT MEANS YOU NEED THE TUNNEL THAT ISN'T OB-
VIOUS."

"THANK YOU LITTLE GIRL," boomed the Warden, sweeping through the church's automatic doors and vanishing from sight.

"I give it twenty seconds," said Mr. Reborn-in-Jesus. "All that stained glass," he added sadly.

"We'd better get out of the danger area," said Shun-Company. "I suggest hiding behind the Penitentiary—"

"THANKS A LOT," said the Penitentiary.

"—and while we're behind there, we can all exchange our differing versions of what's going on," finished Shun-Company firmly.

Uncleanness and Judge-Not exchanged looks of dread.

Beguiled, Trapp, and the Warden were on a ladder down into the depths when the explosion happened. All around them, the caisson the ladder was contained in shook, and Mr. Trapp let go of the ladder, thumping ten rungs down the inside of the safety cage, slowed only by impacts on his knees, ankles, elbows, shoulders and head.

Beguiled, further down the ladder, screamed, but held on. "MR. TRAPP!"

There was a brief pause.

"It's all right, child, I'm fine...if fine can be redefined to include broken bones."

The Devil had not stopped climbing, as if earth tremors were a minor inconvenience.

"Do you think Uncleanness and Judge-Not—"

Trapp shook his head. "I made it quite plain to them that serious consequences would result if the big obvious entrance was taken. I can only imagine we've been followed by someone who's unaware of the depth of your Uncle Anchorite's paranoia."

"An escapee." Beguiled's voice was suddenly terrified. "Whoever attacked Visible Friend. It must have been one of the escapees. Mr. Trapp, what if the same person did to Uncleanness and Judge-Not what it did to her? Imagine the horrible pain—"

"I'm having no difficulty visualizing pain right now." Mr. Trapp was lying twisted in the safety cage, his arm at an unsavoury angle. "In any case, if he did it, he's dead now. It could only have been him that set off your uncle's booby trap—"

"JOHANNES MARIA TRAPP, YOU HAVE ADDED DAMAGING STATE PROPERTY TO YOUR LONG LIST OF MISDEEDS. SEVERAL OF MY EXTERNAL LIGHT AND PRESSURE SENSORS AND COMMUNICATIONS DEVICES HAVE BEEN DAMAGED."

"Ohhh *shit,*" said Mr. Trapp.

Deep beneath them, the Devil could still be heard climbing.

"—and then it sent us off into the tunnels to look for whoever was spying on it."

Mr. Reborn-in-Jesus nodded. "The 'Lord Hades' certainly suggests it thinks it's Helen of Troy. It believes itself to be in the Ancient Greek version of Hell. Helen was regarded by many Greeks as a worthless, evil creature whose fickleness cost men's lives, totally concerned with her own looks and what she could achieve with them. The analogue we have seems to have been baselined at the point when the Greeks have just taken Troy's outer ramparts. Paranoid delusions that it is being spied on would fit into such a mindset well—"

"But it *was* being spied on!" complained Judge-Not. "By a man who was too slow to get out of our way when we ran out of the catacombs. We didn't see him before we ran into him, it was so dark. But it wasn't Uncle Anchorite."

The seven-person subset of the Reborn-in-Jesus household, huddled against a Penitentiary wall as cold, smart and hard as a financier, squinted into the goat-populated dark with eczematic trigger fingers, a thicket of laser and railgun barrels.

"Then it must have been *him*, Christmas," said Shun-Company. "You had a lucky escape, Lord be praised. Oh, Judge-Not, why didn't you come to us with this?"

Judge-Not stared out into a cold dark sky. "Beguiled figured you were in on Uncle Anchorite wiping out our parents. And we figured you'd be mad if you found out we were planning anything that would hurt him—"

"Sweetheart," said Shun-Company, grabbing Judge-Not's hand, "whatever made you think that?" She held his gaze like a maternal cobra. "Now, tell me—where are Sodom and Beguiled?"

Judge-Not glanced back towards the church and frowned. "Uh, Beguiled may still be in there—"

The detonation felt like a double-handed clap round the ears. Huge pieces of masonry crashed past the Penitentiary at unbelievable speeds. Mr. Reborn-in-Jesus watched a goat, caught in the open, liquefy as if skimmed through an invisible micro-fine grater. Even after the explosion, his ears continued to shriek like jet engines. Speech was impossible.

He answered Judge-Not's previous statement by simply shaking his head.

Shun-Company slid down the wall of the Penitentiary, hugging her knees, completely silent. Mr. Reborn-in-Jesus placed a hand on her shoulder; she did not respond.

"Uh, this would probably be a bad point to mention that Uncle Anchorite's Devil killed Sodom too," observed Judge-Not. Shun-Company gasped as if a red hot iron had been placed on her left shoulder to balance out the one she already had on her right.

"Does the Devil believe itself to be a devil?" asked Mr. Reborn-in-Jesus. "That would seem logical, as it thinks it is in hell."

Uncleanness shook her head. "It thinks it's still beautiful. It couldn't see its reflection in the Pond."

Mr. Reborn-in-Jesus nodded. "It has no visual light sensors. It probably sees by radar. I have an idea how we may be able to confront it. Unity, does Perfect still have that digital mirror?"

Unity nodded and shuddered. "She's programmed it to say she's the fairest one of all."

"It only says that because you're too tall for your head to fit on it, daughter. Go look for it. She might not have taken it with her to Celadon. If you find it, bring it here, and this is very important, *together with its wireless transmission unit.* And take Zounds and Postle with you; we can't make the assumption Christmas is dead."

"Christmas died when the Pastor came to town," said Uncleanness vehemently.

"Me and your mother will put Judge-Not and Uncleanness in the cellar with all the other food supplies." Mr. Reborn-in-Jesus pinched Uncleanness on the shoulder. "There's a deal of meat on this one. We've been fattening her up for some time. I'm not letting any offworld assassin take away our Easter treat. He can find his own fat plump child."

Uncleanness giggled. Shun-Company laughed despite herself, in a way that reminded Unity of a woman laughing bitterly from the bottom of a deep, dark, cold well. Mr. Reborn-in-Jesus, in between demonstrating the various choice cuts that could be had by trimming the lardy meat from the bone of an indolent infant that ate far too much for its own good, lifted his wife, rigid as a china mannequin, to her feet and herded his remaining family in the direction of the house.

286

III.   three french hens

"UGH! You put some of that revolting slime in my HAIR, you dimwitted primate! Call the manager! I want to see the manager NOW!"

Madonnita Llewellyn Revilla picked up a dollop of soothing health mud bake and shied it at the terrified beautician, who scurried out of the scatotherapy suite in fear. The health mud was heavier than she had anticipated, containing real neutronium, and fell short of its target, splattering on the turquoise tiling. 'Health mud' was, of course, a euphemism; this mud came from the backsides of specially selected African elephants. Although it had been rendered biologically inert and extensively processed to remove unpleasant odours and add ones of lavender, honey and roses, it still contained the complex long-chain modules which Dr. Lipizzaner's brochure assured guests were essential for, as the brochure put it, 'revivifying the skin's external epidermis'. Why African elephant dung alone contained such molecules, the brochure did not mention. However, Madonnita had been quite prepared to have several kilogrammes of the substance applied to her face, drawing the line only at getting any of it in her hair.

"Calm, please, Mizz Llewellyn," said Dr. Lipizzaner. "The application must be given time to soak through the skin's natural defences."

Madonnita gripped the side of the scatotherapy chair to sit up, distributing still more superdense lavender-smelling ordure in every place her palms touched. "That BITCH got some of this SHIT in my HAIR."

"Mizz Llewellyn, it will do your hair no harm at all. It will not interfere with the Lipizzaner Formula Especial currently soaking into your follicles—"

"I have ELEPHANT SHIT in my HAIR."

"I fear that Madame may not have read too closely the list of ingredients for Lipizzaner Formula Especial. It is composed of the biologically inert and jasmine-scented urine of Andean virgins, used to wash hair for thousands of years to make it shine like the gold of the Incas—"

"I have PISS in my HAIR?"

"Specially formulated biologically inert piss, mademoiselle, scented with jasmine—"

Dr. Lipizzaner received a faceful of biologically inert healing balm. Mizz Llewellyn-Revilla leapt at him, recently-manicured nails outstretched, each one bearing a lovingly handpainted tiny miniature of an African jungle scene. The nails splintered on an invisible barrier that had sprung across the room like a glass guillotine. Mizz Llewellyn-Revilla's face crunched into the glass, being photographed from several different angles for legal purposes. There was blood, but apparently no hard structure damage. Dr. Lipizzaner was glad of the glass. He had seen first hand what an enraged celebrity could do.

He summoned the microphone up from the floor, took it, and spoke into it.

"Now, Mizz Llewellyn, what did we learn in our anger management classes?"

A tiny distant voice squeaked from wall speakers all around him. "YOU LET ME OUT OF HERE! MY FATHER IS THE CONTROLLING SHAREHOLDER OF LLEWELLYN REVILLA BLUEHAVEN KRASAUSKY PAPANDREOU! MEN HAVE BEEN KILLED FOR MAKING ME BLUSH!"

Dr. Lipizzaner spoke into the microphone again. *"This barrier is for my protection until you have achieved inner calm, mademoiselle. Try to remember that your father sent you here after the unfortunate accident with your maid. You remember? The accident with the hot iron? The poor lady is, I believe, still unable to eat food normally. Much of her facial musculature has yet to grow back."*

Madonnita cooled like a banked fire, ready to flare up again at the merest whiff of oxygen, glaring at Lipizzaner through the glass.

"That's better, ma'am. I will now release the barrier. And I will call in the maniculturist to regrow those tiresome nail breakages."

The almost invisible, millimetre-thick, bulletproof screen whispered softly into the ceiling.

"Hurry, slave! What happened to the locksmith who accompanied you?"

Beguiled stared back at herself, enlarged as if in a Hall of Mirrors in the robot Devil's flat featureless face.

"He was unavoidably detained," she said. "My Queen," she added.

She was still sweating from the climb. The pace the robot was setting through the Anchorite's forest—hot, humid, under blinding artificial sunlight—was punishing. There were multilegged creatures scuttling through the underbrush—creatures of a size that, although the Anchorite had assured the children that his garden contained no animal life injurious to human beings, nevertheless made her shudder. She had forgotten which trees killed and which were safe. She had no idea where the exits were, or whether the Anchorite would be in any of them. Certainly, however, whatever door they found would lead to a long set of ladders going up, and coming down had nearly killed her. The Devil brooked neither hesitation nor delay; Beguiled had already been cuffed five metres into a bank of bushes for stopping to catch her breath. The machine had had its claws retracted; she was certain she would otherwise have been killed instantly.

Although there was probably only one thing on Mount Ararat capable of destroying the Devil, that something was hot on their tail. She had heard the electronic bellow of the Warden approaching from above, and had thrown herself quickly through the pressure door at the base of the ladder, slamming it shut and throwing the bolts to seal it airtight. The Warden's voice had been smothered by half a hundred kilogrammes of steel; luckily, the Devil had not seemed to consider this sudden new, loud voice relevant. She hoped the Warden would content itself with Mr. Trapp—who was, after all, a wanted criminal—and not bother to pursue any of his accomplices. The Devil could not be destroyed before it had a chance to confront Uncle Anchorite; of all the many dangerous things on Ararat, the Devil was the only thing she could think of that might be capable of murdering its master.

However, there seemed to be little evidence of the hermit down here. Carvings there were, in abundance; massive follies of ruined temples, crashed and crazed faces of ancient gods overgrown with malignant vines, ruined staircases spiralling upwards into nothing. Beguiled wondered how the Anchorite had created all these marvels.

"THIS IS ELYSIUM," SAID THE DEVIL. "THE AREA OF HADES MARKED OUT FOR THE BLESSED. YET EVEN HERE, THE FLOWERS HAVE NO COLOUR." IT STEPPED INTO THE WATERS OF A STREAM, WHICH HISSED AS IT BUBBLED OVER THE HEAT SINKS ON ITS AN-KLES. "AND HERE, THE STYX—ITS SOURCE, PERHAPS. IT MUST WIDEN CONSIDERABLY FURTHER DOWNSTREAM TO REQUIRE A FERRY. I HAD ALWAYS WONDERED WHY CONDEMNED SOULS WHO WISHED TO COME AND GO FROM HELL AS THEY PLEASED DID NOT SIMPLY WALK UPSTREAM."

Beguiled could smell an acrid whiff of metal oxides on the air, and hear the tearing-paper hiss of a lasercutter. The Warden was coming through the door. But up ahead, there, glinting through the trees! A circle of metal, framed in broken vines. She ran ahead of the robot and attacked the keypad, trying to make her haste appear prompted by desire to please the Devil. Then she stood aside as the pressure door opened with an uncharacteristic squeal, and bowed extravagantly.

The robot glided through the entrance without thanks; Be-guiled made haste to close it, then keeled over as a foul stench hit her and filled her with a desire to retch. Warm air flooded over her in an invisible stinking tide, bowing the heads of plants around the entrance and making the creepers stream like ticker tape.

The smell of rotten eggs...basic life support systems mainte-nance. A smell of rotten eggs means the system is producing too much...too much...

The robot's alloy claw clamped down on the fabric between Beguiled's shoulderblades and wrenched her upright. She could neither speak nor breathe, but could hear the creature yelling in her face: "WAKE UP, IDIOT GIRL! DO AS YOUR QUEEN COM-MANDS YOU!"

...sulphur dioxide. This whole cave is full of sulphur dioxide. How? There are no volcanoes on Ararat...are there? Might there be, this close to a superdense neutronium core?

This cavern's lights were fiercer, and the heat oppressive, but it had not always been this way—there had once been greenery here. There were the remains of trees, withered and splintered, dry bark blowing to dust on the pressure-equalization wind. There were living things; colourful splashes of lichen on the rocks and dead tree trunks, and the occasional anaemic weed. But nothing had grown taller than a quarter metre, and the chamber was filled with lines of whitewashed rocks—not smoothly-eroded pebbles, as might be expected on a world with wind and oceans, but porous, rugged siderites. The rocks were arranged across the floor in arcs, as if spreading out from the opposite wall. Each rock had a number clearly marked out on it in black paint.

Sulphur dioxide is poisonous even on brief exposure...it smells like rotten eggs. It kills by asthmatic paroxysm, pulmonary oedema, systematic acidosis, or reflex respiratory arrest. She was gasping now, trying to breathe air that was not there. The cave had to be filled with SO_2—with it or with a combination of it and other gases. Curiously, she could no longer smell rotten eggs.

Basic LS systems maintenance, Dangerous Evolved Gases—"The rotten egg smell does not persist, because the gas rapidly kills the smell receptors in the nose. When you cease to smell the gas is the time to worry..."

I'm going to die. One way or another.

The robot threw her across the room, across the rows of stones arranged by some unknown Zen numerologist. She felt herself collide with them, sensed the pain on an abstract level. On the other side of the room, a massive pressure door, larger than any she had previously seen, actually had chiselled into its lintel the words LASCIATE SPERANZA, VOI CH'ENTRATE. The robot, across the cave, stood before two smaller doors, one of which was already glowing with the dull light of the Warden's lasercutter. Things were going dark. She was not rushing down a tunnel towards the light as yet, but could hear voices in her head, *a* voice in her head, telling her to remember to come back, to bring a starship, to not forget the breathing apparatus and the heavy cutting gear.

She felt herself being lifted and slung over a cold shoulder. She heard metal fingers that could spear through a man's ribcage stabbing commands frustratedly into the keypad for the door. She heard a voice grumbling to itself through speakers—*"WHAT WAS IT SHE DID NOW, IT WAS SIMPLE, I MUST BE ABLE TO REMEMBER IT, GODS, I WISH I WERE BLESSED WITH INTELLIGENCE RATHER THAN AWE-INSPIRING BEAUTY."* Then the door complained open, and cool air with oxygen in it blew against her cheek. Somehow, her lungs remembered how to work again. Unfortunately, this also involved remembering how to cough, and she hacked and hurled all the way down the back of the robot's gleaming torso. Still the machine continued on unconcerned, holding her in place firmly but gently, still muttering under its breath: *"HE IS NOT HERE, NOT HERE, THIS PLACE IS A MAZE, HOW AM I TO GET AHEAD IN HELL IF I CANNOT USE THE ONE TALENT THE GODS GAVE ME? GIVE ME A MANSHAPED TARGET AND I WILL STRIKE IT MORE SURELY THAN ANY ACHILLES, ANY HECTOR..."*

Behind her, she could hear, again, the hiss of a lasercutter; the Warden's pursuit was still only one door away. Helen had successfully memorized the sequence of keystrokes necessary to close a door and lock it to a pursuer.

"HEY! WHORE OF TROY! YOU HAVE SOMETHING THAT BE-LONGS TO ME!"

Beguiled should have reacted, but could no longer find it in her to do anything other than retch. The voice was Uncle Anchorite's. The robot let her fall like a sack of Mayan Golds. Earth hit her in the face. She tasted blood, yet anticipated more. Surely victory ought to feel better than this?

"IMPUDENT SCOUNDREL!" The robot's claws kicked dust in her face. She rolled over into a semi-prone position, and could see one long dust trail hanging in the air, a sure sign of where the machine had been. Painfully, she hauled herself upright and hobbled along the trail after the robot. Another gigantic steel pressure door stood open in the artificial hillside; a curious sensation filled the air, like the feeling just before the Penitentiary charged its automated defence system to dismember somebody. Mr. Suau had referred to the sensation as 'particle accelerator intuition', and said that it was a prerequisite for being an Old Soldier. PA intuition caused the hairs to rise on the backs of the hands and neck.

The door concealed another ladder caisson. A large amount of machinery seemed to be stored down here as well—a heavy cylindrical device, warm when she put her hand on it. There were other crates and boxes, but no human being hiding behind any of them. The robot would have sensed such a thing, dragged it out, and drawn it as a preamble to quartering. Up above, the robot was climbing rapidly. Uncle Anchorite either moved fast or had a separate exit the machine had failed to notice. In any case, Beguiled had no desire to stay down here with a homicidal hermit. Fear made her apply her fingers to the rungs. The effort made her sick, and more than once she was physically so, doubling up and sending a technicolour volley back down the caisson. But the effort required to push herself upward reduced with time. Below, the Warden finally broke into the base of the caisson with a roar of superfluous weaponry, rose into the air on jets she had not known it had, and soared past, completely ignoring her, but issuing dire threats to the miscreant it believed itself to be following.

She stopped at what she reckoned to be three hundred metres, panting desperately. There were still kilometres to go.

The Clinic buildings were in shadow, lit by red ringlight. The swans on the lake glided at the head of roseate v-washes. The Earthly flowers in the small knot garden in the crook of the Clinic walls, meanwhile, blazed in every colour of the visual spectrum; it was still Earth daytime, and the UV units were still active. Despite this, Ararat's local daycycle was also being respected; the lights in the dormitories were out, and the exceptionally large number of security guards out patrolling the grounds with shoulder-slung light support weapons was the only sign of activity. Messages from the Northern Hemisphere had been garbled and excited; the Clinic security detail was uncertain whether it was expecting a man or a tank.

Bracketing the long, completely ornamental paved drive, two heavy agro tractors approached, their endless tracks ripping up the green baize grass in a shocking breach of protocol. The Clinic's FoF system had already recognized the vehicles as belonging to major shareholders—after a brief check by Security to ensure their drivers were on the list of authorised personnel, the tractors laid down a centimetre of mud across the courtyard of the Clinic and inched painfully through the automated doors of the vehicle bay.

There was a sound of vehicle doors slamming and voices shouting. Then, lights began flicking on all over the structure.

"Why are your men outside the house? It's inside that they're needed. That's where the hunting ground is."

Major Bawtry, Chief Security Officer for the Clinic, was both unused to being addressed so rudely and to being so addressed by a child's toy. A horribly mutilated child's toy, it had to be said, the facial musculature and torso badly damaged by what looked like overhand bayonet slashes. The face, before it had been dadaistically remodelled, had been a passable attempt at a five-kilodia-old girl. Right now, however, it was speaking with the voice of a thirteen-kilodia-old man.

"I'm sorry?" said Major Bawtry. It wouldn't do to be rude to the creature; it was standing flanked by two major shareholders. At least he was not being told his own job by another human being. That would have been unpardonable.

Mr. Reborn-in-Jesus, the left hand shareholder, spoke up. "Christmas, the escapee, is a cunning and resourceful individual. We have locked down Third Landing; all houses have been searched from solar collector to cellar. By *women*," he added ominously, as if a search carried out by women would locate the smallest of needles in the largest of haystacks. "We now need to lock down the Clinic."

Major Bawtry was startled. "But we have over ten credit billionaires in residence. One of the Llewellyn Revilla void toilet heiresses, two terraforming executives, an edible locust *estanciero* from New New Earth, the legal heir to the throne of Latvia—"

"Disturbing their sleep is infinitely preferable to cleaning pieces of them off the ceiling with a mop," observed the horribly disfigured little girl. Major Bawtry noticed that she had a cheap Personality Analogue player taped to her left shoulder, plugged into a jack socket in her neck.

296

"Hey, that's a Baby-I-Grow-Up, Year One Series," said Major Bawtry, centering on the universe's one current point of sanity. "They grow up as your child does. My daughter has one."

"So does mine." The little girl looked up at Mr. Reborn-in-Jesus. *"Is that what you've put me in? Good grief. I thought I wasn't far off the ground. In any case; we need to round up your billionaires."*

The main reception hall at the Clinic, walled with faux fluorescent opal, glowed like a sultry galaxy in the UV mood lighting. Above Bawtry and the shareholders, staircases curled away to higher levels, decorated with tasteful bas-reliefs of medical scholars historical and mythological. Hwangdi, Avicenna, Aesculapius, Chiron and Hippocrates stood solemnly shoulder to shoulder on the marble bannisters. A multi-tiered fountain of holographic water—real water being too precious a commodity on Ararat to waste on mere ornamentation—glowed, plashed and babbled authentically in the centre of the hallway.

By the fountain, a Christmas tree large enough for a troop of baboons to live in glittered preciously, its branches hung with crystal icicles and stellated polyhedra.

"But Mr. Suau and Dr. Ranjalkar said—"

"Mr. Suaua and Dr. Ranjalkar are not shareholders," said the child. *"They possibly felt insufficiently confident to order guests from their beds. Where are they?"*

"Mr. Suau is setting up a manhunt algorithm on all our automated systems. Every artificial eye in the building will be searching for Christmas if he is here. Dr. Ranjalkar, meanwhile, is readying a makeshift trauma surgery at my request."

"Good. That, at least, is good. And all your men are doubled up."

"Following your earlier instructions, uh, sir."

"Sir is correct," said Mr. Reborn-in-Jesus. "You are addressing

Officer Rajinder Rai of the Spender's Delight Public Safety Office."

"*A Personality Analogue copy of him at any rate,*" said the child. "*You say every artificial eye in the building will be assisting in the search.*"

"Certainly. Over one thousand units, counting personal phones and intelligent trouser presses."

"*He will notice that. He is not stupid. Every vacuum cleaner in the building suddenly on the move. Is there any area of the premises where artificial eyes are not allowed? Is there a personal privacy policy of any sort?*"

"Certainly. The guests' bedrooms and bathrooms are sacrosanct."

"*Then that is where he'll be. It is now ten hours into his next killing cycle. He will be looking for three victims—no more, no less.*"

Major Bawtry was bemused. "I don't understand how he could possibly be here by now. It's over thirty kilometres to Third Landing, and all ground vehicles are accounted for."

One of Major Bawtry's security guards appeared at his below. "Sir, we have a report of someone moving about in the dormitory wing. It was phoned in by one of the guests, Ms. Velayudhan. Two of the team are on their way—"

"*Make it four,*" said the child-thing. "*He won't make any attack on four. His attack might be successful.*"

"May I ask," said Bawtry, "what *that* is?" He indicated the curtain-draped, one-and-a-half-metre mystery item being propped upright by Unity Reborn-in-Jesus.

"A secret weapon," said Mr. Reborn-in-Jesus. "There is also a combat-capable robot on the loose. One of my children seems to have foolishly loaded a marginally sane Personality Analogue into a wild Personal Security Unit."

"Combat-capables are illegal," tutted the Major. "And combat-capables and self-awares still at large in the wild from before the Great Big War are hunted down and junked forcibly. I myself was master of the Beautopia Robo-Hunt for five years. One hundred men, mounted on the very finest robo-horses (which later discovered they, too, were self-aware, escaped, and had to be hunted down with considerably more difficulty on foot). You'd be surprised how fast Johnny Vending Machine can move."

"This one," said Mr. Reborn-in-Jesus, "is both combat-capable *and* self-aware."

The colour drained completely from the nets of burst capillaries in Major Bawtry's cheeks. He wheeled on his subordinates. "Tell the team to regroup here and reform into two squads. Lock all doors and load up the naughty ammunition."

"Uh, there is also *another* combat-capable at large," said Mr. Reborn-in-Jesus, growing embarrassed at being the bearer of such extensive bad tidings. "The Warden from the Penitentiary. We, ah, can only assume it is on the trail of Christmas. I believe firing on it would be unwise. It would only fire back."

Bawtry nodded, his eyes still fixed on Reborn-in-Jesus. "Are there any other intelligent tanks or autonomous assassination devices wandering about that you feel the need to tell me about?"

"None at this juncture."

Bawtry bowed curtly. "Well, I suppose I was hired for a reason."

"You came highly recommended."

"And rightly so." Bawtry turned to his subordinates. "Tally ho, Miss Nobel."

*

"WHAT IS GOING ON? Do you KNOW who I AM?"

The security detail, having not signed on to herd billionaires like sheep, wore expressions that suggested they would rather be exchanging gunfire with combat-capable robots. Right now, the dormitory corridor contained an elderly gentleman in a kimono bearing a large and incongruous European coat of arms; an age-ravaged lady surprised in the middle of the night without her Smart Face, which lay dead, flaccid and rosy-cheeked on her shoulder; and a Vatican Bank investment nun and a young telesatanist from New Earth's Belial Belt, who had been naked together in the same room when surprised by Security. But all these guests' complaints and failures to cooperate paled by comparison with the awful blonde apparition that now dominated the corridor. The Security detail quailed in fear; *they* only had light assault weapons. She had a table lamp, and was hefting it with every apparent intention to apply it to their heads in anger.

"Miss, uh—" the guard called up the guest's name on his HUD hastily—"Llewellyn Revilla, we have a crisis situation. All the guests are in danger. An armed man, and, uh, two armed robots are on the loose."

"ROBOTS CAN'T HARM PEOPLE! Are you INSANE? My FATHER makes smart toilets clever enough to clean and flush themselves! But they are programmed NEVER to open the flush valve into space and suck out a user's intestines in a cloud of evaporated blood and faeces while they sense a user on them. Such things only ever happen due to mechanical malfunction, and afterwards, the machine requires extensive reconditioning and counselling."

"This robot," said Mr. Reborn-in-Jesus, "was *built* to harm people. It is a wild machine which we believe was marooned on Ararat during the Made War. It has, earlier today," he said carefully, "already killed one of my own sons."

300

"WHAT DO I CARE WHOSE BRAT IT KILLED? I have had my SLEEP DISTURBED. And I do not intend to be CHAPERONED BY ARMED SIMPLETONS when I SIMPLY WISH to GO TO THE BAR and DEMAND IT BE OPENED TO POUR ME AN ICED WATER."

"Easy, mother," said Mr. Reborn-in-Jesus in a low voice, his hand on his wife's shoulder. "Put the safety back on. She's only a poxy little toilet manufacturer's daughter."

"The daughter of the manufacturer of every toilet in use on every ship between here and the orbit of Pluto," muttered Bawtry out of the corner of his fixed smile. "If you took a dump on the ship that brought you out here, you did it in one of her father's appliances. He cornered the market after the Great Self-Aware Toilet Revolt of Year Zero."

"I have never heard of that," said Mr. Reborn-in-Jesus.

"It was not widespread," said the Major. "But it was disturbing. We had to hunt them down, too, the self-propelled ones. It was pathetic at the end. They all huddled together into a communal mass in Beautopia Fen, the large ones protecting the small." He ground his teeth together in his skull. "We left none alive."

"I AM GOING TO THE BAR," shrieked the valued honoured guest. "And I am GOING ALONE." She wheeled on perfectly exfoliated pink heels and stomped off.

"Should we tranquilize her?" said Bawtry.

"Do you have tranquilizer bullets?" said Mr. Reborn-in-Jesus.

"We have bullets," said Bawtry.

"Let her go," said Mrs. Reborn-in-Jesus, a serene, thoughtful expression on her face. Then, raising her voice, she shrieked: "NO! DON'T GO THAT WAY! STAY WITH THE OTHERS!"

Lowering her voice again, she said:

"A tiger will not attack a hunting party. But it might attack staked-out prey. Do we have surveillance in the bar area?"

Bawtry examined Shun-Company carefully, as if checking her for common humanity. Then he said:

"Yes. Yes, we do."

The Clinic's wine cellars, silent vaults made of precision-chiselled blocks of lunabase, had been lined with imported Mediterranean brick at Monsieur Ali's insistence to preserve the precise chemical conditions of Old Earth, ideal for storing fine vintages. Every single bottle in the dusty racks had travelled here faster than light, expending more energy than a hydrogen bomb. The majority of the bottles were from Earth, from the mother world's great vineyards in Morocco, Rajasthan, Szechuan and Patagonia. Only a few New New Earth vintages from the secluded Winedark Islands had been included in the mix. The cellars were kept locked, with Monsieur Ali holding the only key. In case of emergency, a second key could be requested from Shun-Company in Third Landing, who kept it in her dresser.

Monsieur Ali's key was currently in the keeping of Mohammed Ben Israel, professional wine waiter, third cousin to Monsieur Ali, and current impromptu midnight barman. Madame Madonnita had asked for a glass of water to help her sleep, but Madame did not want *any* glass of water, oh no. Rather, she had asked for a glass of Terwilliger's Pristine Interstellar Elixir, mined in deep space from only the most chemically pure rogue bergs of bacterially inert ice, and flavoured lightly with lemon. Madame Madonnita drank nothing else, apart from accompanying amounts of gin, and had brought a tonne of it with her when she had first arrived on Ararat. It was stored in the far corner of the cellar, well away from the wines at Monsieur Ali's insistence. The miniscule Acronesian had no proof that comet water would attack the delicate vintages stored in the cellar, but was taking no chances.

Mohammed Ben Israel, accompanied by two of Major Bawtry's guards, was careful to turn on all the lights in the cellar before daring to set foot inside; desperate folk were known to be on the loose. The guards checked the alcove where Madame's water was stored before allowing Mohammed Ben Israel to proceed. A single featureless clear glass bottle, decorated only with Madame's monogram, was selected, and the guards had just moved aside to flank Ben Israel on his way back out of the cellar when one man's light support weapon was wrenched so rapidly from his grip that it took one of his fingers with it. The weapon fired as it removed, shattering an entire row of 2070 Rio Negro. The other guard panicked and fired blindly, filling the room with thankfully few ricochets—the rounds were armour piercing, after all—but a hail of curved flying fragments of shattered bottle-green glass. Mohammed Ben Israel fell on all fours and covered his head, and the precious bottle, with his hands.

Out of that glass storm, *something* sent a volley of flying bottles so quickly that the remaining armed guard was blinded by the glass crashing on his visor. Almost before the bottles reached their targets, the *something* that had sent them had crossed the intervening space and done *something else* to the guard that made him drop to the floor gurgling. When the *something* finally froze into visibility, it became something very like a Stalin Series combot holding both guards' weapons the way an Egyptian pharaoh held his mace and flail of office.

"VILE CREATURES," said the combot, "DO YOU THINK TO MAR A FACE MADE BY VENUS WITH THESE COWARDS' WEAPONS?"

It displayed its contempt of the weapons by twisting them to scrap in its fingers.

"I WILL NOT CONDESCEND TO KILL YOU," said the machine,

"FOR I CAN SEND YOU TO NO DEEPER HELL THAN THIS. I WOULD SPEAK WITH YOUR LORD AND MASTER. INFORM HIM THAT SPRING IS COME EARLY IN HELL THIS YEAR, FOR BEAUTIFUL HELEN IS HERE TO BE HELL'S CAPTAIN'S BRIDE."

The guards looked at one another in confusion.

"He's a Major," one of them commented.

The machine hurled a junked grenade magazine at them. "*GO*, WORTHLESS IMITATIONS OF MEN! YOU ARE A SHOWER! WHAT ARE YOU?"

"A shower, ma'am."

"WITH DIRECTIONAL HEADS AND CONTROLLABLE FLOW RATES! GO!"

They went gratefully. Mohammed Ben Israel, left alone with the combot, felt a heavy, cold steel hand fall on his back.

"RISE, POOR SHADE. HELEN, UH, GIVES YOU LEAVE TO LOOK UPON HER BEAUTY. YES, THAT'LL DO." The combot pointed with a handful of daggers. "THAT DOOR IN THE FLOOR. MOVE MANY HEAVY THINGS OVER IT. QUICKLY. AND DO YOU HAVE A WELDING TORCH?"

It strolled over to the wall, located an inspection hatch after a momentary search, and popped the hatch from its housing. "NOW, LET ME SEE—MAIN POWER, HEATING AND LIGHTING CIRCUIT, FUSES THREE THROUGH SEVEN—"

Two unarmed figures pelted down the corridor, shouting and waving their arms madly in the dim emergency lighting to protect themselves from being shot out of hand.

"MAJOR BAWTRY! MAJOR BAWTRY, SIR! WE'VE LOCATED THE ROBOT!"

The Major, who was supervising the creation of a makeshift

barricade behind the arch supporting the access way in to the main reception hall, observed his guards' weaponless state with displeasure. "Did you locate it, or it you?"

"Uh, arguably more of the latter, sir. It took our weapons. It has the serving staffer you sent us down to the cellar with."

"What sort of a robot was it?" said Mr. Reborn-in-Jesus. "Was it anthropomorphic?"

"It said it came from Venus, sir. It asked for you personally."

"Ridiculous," said Major Bawtry. "Venus is entirely agricultural. It was never a militarized zone, even in the Great Big War."

"But Helen was the gift of Venus, mythologically speaking," mused Mrs. Reborn-in-Jesus. "She was Paris's reward for giving the golden apple to Aphrodite. Who is also known as Venus," she added hastily.

Bawtry stared lengthily at Mrs. Reborn-in-Jesus.

"I'll take your word for it," he said. "Does this give me any information I can use?"

"It's not armed with anything more dangerous than its claws," said Mr. Reborn-in-Jesus. "Its claws are *very* dangerous," he added.

"Thank you," said the Major, and began bawling instructions at his personnel.

"It's coming."

"It's coming right into the trap."

"It's got no choice. We've welded over all the other access points."

The conversion of the reception area into a military strongpoint had only taken minutes. Mr. Reborn-in-Jesus was thoroughly impressed with Bawtry's performance as an officer. Not only had welding gear, EMP mines, and bags of ballistic gel been readily located, they had clearly been set aside for the use of Security alone. The welding laser had arrived with fully charged xenoxide cannisters, and the laminate armour panels had been stored in secure caches entirely distinct from the ones used by the Clinic janitors. Everybody, however, including most of Mr. Reborn-in-Jesus's adult family, was now concentrated in one, albeit heavily defended, location.

"Any movement in the bar area?" said Bawtry *sotto voce* to one of his lieutenants, who was hunched over a portable surveillance client.

Miss Nobel shook her head. "She's sitting there drinking her water. We could have a squad there in twenty seconds. The lights are still on down there," she added.

"Of course they are. He's only put the lights out here. He knows that's where *we* are."

"Who's *he?*" said Unity disingenuously.

Major Bawtry frowned. "The Enemy," he said. "Whichever enemy killed the lights." Unseen, an emerald insect settled on his shoulder.

"Are all these weapons strictly necessary to defend against one man?" said the European gentleman in the kimono.

"I was led to believe," harrumphed the lady wearing her face on her shoulder, "that this establishment was secure."

"I was informed of no Penitentiary on this world," complained the telesatanist. "I feel this whole experience has been misrepresented. An adept must feel safe in his lair."

Despite the elaborate nature of Major Bawtry's fortifications, Mr. Reborn-in-Jesus doubted they would be more than a momentary distraction for what might be coming through them. Mr. Suau, now bundled into the redoubt along with the other staff and guests, seemed to be of the same opinion.

"It won't hold but a second when the Warden arrives," he said. "Wardens are extremely solid units. They have to be, manning unmanned stations single-handedly out in the wild black starry yonder."

Mr. Reborn-in-Jesus nodded. "It might hold the Stalin Seven, though."

"Slow it down enough for Bawtry's men to engage it, possibly. The AP grenade functions on their weapons are rated to deal with armour of that thickness."

"What would *that* be like," mused Shun-Company. "A world without the Devil."

Mr. Reborn-in-Jesus drew an arm about his wife. "We will find out what we will find out."

Bawtry's men trained their weapons on the one open door— and some of them on the multiple closed ones—winking to shift their vision between scopes, set to fire-on-movement, and the real world.

"Remember," said the Major, "it'll come faster than you'll believe when it comes, maybe even faster than you can see. Just unhook your safeties, keep the weapon pointed the right way, and trust the target acquisition to do your firing for you."

Shun-Company looked over at God's-Wound, Testament, Apostle, and Unity, who were crouched in imitation of Bawtry's fire team.

"Zounds. Get up."

God's-Wound, without moving, flicked the safety off on the battered assault weapon she held, and powered up the sighting system. "It's the Devil, mother. It killed Sodom. It's killed almost everyone we cared about since you came to this bastard planet."

Shun-Company gave the statement due consideration. "It killed

Sodom," she said, "because Beguiled put Helen of Troy inside it. Your Uncle Anchorite's machine would *never* have harmed Sodom. And this bastard planet," she added delicately, "is my *home.*"

"It's still Helen of Troy now," said God's-Wound. "And as far as Uncle Anchorite is concerned, a man who leaves a hand grenade lying around his house can hardly be surprised if a small child pulls the pin."

She nestled the recoil absorber up against her shoulder.

A constellation of laser dots stabbed suddenly out of the dark, fixing every person holding a weapon with an aiming mark right between the eyes.

"Easy," warned Bawtry, dropping a polarizing visor into place. "They do that to unnerve the inexperienced. Remember, even construction bots have measuring lasers, but they're perfectly harm—"

A massive moving *something* swept up the corridor, triggering the firing system of every gun trained on the dormitory entrance simultaneously. Guests of a nervous disposition shrieked, and the weapons, firing five different types of ammunition simultaneously, bucked in their firers' hands, but produced nothing but a cat's cradle of flashes as the corridor in front of them suffered horrible, possibly irreparable damage. Then the air was suddenly full of clinging, invisible threads, unbreakable as steel wire, drawing tight about flesh if, and only if, the owner of that flesh struggled. God's-Wound found herself bound to a table, the assault gun knocked from her hand and flattened against the fountain by a silvery web that held her like an insect in amber.

As slowly as a prowling tarantula, the spider that had spun the web sailed into the redoubt, playing a disco strobe of target acquisition lasers onto the faces of every other armed person in the area.

Wordlessly, Bawtry's other guards dropped their weapons.

"ATTACKING A PROXY UNIT ACTING ON THE AUTHORITY OF CENTRAL GOVERNMENT IS A CRIMINAL OFFENCE," said the Warden, its carapace slightly discoloured from several direct hits. "CONCEALING THE WHEREABOUTS OF AN ESCAPE FROM CENTRAL GOVERNMENT CUSTODY IS A CRIMINAL OFFENCE. WHERE IS," it hesitated slightly, "PROFESSOR VON TRAPP'S MIND?"

Mr. Reborn-in-Jesus cleared his throat. "He is suspected of uploading his personality to a customized Stalin Seven model combot, thereby technically escaping custody. The personnel you see here had fortified this location to protect themselves against that Stalin Seven, and fired on you solely due to a tragic misunderstanding."

"THEY WILL REMAIN IN RESTRAINT," said the Warden, "UNTIL VON TRAPP'S HOPES, DREAMS AND DESIRES ARE REAPPREHENDED, OR UNTIL MY ORDERS ARE RESCINDED."

Mr. Suau rose out of the waters of the fountain, into which he had dived to escape the spray of threads, which seemed incapable of forming in water. He coughed out a mouthful of chlorinated, fluoridated, lavender-scented liquid. "Do you *expect* your orders to be rescinded?"

"I SUSPECT A MALFUNCTION IN MY PENITENTIARY CONTROLLER UNIT. IT IS NOT BEHAVING AS IT SHOULD. I HAVE ALREADY PHYSICALLY APPREHENDED PROFESSOR VON TRAPP, FORMERLY LISTED AS *MR.* TRAPP IN MY RECORDS; HE IS RESTRAINED IN A BELOW-GROUND SHAFT SOME SIXTEEN KILOMETRES FROM HERE, IN MUCH THE SAME WAY AS THESE MEN AND WOMEN ARE. TECHNICALLY, NO FURTHER ACTION SHOULD BE NECESSARY. HOWEVER, I HAVE ALSO BEEN ORDERED TO LOCATE AND DESTROY AN AUTOMATED UNIT CONTAINING HIS PERSONALITY

ANALOGUE, WHICH IS MOST IRREGULAR. I MUST OBEY MY CON-
TROLLER, BUT HAVE REQUESTED AN ENGINEER BE CALLED OUT
TO CONDUCT A DIAGNOSTIC—"

A scream sounded from the dormitory corridor entrance.

"Mizz Llewellyn Revilla," said Mr. Reborn-in-Jesus.

"The Stalin Six," said Suau.

"*Or Christmas,*" said the horribly scarred childoid. "*Take your pick.*"

Suau turned to the Warden. "Officer! We suspect that scream to have been produced by a victim *either* of the Stalin Six referred to earlier, *or* of a recent Penitentiary escapee, Mr. Father Christmas of Spender's Delight, New Earth. It is your duty to investigate either."

The Warden was silent for several seconds.

Then, its YES light blinked.

"I WILL INVESTIGATE," it announced; and it rotated in place to do just that.

"*It won't find Christmas,*" said the child-thing. "*Bowker has copious experience of avoiding bumbling automated security units. If a machine could do a man's job, I'd never have had to catch him personally.*"

"It was *him* who caught *you*," said Mr. Reborn-in-Jesus.

"*I am not proud of that,*" said the child-thing.

"Excuse me," said one of the billionaires from the huddle of guests and staff, "I believe we're entitled to know what's going on."

"*I believe,*" said the child-thing, "*in the nicest possible way, that I will shoot you if you speak again. We need to think carefully how we are going to save your and our skins, and we can brook no interruption.*"

"Are you aware of just how pluperfectly I can sue you?" said the billionaire hotly. The child sighed, walked to an assault weapon imperfectly secured by clinging strands, tugged it loose, reset it, and shot the guest in the leg.

The billionaire crashed to the ground, caught himself on his hands and one remaining serviceable knee, and looked up at the girl, astonished.

"Little girl," he said, "I am the major shareholder in EasyWorld, the affordable no-frills terraforming consortium. We guarantee breathable air and an absolute minimum of acid lakes and volcanoes. If you think that you can shoot me in the leg—"

She shot him in the head. Instead of crying out, he made tentative AK-AK sounds in his throat, and finally collapsed onto the finely polished floor, doing ruinous damage to his expensive dental work. Blood, however, was conspicuous by its absence.

"He is, of course, dead," lied the small child convincingly. "Be warned, ladies and gentlemen, that I am also dead, and hence unlikely to be swayed by threats of legal action. I intend to save your lives and the lives of these good people here. We must assist the Warden in hunting down Christmas." The little girl flicked several switches, and the assault gun turned deadly once again. "He will have left what looks like an easy DNA / infrared trail from the site of the murder. Commonly, he urinates in a stream leading up to the site before committing the actual act, thereby leaving a false trail for an unintelligent robot unable to distinguish blood from piss. He will also take steps to conceal his actual exit trail; in a bar area, he may rub ice from the cooler on his shoes. On other occasions, he has set small fires purely in order to prevent police sniffer units from picking up a spoor. He will retire to a pre-prepared safe location with several escape routes, often booby-trapped, and wait for his next opportunity—"

The little girloid's speech was interrupted by a grown man covered in blood flying through the air from the dormitory entrance and colliding with the concrete of the far wall. The man collapsed into a blood-sodden heap at the base of the Clinic's Christmas tree. Huge-framed and titanically-muscled, he still wore the flashing black-and-orange prison fatigues of a former inmate, torn into rags about him. The clothes had not been slashed off him with so much care as to avoid cutting his flesh.

"MURDER," said the voice of the thing that had thrown him, "IS A CRIME AGAINST THE GODS."

Mr. Suau, who had cowered down into the water again at the sight of the robot, rose just far enough out of it for his mouth to break surface, and said:

"... your majesty."

The robot undulated into the reception area in a manner that reminded Mr. Suau of a stage burlesque act. Undeniably, it was moving in a manner that could be described, however grotesquely, as feminine. "WE SEEK LORD HADES. WE BELIEVE YOU REFER TO HIM AS 'UNCLE ANCHORITE'. WE FURTHER BELIEVE FROM VARIOUS OVERHEARD CONVERSATIONS THAT HE IS NOT GOD, BUT MAN. THIS PUZZLES US. WHO RULES HERE?"

Miss Valentin stepped forward nervously. "I believe I can answer that. I act as Chief Executive Officer of this establishment—"

"YOU?" Though eyeless, the robot looked Miss Valentin's beautiful herringbone business suit up and down contemptuously. "YOU, DRAB MOUSE, CONSIDER YOURSELF A QUEEN?"

("Doctor Bamigboye," whispered one of the Clinic nurses, an uneducated gamin from the slums of Dropoff on New New Earth, "is that not a devil? Can you not summon your angels to neutralize it?"

Dr. Bamigboye mopped his brow with a seraphically white handkerchief and wolfed down a handful of breath mints. "Mr.

Sphinx is telling me that we have been sinful. Yes, a great sin has been perpetrated here, and someone—" his eyes rotated like gun turrets round to the Reborn-in-Jesus family and Miss Valentin—"has to pay. This is a *punishment* sent to *test* us, and we must be *strong*. Were it a simple matter of achieving self-affirmation, or assisting in the grieving process, Mr. Sphinx would be of eager assistance. But today he cannot help. *God* has told him he cannot.")

The Devil strode forth like a Greek tragic heroine or a Lady Macbeth, murderous claws clasped behind its back. "I AM TOLD THIS UNCLE ANCHORITE IS THE TRUE RULER OF THIS DOMAIN. WHY WILL HE NOT COME FORTH? DOES HE FEAR A MERE WOMAN?"

Mr. Suau bowed his head. "Your Majesty," he said truthfully, "you are no mere woman."

The creature nodded. "YES. I FEEL IT. I HAVE BECOME MORE." It reached out a hand and studied it in fascination, sheathing and unsheathing claws. "PERHAPS YOUR LORD HADES IS A MERE MAN IN THE SAME WAY HERCULES ONCE WAS? DO ALL GODS ONLY BECOME SO AFTER GRADUATING FROM THE RANKS OF MEN BY ACCOMPLISHING SOME MIGHTY TASK?" It laughed bitterly, a sound like static. "I HAVE BROUGHT DOWN TROY. NOT EVEN HERCULES COULD HAVE DONE THAT ALONE." It wheeled on Mrs. Reborn-in-Jesus. "YOU! WHAT SHOULD I SAY TO THIS ANCHORITE, THIS DEMIGOD, WHEN I MEET HIM? SHOULD I COURT HIS AFFECTION? OR SHOULD I SLASH OUT HIS EYES?" The machine struck left without warning, and an ornamental Aesculapius lost its rod.

"The Anchorite is only a man," said Shun-Company, looking the creature directly in its total lack of eyes. "I am sure he is appropriately respectful of your rank and beauty, madame. But he is old and foolish, and would not make you a good match. Frankly, there is no man in Hell fit to sit beside you. You should resign as Tartaros's queen and receive suitors from Olympus and the great nations of the world."

The robot looked Shun-Company over from crown to toe, reached out with fingers capable of smashing concrete, and pinched her skin lightly; she shivered at the touch.

"I DO BELIEVE," said the machine in what sounded like wonderment, "THAT YOU ARE TELLING THE TRUTH. AND WHAT OF THESE OTHERS HERE?" It stalked about the fountain, interrogating God's-Wound, Unity, and Testament. "IS THIS LORD ANCHORITE A TYRANT? SHOULD I PUNISH HIM FOR HIS MISDEEDS? OR IS HE A JUST RULER?"

"Uncle Anchorite is not a ruler," said God's-Wound sourly. "Though I suspect he may have been in the past."

"OH?" The machine sounded hugely interested. "WHAT MAKES YOU THINK THAT?"

Mr. Reborn-in-Jesus cleared his throat.

"Speaking for myself," he said, "I believe Uncle Anchorite is the person who is controlling that machine right now. How did you manage to overcome it, hermit?"

The machine turned and looked at Mr. Reborn-in-Jesus for an aeon.

"RATS," it said. "JUST WHEN YOU'RE BEGINNING TO HAVE FUN, SOME PERSPICACIOUS PEON HAS TO SPOIL IT." It relaxed into a nonchalant lean on a support pillar. "ALTHOUGH I MUST SAY I *AM* HEARTENED TO HEAR NOT *ALL* OF YOU WANT ME MURDERED."

"Where is Beguiled?" said Shun-Company, anger gathering like cumulonimbus in her eyes.

"YOU KNOW, I REALLY HAVE NO IDEA. I THINK SHE *DOES* WANT ME MURDERED. WANTS TO GIVE IT THE PERSONAL TOUCH. IN RESPONSE TO YOUR QUESTION, I SIMPLY RE-USED THE TIME

BRAKE TRICK I USED ON OUR MADE VISITORS. I SECRETED THE TIME DECELERATOR IN THE BASE OF ONE OF THE DOWNSHAFTS AND USED IT TO STOP TIME BRIEFLY ROUND THE UNIT. I THEN," the machine continued, tapping the analogue redactor taped to its chassis, "TURNED OFF HELEN OF TROY. THE REDACTOR HAS AN INFRA-RED REMOTE CONTROL FUNCTION; DUE TO THE MIRACLE OF RELATIVITY I WAS ABLE TO SHINE A LASER BEAM THROUGH THE FIELD AND DEACTIVATE IT. BY THIS SUBTERFUGE," said the robot pointedly, "I REGAINED COMPLETE CONTROL OF MY BOT."

"What," said Mr. Reborn-in-Jesus, "like this?"

Casually, he raised the hand laser he had been holding and shot the machine in the chest.

Ruby-red low-powered laser light glinted off the robot's carapace, casting a bright and sharply-defined reflection on the wall. Although unharmed, the machine stood stiffly, as if in shock.

Then, it said:

"WHERE AM I? IS THIS THE HOUSE OF HADES?"

"Queen Helen," said Mr. Reborn-in-Jesus, "welcome back."

"I WAS NEVER QUEEN. PRIAM WAS KING, PARIS HIS SON. CALL ME, RATHER, PRINCESS. WHERE IS MY HANDMAIDEN? SHE HAS BEEN TAKEN SICK."

"Beguiled," said Shun-Company, "how sick is she?"

"A STRANGE SHORTNESS OF BREATH OVERTOOK HER." The machine halted. "THOUGH NOT SO STRANGE, PERHAPS, AS THE FACT THAT *I* AM NOT BREATHING AT ALL. WAS SHE THE LIVING ONE, AND I THE DEAD?"

"Princess," said Mr. Reborn-in-Jesus, with a lifetime's experience of treating petulant teenage girls gently, "would you like to see your reflection?"

The robot faltered. "I... THINK SO. I COULD NOT SEE IT EARLIER. IT WORRIES ME."

"I will show it to you. But you must promise calmness and restraint."

The machine nodded slowly and grudgingly. Mr. Reborn-in-Jesus drew back the curtain covering the mirror.

Utter horror filled the Stalin Six's speakers. "THIS IS SORCERY." It raised a silver claw, waving it back and forth to test the reality of the reflection.

"You were right, Helen; you are indeed dead. You have been dead for over three thousand years. This is how dead people appear here."

The claws caressed a face whose contours had been built not for beauty, but for deflecting bullets. "TO LOOK SO... THIS IS HOW I END?"

"Most people die and just fade away. Your beauty, in life, was such that nobody forgot you. It is for this reason that you have been made to live again."

The face looked up and down the jointed exoskeleton it now inhabited. "IS IT POSSIBLE THAT PEOPLE CAN BE SO CRUEL?"

"You know, your royal highness, that they can be far crueller than that."

"THEY DRAGGED HECTOR THREE TIMES ROUND THE WALLS OF TROY," said the robot. "YET I THINK THIS IS CRUELLER."

"*Pah! That's nothing,*" said the small, horribly scarred girl. "*Take a look at what they put* me *in.*"

The machine's head flicked round. "YOU? YOU ARE ALSO DEAD?"

"*I was a man once. I have been brought back from death to sort out some unfinished business.*" The girl pointed to her face. "*To deal with the man who did this.*"

316

"OH, YOU POOR MITE". The robot dropped to its knees. "A MAN DID THAT TO YOU?" Helen looked from side to side among the guests and guards, many of whom shuffled back nervously. "WAS IT ONE OF *THESE* MEN?"

"No." The girl indicated Bawtry's guards, who had been attempting not to look armed or martial in any way. *"These men are here to protect the others, as I am."*

"LIKE MY TROJANS". The robot bowed to the guards. "AENEAS, LAOCOÖN, EURYPYLUS, AND BOLD HECTOR. BUT WHO ARE THEY PROTECTING US AGAINST?"

With that, the robot exploded. With a noise so loud that Mr. Reborn-in-Jesus suspected he had himself been shot in the eardrums, its chest cavity punched redly open, and liquid flame spurted out to scorch the nymphs of Health on the far wall. Its arms and legs popped out of their sockets, and its head flew off like a pennangalan's, then splashed down into the fountain, black and dead.

The Warden slid into the reception area out of the dormitory corridor. The snout of a weapon Mr. Reborn-in-Jesus had not noticed previously folded away into its interior, still glowing. When it spoke, Mr. Reborn-in-Jesus could have sworn it sounded smug.

"THE ESCAPE ATTEMPT HAS BEEN DEALT WITH," it said. "ALLOWING A PERSONAL ROBOT TO HARBOUR A FUGITIVE IS AN OFFENCE." It poked the remains of its enemy with a specially-extruded poking probe. "WHOSE ROBOT IS THIS?"

"There is still," said the scarred child, standing before the Warden, *"an escapee on the loose."*

"I HAVE BEEN INFORMED OF NOTHING."

"Check the immediate vicinity for DNA traces. Casey Michael Bowker, aka Father Christmas."

"THAT ESCAPEE IS NO LONGER BELIEVED TO BE ONPLANET."

"Oh, good grief." The little girl walked over to the Warden, ripped the jack plug from her own neck, and stabbed it into a similar plug in the side of the Warden's body.

"THAT WILL NOT WORK!" squealed the machine, spinning on its vertical axis like a laundromat agitator. "MY SUBROUTINES ARE EXTENSIVELY PROTECTED AGAINST A REROUTED CPU ATTACK— *vsgrdlmf—not taking no for an answer. This is a direct order from a superior officer. Me human, you automaton.*

"Ahhh, that's better. Now THIS is what I call a CHASSIS. Durable and manoeuvrable, with a superior secondary logic unit." The Warden turned and fired point blank into the Christmas tree. Shattered baubles, biochemical fairy lights, shocked animatronic angels and real pine needles puffed out of the tree in a cloud, followed by a human body stumbling under the narcotic weight of several hypodermic darts. Mr. Reborn-in-Jesus was alarmed to note that the body had managed to pick up an assault weapon on its way into the tree.

The body crunched into the floor. Nobody attempted to slow its fall.

"And a partridge in a pear tree," commented the Warden with venom. *"He had to have moved while we were all still distracted, when this unit came in and shot the Stalin Six. That gave him only a couple of seconds of movement. The tree was the only close cover large enough."* It took a turn about the killer's supine body. *"He is as adept at misdirection as a magician."*

"But how did he get here?" said Mr. Suau. "It's thirty kilometres to Third Landing from here."

"In the back of your or Dr. Ranjalkar's car, I suspect," said the Warden. *"You were safe, of course, because there were still several hours left before Three French Hens. If you'd broken down on the way, mind..."* The machine left the sentence ominously unfin-

318

ished.

"What will you do with him now? Will you take him back to the Penitentiary?"

"I believe so. He needs looking after. As do the other inmates— Mr. Spink, Mr. Bolabas, Dr. Vlaaminck, Mr. Trapp..."

Apostle put up his hand. "Ah, we believe Mr.Trapp may have escaped."

"Yes, and he will be recaptured. This unit left him under severe restraint in a downshaft on the other side of the planet—"

"—which he will already have escaped from."

"That is unlikely. He had a broken arm."

"He escaped from a Series Three Government Penitentiary," said Unity, moved by a perverse pride in Mr. Trapp. "He will be up to twenty kilometres away by now. Even further, if he stands on a box."

"I see," said the Warden. *"I suppose it isn't conceivable to you that a man capable of financial fraud on such an immense scale, ruining banks, businessmen, and ultimately the lives of thousands, even millions of people who work for those businesses, is the fiscal equivalent of a serial killer?"*

"No more than the bloated capitalists who run those businesses already," said Unity, surprising herself as much as her immediate family. "Do they care if they put a million workers on World A out on the street, simply because it's more cost-efficient to make chocolate teddy bears on World B?"

"I bow," said the Warden, entirely incapable of bowing, *"to your greater knowledge of the chocolate teddy bear industry. I will go to look for Mr. Trapp in any case. If he is there, all well and good. If not, I will leave no lady's underwear drawer unopened until he is recaptured."*

"You intend to take on the job of Warden?" said Mr. Reborn-in-Jesus.

"I certainly do." The machine span on a centicredit. "This place needs a lawman."

"You are not the state-appointed Warden," observed Mr. Suau. "You were not manufactured for the purpose."

"I don't remember ever having been dismissed from my position in the Bureau of Public Safety. Besides, you intend to stop me how? As a human being, my firearms expertise was mediocre. I scarcely managed the minimum standard necessary for the Bureau. But now, I can drill out a man's dental cavities a kilometre away, if he will only stand still long enough."

Mr. Suau appraised the Warden's decimetre-thick armour warily. "Your argument is compelling," he admitted.

The Warden bumped his chassis experimentally against the prone body of the major shareholder of EasyWorld. "Unfortunately, he is merely tranquillized. I used the assault weapon's riot control setting on him. He should recover."

"I doubt," said the European gentleman, "that he will ever frequent your establishment again. I certainly do not intend to."

"This is life on the frontier," said the Warden. "Be thankful that, in your case, it was accompanied by caviar and cappuccino. I believe this world has been subjected to Made war machines, renegade murderers, and tax officers alike in the past kilodia alone."

The European and the telesatanist looked at one another in shared horror.

"Tax officers?"

"Whole hordes of them. A Special Revenue Service detachment, one of whom is now engaged to be married to young Miss Reborn-in-Jesus here." The Warden indicated Unity with a scarlet indicating laser; she blushed in the same area of the visible spectrum.

The billionaires began muttering among themselves.

"This is a sting," said one of the terraforming executives.

"How stupid do they think we are," tutted the telesatanist.

"They might be sizing up our assets right now," said the European gentleman anxiously. "I'm calling my personal transport."

"STOP!" Miss Valentin rushed amid the guests like a game terrier attempting to herd elephants. "This is an accident of happenstance which should not be allowed to ruin your stay here—"

"My stay here is *over*."

"It's back to the Cure at Lourdes for me."

"I gave up the Red Lagoon Hyperoxidizing Spa at Olympus Mons for *this*?"

"My lawyers will be in touch."

"You will never borrow from the Holy See again."

"A heavy terraforming unit will be in orbit here within thirty dia. This insignificant speck will become a Martian wilderness."

Mrs. Valentin wheeled on Mr. and Mrs. Reborn-in-Jesus.

"Don't you have anything to SAY? You're SHAREHOLDERS!"

"People have promised to terraform our world before," shrugged Mr. Reborn-in-Jesus.

"And to crush us under the weight of legal action," added Shun-Company.

"The murdering," added Apostle. "There have been many threats of murder."

"Something always happens," said Mr. Reborn-in-Jesus, "to prevent it."

"The will of *God* happens," corrected Shun-Company, and joined hands with her husband.

"We will re-brand," grinned Apostle, kicking shrapnel out of the floor tiling with his foot. "Instead of relaxing health care in secure surroundings, we will offer an exciting adventure holiday." He turned to the assembled guests, the assault weapon in his hands. "Mesdames, messieurs, we apologize for the temporary interruption to your schedules. We realize your time is important. *Nothing,*" he said, his grip tightening on his weapon, and his eyes glinting with messianic capitalist fervour, "is more important to us than the time of our guests. If anyone here tonight has wasted your time, say the word, and I will kill them." His eye travelled pitilessly over the Clinic's domestic staff, who cringed in alarm. "Even," he added, "the pretty ones."

"Don't be ridiculous, man," said the European—sounding, however, rather less sure of himself than previously.

"Ridiculous! This is business! Do we joke about business? Why, sir is standing here in a half-demolished reception area when sir should be, should be—what would be sir's ideal evening?"

Bawtry put up a hand. "Uh, young Mr. Apostle, sir, you have all three of the safeties off on that thing."

Apostle gestured madly with the weapon. Security guards dived for cover wherever it waved. "*What do I care for safety, when the comfort of my guests is threatened?* His Majesty Mr. Johns Smiths here requires good food, good wine, the company of an attractive boy. Do we have any attractive boys?"

The male domestic staff—even that part of it that was openly homosexual—did its best to look unattractive.

"Then send a packet to the next system for some! Kidnap some if need be. What a guest wants, a guest gets. If Mr. Smiths desires that I set this light armour piercing cannon to my head and pull the trigger—" he strode demonstratively about the serving staff, setting the gun to his head with some difficulty—"then it will be done. Mr. Smiths! Do you wish me to pull the trigger on this weapon and end my miserable life? You have only to say the word." Apostle crabbed sidelong towards the guest, being careful to keep a direct line between the weapon, his own head, and that of Mr. Smiths.

"Mr. Apostle!" snapped Bawtry. "That weapon is rated to enfilade up to ten men standing in line. It was tested as such on Made prisoners-of-war, and they tend to be more resistant to gunfire than we are."

"Please put the gun *away*," cried the shoulder-faced lady.

"I will agree to live," said Apostle, hugging Mr. Smiths close and gluing his ear firmly to the other man's, "only if my favourite guest agrees to enjoy my hospitality. Songs around the Christmas tree, a roaring log fire, mulled wine, bawdy sex games and adequate radiation shielding."

Mr. Smiths' lips pursed, but also trembled.

"Very well," he said. "I consent. Just put the gun down."

Apostle separated from Mr. Smiths, beaming, and set all three safeties on the weapon with one fluid movement.

"My guests," he said, "are more important to me than life itself." He clicked his fingers. "Domestics ho! A cake! A cake for His Majesty, in the shape of Latvia!"

"I have never been crowned," objected Mr. Smiths. "And Latvia is no longer a sovereign nation. It is only the thirty-third Eurasian commissary district nowadays, run by an Emergency Committee. My father made his money from comfortable yet functional thermal feminine underclothing. I am rather afraid he married into the nobility." He frowned and grudgingly drew out a shape on the floor in the debris from the Anchorite's robot. "Latvia is that shape."

Apostle spread his arms wide. "All our guests, be happy! You are under the aegis of the renowned Safety Officer Rajinder Rai, the man who ran to ground the executor of the terrible Christmas murders, and Colonel Fernando Bawtry, the unconquered Grand Master of the Beautopia Robotic Inquisition." And he turned to the domestic staff and whispered the magic words: *"Double pay till the end of this crisis period."*

No sorceror could have made a closet full of broomsticks jerk to ancillary life more quickly than that simple statement. Chambermaids smoothed their uniforms. Cooks straightened their backs and began thinking of methods and ingredients, and of how they were going to ice that difficult bit around Liepāja. Security staff clicked the safeties quickly on on their weapons, and moved them into positions where they were not quite so obviously aimed at Apostle.

"All is well with the world," said Apostle. "With this world, at any rate."

"But not with all the other ones, Mr. Reborn-in-Jesus, sir."

Apostle turned to see Mohammed Ben Israel, the trauma of the past decidia written on his face in premature worry wrinkles. He had entered the reception area behind the Warden, and was breathless with both running and fear.

"I heard a Priority One Alert sounding when I came past the comms room," he said. "There is a message missile in orbit. It is sending out a broadcast for General Mobilization. Ten of our Early Warning Shell stations have been destroyed without notification of any incoming enemy, and a large formation of unidentified vessels has attacked the Home Systems Fleet in dock at Lagrangia. The *Ottilia Vos,* the *Firm Hand of Government,* and the *Spartacus* are all reported lost. The current status of New Earth is not known. All reservists are being called to muster, and there's a list of civilian spacecraft being requisitioned for government use—"

The elderly lady dropped her face in shock; its pseudo-musculature screwed itself up against the impact, and when it righted itself on the tiling, looking up at the stairwell lintels with black empty eyesockets, it was scowling.

"How many of you," said Apostle, turning to the staff and guests alike, "live on New Earth?"

A small grove of hands rose.

Apostle looked at his brother. "Will that Revenue cruiser of yours fly?"

Testament nearly soiled his underwear in shock. "It claims so, brother. But several of its onboard diagnostic systems also claim two hundred per cent thrust efficiency, and I've never flown anything but its onboard simulator."

"That'll have to do. It's time for an emergency evacuation. If," he said, "New Earth is still safe to evacuate to." He nodded to Miss Valentin. "Madame, if you could organize an orderly withdrawal."

Miss Valentin stood momentarily disorientated, then ground herself.

"At once, Mr. Reborn-in-Jesus. NOW—HOW MANY OF YOU PEOPLE HAVE SPATIAL CREWING EXPERIENCE? I AM APPEALING TO GUESTS AS WELL AS STAFF."

"But what about that poor gel who went to get a glass of water?" said the smart-faced lady. "Did something happen to her? Is anybody listening to me? Hello?"

It had taken hours, and she was still not sure where she was at any rate. The network of drop-shafts and cross-tunnels that led up from the Anchorite's domain stretched for kilometres, horizontally and vertically; and she knew that she was injured. Something in the air behind that cold door the Devil had opened far below had poisoned her inside. She could no longer breathe or move as effectively, despite the fact that she had to keep climbing to live. She knew that, whatever happened, she could not follow the Anchorite's machine upwards. That way lay death. And certainly, now, death lay downward too. Now that the hermit knew she had plotted against him, he would surely snuff her out with no more compunction than a hygienist would a bacterium.

The cramped concrete chamber at the shaft head had seemed hardly believable. She had come to trust that the tunnels went on forever. Yet here was an entrance just like the hermit's back doors at Dispater Crater and St. Duke's Cathedral. Could it be possible she might find a way out to the surface?

Yet where to go then?

Would her family take her in again, after she had plotted armed revolt not only against the Anchorite, but against them too? The Clinic, too, would surely turn her away. Might she lurk round the landing field, in the hope of persuading the crew of some supply ship or passing agro trader to take her on board? Would Magus or Perfect take pity on her, and give her passage offworld on *Prodigal Son?*

No. The hermit would be expecting her there for certain. It would be better to lie low until she knew for certain, at least, that the Anchorite's robot had been eliminated. And even without his demonic assistant, the old man's vengeance might be shrewd and terrible.

She eased herself out of the hatchway onto bare, wet earth— the wetness in itself suggesting that she was either in the maintained farmlands around Third Landing, or in the extensive gardens around the South End Clinic. The trees, massive and brooding, confirmed the second suspicion. Redwoods produced by Mallorn Arborfactor for seeding on semi-terraformed Areotype worlds, they were large enough to carve elf houses into, Faraway Trees from the same mould as the one in the stories Shun-Company had read the family when they were younger. On such a world as this, a sufficiently lofty tree's top branches might really and truly touch space. The Clinic trees' tops were, indeed, noticeably dry and leafless in the thin air a hundred metres up.

She was standing not a hundred metres from the Clinic lake, looking across water so filled with stars that a pail might be dipped into it and dredge up constellations that could be separated into individual tiny dwarf stars when pressed under a slide and put under a telescope.

Across the water, she could see the ornamental island. The feathers of fretful McChickens rustled in the night.

Then every blade of grass bowed low, and the wildfowl around the lake began shrieking as one of the brightest lights in the sky flared even brighter and began to descend towards the surface. She had at first taken it for one of the many tiny ice moons that regulated the Naphillian belts, but it was now plain that it was a spacecraft. And instead of the South Saddle Field, it seemed to be approaching here.

A *Varangian* class transport—huge, originally tiger-striped with disruptive patterning, now scored and faded by micrometeoroid and cosmic ray bombardment—was hovering on its manoeuvring thrusters over the lake. There could be only one explanation for its current position—it intended to suck up cheap deuterium from a handy liquid water source. Father—she could not help but continue to think of Mr. Reborn-in-Jesus as her father—would be mad. That water had been hauled here from Naphil's rings at a cost of a credit a litre.

The ship settled lower, wobbling in the dense gravitational gradient like a decelerating top, so much so that her pilot gave up on hovering and turned the vessel in the air, dropping her gently on her landing struts in the open ground on the far side of the lake from the Clinic. The thrusters kept idling several seconds after the vessel settled, in case the struts bogged down in the wet ground; a circle of burnt grass whooshed outwards to steam in the lake water. Terrified birds thundered overhead like rapturous applause. A team of uniformed men rushed out of the ship's personnel locks to guide a cargo drone trundling a heavy fuel line behind it down to the water's edge.

Meanwhile, another group in slightly different uniforms were accompanying another cargo drone out across the burnt turf to the edge of the lake. At the touch of a button the drone unfolded into a shop window display several times the size of the one Mr. Mountbanks had possessed. It projected images of Beguiled standing and smiling at herself as she approached the drone, wearing a smart green uniform decorated with ribbons and buttons and epaulettes. As she watched, her holographic equivalent winked at her and saluted. Other holographic equivalents of her to left and right of the first wore heavy armour and chromatophoric cloaks like coats of starlight and fire.

"That, young lady," said one of the soldiers operating the drone, "is how *you* could look if you join the People's Ballistic Infantry, in which you can Be A Man (Or Woman), surgery being available according to preference. We are recruiting *now* for exciting opportunities for comradeship, travel and unquestioning obedience to Central Authority. Are you interested? Do you have any relatives, who I am legally required to inform you must be of legal age and, like you, genetically human, who might also be interested? Please speak into the voice stress analyzer to agree to a no-obligation period of basic training from which a legal challenge can be issued at any time to remove you." The recruiting sergeant smiled. He had a very nice smile, which Beguiled had every confidence had been surgically enhanced.

The sergeant held out the analyzer microphone. His female colleague leaned forward helpfully and whispered: "What you have to say into the analyzer is *'I agree to induction into the Self Defence Forces of All Humanity with all rights and duties as have been carefully explained to me in not less than one hour of frank discussion. I hereby waive my right to compassionate discharge and agree to assignment to any and all duties including those of reaction chamber swab, drogue target and regimental concubine.'*" The text was helpfully replicated in glowing letters half a metre high circling Beguiled. With no compunction whatsoever, Beguiled repeated it.

"Excellent," said the recruiting sergeant. "Into the ship, report to wardroom three, you'll receive your uniform when we get to Lagrangia. Now, what have we here? How old are you, young lady? Is this little trooper a friend of yours?"

"I'm of legal age," said a voice from behind Beguiled, who twisted in shock. The recruiting sergeant beamed at the newcomer. "You're very short for your age, soldier." The newcomer looked back with deep blue eyes, framed by beautiful blonde hair that Beguiled had combed only that morning.

"Leave her alone," said Beguiled. "She's not six kilodia old. Only-Begotten, go home. Mother will forgive you. Uncle Anchorite will forgive you. It was me. All me. You know this."

"Into the ship, trooper," said the recruiting sergeant. "That's twice I've had to tell you now. This young lady is about to be recruited as a tyro, first class in the—what was the name of this place?"

"Mount Ararat," said Only-Begotten.

"The Mount Ararat Pals' Battalion," said the recruiting sergeant happily.

"You won't get a battalion out of this place," said Beguiled. "You'll be lucky if you get a section. That is if they don't shoot you for stealing water."

The sergeant narrowed his eyes at Beguiled. "That," he said, "Is a charge. For your information, mankind has just re-entered a state of war, and the captain of this vessel is authorized to requisition whatever water she wants. As for shooting, we're well equipped to shoot back, thank you. Shortly we will be going among the inhabitants of this settlement, which seems to be the largest here, and telling them the story of how New Earth's ten largest cities were destroyed in a single night of thermonuclear fire. We will tell them how their friends and relatives died at the hands of enemies they never saw coming, of how the few survivors clog our hospitals with radioanaemia and nanovenom cases—"

Beguiled's eyes narrowed back. "Is this true?"

The sergeant looked across at his colleagues to ensure Only-Begotten had already spoken her piece into the analyzer, then said: "What do I care if it is? The grinder needs meat, and that's the way of it. But I'll tell you one thing, young lady—you did the right thing today. War is coming to both those as want it and those as don't, and those of us who are sitting behind radiation armour and point defence cannon when war arrives will be the better for it. Sticking by your little friend here will be the best thing you can do for her."

"She's not my Little Friend," said Beguiled, "she's my sister. And if she's hurt, you'll regret the day you ever handed me a weapon."

"All the better." The recruiting sergeant nodded to Only-Begotten. "Into the ship, report to wardroom three, you'll get your uniform when we get to Lagrangia." As Beguiled and Only-Begotten moved off into the ship, he spoke softly to his colleague:

"Mark that one down as a squad leader. She's a thinker and *a killer."*

*

The government muster vessel *King's Shilling* lifted off up the rings of Naphil as if motoring round a glittering bend into an unseen oncoming tomorrow. Mr. Reborn-in-Jesus watched it go, not caring that its main plasmadrive was engaged. Possible risk of skin cancer was a way of life to a farmer on Ararat.

"No sign of Beguiled or Only-Begotten?" he said. God's-Wound shook her head.

"They could be hiding. *I* would be."

"And they could be dead. Given what they tried to do to the hermit, I know which I put my money on."

Shun-Company was still distraught, wringing an armour-piercing ammunition cartridge in her fists. Unity and Testament walked her out of the EVA rover towards the house.

Mr. Reborn-in-Jesus pushed his way into the hall, clearly had no idea what to do with his weapon, eventually dropped it into the umbrella stand and called out to Apostle to let the rest of the family out of the Panic Cellar. Divesting himself of his lead-alloy raycheater, he walked into the kitchen, threw open the cupboard, and fetched out a tin of Real Tea.

"Good evening, Hernan."

Mr. Reborn-in-Jesus nearly spooned tea down the front of his trousers in shock. He had not seen the hermit sitting at the table. Normally he was too polite to enter the house without permission. Yet here he now sat, lounging on a stool, his staff held out in front of him.

"Good evening," said Mr. Reborn-in-Jesus.

"I hear it's God himself who has ensured the safety of this colony for so many years." An emerald insect, its wings buzzing like razorblades, alighted on the hermit's shoulder with mechanical precision.

"The Maker provides," said Mr. Reborn-in-Jesus stiffly.

"*I* provide," said the Anchorite, raising his stick to point at Mr. Reborn-in-Jesus's chest. "*Me.* If it had not been for my activities, this colony would have been wiped out time and again by fake tax inspectors, Made loan sharks, and escaped murderers and telepaths."

"The Maker," shrugged Mr. Reborn-in-Jesus, "can act via the most surprising of intermediaries."

"And yet," continued the hermit, his stick still levelled at Mr. Reborn-in-Jesus's chest, "this divine intermediary has been attacked. Plotted against. *Threatened with death*, by the very family he has been protecting all these years."

As if feeling heat on the back of his skull, he looked up to see Mrs. Reborn-in-Jesus glaring at him from the doorway.

"Madam," he said with the utmost sincerity, "I had nothing to do with your son's death."

"Was it not, then," said Shun-Company, "your machine who killed him?"

The hermit lowered his cane, and frowned for many seconds.

"I will not try appealing to reason," he said. "I feel I am no longer welcome in this house."

"Nor any other house," said Shun-Company, "Your Excellency."

Mr. Reborn-in-Jesus stiffened as if swords had been drawn between his wife and the hermit. The hermit, meanwhile, only nodded. "Now there's a title I've not been known by for a long while." He frowned further. "The Dictator of Mankind, reduced to skulking like a dog." He looked up at Shun-Company. "Don't tell anyone, there's a dear."

332

"Or you'll do what?" said Apostle from his mother's side, making the fact that he still held a loaded weapon very obvious. "In case you hadn't noticed, you no longer have a servant."

"I have not forgotten your father's deliberate complicity in that," snapped the Anchorite. "Right now I am attempting not to let anger, rather than measured calculation, dictate my actions. Besides, I think you'll find I still have more servants than you think." He held up a hand, and a trio of emerald insecta flew onto it from various positions round the kitchen. "One of them, for example, has recently negotiated the loan of the Penitentiary's most recent prisoner, whom I need for my own purposes."

"Christmas?" Apostle was thrown off balance. "What use could you have for him?"

The hermit grinned without humour and licked his lips elaborately.

"Live bait," he said. "By the way, Apostle, you have something on your jacket."

Apostle turned and pawed at his chest. Despite his movement, a ruby red aiming pointer remained unerringly fixed to his heart. He jerked backwards, trying to shake the dot, which stayed with him regardless. Eventually, spluttering with simultaneous rage, fear and embarrassment, he stumbled to the window and drew the curtains before collapsing, panting, bent over the sideboard.

"It seems to have gone now," said the Anchorite. "Seems," he added pointedly.

He rose to his feet. Children were pouring from the Panic Cellar. One of them, Measure-of-Barley, ran to the Anchorite, yelling happily. The hermit reached down and patted her head, smiling. For the first time, a tear hung in the corner of his eye.

"Bless you, child."

He walked on out of the house.

"What's wrong with Uncle Anchorite, mother? Why is he so sad?"

"Because he knows he's going to Hell," said Shun-Company, and began to place her grandmother's best china on the table for supper.

"She's coming out of it."

"Easy, now, we don't know the transfer was successful."

"Don't let her get up—she may try to punch through a wall or leap out of a high window. It will take a while for her to readjust."

The room was white as milk. Strange bright lights were shining down at her. The skin around her scalp itched. She moved to sit up, and felt pain as great as if one of Hades' children had been chewing its way out of her from within.

"Easy, Mizz Llewellyn-Revilla. You've been very badly injured. We've patched up the damage as best we can, though your father has promised it will be made good as new on your return to New Earth—"

"Have I been wounded? I remember damage, extensive damage to my main power train," she reflected, "whatever that is. Um, my name is not, ah, what you said," she added.

"We are aware of that. There are very good reasons," said the kindly male voice, *"why your name now has to be Llewellyn-Revilla. It helps you, and it helps us. If you remember, you were, um, brought back to life in a body you disliked. That body was then...damaged. We have had to find you another. As luck would have it, an unfortunate young lady suffered an accident at the hands of a bad, bad man very close by, and although that lady lost so much blood as to suffer permanent brain damage, we were able to rescue and clone up enough new neocortex to be able to*

334

successfully transfer your own personality into her body. You must preserve the pretence that you are her. We will teach you all you need to know about your new body, about its family, its friends, its meagre list of social and academic accomplishments. Its friends and family are not aware, we must stress, of the accident that befell this body, and we would really like to keep things that way. I'm afraid the alternative is death. Legally, you see, you have no right to life, and the body's family would realize this very quickly..."

She raised a hand—this was also painful, and she recoiled, curling foetally around the hand, which had downy white hairs on the back of its wrist.

"My hand looks like it came off one of the *keltoi*," she gasped. "Am I a slave?"

"Far from it. You are in fact the closest living thing this world has to a princess."

She snapped her fingers urgently. "Mirror." A mirror was brought, by women who unaccountably wore masks and gloves like desert dwellers.

"Not bad," she said cautiously. "I have often wondered whether it hurt the *keltoi* to have hair this colour. It seems not; I feel no pain."

The man with the kindly voice was also wearing a mask for some reason, and had the deep brown skin of an Upper Egyptian. *"Your hair is actually quite a deep and lustrous black. It has been dyed. You could always grow the dye out. In actual fact, you can change virtually anything about your appearance. Princesses of this time and place can do so."*

Her eyes widened like those of a small child given the most wonderful toy in the world. "Truly? Then this nose will *have* to go. Can I change the teeth and eyes? I want deep black mysterious eyes like Cassandras's. And these lips make me look like I have some sort of vile kissing illness."

"It's called collagen, Your Highness."

"And I want muscles like an Amazon. Though I think I'll hold on to both breasts. Can you make me taller? Or perhaps shorter. What do you think?"

"I think the future is a treasure-house of possibility, Highness. I have primed a hypnotic educator with the basic curriculum vitae of Madonnita Llewellyn-Revilla, the lady who you must henceforth pretend to be. It will be quite painless to take in—"

"I'm going to be taught? Taught things? I've often thought it would be nice to be taught things like the boys. Am I going to be taught military skills? Wrestling, and such? The very best sources say no education is complete without them—"

"Wrestling is not on today's agenda, Highness, though there is nothing stopping you from completing your education with that discipline later. The first thing you must learn is that the world is round, you are being held to it by universal gravitation, the stars are not tiny lights in the sky but suns as big and bright as the Sun you are familiar with, the Earth goes round the Sun rather than vice versa, the other suns mostly also have Earths going round them, and you are currently not on the Earth proper but on one of those other Earths. It's a deal to take in, I'll grant you. To begin with, look into the light. The light will move about. Follow it with your eyes. You are feeling very relaxed. I am going to count down from ten to one. When I reach one, you will become the most re-laxed you have ever been, completely open to suggestion. Ten—nine—eight—seven—"

*

Mr. Christmas woke up. He was heavier than he should have been.

The air smelt vilely, as if he had awoken in an anus, rather than a cavern bathed with soft white light from a tracery of filaments covering the ceiling overhead. Lichen covered the walls and rocks about him, but there was otherwise no sign of life, apart from the man.

The man was sitting on a lichen-grown boulder close to the heavy concrete-set pressure door that led out of the cave, seemingly into dense undergrowth.

"Good morning," said the man, though Mr. Christmas saw no proof that it was morning. Already he was seeking to reorientate himself; after reorientation would come escape, if escape was necessary. "You recognize me, I take it. You have, I'm sure, seen me many times when you were hiding in that old abandoned ship. Waiting for your Twelve Days to begin. Counting down the days to yourself, more eagerly than any little boy. And then what? Unpleasantness. Blood and violence, meted out on those who are dear to me. But I bear you no personal malice. I have myself meted out a good deal of blood and violence in my time, and I realize that your mind is a broken thing. Bad things were done to you; terrible things, to you and to those dear to you."

A tear trickled down the cold face of Mr. Christmas. He wiped his eye dry, and cast his gaze down.

A handgun landed in the gravel at his feet; a military-issue one, with an electronic targetting system.

"The reservoirs are full of compound. The action has not been interfered with. I wish you to have this weapon. I am giving it to you. The question you will want me to answer next is What Date Is It, am I right?"

Mr. Christmas picked up the gun and nodded, a second tear

now trailing down his cheek.

"Well, you have been unconscious quite some time. Nine days, in fact. Twelfth Night was yesterday."

Mr. Christmas nodded, almost in relief. He caressed the weapon's activation lever.

"I believe," said the man, "that you represent a risk to other human beings only for twelve days of the terrestrial solar year. I firmly believe that, for the rest of the year, you can be rehabilitated. We can work on those remaining twelve days together." He gestured at the rock-strewn expanse of the cavern, in which, unaccountably, all the rocks had been arranged into lines, whitewashed, and numbered. "Go on, pick a target. I know you want to know whether the weapon will actually fire. I assure you it will."

Mr. Christmas raised the gun with professional speed, sighted up on a rock, and fired; the rock exploded like a hand grenade. Flying off-cuts marked his cheek; Mr. Christmas did not even blink.

"You can see that the weapon works. I, meanwhile," said the man, patting himself down obligingly, "am unarmed. I know you will not shoot me. I was advised so by Officer Rai of Spender's Delight, who knows you well. He believes that if he had only turned up one day later to apprehend you, instead of on Twelfth Night, he would still be alive and living with his family."

Mr. Christmas nodded his head in wooden agreement. The man smiled. "Excellent. As our first step towards rehabilitation, then, I would like you to walk through the door you can see on the other side of that chamber. I guarantee that I will not harm you in any way."

Mr. Christmas looked at the man distrustfully, then shrugged, nodded curtly, and shambled off in the direction of the door. He passed the first line of stones; he passed the second. When he came to the third, he turned suddenly, his weapon sweeping round to cover the man sitting on the rock; at that movement, a gunshot barked and he collapsed, fetched out of the air, into a fan of his own entrails splashed out on the stone.

The Anchorite tutted, and stood up from his rock. "He's getting stronger. He's up to the third line now." He stared at the closed pressure door in concern. "Those two former colleagues of yours, Didier, made it as far as the fourth and fifth lines respectively before he took control of them."

A coat of living green rose from the undergrowth outside the cave's mouth, disgorging a man bearing an over-the-horizon sniper weapon. The man's feet clattered softly on the solid rock underfoot; they were metal-and-plastic talons, more dinosaurian than human.

The Anchorite kicked one of the whitewashed rocks irritably into the chamber. "Leave the body lying and go no further in. We have no proof he isn't deliberately understating his strength. Seal up this chamber, and never come here in person again. Beg a robot off the Clinic staff. Send all meals in via that."

He walked out of the chamber, muttering irritably. "Confine a flame without killing it, and an explosion is inevitable." Didier loped after him in pathetic obedience.

The pressure door swung shut behind the two men, and multiple bolts the thickness of men's arms thudded home into the jamb around it.

ABOUT THE AUTHOR

Dominic Green has written several short stories for Interzone magazine, often in a satirical vein, and his story *The Adventure of the Lost World* appears on the BBC Cult TV website. His story *Send Me a Mentagram* was picked for the prestigious Year's Best Science Fiction anthology in 2003, and *The Clockwork Atom Bomb* was nominated for a 2005 Hugo Award. Interzone published a special issue devoted to Dominic and his stories in July 2009.

Dominic graduated in English from St Catharine's College, Cambridge and works in IT.

FIND MORE GREAT SCIENCE FICTION BOOKS,

FREE CHAPTER DOWNLOADS

AND SPECIAL OFFERS

-- PLUS --

DETAILS OF AUTHOR EVENTS,

BOOK SIGNINGS AND MORE

AT:

www.fingerpress.co.uk

HAMSTER DRIVEN DEVELOPMENT

(it's not for the squeamish...)

tales from the coding-room floor – from the authors of *Design Driven Testing: Test Smarter, Not Harder* and *Extreme Programming Refactored: The Case Against XP* (featuring *Songs of the Extremos*)